ABOUT THE AUTHOR

Photo by Joachim Veselý

Martin Patrick lives in London. He's a former university professor of film, drama and cultural studies. As a Black British author, Martin started his professional writing career in the theatre. His Undergraduate, Masters and PhD studies have inspired him to explore diversity, identities and sexual politics in 21st-century multicultural society.

MARTIN PATRICK

Son of a
Dish

AUSTIN MACAULEY PUBLISHERS™

LONDON • CAMBRIDGE • NEW YORK • SHARJAH

A CIP catalogue record for this title is available from the British Library.

ISBN 9781788788694 (Paperback)
ISBN 9781528953993 (ePub e-book)

www.austinmacauley.com

First Published 2022
Austin Macauley Publishers Ltd
1 Canada Square
Canary Wharf
London
E14 5AA

DEDICATION

I dedicate this novel to Anton Dell. You are a diamond bloke, and a great father to your children.

ACKNOWLEDGEMENTS

To my son – You're a really good reason to live.

This novel wouldn't be possible without my profound love and admiration to all the American great Jewish writers who have inspired me throughout my life.

Book One

LIFE SAVER

CHAPTER ONE

2019

Aaron strode down the street like a man who was too big for his britches. His black leather shoes hit the ground like the sound of a soldier on the march. It was a sunny spring day, but his face was clouded because he was mentally preoccupied. Marylebone High Street was packed with the usual herd of overprivileged London shoppers and lounge lizards. These fashion-conscious men and women had their counterparts in New York's Upper West Side, on the Right Bank in Paris, the Museum Quarter in the South of Amsterdam, as well as every chic pocket in just about all the major cities of the world.

Even in his Ted Baker casual attire, Aaron had a proletariat substance that was made finite, not merely in his robust six-foot physique; it was pronounced in his rugged face, which marked his Jewish and Jamaican background. His smooth skin was a delicate mix that left him an opaque shade of gold. His brown lion eyes were alive as he muttered to himself, but strangers that walked past him thought he was singing as they caught sight of his lips moving. He wasn't singing; Aaron was cursing as he appraised the clients he had interviewed earlier that morning.

There was no doubt that Aaron was in a prosperous part of town because the traffic was congested with a few vintage cars and high-end vehicles flashing past boutiques and emporium shop windows on that bright spring day. If anyone was in doubt as to what class of neighbourhood it was, one could spot models popping in and out of doorways, strutting about with their pedigree dogs, and London's stage actors dining al-fresco at sidewalk cafés like beautiful 'Lovies'.

A Nordic model and her gay boyfriend eyed Aaron as he approached them because, in a world of imitators, he was authentic. She liked the look of him due to his irrefutable masculinity and his casual attire. Striding along the tidy street, he wasn't aimless, nor was he distracted by an app on his mobile. He looked like a man out of uniform, but at ease in civvies, while his mind and body were on alert. He gave the fashionista a look that made her nipples tighten as he passed by, so she unconsciously placed her palm flat against her neck and cleared her throat.

Thirty seconds later, Aaron saw the silver-coloured sports car pull out of Moxon Street, next to the trendy *Marylebone* pub, and turn left, speeding as if the brakes had gone. Aaron estimated the driver would hit the young woman walking across the zebra crossing in less than five seconds, so he yelled, 'Oy gevalt!'

Aaron dashed in front of the woman, yanked her aside, covered her with his body and screamed, "No!" so loudly, everyone within a 25-metre radius turned to them. Aaron brought traffic to a halt, forced the driver to stop, and made people stand still. She screamed, and her hot breath penetrated his jacket and shirt, and then spread across his chest.

The thirty-year-old public schoolboy attempted to reverse, but he crashed into the car behind him. Aaron told her, "It's alright, darling. I'm here," and kissed the top of her head. As she screamed and held on to him, he became aroused and breathless, panting while holding her tighter. When he pulled back, he saw her fear, and so he embraced her once again, and her vibrating body and breasts touched him deeply.

Violence blazed into his eyes as he told the driver: "Get out of the car!" The veins in Aaron's neck and temples pulsed, and his wide mouth revealed his teeth. The pale-faced driver was utterly panic-stricken. He shook his head and his ginger hair fell into his eyes. Innocent passers-by watched them as though it was an on-location action scene. Aaron let go of the woman and then lunged towards the car in seconds. He kicked the driver's door seventeen times. The sound of his boot denting the metal terrified everyone. The reckless youth eventually opened the door, pleading and crying, 'sorry'.

"You nearly killed her!" Fifty-four people in the direct line of sight watched, and more people from inside shops looked out because Aaron's voice sounded like an air raid preceding an invading enemy. The crowd of strangers tingled with fear of impending violence.

"You dirty son of a Nazi whore."

The bloated driver yelled, "It didn't happen! Calm down, alright, mate." In Aaron's mind, the driver's words sounded like an offensive denial; therefore, Aaron punched him in the neck, and the driver choked and fell to the ground. Looking down on him, Aaron spat on the driver's head.

A woman dashed up to Aaron and said, "He's a piece of shit, luv, don't hit him again and get yourself into trouble. I've called the police. They'll be here in a couple of minutes." She was from Leeds; in for a day's shopping to find something for Mother's Day. She looked like the kind of woman you wanted to meet if you ever had to go to customer service and complain. Aaron looked into her blue eyes, and she silently spoke volumes to him in seconds. He dashed back to the young woman and put his arm around her, and she was still shaking, but her level of panic had dropped to pure distress.

"What's your name?"

"Amber, Amber Shapiro." Later on, recounting everything he felt to his best mate, Roy, Aaron said he glanced down and saw her lipstick, mobile, tampons, face-wipes and gold pen scattered over the zebra crossing. Aaron's mind flashed like a lightbulb, and he saw:

A young woman horribly twisted as her body lay contorted into an unnatural position. She was splattered with blood. A foot away from her, a man lay dead, with his arms flung upwards and his clothes ripped, exposing his knees and his stomach. Blood dripped from his jacket, his eyes were wide open, and his medical equipment, fruit, and vegetables lay between him and the girl on the zebra crossing.

Aaron picked up her things and gave her the bag. "Thank you..." Her tone of voice indicated she needed to know his name.

"Aaron Rapchinski—"

She interrupted him unexpectedly. "You're Jewish?" Amber asked, confused, and then she remembered Jewish history existed throughout the world, therefore even though his complexion and his features might perplex ignorant people, she wasn't one of them.

"Yes," he told her, nodding in a manner that acknowledged he'd dealt with the question and issues all his life. They moved to the side of the road, and she kissed him with all her heart, and it aroused everything in him.

When they broke their kiss, she asked him why he was crying and he said, "I'm not," but tears were slipping down his face. All at once, he realised she was wearing a red, long-sleeved dress, and he imagined her covered in blood that dripped onto her black Mary-Jane shoes.

Aaron heard cries and moans screaming in his ears, but he couldn't block them out. Consequently, he moved away from Amber to confront the bloated driver and looked at him with hatred blazing in his eyes.

The driver's fidgeting indicated that he might bolt away from the scene, but Aaron's inability to restrain his tears arrested the driver and so he couldn't run. Later in court, the driver testified he was so afraid, it spread through him like poison. He told Aaron, "It could have been worse," but in the ears and minds of witnesses, it sounded like the type of denial cowards utter when they refuse to accept the consequences of their actions. People turned around when they heard a police siren, but Aaron didn't take his eyes off the driver. The look of rage in Aaron's eyes accused the driver of depraved indifference, therefore he looked ferocious.

The driver became increasingly agitated as the sound of the police came closer, and Aaron's scornful eyes condemned him. The driver felt like he was swallowing an ocean that drowned him in despair, so he screamed, "It didn't happen; stop looking at me like that!"

Amber went over to Aaron, and she saw a mixture of hatred and rage darting out of his eyes along with the tears running down his face. She took his fist in her delicate hand, and he looked at her. She was a sight to behold. As the police cars came to a stop and they got out, Amber opened his hand and locked her fingers in his. Her manicured fingers spread across his tanned fist.

Aaron told her, "I'm alright now, really, I'm okay."

"Why are you crying?"

Reluctantly, Aaron replied, "My father and sister were killed by a drunk driver." Upon hearing that, Amber immediately felt grief-stricken. Tears rose up in her, and so she hugged him. They stood there paused for a moment before the police began the inquiry. A CCTV camera had captured the scene, and in court, it would be the most damning evidence against the driver. Aaron's mobile rang, playing Stevie Wonder's *Superstition*, which scared the bejesus out of the driver, Harry Beaumont, of Kensington London, and Clifton in Bristol.

CHAPTER TWO

Donna and her son, Aaron, were born into the best of both worlds in the London Borough of Hackney, where they were sandwiched between Orthodox Jews in Stamford Hill, and Caribbeans in Stoke Newington. Since the 1950s, the Borough's history had changed from its deep-rooted poverty—with its rich dialect of Cockney, Yiddish, and Patois, into one of the most aspiring piss-elegant areas of London. Unlike Whitechapel in the neighbouring Borough further to the east, Hackney didn't have a 19th century history of Jack the Ripper infamy. Hackney was scarred by WWII bombings, criminality, unemployment, and poverty. During the Millennium era, the local villages within Hackney; from Clapton and Stamford Hill in the north and east, to Dalston, Hoxton, and Shoreditch in the south, bordering on the City of London had redefined the meaning of 'hip' by its constituents' Hipster fashions and left-wing political mindset.

In 1970, going out for a meal in Hackney gave you a choice of pie and mash or fish and chips; neither of which would cost you more than £5 for two people. Now, dinner in Dalston can set you back over £100 for two, and if you're lucky, the piss-elegant menu might have character instead of a 'persona'. If you want to find real characters in Hackney, you have to hang out on the streets because the area is loaded with talent. They come in all sorts: intellectuals, criminals, entrepreneurs, artists, and socialists who can justifiably tell you how to run the country and look after 'the people'. Any conversation with a Hackney constituent promised to be thought-provoking. The best of them were thoughtful, and the worst of them were provoking.

I'm in a position to tell this story because I know everyone involved, and people confide in me; or I'm always in the right place at the right time. Phrase it any way you like, I saw just about everything unfold in 2017 and my best friend, Eugene, used the facts and his imagination to co-write this novel with me, based on everything I told him and his skills as a novelist. So, let me take you back to Mother's Day 2017.

* * *

If Jane Fonda had been cloned, she would now be living in Hackney, as Donna Rapchinski-Blackmon: a true figure of a woman who is as gracious as she is feisty. Today, Donna sat in front of her four friends and her greatest enemy, Judy Sapperstein. Judy dressed like 1975 was the best year of her life and nothing could change her. She was the elder sister of Donna's close friend, Beryl. I watched Judy surreptitiously eye Donna, and I could mentally hear her scream...

Who gave you the right to flash those long legs, and wear lace-top stockings instead of tights like a normal woman? And how the hell do you have the audacity to wear a red skirt, as short as that, and a white silk blouse, with those boobs stuffed in there like a butcher's window packed with Ox tongue! Your hair dyed the colour of whiskey, and a face like some glamour-puss retired from show business!

Some people think I have an overactive imagination, but I can read people quite accurately because it's my defence mechanism. Survivors have sharp instincts because I am a product of a violent home environment, so I've honed my senses to know when a punch, plate, or plastering is coming my way. The weather bureau uses all kinds of sophisticated technology to detect storms, but I can sense when people's pulses are racing, and their fists are gonna fly. I can thank my father for that, but I'll get to him in time.

Right now, I can feel Judy's malcontent. I'm sure she was born with the umbilical cord up her arse. From what I've heard, she's been as uneasy with her feelings, as she is with her footing. Imagine a horse moving around for dressage, and you've got this 'ain't-sure' woman down to the hairs on her face. That sounds bitchy, but I don't mean it that way, she *does* have light hair on her face.

Donna's eyes darted between her friends, and she said, "Judy, I don't know if you're constipated or about to give birth, but you look painful." The seven Black women standing in a circle laughed as only Caribbean women do, at moments like that—with mocking vulgarity. They filled the room with laughter, and Beryl was energised by the life and force of the West London ladies. Donna got up and crossed the room to bring Judy another drink.

Donna's vitality emphasised Judy's vapidity. In totally different ways, each of the seven Black women watched Donna, knowing she was on good form and ready to make the most of Mother's Day. Donna sashayed through the room as if she was on stage and knew she had to keep the audience enthralled with her star quality. Trust me, I loved that about Donna.

After twelve years of friendship, I knew, in Donna's mind, she was playing to an audience. On the best day of my life, Aaron invited me to dinner at his home. Donna and her husband were 'tipsy' when I arrived, half cut by lunchtime, pissed at seven, and flying high by nightfall. I can still remember everything that happened.

Aaron's dad, Humphrey, as fine a looking man as I ever saw in Jamaica, filled his voice with ministerial pomp, as only the best Jamaican Pentecostal preacher can. He stood before Donna, filled with virile admiration, then pointed at her and proclaimed...

You boys are too young to know, but this Goddess of a woman, my wife, can put all those flat-arse, surgically enhanced film stars to shame! She's greater than Raquel Welch, and Julianne Moore rolled into one. Plus, Donna has more mystique than Madonna can fake.

Responding to Humphrey's compliment, Donna rose and took a bow, as though someone had pulled back the curtain. Her daughter, Zara, had a beautiful stillness to her. She had pre-Raphaelite brown hair and a butterscotch complexion. I think Zara was stirred by her mother and so she admiringly smiled at her mum. Humphrey gave Donna a rum bottle as a substitute Award. Donna gestured in a manner that could top, Bette Midler, and said, "Thank you." She looked at us, and the unseen audience, and continued with true mock humility,

"My whole life, I wanted to be a great actress, but I decided to settle on being a star. There are so many people to thank..." I quickly turned and looked at Aaron. In his face, I saw adoration for his mum that just fell short of religious devotion. He watched her as though she was the goddess of ethereal and maternal love. That was in sharp contrast to Humphrey's stare. He gazed at her as if she was the source of erotic love.

Donna continued her speech, admired by her family, and I loved the moment when Zara winked at Aaron, and he took her hand affec-

tionately and the kinship between the family energised me. However, I couldn't hear Donna because I fell in love with the entire family right then and there. Humphrey had all the kindness my father considered a weakness, and Donna had the love my mother was incapable of giving. Aaron and I were new student friends, but after that Sabbath dinner, he became my best friend, and our whole Jamaican Jewish circus pitched camp and never stopped doing the rounds.

Anyway, back in Donna's living room, the ladies of the two J's: Jamaicans on one side of the living room, and the Jewish women on the other, made an impressive Greek chorus from where I was sitting. Judy said something that she thought was a retort, but it wasn't worth repeating. Donna was determined to win back the Jewish women who had rejected her in the past, but they'd come over on Mother's Day to assuage their guilt.

Clarissa, a horrid battle-ax that I loathed, told Donna, in a distinct Jamaican accent. "Donna! No lie, the house looks fantastic! I'll bet no other woman in Stoke Newington has your taste! I've been in uglier houses in Golders Green! And that area prides itself on being high class!" Golders Green has a significant Jewish middle-class population. Therefore, several of the Jewish women didn't care for that remark, and it showed, which made no difference to Clarissa—her mouth was set on springs so she couldn't shut-up. Donna had recently come into some money, and she spent it on the house, so now it looked just like a swanky home in *House & Garden* magazine, modelled after an elegant property in Chelsea. The thirty-foot living room was decorated in plum and caramel cream-colored furnishings.

I don't know much about interior design, I'm a journalist, but the entire house felt as though you were walking through the best-decorated display rooms in the Conran Shop. Everything, from the curtains to the lighting, felt cosy; and I could also smell potpourri everywhere. I was propped up in a throne-like, big leather chair that was the most wonderful pomegranate red, with black silk cushions, and I felt grand.

The doorbell rang, and Donna left the room. I'm telling you, that lady knew how to move it. One of the other things I like about Donna is that she's a woman who looked like she went to RADA, and on some occasions, she could pass for an elder Joan, the character in the TV series, *Mad Men*.

"Roy, you're very quiet, what's wrong with you?" Clarissa asked insincerely.

"If you want to chastise somebody, call your son, OK." At age sixty-two, Clarissa was just ugly, and she had the stamina to overpower her forty-year-old son who could kick the shit out of younger and stronger men than himself.

Clarissa said to a friend, "These kids today are too damn cheeky."

"I'm thirty: it's your routine that's old." I kissed my teeth and got up. Clarissa reminded me of my mother, with her willingness to criticise, just to exercise her mouth. Judy and Beryl looked like they enjoyed hearing Clarissa being told off. Clarissa told me, in that, oh so familiar Jamaican 'ready for a fight' manner.

"Oh, so you're a man, are you?" She reminded me of a vicious 'church-lady' who never had a kind word for anyone. But unlike her son, I didn't have to live with her wretchedness.

Her scornful eyes hit me in the face like snake spit, so I facetiously told Clarissa, "You should go home, and change." She didn't get it.

"I don't have anything as flamboyant as you're wearing to put on," Clarissa replied to conspire with her friends.

"This is a 1950s baggy grey flannel suit, white cotton shirt, and loafers."

"And pink socks." She sneered and glanced at her friends, amused.

"I'll dress properly for your funeral, I promise." The Jewish ladies' intake of breath was audible, and suddenly, I noticed Miriam.

Miriam had feline features, an exotic look, and a spirit about her, reminiscent of sirens that populated Bond films. Donna had introduced Miriam when I arrived, and she looked up and smiled at me. Dressed in her cream and brown polka dot, figure-hugging dress, that featured her breasts, she looked impressive. Miriam reminded me of someone who had a secret, and *that* kept her happy. But I hadn't paid attention to her until after I cleansed Clarissa's existence from my mind.

Miriam's smile shimmered with a touch of sin. I could imagine her seducing a married man at work who flirted with her, and after she had him, then kept him on the boil; she'd cut him off just to prove she wasn't his plaything. The look I saw in her eyes might be me projecting my favourite fantasy onto her, because playboys, who think they're born to rule 'lesser men' or 'the weaker sex', as so many of them referred to women, make me want to kick them in the balls.

You might think, I'm one of those Black guys with a temper and a grudge, and you'd be right. Bigots and bullies disgust me, and I have been known to explode, which leaves a significant shockwave around me. I've seen people brace themselves just before my rage detonates and shames me, which it does. Even though I am glad I've expressed myself, the fact I've scared people leaves me feeling a bit dirty. It's one of the reasons at university that my 'Don't Fuck with Me' T-shirt was as emblematic of me as any character in *Star Wars*. My T-shirt made Aaron smile the minute we saw each other during Fresher's Week at the Two-Tone music gig they put on.

Aaron then entered the living room, and it was as if someone plugged in the electricity. Some blokes are imitations of what a man is. Other guys are male, but they fall short of being a man because they're heartless. There are also gentlemen who call themselves men because their class asserts the myth of masculinity, which they flaunt as their true character. Then there's Aaron, who is a man because as they say in his circle of friends, he's a mensch! He filled his suit as a middleweight boxer and every woman in the room looked at him and Miriam suddenly shifted out of her repose like a tigress that's spotted a lion. Aaron's hair dries rather like a curly Afro, but sometimes he brushed it out. No matter the circumstance, his face reminds me of heroes from the Old Testament. His voice has a rhythmic timbre, which reveals his Estuary accent rather than a posh voice.

Standing beside him was a girl, all 10 stone of her, about twenty-two years of age, and lovely, in an Audrey Hepburn sort of way. She had delicate features, shoulder-length brown hair, a charming smile and a somewhat shy quality that was evident by the way she hid beside Aaron when he presented her to Donna. Miriam stood taller and bolder and looked at the girl as if she were going to scream in her face. Something about Miriam's tight busty dress could have blotted the girl out, but Aaron said.

"Mum, this is Amber, I haven't told you anything about her because we've just met. Isn't she adorable?"

Amber told Donna, "Aaron hardly ever stops talking about you. I feel as if I want to know you. When he talks about you, it's like he remembers his favourite parts of a film." Amber smiled in her eyes while holding onto him. In her pink dress with a primrose sash tied into a bow at the side of her waist, she looked rather like a princess.

Donna asked, "Where are you from? Your accent is full of everything."

"Except distinction," Miriam concluded.

"I'm from Luxembourg, so there are three accents playing about in my vocal cords. But everyone has an accent, so it doesn't matter."

Aaron reproachfully added, "Not when half your family was slaughtered by Nazis and you're a survivor." All the Jewish women led Amber to a seat. Walking past the room full of women of all ages, Amber looked young and dainty in her pink dress and primrose sash. The most grown-up thing about her was her high heel shoes with ankle straps.

"This is such a pleasant room," Amber said. "I love the colours and—everything." Her voice lacked resonance, but it was full of wonder and joy, with a special touch of innocence that was lyrical because her accent was particularly French and rather German.

Miriam said to Aaron, "Where did you meet this delightful child?" Her New York tone had a lascivious cadence that was reminiscent of Cher's nasal voice.

Aaron said, "Some bastard, speeding, almost ran her down on Marylebone High Street. Amber was frozen with fear, screaming, and I ran to her."

Startled, Donna stared at him and for the first time all day, she looked upset. Aaron saw her concern, so he touched her shoulder. "We're fine! I bought you two Mother's Day presents." He took a little box out of his jacket pocket and gave it to her. Donna slowly opened it, dividing her attention between him to be sure he was OK, and the box. I'd spent the past four days away from home on a business trip with my partner, so I hadn't heard about the car incident, and I needed to know more, but I'd trained myself to maintain a low-key response to certain things, but the look Aaron threw over to me was reassuring.

In a creepy manner, Miriam tucked her arm into Aaron's and eased him away to ask, "And what do you do when you're not rescuing girls?"

I don't know whether she was disinterested in the near-accident Amber and Aaron experienced, but her pushy flirting needled me. However, I calmed down when I realised, she couldn't be a close friend of Donna's, or else she'd know Donna lost her husband and daughter because a drunk driver killed them.

Aaron casually replied, "I help people find their dream jobs to build their careers. And I amuse myself."

"How do you do that?"

"Aren't these too many questions considering we've only met once before?" "But—" Aaron walked away and left Miriam standing, so I went over to her.

"Easy does it; he's big-game and you're too much. Tread lightly."

"Have *you* trapped him, or is he strictly a ladies' man?"

"In England, statements of that kind can get you in trouble. I know some Black guys who'd slap you in the mouth for talking like that."

"You don't look like the type."

"You haven't seen me deal with bigots." She went red in the face, and I wish I knew what she was thinking.

"Excuse me," she said.

"No. Why are you here?" She gave me a look as if to say, *do you have the right to question me?* "I'm Aaron's best friend. If you'd like to get to know him, I can help." She shifted her weight and re-evaluated me; I could tell from the way she twisted her lips. Twenty seconds later, she smiled.

"Donna and I meet at trade shows. We both buy menswear for the over forties. She invited me to stay on my next trip to London, so I'm here." I led her out of the room into the kitchen, where the food and drinks were laid out.

"You and Aaron been friends a long time?"

"Twelve years. We met at college. What do you think of the girl he's brought; she's pretty, isn't she?" Miriam gave it some thought and right then, a Black lady pointed into the kitchen and showed Amber the house while they stood in the doorway.

Miriam's hostile examination made me turn to Amber, who was clearly absorbed by what she was being told before the lady led her away to another room.

"She's lovely," I honestly said.

"If anorexic kittens appeal to you," Miriam replied tersely, as she picked up hors-d'oeuvres and bit into it. "Do you like girls like her?"

"Do you really think she's a kitten?"

"With her bright-eyed look of wonder and 'everything is *so* amazing'—yes."

"Why are you so angry?" I asked with a smile.

"You men can't resist that type. It makes you feel so self-assured and masculine."

"Oh, I thought you accused me of being gay a minute ago."

"You're not? Oh sorry. In England, I don't get you guys or know anything about blacks really, so I was just picking up on the vibe in the room. The women in there think you're gay," she said, waving the food around as her bracelets jangled off-key.

"They can't see past their prejudice. Aaron's my best friend and if you like him, I can put in a good word for you. Did Donna setup a date or something?"

"No! Well, not exactly. She said… Look, we were just talking, and she mentioned her son." Miriam obviously recalled the conversation and smiled to herself. "Donna said he wasn't a typical Jewish guy. When I first met him a couple of weeks ago, I understood. Black and Jewish I'd never met, but when he came over, I could see he was one hell of a guy. He adores Donna."

"Yes, and that's not even his best quality." Aaron came into the kitchen and so we shut up. Miriam watched him and tried to suss him out.

"Mate, are you hiding out, in here? Don't tell me, the bubbies giving you the treatment, right? They're just grannies, they live to complain."

I told him, "No more than usual, except for that cow, Clarissa."

"Ignore her. And how are you, Miriam?"

"Great, you look dapper. Where'd you buy the suit?" She went up to him to feel the material, finger the lapels and check the fit. She knew how to turn it on. She went from naught to sexy in seconds.

"I have my suits tailor-made. A great guy in Shoreditch sees to me." She went behind him and eyed the cut, touched his shoulders, felt the jacket in the waist and opened the vent. Unseen by Miriam, Aaron glared at me bug-eyed by her boldness and mouthed the words, 'fuck off, lady' silently and I gagged while he pulled a face, stunned by Miriam's impudence.

"You like?" he asked her and I could hear his sarcasm.

"Very nice," she replied. Aaron remained cool. He could have stepped away or pushed her away, but he turned around to face her.

She said, "I love the way you wear shirts buttoned, without a tie. Is that a British thing?"

"You're the fashion stylist, you tell me. I just dress how I feel." She smiled and her face lost its tension. Behind her, Amber appeared in the doorway looking for him and when she saw Aaron standing in front of Miriam, Amber looked vexed. But slowly, I saw that vanish as silence settled in. Because Aaron had his back to me, I couldn't see his face. But in the space of ten seconds, I did see an engaging smile light up Miriam's face because she thought he was looking at her; even though Amber's face clearly told me, Aaron was watching her.

"You fill out those pants real good," Miriam said, eying him, unaware that if he was getting a 'swelled head', so to speak, it was for Amber, not her. Caught in her own passion, she was unaware of Amber.

Aaron stepped away from Miriam and the disappointment on her face made her crumble. I saw her hand drop in mid-air and fall by her side. Behind her, a smile rose across Amber's face and lit up her eyes. The two women couldn't have looked more incongruent. Aaron walked the nine and a half strides over to Amber and took her in his arms and kissed her. Miriam turned to look, and their kiss pulled her uptight. I saw her back muscles turn rigid as Amber and Aaron filled the doorway, framed as lovers in an old fashion photograph. They only stopped when a burst of laughter echoed through the air. It was Donna. I left the kitchen quickly.

I entered the living room and Donna, and the other ladies were weaving about as though they were passengers in a cabin on-board a ship. Everyone looked slightly distorted because of the intensity of their laughing faces.

"What?" I asked.

"Get that son of mine in here." Aaron came in and Donna staggered over to him and wrapped her arms around him.

"Darling, thank you so much!" She continued laughing. "Who else but you would give me Valium for Mother's Day? I love that!" She kissed his forehead and he regressed from a tough guy to a boy in seconds, held in his mother's arms.

Aaron told her, "I knew you'd get it!"

"Only my baby would be the kind of man to know what a woman needs. If your father was here, he'd..." She struggled to find the words and so he held her and rocked her from side to side. Amber came in and Miriam followed behind her. All the women watched them, and the atmosphere slowly turned sombre.

Aaron began singing Aretha Franklin's song, *Angel*, and you could hear he was Black even though he didn't look it. The seven Black women and most of the Jewish ladies clapped their hands as the Black women sang. I watched Miriam shift from tension to tenderness watching them and I saw Amber scrutinise Aaron. Before long, Amber watched all the women singing and clapping and she folded her arms in front of her tummy.

"Daddy's right here, mum. I can feel him watching us and showing Zara, I'm looking after you and he's looking after her because that is the will of God." The Black women said, "Amen!" and "Hallelujah!"

"Until we're united with my sister and my dad, I *will* be my father's keeper and do what he'd do on a day like this or any other day. Make sure you're alright." The Jewish women said a prayer and Amber knew it, so she joined them. Miriam saw the comfort Donna took from their prayers, so she joined in: but I felt so alone. This was one of the countless moments when I wanted my family's love and I had nothing until Donna called to me.

"Come here, Roy. I want both of my boys near me." She began giving thanks for her life, her son, her family, and I felt that intangible yet powerful feeling of grace within the heart and soul of decent people.

Donna told her mother-in-law, "Mum, come, he needs you too. Aaron, move over to make space for grandma." His father's mother, Violet, got up and joined them standing in the middle of the room and I was struck by her willingness to accept me. She was from the Parish of St Thomas in Kingston, Jamaica and came to England in 1953 as a young bride. She'd been here long enough to see everything change, but in the depth of her heart, she always told me she felt Jamaican.

For a woman of seventy-five, Violet sure could move and so she held my hand and Aaron's hand and led us into the gospel classic *Mary, Don't You Weep*. Donna began singing and I swear to God, the meaning of existence took hold of me because there is so much hate in this world. Hearing Donna and Aaron reached into me and told me even though I don't have a family anymore, I have them, my faith and I have a man who loves me, even though he's not here.

Aaron invited Amber to join him, but she shook her head and stepped back. Miriam stepped forward and joined in and the Jewish women gave a little shout. Miriam rocked side to side, clapping out of time and I took an instant dislike to her. I saw that Donna was pleased to have her join us.

Aaron caught my eye and he silently asked me what was wrong. I cast my eyes towards Miriam. He couldn't read my complex thoughts, but he indicated I should relax.

I told myself to stop it! Whatever Miriam is or isn't, she is not my business. Brian, my ex often quoted his dad and his Papi when he'd say: 'Don't busy yourself with what's not your business!' Brian's African American and Latino fathers were wealthy and very powerful, so they taught me a lot. In fact, that's what I loved about Aaron and his father. They taught me great things because they were tough guys with tenderness and that's my ideal kind of bloke.

* * *

Shortly after Mother's Day, I went to the Whitechapel Gallery for the group show exhibition in which my boyfriend's work was featured. I walked away from the 'hip' crowd of people swanning around and took Dr Eugene Martins' elbow and led him to a corner where we could talk privately. There were lots of people everywhere, so we huddled near the entrance. As always, Eugene's post-apocalypse clothes and hair made him look more interesting than anyone in *Mad Max* because he's a Black man steeped in wisdom and erotic power, even though he's over sixty.

"Dr M, I've read the opening chapter. You've captured the spirit and fear I told you about when Aaron recounted the near-fatal accident to me. The fear, drama and circumstance are all there in your opening chapter. I love it!"

"And I've read your chapter where Aaron introduces Amber to Donna with Miriam there and the Caribbean and Jewish women in the house on Mother's Day. I like it too. You should just write the novel yourself, Roy."

"I can't, I'm a journalist; you're the novelist. You write so much better than me. I get bogged down with the emotional weight of what's happening."

"All novels need that."

"But I'm too close to Aaron to write about him objectively. When I feedback to you, you interpret him so well." A group of Indian people stopped near us and praised my partner's work. There was a feature on him in *Time Out* and *The Metro*. "Narj is their hero even though they haven't seen the work yet."

"Roy, you did a pretty good job of boosting him in your article on the show."

I waved it away. "Eugene, I've told you everything that's happened so far. Help me to write the novel. There isn't another man who can do justice to this story about us. I can't write about myself. You know me, you can."

He gave me a tentative look, evaluating the cost and scrutinising me. "Eugene, please. You're an award-winning novelist, Broadcaster and Cultural Critic. Can't you see yourself as the envy of the Black British elite if you write this novel? Nobody is dealing with this subject of Jewish Caribbean identity and sexual politics."

"You're a very persuasive son of a bitch."

"I *am* a son of a bitch. But unlike the woman who gave birth to me, Donna's a mother to me. She's turned my life around, so I'm not the victim I use to be. Of course, the writer's credit will go to you, citing me as your researcher." Someone rushed into the gallery and bumped into me, which pushed me nearer to Eugene. I took off my trilby hat and looked at him.

"You're lucky you're smart and handsome. OK Roy, I'll do it." I felt relieved.

"I've told you what happened when Aaron left Donna's with Miriam and then when he contacted Amber. This is exciting: you and I working together. I have no objection to working out of the spotlight just so long as I get credit for my input and ideas. I'm not a star and I don't want to be that."

"What do you want, Roy?"

"Ask me that after you continue writing and I'll tell you." He shook my hand and gave me the nod every Black man knows and then he headed out. I stood there, knowing who meant the most to me and then I walked back into the gallery. It was a group show, but my fella was the press' star find. Proud of his Sri Lankan identity, Narj positively shone at the centre of the public's adulation.

Surrounded by other paintings and works of art, Aaron walked towards me, and I gestured and fidgeted. "Well, three years of hard work have paid off for your boy. He looks super trendy and full of bliss tonight! It might not be long before Asia wants him back. He's not *my* best friend, but that portrait of you is the best thing in this exhibition. It's so obvious he loves you."

"And who do you love?"

"Don't think I'm loved-up and crazy, but I feel something amazing in my guts and my head about Amber. Saving her life like that. I've invited her to our Prince Memorial Party." Aaron led me into the crowd and Narj came towards me.

"Go on, *lover*; take care of your boy." I swore at Aaron and went to Narj.

CHAPTER THREE

Miriam happily walked with Aaron down Stoke Newington Church Street past many warmly lit bars and restaurants, filled with people carousing. Everyone they passed looked as though they were members of a Hackney 'alternative' clique, aligned to entrepreneurial capitalism and local community style. A Mediterranean girl with blue hair and a Black guy with bleached blonde hair caught Miriam's attention. She later told Donna; Hackney's swaggering Hipsters all looked gainfully employed in small niche businesses.

Walking down the street, few shops had darkened doorways. Almost everyone was open for business that Mother's Sunday and everyone looked as if they wanted something. Aaron, as well as passer-by noted that Miriam sashayed as she walked.

"Interesting," Miriam said. Aaron looked at her with an inquiring expression. "There's no one begging. In Manhattan, a neighbourhood outside of the prosperous parts of town, have lots of panhandlers. Over here, I haven't seen people on the subway hustling for money."

"Oh, they're here," he said, without correcting her.

"And this neighbourhood; isn't it kind of poor, compared to the West End? But look at the girls. They wear designer Brands. But anyway, my job is men's fashions. In Hackney, the guys have combined early 1980s style with 21st century menswear. Their hair and faces are an odd mix of 1950s thrift-shop jazz style and a self-conscious parody of their post-war parents." Aaron took her arm and held her hand as they walked.

"Mum told you I'm fascinated by fusion, didn't she?" Miriam tried to stop walking, but Aaron led her and kept her moving. She smiled at him beguilingly.

"No, I was just observing—"

"That I'm thirty and single and need a strong but alluring wife who'll excite me?" Miriam pulled herself free and stopped walking. She eyed him and looked away and saw merry-makers in a bar in groups of couples. Suddenly, her mother's 'words of wisdom' echoed in her ear about how to deal with men. She decided to strike a pose and search in her handbag. Her cream and brown polka dot dress made her feel as though she'd broken out in a rash because Aaron was onto her, and she hadn't prepared a defence because she didn't think she needed one.

So, she held her stance, with her shapely leg slightly turned and found the pack of cigarettes. She offered him one and he shook his head, no. She lit up, tossed her head back and settled herself as the nicotine rushed through her. She looked like Miss TWA 1963 standing there and the fifteen men that passed her from the left and right noted her figure, her feminine aura, and her defiance.

"I'm quite capable of handling my love life without mum's help. I wish she'd stop doing this." Miriam tried not to look surprised, but she was. "You must be the nineteenth woman she's put in front of me."

"What was wrong with the others?"

"You're asking the wrong question."

"You sound angry. You mustn't be mad at your mom. She's—"

Aaron abruptly interrupted Miriam, "Just too worried I won't find the right girl."

"I'd never think the two of you have issues, she never stops talking about you and obviously, you're very close to her."

"I often get angry with mum because I love her and know her."

"That's a strange thing to say."

"Well, we're an odd couple." She looked at him judgmentally, but he didn't care. "You're sexy. If it weren't for that disgusting habit you have, I'd kiss you." That threw her out of her comfort zone as she pushed her red velvet coat back and stood like a Dior model at the end of a catwalk.

"These keep me slim and stop me from drinking too much."

"Yeah, and they kill you too." She dropped the cigarette and twisted it with the toe of her shoe. Aaron couldn't figure out why he was reminded of women in film noir and pouty Italian actresses, like Monica Bellucci, even though there was nothing Italian about Miriam, except she was loaded with style and typified slinky women.

"Are you an early riser, or would you like to stop in for a nightcap?" She indicated pointing at the trendy warmly lit bar with its young carouser's clearly cavorting inside the bar, behind them.

"I'll get you a cab and—"

Miriam gestured disapprovingly. "There's plenty of time for me to go to bed. I'm in London and I want more than that."

"Oh, such as?"

"Theatre! Cocktails! Sightseeing, romance..."

"A husband?"

"Marriage is something most girls do when they're not very ambitious."

"What are *your* aims?" he asked, indicating they should continue walking. She agreed and they headed along as police sirens assaulted the air. Various Hackney 'Stokey' nationalities turned left and right checking the streets and then gave way to each other on the pavement.

"I want to make a million! And I won't stop until I've done it. I'm not looking for a rich husband to keep me shopping or stupid. Work is the one true thing that defines us. I want my status to be my living. And any man I marry will know I'll respect him if he aims for more than what most men settle for."

Coming up the street, a bunch of playful gay women approached, singing. Four of them were aging Butch's and three Femmes, as well as a couple of Genderqueer 'girls' whose joy in life was exploring London's 'underground' scene and finding creative artists. The array of clothes on each one of them and the drunken joy that came out of the mouths of each of them shocked Miriam.

Aaron asked them, "Hey girls, did you do it right tonight?" They screamed and whooped. Aaron then sang "...Aaar Haar! *Constant Craving*..." in a joyful exclamation. The women whistled and cheered and then joined in to enjoy k.d. lang's song.

"What's up with you?" Miriam asked.

"I'm good. Do lesbians bother you?" His smile warmed her as she watched him gesture with his hands and weave about, asking her to respond to him. Aaron looked like a marionette out of control as the dip and bend of his joints seem to discombobulate him and Miriam knew somewhere in him there lay a maverick.

"They have nothing to do with me and I'm not involved with gays' lives."

The look on Aaron's face meant something she could never figure. She had gone on over sixty 'first dates' in her life and walked out on over half of them because some men are so obvious, she didn't need to hear their chat all over again. Aaron, on the other hand, was puzzling because she couldn't read him. She sensed he wasn't impressed with her and that was unusual because ever since the age of fifteen, her curvaceous body appealed to a line of men that could stretch all the way from Brooklyn to the Lower East Side.

"I know how this evening should include another meeting," he said to her. From the look on his face, it seemed that he had changed his mind or come to his senses as far as she was concerned. She did a quick spin and her retro 1950s Swing-coat flared as she reached above her head.

Miriam happily told him, "So! You've got your mother's good sense, great! I hate weak men. It sickens me when a guy can't see a good thing and go after it. You're cagey, but you've got brains."

"I like to think I have what it takes to get ahead."

She threw her head back and clutched her waist with one hand and gripped her red leather clutch purse with the other.

"Did you just say, 'get head'? Oh no, I don't do that on the first date. We have to build trust before I go there."

"I didn't say, 'get head', I said to get ahead." Her guffaw was totally false. "I'll bet you make better friends with men than you do with women."

"Oh yeah; why'd you say that?"

"I think a lot of women would be either jealous or threatened by you."

"Oh?"

"Come on, you're a knock-out! On Sunday afternoons, dad, mum, my sister and I used to watch those great black and white thrillers from the 1940s and '50s. Those babes were so smoking hot; I'd have to leave the room to adjust myself."

"What do you mean?"

"I'd go to the kitchen, take out a can of cold drink and put it down my pants to cool off!"

Miriam laughed once again and her breasts jittered, held in by the overlapping material, gathered across her cleavage. She saw him eye them, so she moved towards him, and he stepped off the pavement to allow a couple to pass by.

"Did mum tell you that I always date the wrong girls?"

"Not exactly, but she said you've never met the right one. And if you don't mind me saying, you're still off the mark."

"Oh?" he responded inquisitively.

"That girl you brought today. What is she, nineteen? A waif with a tragic past; she's a classic Anne Frank heroine. I don't know a single man who wouldn't want to rescue her. She's our sisters and mother goddess. Not some vague Renaissance Madonna or Venus. She's the Jewish girl every one of us couldn't save. And men are naturally drawn to her type. It makes you guys feel heroic. Saving her and loving her is a reversal of what really happened. The war made so many men impotent; we lost our grandparents. The Anne Frank syndrome helps men to reclaim the past. But I think you're more than that."

'*What kind of woman is this?*' "Why, you don't really know me."

"Oh yes I do; Donna's told me you're one hell of a guy. You own your own agency."

"Earlier, I thought you didn't know what I did?"

"I was just playing with you." She continued, waving away his interruption. "No, you need a woman. I'm going to make my fortune. Only an ambitious man appeals to me. The trouble is men today are so weak. They're desperate to protect themselves. Sure, no guy wants to get stuck with a skank who marries to bleed him dry. But you guys must deal with commitment! I mean, where is it written every guy on the planet has to bang every broad they can con into bed?"

"That's never been my ambition."

"Oh, come on."

"My dad would have beaten me until I was really black if I conducted myself like a thug."

"Was he mulatto or full-blooded black?"

"You're referring to my dad as black with a little 'b'. He was a British born brown skin Jamaican, **B**lack man. And for the record, I'm not a mulatto."

"No, but you're not like the black guy who was at the house." Only Donna and Roy would have accurately understood how insulted and angry he was. He lowered his voice and contained himself.

"Roy is not some 'black guy'." He shifted to an even more conciliatory tone. "He's mum's dearest friend." She quickly nodded and stood corrected. She was annoyed with herself that they were off track again. Even though he wasn't shouting, his clenched right fist and shaking left hand told her he was angry.

"I'd love a drink: my treat."

"I have work to prepare, but why don't I call you. Where are you staying?"

"At the *Nice* Hotel, in Old Street."

"They did a big to-do about the launch of the Hotel chain, is it 'nice' there?"

"Yeah, listen. I hope we can get to know each other a bit while I'm in town."

"Count on it, Miriam."

"Would that be alright with Amber?"

"We've only just met."

"Well, if it isn't going to be a conflict of interests, it'll be great to meet early next week?" Her flirtatious wordplay appealed to most men.

"Yes, maybe Tuesday?"

"Tuesday is good. You pick the place and call me. She opened her purse and gave him a card with her numbers on it."

"I'll take you to *Le Relais de Venise*, it's a French restaurant in Marylebone, they're famous for their steak and chips, do you like—"

"Steak, yes, I love it." Aaron saw a cab, flagged it, told her to get in and she liked that. He told the driver, "Take the lady wherever she wants to go, now!" He gave her a last look and said, "See you next Tuesday," slapped the roof of the taxi and the cabbie drove off.

He watched the cab diminish into the night traffic and as it was swallowed into congestion, a sneer twisted Aaron's lips. "What a bitch!"

Aaron walked in a circle shaking his head and then he pulled himself together and walked on. "The mouth on her! 'A classic Anne Frank heroine', my arse. What a bitch!" He scratched his balls and stretched his neck with a jolt. Aaron then marched off down the street as though he was on his way to a fight.

CHAPTER FOUR

Aaron walked through the door of his house on Greenwood Road, near London Fields, in 'Hipster' Hackney, and made his way through the hallway. It was one of the Edwardian houses that people were buying up because they couldn't afford to live in trendy Islington. The entire house had been rebuilt into a fusion of Contemporary meets Warehouse. Aaron shared the place with Roy. It was a three-story townhouse that was worth millions in the Borough and would have sold for five million more in the Royal Borough of Kensington and Chelsea; however, no one could pay Aaron to live in Chelsea because he felt he didn't belong to the 'toffee-nosed' clan that occupied that Borough.

He walked down to the lower ground floor kitchen and dining room that ran the length of the house, from the backyard to the front garden. The steel and white tiled kitchen was modern. The white tiles faded into brickwork that was treated for interior decoration in the dining area which created a very cosy rustic feel. This was offset by the framed hanging prints of Jackson Pollock and Clyfford Still's Abstract American artworks on one wall. On the wall opposite, there was a six-foot-wide painting of Superman in comic book style as a Blaxploitation big Afro dude, being crucified. In the scene, his cape was swirling off to the side and 'foxy chicks and funky brothers' circa 1974 filled the landscape looking up at the brown skin, broad chest, 'well-hung' action man, in blue and red.

In the painting, the words *Living For The City* formed clouds floating through the sky. Aaron took off his shoes and went and made himself herb tea. The lighting and spot-lit areas on the brick wall shimmered between dusty white and brown stonework. There was a dining table made of Redwood, carved into a narrow 'S' that balanced a 10ft glass tabletop. The table was surrounded by six elaborately carved Redwood chairs with Japanese silk cushions. The lacquered cabinets and painted screens in the room distilled an Oriental atmosphere.

Several Japanese Samurai icons also hung, and everything created a balanced stillness within the room because the painted black floor with a high varnish, had four large red carpets around the table. The overall impression was that of a tranquil Kabuki scene. Yet sometimes the street beyond the dining room window could be transformed into fringe theatre because in Hackney, people's personal lives were acted out on the streets. I'd been there on several occasions and witnessed couples' breakups and East End culture clashes.

Aaron brought the mug of tea into the dining room and slumped onto the sofa. He took off his trousers and sat in his bright colourful boxers and felt free. Aaron took his mobile and called Amber. "Hello darling, how's it going?" He listened to her light voice and slowly happiness crept into him, as he breathed.

"No, I put that bitch in a cab. Amber, you should have heard her! I'll tell you when we meet. How's your mum? I felt weird having to let you leave to go to your mum's. Also stupid, because I don't have the right to tell you to spend your time with me." When Amber replied, he put his tea on the floor and put his hand down his boxers.

Amber confided in him for ten minutes before he spoke again, "If you'd like, I'll take your parents to dinner and tell them about us. I hate to think they didn't like me when they've only seen me twice."

"They don't think anyone is good enough for me."

"Tell them, I'm so serious about getting to know you, I'm prepared to travel down to Wimbledon to see you. Believe me, that's something! I don't go to South London, but I will for you." He listened. "Why...? South London. Oy! I'm choking back vomit at the thought." She laughed and he laughed with her.

"South London makes me sick. Hackney is happening! For real: listen. I could take you to some swank place in the West End, but I know places around here... There's a great place opened up in Broadway Market, London Fields..." He listened to her for a time.

"They won't come to Hackney. Tell your parents to come home; we have real Jews in the Borough." She was laughing so much he sat up and kissed the mobile phone. "No *real* Jews live in bloody Wimbledon!" He smiled broadly and sat forward. "Jews and Jamaicans Da-ya!" he said in mock patois.

His voice dropped several octaves when he said, "What you mean you don't understand 'such words' or my accent?" He stood up and began strutting around the place. "I've told you already, I'm comfortable being a Jamaican Jew. You like Lenny Kravitz?" She told him yes. "OK! He's the Jewish African American; I'm the Black British Jew!" he concluded in a high tone of voice. "Stop laughing! Stop laughing!" He switched to patois. "Don't mak me come down South and fix your business since you don't know better."

"Daddy fends off all suitors until he's investigated and disqualified them."

"I'd love to tell you the truth, but I don't walk the line of sexual harassment. A man tells a woman he's excited by her and that's misread—" Amber interjected, and he listened.

"Oh, you're cool with that. This conversation just got better. Keep talking, darling, you're just making me harder." Amber screamed with laughter, which made Aaron strut about whipping his fingers and laughing with her.

"No lie! I'm stiff right now, but since I'm up here and you're down there, you're safe. Besides, I'd never force myself on you. That's the relaxed Hebrew in me speaking." He listened to her for four minutes without talking.

"Your voice sounds like music from a balalaika." He listened. "That's not flattery; it's the tonal quality of your voice." He kept listening. "Yes, accept a compliment. Now, those French boys are fuckin' mutts." He captivated her.

"Amber, behave yourself: there's a reason why you're lovely." She told him about a flirty girl she knew. "Oh please, I've met some trampolines in my day." Again, he listened then told her. "Oh, 'trampolines'? I mean nasty girls blokes bounce on because they're wide-open tramps."

"Boys like easy girls," she said knowingly.

"I wouldn't dirty myself on those meshuggeneh muffs." Aaron opened the cocktail cabinet, fixed himself rum and Pellegrino and then took a sip.

"Let me come by Selfridges tomorrow after work and I'll pick you up and take you anywhere you want to go for the evening.

There are so many things I want to tell you, but 100 words can't say it. I'd just babble." He broke out and sang The Police, *De Do Do Do, De Da Da Da*; moving in the classic Two-Tone shuffle that Sting and Madness mastered. Amber's laughter came through the mobile loud and clear which kept him singing and dancing. He held his mobile like a microphone and sang his heart out to her. Amber's laughter lifted him higher and higher. When he stopped, he picked up his drink and smacked his lips, 'Aarh!'

"Aaron, you're going to far too much trouble. I don't know what's to become of us: a relationship, a friendship, because my father is not impressed or cosy with any boy I've ever seen or gone out with. Maybe I'm putting myself in harm's way."

"What has he said about me?" he asked, suddenly overtaken by a dreadful feeling. Amber wouldn't answer. "What?" She still wouldn't answer. "Amber, please tell me."

"You're Black."

Aaron put his drink down and stopped strutting. He sat at the table, and he squeezed his lips together and slowly he felt debilitated.

"OK, listen, if that doesn't make any difference to you, call me tomorrow." He listened to her. "I know my working-class background and accent isn't posh. But I have a Masters degree, two professional qualifications and I run my own business. Sweetheart, I just need to understand your side. I know some people think Blacks are dreadful. Goodnight." He turned the phone off and tried to steady himself, but he saw Roy standing there.

"How long have you been fuckin' standing there! You creep around—" But then he stopped talking before he said something stupid. Roy came over to him and Aaron reached out and pulled him closer. He buried his face in Roy's shirt and cried out.

"When will it stop? 'Oh, you're not Black enough!' 'Oh, you're a Jew?' I'm fuckin' sick and tired of it!" And then he tried to control the emotional chaos tearing through him.

Roy kissed the top of Aaron's head and hugged him. "I know. I know."

"I'm sorry I swore at you just then."

"I know." He patted Aaron's back as best friends do.

"And you know what? That Miriam thinks she can lead me up the aisle. Over my dead body!" he roared furiously. "You should have fuckin' heard her: trying to play me. And guess what?"

"It's a setup: Donna's matchmaking again."

"When is she gonna stop? Those bitches are venal, capricious and vain. Today every man better check his mouth before he talks to a girl. No woman's gonna bring me up on charges or hold me prisoner in marriage: fuck no!"

Aaron shoved the air out of his face. He mocked their voices: "Always, you hear: *I want, need, must-have, where's mine?* Those vixens will suck you dry!"

"If you're summing up for the jury, you should put your trousers on."

"Fuck that," he sneered, standing in his boxers, heading for his drink.

"When is mum going to stop trying to marry me off?"

"When you get married. Aaron, I could tell your life story and do you and Donna justice. I know you two better than my own mother and father. I've seen you both at your best and worst. Instead of writing for my news agency, I could write your biography and tell—"

"Roy, no joking mate, don't. You're a great journalist. Your by-line exposé, your investigative journalism and uncovering celebrities' shit: but you know too much about all of us and me especially. Don't write about me. Never tell my story." Roy felt Aaron's Caribbean spirit overtake his Jewish kvetching.

"As juicy as it is," Roy said playfully.

"Bubala, I'd never hurt you, never." Aaron touched his face and looked right through him. "I know, I'm just saying."

"That bitch has gotten under your skin. You always get defensive when you're with people like that."

"I'm not playing! Keep your mouth shut!" Aaron yelled, punching the air into Roy's face as he stormed out of the room looking like a middleweight boxer. At university, Roy once saw Aaron deck a loudmouth punk for talking trash about 'Jews' and Roy loved Aaron's anger, but not at that moment.

The following morning Aaron was in his office with his six members of staff. The phones were ringing, and his staff was screening candidates over the phone. There were three men and three women in the office with him; all of whom, with one exception, was under thirty and from different parts of the world. Aaron abruptly got up and walked through the basic modern office that looked like thousands of offices in London. He stepped into the grey and white hall outside and then went into the hollow stairwell where he was alone. He switched on his mobile and a picture of him with Roy and Donna laughing at a bar loomed large.

The next day I was called in for a development meeting with Roy and his department manager at the News Agency. Roy's workplace is one of the Hi-Tec, multimedia Corporations that occupy a skyscraper in Canary Wharf: the glittering steel and glass new financial centre of London. The security at reception could rival MI6 and while that reassured and impressed some people, it got on my blasted nerves; after all, it wasn't Scotland Yard.

Our meeting was held in the glass bowl office titled *Paris*. All the meeting rooms had names of cities. I worked for a big pay-for-view Television Network that rivalled the BBC. In the labyrinthine high-rise steel and glass maze of ergonomic chairs, mobile and desktop technology; hundreds of keen and eager British and Europeans were diligently at work. Roy was the only Black man on the 33rd floor; along with one Asian woman at a desk that looked a mile away from our *Paris* glass bowl meeting room.

Roy was investigating a story about the Empire Windrush Generation of Caribbean immigrants who were being discriminated against by the government. With cold objectivity, Roy was talking to eight members of staff and leading them through a presentation on a feature article he had written. He presented me as the man who should turn the story into a TV program.

The aging white status quo listened closely to Roy as he continued to explain the news report he'd written, using photographs and video he had filmed with the help of his contacts. Roy's youthful maturity and his authoritative voice commanded attention which the men in the white shirts and ties gave him; until a young woman came in and said there was an important call for Roy. He told her to take a message. She told him, "Mr Rapchinski said it's imperative."

"Gentlemen, excuse me for three minutes, I'll leave Dr Martins to tell you his plans for the television series. His people want him to do this because their TV Network needs a cultural show that covers matters related to Black British social diversity in our current immigration climate and Dr Martins can do it ten times better than the BBC." Roy picked up his notepad and took out his gold Parker pen and left the room. I admired the way he dressed, rather like a Jamaican Windrush immigrant: in his baggy suit, braces, white shirt and tie and brogue shoes. I turned my attention to the managers and then went into my pitch for the TV show.

Standing at his desk surrounded by countless newsmen and women, Roy sat down. On his desk there was a picture of Humphrey, Donna, Zara, Aaron and himself. Roy turned around to look out of the window onto Docklands, with City Airport in the near distance where planes took off every two minutes. Roy lowered his voice. "Roy Burton, good morning."

"You sound very butch when you do that."

"Bitch, what do you want?"

"About last night, I was tired and upset. I didn't mean to yell at you."

Roy took five seconds. "Aaron, there's no way I'd betray the family. We've got something; don't you know what that means?"

"That you love me."

"No, you dick! It means if a guy has no honour, he isn't a man."

"I know, I do—sorry for being a knob." There was a long silence. "Are you nodding your head, but I can't see you?"

"Yes," Roy replied plaintively.

"Do you want some chocolate cake from *Maison Blanc?*" Roy hummed. "I'll have it sent over to your office for lunch." Roy laughed and Aaron hung up smiling. He felt lighter and energised now.

* * *

A few nights later, Amber walked around Roy and Aaron's house glancing and staring at their friends dressed in iconic costumes that Prince, The Revolution, and the New Power Generation wore from the 1980s to the 1990s. Aaron's university alumni friends and Roy's mates and activists roamed around their house which featured comics, video games, R2D2 & 3PO, a sculpture of Darth Vader, Batman and Superman. It was their first-year memorial for Prince; and his signature songs continued to play throughout the house. Amber noticed how at ease Aaron was greeting and hosting. She loved the fact he was styled like Prince during his

Purple Rain era. Aaron was wearing a copy of the silver and cream suit with the white ruffled shirt Prince wore in the *When Doves Cry* video and now his curly hair looked right; styled as it was.

Amber passed him in the purple lit hallway, and he said to her. "See, I've got degrees, I own my own home and I run my own business. All my friends are smart, employed, qualified postgraduates. So, tell your dad, I'm not an East End 'black gangsta'."

Amber felt guilty and embarrassed. "Aaron, please; my parents are idiots, not me." He took two steps away and then turned back. Her hazel-coloured eyes implored his forgiveness. He kissed her on her neck and held her flesh between his lips and she quivered. When Aaron looked into her eyes, she gazed at him, conscious of her own dignity.

An hour later, Roy stood in front of everyone in a see-thru purple jumpsuit, black underwear, and Doc Martens. He usually wore baggy clothes that covered him up, but everyone could see his gym-toned body through his Prince-inspired costume. I liked Roy because he translated facts into human interest journalism. What I love about him is that he's a Masters graduate who is astute, handsome and bashful. With plaintive eyes, that only people who've been subjected to violence have, Roy said.

"There are no heroes left that I love. We all have our fantasy narratives in comics."

Their forty guests, spread throughout their reception room yelled, 'Yeah!' "The *Falcon* and *Black Panther* still kiss my balls with narrative pleasure." Aaron and their friends responded with a roar! "It's important to cultivate friendships. My boyfriend's not here because he's swanking it up at a gallery's collective exhibition in Paris. So, with Prince and my fella out of sight, I'm here with you lot because our blogs, our discussions and our quest for equality keep me alive. With that in mind, let's get my mate up here. To paraphrase Prince: sexy motherfucker, shake that arse and get up here."

Aaron went to the front of the room. "Prince, 'Rest in Peace'. We all love you."

They cheered, which thrilled Amber. "Next thing: our anti-Brexit blog has now reached one million. You know, I'm obsessed with fair and equal employment, but we're Kings College alumni. We're employed by powerful organisations, and we can disrupt corporate thinking. Anyway, I won't bang on, *as usual*," he said self-mocking. "I'm just glad we're friends, committed to social change. So, let's turn to *more* good news."

Aaron looked at Amber and visceral energy rush through *me* because of the look that rebounded between them.

"The other day I met a fantastic girl! This woman loves fashion, comics, and Tudor history. The rest I've yet to find out, but I'm going to because she lights my fuse. Amber Shapiro!" In front of their house full of guests, she blushed, covered her face for a moment and then smiled and Aaron's friends took a shine to her. Roy went and got Amber because he could see she wasn't going to move. He brought her to the front of the room to join Aaron.

Watching Roy in his purple see-thru jumpsuit and Amber in a mint green silk and chiffon dress, they resembled something out of a 1950s delinquent cult movie John Waters hadn't made yet. Roy handed her over to Aaron and he put his arms around them. Sex appeal is an indefinable thing, but the three of them were tantalising and mysterious. I couldn't think of a Pop Star with more authentic magnetism than Amber standing between two blokes who conjured up images of R&B and Rock & Roll. Aaron gestured for Amber to speak, but whatever she said didn't fully connect with me, because her European accent created a luxurious rhythm and tempo in my ear that warmed me.

I knew Roy well and within a year, I would discover Aaron, Donna and Amber's family lives in intimate detail. It took time, but Aaron's entire extended family and Roy's past filled me with creative inspiration and respect for the bond between them.

A young woman came up to me and said, "Eugene Martins! Oh, this is great! I love your shows, your books. Can I get a selfie with you? I must be seen with the man who ties Bauhaus, Black politics and British identity into a style of his own." She had no style, but she was warm-hearted.

At sixty-one, I had my hair-coloured silver, so I sported a high-top Afro with shaved sides that came to a **V** at the nape of my neck. Fortunately, my brown skin was in good nick, so I looked like an ageless man whose style rather than age identified me. My bright silver hair, brown skin, 'next-century' style and post-nuclear boots were my iconic image in the newspapers and on TV. She took the Selfie, and I showed my best side.

Roy gave me a funny look and after she dashed off, I asked him if we looked silly. He said, "I have everything she doesn't." He then introduced me to some of his and Aaron's anti-Brexit support-ers and I must admit his friends and his politics impressed me further.

Half an hour later, Aaron came up to me and quietly said, "You won't get any sleep tonight if you keep looking at Roy like that."

I came to my senses and turned towards him. "His trilby and those baggy suits he wears, they don't do him any favours, do they?"

"Who cares how he dresses, he's a great journalist and a good friend."

"Yeah, who makes you hot and bothered." I did my best to conceal my feelings.

"About this girl you've just met." Aaron glanced around to find Amber among his friends. When he spotted her talking to a Persian Jewish woman who worked for a City Bank, he scrutinised her.

"She's gorgeous. I can talk to her without worrying she's going to accuse me of sexual harassment." He gazed at Amber. "We've got a good vibe. I want her to see that my friends are thinkers and activists. She must know I'm not 'the black' her father takes me for." He said it more to himself than to me. It was the only moment, all evening that he looked troubled. Roy came up behind us and patted me on the shoulder.

"This is the best turn-out. I thought some people were losing their stamina in our Remain in Europe against Brexit and Employability campaign. It's an odd mix of Prince clones and politicos, don't you think, Eugene?" I nodded, but Aaron jumped in.

"Come on, Dr M, what I like about your programs is the hybridity... Wait a minute! She's coming over—God! You just smile looking at her." I saw Aaron inhale as Amber twisted and turned between the party people and made her way towards us.

Amber told him, "You have fascinating friends." I couldn't think of two film stars who generated more sexual sparks than Aaron looking at her and Amber sizing him up. She was rather like Diana the Huntress, to his Perseus the slayer of Medusa. Their energy was primal and mythic; rather than ordinary.

Amber said, "I bought two bottles of Moët. Can you make a champagne cocktail?" She took Aaron's arm and led him away through the room filled with forty people, all dressed in their

Prince iconic costumes. From the triumphant look on Aaron's face, Amber must have made him feel like one hell of a man.

CHAPTER FIVE

A *week later* at Aaron's grandparents' house, Aaron and Saul took hold of the brocade red and black couch and moved it further away from the electronics he was installing for the widescreen conference video monitor and the 4ft high stand that Aaron had erected. Both of them were a sweaty mess. Saul was Humphrey's best friend and Aaron considered him family. Saul looked strained as he carried the other end of the couch, walking backwards through the typical Caribbean rumpus room, filled with electronics and family trophies.

"Uncle Saul, are you OK?"

"I'm thinking, who needs furniture like this, in this day and age?"

Aaron replied in the sarcastic Jewish tradition, "This relic is a necessity in the 'House of Chintz', what are you talking, Uncle Saul!" They staggered about carrying the couch, with Aaron's arms bulging in his sloppy old T-shirt and Saul sweating in his old vest. They put the couch down and Aaron glanced at Saul's wet hairy chest and pale skin, as Saul took a dinner napkin out of his pocket to mop his balding head. Aaron turned to his grandparents and told them.

"This is totally incongruous! You got this Hi-Tech satellite hook-up in this museum. Make up your mind already, modern or antique, but not both!" Saul found it easy to laugh because Aaron's body language underlined his Caribbean bravura and at the same time, emphasised his Jewish compulsion to kvetch. Saul looked like he was straight out of a Neil Simon comedy, as an over the hill playboy.

In his youth, Saul resembled a stand-up comic, with an ability to talk to someone as though he was addressing an audience and women loved him. As twenty years of marriage, three kids, two houses and kidney failure set in, it took its toll on his body and his posture; but his smile was all his own: he looked impish. Aaron and Humphrey considered Saul, a real mensch because he didn't have a mean bone in his body.

Aaron's grandfather, Harold, had shiny silver hair and a beard that distinguished his Jamaican face. He proudly said, "This house is a monument to a family that doesn't owe a penny to anyone." On all the walls, his family history was told in pictures of his family's achievements in Britain. "We raised five children, sheltered thirty-seven battered women and lived through prejudice and poverty. I'm not looking to make *no* statement about fashion!"

"It's just as well," Aaron said, pointing to the oh-so-typical Caribbean room packed with the knickknacks he remembered in other people's family homes.

Aaron's grandmother added, "And don't think your fancy mansion makes you better than anybody." Aaron's grandparents were as Christian in their fastidious humility as they were in their dress. The pair of them had a social education that trained them to argue with intellectuals. They represented the 1970s. Violet had all her clothes made by a dressmaker and Harold had all his suits and trousers made by a tailor in Stepney, East London. They were like a thousand other grandparents.

Aaron stated, "Please don't start, because I don't need to hear again how you raised dad on cornmeal porridge, chicken and Nutrament! Uncle Saul, did you know that made dad a *true* doctor?" Aaron's tone was so sarcastic his grandfather marched up and faced him with barely a space between their noses. Even aged seventy-seven, he looked good.

"You're not too big to get a damn good slap, boy!"

"I'm thirty and you're out of your mind!"

"Alright! Punch me down since you're so big and bad," his tough granddad told him. Harold was one of a dying breed of Jamaicans who would kick Satan in the balls rather than knowingly give in to temptation.

"Granddad, sit down, I'm trying to install a satellite conference between you and your people. Now you're King of the Manor and we're your loyal subjects, give it a rest." His grandmother pushed them apart. At seventy-five years of age, she'd live through the National Front, Thatcher's lies and her self-generated strength in Black British dignity in the face of economic disadvantage.

"Just like your father: cheeky!" she told Aaron.

"Dad *was* cheeky." A smile crept onto Aaron's face and Saul put his hands together and gestured a prayer.

Saul happily recounted, "I remember when the police stopped us; we were running to catch the night bus but missed it. Coppers drove up and stopped us. One asked why we were out that late and demanded ID. Your dad gave him his ID; it said, Dr Blackmon."

Donna came up to them. She had on a poncho and plain white Capri pants; her hair was pinned up which elongated her neck. "Oh yes, I remember that!"

"They couldn't believe he was a doctor and they asked: 'Where did you get this?' Humphrey replied. 'Will you stand up to cross-examination when I have my lawyer prosecute you?'. That dirty bastard looked like he shit his pants!" Aaron embraced him and then Donna kissed Saul, while her mother and father-in-law screamed with laughter.

"Humphrey said: 'I save lives, what's a schmuck like you do?'"

Donna was arrested by the memory of her husband and the absence of her daughter.

Donna said, "Nobody could mess with my man, not my father or anyone."

Aaron reminded her, "Mum; me and Zara didn't get away with much either." His grandparents recalled the Jamaican pride they had instilled in their son so he'd know he was a British citizen.

Donna stepped back and pushed her fists into her waist. The way she cocked her head to one side told everyone she was going to testify. She merely said: "The missing Richard Prior album!"

Aaron winced. "Oh mum, please, not that. That wasn't my fault!"

"Tell your grandmother what you did." Aaron walked away, but he suddenly turned back to see his family waiting for an answer. Their Jewish and Jamaican faces were insistent. The memory was as vivid as it was hot in Aaron's mind. But he refused to be distracted.

"Mum, I have no intention of reliving my shame to entertain the folks. I actually want to talk to you after I've got this hooked up and ready to receive messages." There was a strain of derision in his voice that his granddad picked up.

"Donna, how do you let him talk to you like that?"

"How is he supposed to talk to her?" Saul replied. "They're not formal. They're in tune."

His granddad insisted, "It isn't right. You should have more respect, Aaron." "There's no one else I have more respect for. That doesn't mean I'm going to put up with shit because she's my mother."

"In my day—" Harold began, and Aaron cut him off with deliberate intent.

"They'd beat the shit out of the kids! Thank God that's illegal now. You used to beat dad, but that didn't make him love you anymore." *Fuck!* "I get tired of hearing how much better everything was back in the '60s and '70s when we were at the mercy of the National Front and anti-Semite Oligarchs. All that oppression twisted our lives and minds, granddad, so deal with the change; it's liberated you more than you know."

"Your book learning has turned you into an educated fool."

Aaron said, "Oy! Help save the planet by stop talking!" Donna took Aaron by the shoulders and turned him to face her.

"Hey...what's the matter with you?"

"I'm very pissed off at you," he replied in a flat light tone of voice. "You set me up with Miriam like I'm some miskite or schmuck who doesn't know better."

"I'd never do that. Miriam and I work together from time to time, I know her, I like her. She's nice. We were talking on a flight back from New York. She mentioned she never meets nice guys, I said you were one. She asked about you and I told her you're great: run your own business, single and no victims cursing your name like some of the guys we've known."

"What makes you think she's right for me?" he asked, half smiling, ready to pounce.

"I like her. She's very ambitious, no leech, she's independent— she's kind."

"Why is she *right* for me?"

"What, she's nice, she's attractive, I like her, she's no slut... what?" Aaron pointed at himself and twisted his face.

"Why would she fancy me? What have we got she'd marry into?" Saul watched the two of them and he remembered that Donna and Humphrey could face off and snap at each other. He felt awkward, so he tried to buffer their exchange by arbitrating.

"I think what he's saying, Donna, is—"

"Saul, let him speak for himself. He's a big man."

Aaron's grandparents felt the oxygen in the room thin out, as tension crept in. They looked at their grandson and daughter-in-law and it reminded them of the early days when Donna and Humphrey argued about the intent and treatment her family put her through and the level of distress it caused her.

"You're young, virile, you make money, you're kind, you're handsome; what's not to like?" Donna stated, opening the palms of her hands.

"I'm not her type."

"Since when are you an expert on women? What do you think a woman is looking for in a man?"

"Today...now? A man without choices because she'll make them for him."

"You think that's why I married your father?"

"Mum! Don't do that. You switch gears when you're losing an argument to a point you can win. Dad married you because he adored you! He married you because he believed in integrity, love and faithful service to ease people's suffering. We all that! He constantly told me, read Marcus Garvey and David Dabydeen. I did. Miriam isn't interested in any...of...that!" he concluded, sticking his neck out.

"How do you know?"

"I'm *your* son with my father's bloodline," he stated as irrefutable evidence. "I know that Miriam is shopping for insurance to make sure she doesn't end up single."

"You're wrong. You're not the only man on her dance card."

"How old is she?" he asked, pointing in Donna's face.

His grandmother pushed her way in. "No mum, I'll deal with him. She's thirty-three, what of it? You think she's finished at that age? I thought I taught you better than that."

"She's desperate, she is!" he replied, flinging his arms about.

"She isn't, she's a very nice person, I like her! You think I'd introduce you to a Shlooche!" The two of them became angrier and started arguing in Yiddish for two minutes. They looked like the 21st century classic comic duo Mike Nichols and Elaine May in action.

"What are they saying?" Harold asked Saul, who whipped his head left and right between Donna and Aaron.

"I'll tell you when it's over."

Violet shouted, "Quiet! Both of you!" So they stopped.

"Mum, it's my fault for caring. He'd end up alone because he thinks he's got all the time in the world. Then he'll marry some 'save the earth' idealist because he's drawn to that kind of graduate intelligentsia, bag-of-bones who doesn't eat because God forbid, she should look fat!" Donna began tip-toeing around the room like a ballerina who constantly covered her body with silly demure gestures. Aaron watched Donna do it and she was an accomplished mime.

Donna then mimicked a girl picking at food. A girl fluffing her tutu, covering her privates and looking shocked. She mimed the actions of a hoity princess and someone who begged for love and then backed away. Considering Donna wasn't a dancer, she did the balletic mime with real conviction and translation. Saul thought she was wickedly funny and Aaron's grandparents thought she was half-mad. Aaron's anger diminished because he was always amazed at how effective his mother was at mocking things she hated.

"Mum, right now, you're twelve; you're a 12-year-old nutcase, OK!"

Donna stood still and tried to calm down. "You don't know what's good for you!"

"Is that why you agreed to send your friends' daughters to me?"

"Why shouldn't sons and daughters from good families meet?" Donna's feminine gestures were shaped by her effusive and bold movements.

"Because it's the 21st century and this isn't Israel or Spain where your family arranged their marriages."

"My family have never divorced in over ten generations."

"Yeah, how right were your parents when they renounced you for marrying dad?" Donna lunched forward.

"Watch yourself because you're going to piss me off any minute now!"

"No-no-no, this is not the time or place. If you want to get serious, how about you deal with that sloppy cleaner and broke-arse useless husband who supposed to clean my house properly but can't. You found them, you sent them to my yard and they're bloody hopeless! Deal with that. Get on the phone and deal with that!"

Donna said, "Mum, give me a fucking phone!"

Grandma Violet was in shock, so Saul gave her his mobile. "Shit, the bitch's number is only in my phone. Go and get my bag...no, I'll get it." She went to the corner of the room where the furniture was crammed together and got her handbag. She took the mobile, found the number and dialled.

"Miss former Yugoslavia, this is Mrs Rapchinski-Blackmon. My son tells me you and your worthless husband can't do your job! Get this, Bitch! Clean that house properly! Or you'll find your arse on a boat back to the 'old country'! You hear me!"

Aaron watched her amused. "Shut your Catholic mouth and do your job!" Saul covered his mouth and gagged listening to her.

"That wasn't politically correct!" Aaron said.

"Piss on that dogma! What else you want from me, Aaron?"

"Stop sending me these witches. I don't like them. I can choose the girls I want."

Donna grabbed him by his T-shirt and told him eye to eye. "I am not gonna let you throw your life away on some 'new age gal' who doesn't know how to take care of her man because she is on some half-arse mission to bring *equality* and harmony to the world—which is your type! Don't deny it; I've seen the 'Millennials' you've gone out with," she sneered.

"What's wrong with women who are committed to equality, eco-politics, or empowerment of downtrodden people?"

For a woman of Spanish Israeli heritage, Donna's stance and gesture couldn't have been more Caribbean. "They starve themselves to save the world and end up childless. My friends are building a future for progressive Jews through ecumenical marriages."

"You cannot change the world this way! Arranged marriages... The days of..." He suddenly stopped in the middle of his tantrum when he realised his mother *was* visionary. He smiled curiously and Donna sensed his mind was shifting. Aaron said, "Suppose I set *you* up on a date with a man who wants to get married." Everyone in the room laughed.

"Remarry?" Donna asked. "Don't make me laugh! Replace your father? Your dad was unique!" She walked around him and pointed. "Look at dad's parents. Your grandma's lifelong service to Royal Mail and her network of retired friends: plus, grandpa's commendations for services to London Transport as a driver. That's in addition to his Union leadership reputation. Everything they fought for and won they instilled in your dad and helped raise a doctor! Your father had kindness, pride—not to mention sex appeal, so you can't find *his* like!"

"I know you. I could find you a husband to cure your neurosis."

"Who are you calling neurotic?" she jabbed and shoved him.

Aaron adopted a crucifixion pose and said, "You! Me! We're narcissists *with* a guilt complex!"

"You're the neurotic: I've learnt to cope with deprivation."

"Mother..." He eyed her knowing every desperate minute of their shared bereavement for Zara and Humphrey. His face slowly reverted to the times they wept and drank together after they buried his father and her daughter.

Watching them, his grandparents became deeply upset. Donna watched him and she knew he was reliving their past. "Bubala; sorry." Aaron tried to block out the grief, but he still felt for Zara.

"What's all this drama? I don't need a husband!" Harold and Violet tried to cheer Donna and Aaron, but the memory of their son and granddaughter left a pall over them.

"Aaron, I just want to enjoy your wife's friendship, and help the two of you raise my grandson and see my granddaughter married," Donna concluded, looking at his grandparents and they agreed with her.

"Mummy," Aaron shook his head and gave in. "Mum, you'll get your wish, I want a wife and kids." His family looked pleased. "But arranged marriages..."

"I'm introducing you to nice girls because I can't deal with a bitch that'll separate us!" She screamed and tore her angst out of the air and threw it towards the open window. Saul watched her and he understood as well as he knew his dear friend Humphrey, who always bragged about his beautiful wife.

Saul liked them as a couple because they were much more receptive to ideas and diverse people. Saul couldn't remember an occasion when Humphrey made fun of his religion or mocked him for being a white-collar worker who played it safe. As the son of Eastern European survivors, Saul had the most profound respect for Donna. If *he* had been cast out of his Jewish community, as Donna was, Saul couldn't have coped, but he saw Donna change over time and he admired her. When Humphrey and Zara were killed, he remembered Donna and Aaron sliding off the deep end into depression and grief he couldn't pull them out of.

"I want to meet your father's like! Or better yet! Bring your father back to his family because his parents miss him as much as we do! Do that for me, if you're so fucking smart, son of mine!"

Her strut stalked Aaron just before Donna's temper moved up a gear. "And no anaemic bitch is taking you from me because I'm too Spanish! Too Jewish, too Jamaican and she can't cope with my *fabulous* energy that just might burn up her 'millennial egalitarianism'," Donna said with dripping contempt for girls like that.

"Mummy, I'm not interested in girls like that." The scorching look she gave him could have shrunk a weaker man. "Mum, I'd never marry any woman who'd cut you out of my life."

"I've lost enough already!" she fervently declared. Everyone knew how much she adored Zara and Aaron realised she hadn't recovered as well as he had adjusted to the death of his sister and father. The rumpus room became claustrophobic, so Donna left and they watched her.

Violet smacked Aaron's face lightly. "Where's your sense?" She went after Donna.

His granddad told him in a scolding and reproachful tone, "*Your* analyst is working; your mother's therapist isn't." It saddened all of them.

CHAPTER SIX

Aaron waited for Miriam at the *Sanjay Café Bar* in the heart of St Christopher Place; an overpriced, upstart, self-conscious imitation of chic. The Bar was one of the best-reviewed new places in London's West End. The soft gold lighting and retro style was anything but exceptional to Aaron. Where the Café excelled was in attracting pretty girls who were periodically joined by their self-conscious boyfriends. It was the perfect new media social space. On all the Café walls, it displayed posts of events happening online and diners could read comments on what was 'out there' if the patrons ran out of conversation.

The colour scheme and the feel of the place reminded Aaron of Rotterdam's airport's *Grand Café Horizon. Sanjay Café Bar* appeared to be an exact replica of the departure lounge with its mustard yellows, orange, browns and black décor. Coleman Hawkins' greatest hits played through the sound system and Aaron sat still writing to Amber in his notepad. His use of a fountain pen and his ability to turn the nib to make thick and broad calligraphy was most skilful. His handwriting was a combination of disconnected letters that looked independent yet interdependent as each letter formed words and sentiments on the page.

Our conversation on Sunday convinces me that we have a lot to talk—

Miriam came walking down the side of the bar near the glass wall window and Aaron noticed the looks she attracted. It could have been the black lace dress with a red silk slip that shone through, or it could have been the red shoes and black purse she held in one hand, but she commanded attention and got it.

Aaron glanced at people because they were all younger than Miriam, but they didn't have the vitality she possessed as she came towards him. When he stood up, his light grey trousers, white bomber jacket and black T-shirt had just the right level of casual smart that Miriam liked. If he'd have overdressed, she'd have been less impressed. Miriam sat down, took out her mobile and turned it off. "You look lovely," Aaron told her which made her smile in an enticing manner.

"I'm all yours now." If she had a cigarette, she would have been mistaken for an enchantress of the German Expressionist era and most certainly a femme fatale of the neo-noir age. Her body language and husky tone of voice were ripe with sass and sin and her fingernails were squared off and painted with glittering gold nail polish.

When she saw him looking at them, she wiggled her fingers and placed her hand above her cleavage near her throat. "This is my first date in London, so I decided a manicure was a must."

"What would you like to drink?"

"Cosmopolitan."

"That's very *Sex and the City* of you."

"I hated the films. They took those smart girls and turned them into greedy, stupid, shopaholic bimbos; what a let-down!"

"Mum liked the series. I didn't because Mr Big had no meaningful life. For a guy who posed as an existential character, conscious of the choices he made that shaped his life and defied his destiny, he was a schmuck!"

His comment arrested Miriam. "What were his politics? Who's his Rabbi—And no 'best man' for his wedding. Ridiculous! That 'character' showed me a very rich guy who was possibly just a prick in a suit. There was no way I could consider him a man. If only I knew what he did for a living and how his job fulfilled his life I could have considered him a man." Miriam's scrutinising gaze didn't perturb him, instead, he examined her.

"You really hated it, didn't you?"

"No, watching it with mum was a million laughs." He got up to go and buy her a drink. At the bar, a girl threw him a glance and the lady behind the bar also gave him the eye. The girl beside him waited for Aaron to talk to her.

"I'm on a date. No idea if it's going to be nice or nasty yet." The young beauty looked around and attempted to give him a card from her bag, but he shook his head no. Miriam saw some of it from thirty feet back and remained at ease because he moved away from the girl.

He came back and as he approached her, he held the drink up high and she saw the line of hair that led up from the waistband of his trousers to his tummy under his T-shirt, which she liked. When he put her drink down, he noticed the smile on her face. "What?"

"I like this place. It's very European."

"Once I was delayed at Rotterdam airport; this place reminds me of the departure lounge."

"I love the media messages on the walls. I looked this place up when you called and now, I see what they mean by city news updates." She had her drink and nodded.

"How hungry are you?"

"I could eat a horse."

"The restaurant is French, so it might be possible."

"You seem to be in a good mood tonight."

"I spent yesterday with my family. Moving furniture and connecting a conference screen of all things. But grandpa really wants to see his family, so it's the least I could do. Tonight, he's talking to the whole clan back in Jamaica."

"What's that like for you? Donna told me how her family cut her off and—"

"I couldn't want more from my family. If that's not good enough for the orthodoxy, forget it! My dad was a GP." Miriam didn't understand the British meaning. "Mum told you dad was a doctor?"

"Yes..."

"Over here, doctors are general practitioners: GPs are local family doctors."

"Oh, right, OK!"

"Anyway, he was great. I remember him reading bedtime stories to me until I was twelve. I just loved how he could dramatize Br'er Rabbit, Caribbean Folktales and most of all, King Arthur and his Knights, the destruction of Arthur's Camelot, adulterous Guinevere and backstabbing Lancelot. Dad would really go off on one about adultery and make up all kinds of stories for me to learn from."

"Was your father very religious?"

"100% a true Baptist."

"How close to the faith are you as a Jewish man?"

"Good question, I'll answer that another time. How was work today?"

She drank her Cosmopolitan and took ten minutes to explain the difficulty of working with Brits. "Over here everything is veiled, shrouded in polite rejection. I'm used to a more direct approach. 'Are you buying or not?' Yes or no...' Over here, everything is 'maybe' or 'later on'. That shit drives me crazy!"

"Let's take a stroll before dinner."

She agreed. They talked about nothing and then left. Out on Oxford Street, they looked good together. As he walked her past fashionable shops in the area, he pointed things out to her and she was most attentive. Miriam liked the Regency houses in Manchester Square as it epitomised London's smart history. Aaron noticed the number of men who eyed her as they walked by and the evening light complemented her snazzy demeanour.

* * *

Heading back from the restaurant in the taxi, Miriam and Aaron sat with a polite gap between them in the black cab. The West End streets, shops and people glittered and flashed past them in the cab.

"It's funny how people go out on a date and end up agreeing on their political views. Mum told me you felt strongly about terrorist factions and..."

"I can't seriously talk to anyone about this back home. I think that's the amazing thing about Europe. You guys are so much better informed about global news than we are. I just know all these people who go about their lives and end up dead in a concert auditorium, sports arena, restaurant or subway: it's made the reality of death so real to me. Before 9/11, I thought we'd die of old age. I never go to the Middle East for business; I can't even share my thoughts with you or anyone about that part of the world."

"These attacks and suicide bombings are such a twisted reading of religious enlightenment and faith. It hasn't called *my* faith into question; it's made me question people's idea of worship."

"And we're back to earlier in the evening before dinner when I asked you what kind of Jewish man are you."

"You'll only find out if we get naked, but in the face of Third-wave feminism and Rebecca Walker's insightful discourse as a Black Jewish woman, that won't happen unless you email to confirm that you want me. No woman is ever going to accuse me of sexual harassment." His stone face detachment revealed a lot to Miriam. She reached for her handbag, took out her mobile and sent him an email while he sat back and watched her. After she sent it, he got out his mobile, waited and then read it. His pugnacious face was changed by a beguiling smile.

Aaron then sat back and laughed for the first time all night. "You're more interesting than you know," he told her. "I like that you're pro-Israel and I admired the fact you're a feminist who dresses like this and cannot imagine her life without a husband and kids."

"I didn't say 'cannot imagine myself'. I said in my forties, I'd feel unfulfilled if I wasn't married with children and a loving husband."

"Is that the new-age feminist doctrine?"

"Don't mock me, you put on that cavalier pose, but no one who loves his mom as much as you do and speaks so highly about his sister, is a son of a bitch."

"I'm the son of an amazing woman. I see blokes give mum 'the look' and she never lets them close. She was dad's lady; to see them together, you'd understand real love."

"And you're looking for someone like her to marry," she stated, but he didn't answer. He moved closer, leaned in and stopped. She closed the small gap between them and eyed him, searching for answers she hadn't asked. His honey-coloured lips and lion eyes moved her, so she kissed him. When he responded with intent, she felt a bit giddy and pulled back, but the smile on his face warmed her.

"Shall we see if three makes it the magic number: we've met three times. Maybe we should go to my hotel…"

"Yes, let's go to your hotel."

* * *

Roy met me for lunch in Canary Wharf and I listened to him as we walked around the concrete and steel maze of a place. The shiny sterile imitation of reality flummoxed and disquieted me. Every phallic tower in the vicinity disgusted me. To me it was the quintessential heterosexist monument of deluded potency.

Anyway, we walked and ate our lunch from cartons and cups, dodging businessmen who ate and drank on the move in the steel glass cage.

Roy told me, "I've seen Aaron in action when we used to go raving, in Ibiza. He's got the right stuff to fuck four girls a night. He told me that he took Miriam over the edge seven times in two hours. He isn't lying. He's studied *The Hite Report of Female Sexuality* in the '70s and the 21st century Women's agenda. When he's aroused, he's another person. He gave Miriam a going over. It made her text him eleven times yesterday."

"To say...ask what?"

"Wreak her pum pum: me-no-know!" Because he quoted the Prince Buster classic tune, with a distinct Jamaican accent, I burst out laughing and people in the bloodless environment made me feel Caribbean Black instead of Black British.

* * *

A few days later, Aaron sat at *Searcys, St. Pancras Champagne Bar*. It was elevated above the main railway station concourse, under the giant curved roof. When walking below, the Bar always looked out of reach. The leather chairs and first-class fittings pleased Aaron, but he looked at his watch for the fourteenth time. Three minutes later, Aaron looked up because he heard the sound of high heels walking towards him and then he saw Amber approaching.

Even though he couldn't identify Issey Miyake's fashions, he loved the green and white dress Amber wore; complemented by her decorative shoes and bag which affirmed her demeanour and elegance. Her hair was styled into curled waves, so she looked lovely. He got up and took her hand and her smile penetrated his senses. "Bloody hell, you're so beautiful," he said sincerely.

She looked him over and he could see her studying his appearance. "Just Ben Sherman casuals; I'm not very fashion-driven."

"You don't need to be, you're..." the playful look on her face made her all the more adorable to him. "...smart. May I have a champagne cocktail?" Aaron ordered and three drinks later, they were both making circles around the six glasses on their table. Aaron's index finger moved clockwise around the rim and Amber's middle finger moved counter-clockwise around her glass.

"Miriam's all wrong for me. I took her out mainly because I promised mum I'd give her a chance. But I'm telling you—until the day men give birth, she stands no chance." He took a moment. "What did you think of my letter yesterday?"

Amber sat back and composed herself after listening to him, tell her about Miriam. She looked up and recalled her joy at reading the letter and a smile came over her. "I've never received a love letter in my life, I liked it. There is so much philosophical discourse in your explanation of your life and hopes."

Aaron went into his jacket pocket and took out another letter in a black envelope.

Amber took it and looked at the gold ink wording: To the girl of my dreams.

"Your handwriting and this gold ink...I love it!"

"The parchment is specially made, and the gold ink is specially made. My sister taught me how to use a fountain pen. The rest is all me."

Amber opened it and sand and glitter fell out of the letter when she unfolded it.

"The sand is from Israel."

"Oh, you're too wonderful!" she declared breathlessly.

"No, I'm a bit of a bastard; but I'm working that out." He leaned forward and kissed her and then sat back. Both of them had stardust and hope in their eyes.

"Your dad really doesn't want me to see you because my father was Black British?" Amber's entire mood changed, and a feeling of shame came over her. So, she grabbed the champagne flute and hoisted her arm as if she was going to throw it. She took several deep breaths to calm herself and as she put the glass back down on the table, Aaron noticed that her hand was shaking.

"I'm a very good girl, you know. I do as I'm told. I went to finishing school in Switzerland. I'm this 'pretty' because I've been carefully trained." She opened her purse and took out a small, wrapped piece of chocolate. She was about to unwrap it, but she shoved it over to Aaron and searched her bag to find another piece. For about ten seconds, she thought it was her last one, so Aaron pushed his back to her and then Amber found another piece, so she pushed it back towards him and they ate with smiles on their faces.

"Aaron, my problem is that I have rebellious thoughts, but I don't..." She pushed her hands out. "...I lack courage." Again, she took a breath. "In your letters, you explain how your mother defied her parents and married your dad. That's so fantastic! I am trying to be that...brave. My father's a diplomat: people don't defy him." She played with the sweet-sixteen ring on her middle finger. "If I understand your letters clearly, sometimes you defied your dad's authority..."

"I was such a 'git' growing up." Amber was unfamiliar with the word 'git'. "I struggled with being Jewish, but not raised Jewish: and being Black, but looking European. Unless people know me, they don't know I'm Black. I could pretend, pass for white but—"

"If you did that, I would get up right now and never speak to you again."

"It wasn't until I met Roy, that I found the perfect friend. At school, I use to win friends by doing a wicked Ali G Jewish Jamaican—"

"Ali G?" Again, he had to explain to her who and what that meant; and relive some of the gestures and mime which made Amber laugh uncontrollably.

"But dad use to take me for survival lessons in the woods. We talked about how the world is shaped by philosophy and psychoanalysis. Deep conversations, me aged sixteen and him a grown-up. So, when I met Roy, the first week at Uni'; we got talking about our love for British Two-Tone culture. Roy's from Jamaica, so I just fell in love with him! I took him home and we've been mates ever since."

"Wonderful! I don't care if my father thinks he's going to marry me off to...someone. Keep writing to me because I'm going to continue seeing you—yes?" Aaron's heartfelt smile was as becoming as always.

* * *

According to Roy, a week after Aaron and Amber had their heart to heart, he was still intensely happy. Consequently, the afternoon

Aaron ran his 'Personal Services' workshop, he invited Amber to his office in the City. Amber eyed him, standing at the head of the boardroom table, in his grey flannel suit, pastel yellow shirt and blue tie. He was surrounded by flowcharts of employability strategies and goal objectives, mapped out in different colours projected on walls around the typical boardroom.

Aaron said, "I've contacted my network of confidential informants," he told them as if he were running a secret 'Agency', and his clients liked it. It looked like a staff meeting, but the men and women were all job-seeking executives.

"They've told me everything I need to know about the firms you're interested in. I'm not charging you five grand just for personal counselling, in-depth psychometrics training and professional skills development; or to give you lip service. I have personally put together all of your recruitment campaign reports based on your individual skills. It's packed with background info on the firms you want to work for." He looked at each one of them with a foxy smile.

"These companies don't use recruitment agencies, but we'll see about that!" He laughed with absolute glee. "I'm going to mock interview each of you and get you up to speed! Any questions?"

Amber asked, "Are these reports 100% accurate of what it takes to get an interview and impress the HR and hiring managers at these listed companies?" St John, a debonair fifty-five-year-old gentleman, born and bred in Bath told Amber. "Our man here knows his business. I've got six interviews based on his research."

Amber asked, "Why didn't you get the job? I've heard everything you've said. You're a top director with an MBA and over £16 million in account billings—"

"Yes, my dear: I'm also crowding fifty-five and these ahistorical numbskulls think you have to be under forty to be brilliant."

Frederick, a trendy account manager who looked like a £100k a year, London top sales executive interrupted, "Gregory, we know most hiring managers are a bunch of tossers." Because Aaron's clients were well educated and some of the elite business people on the market, they all sounded posh. Therefore, Frederick's lewd comment made him sound like a naughty public schoolboy.

Kim, the perfectly dressed, Caribbean dark-skinned woman, turned to Amber and said, "And let's not forget that most businessmen lack any sense of equality, so we have to double our efforts." The job-ready executives in the boardroom all agreed with her.

Amber told them, "It's my first time here, so forgive me if I sound like I'm cross-examining you."

"We all have the right to get our money's worth," a mid-thirties German salesman said, clearly joshing Aaron and flirting with Amber. She knew he was flirting, so she looked at Aaron, confident in his advice.

Aaron told them, "If you get stuck on anything, as you fill out the template I've provided, you know you can contact me right up to nine o'clock. All of you remember this. I promised to get you into top firms in London, based on your choices and my contacts. I swear on my balls! I'm going to do that." Aaron's statement hit Roy and the others. Aaron shut the lid on his laptop and the others prepared themselves to leave.

Kim went over to Aaron and he walked her towards a corner of the room as they spoke privately. Roy went up to Amber as the other men and women gathered their things from the table. "What do you think?"

"He should do motivational speaking at events. He commands like an American corporate leader. She looked over and studied him.

"Not even my old professors at university dragged that much out of us in seminars. Everybody had so much to say. When that guy said he cried because he didn't get the job, I knew Aaron must be working closely with all of them. It's recruitment and career management therapy. I've seen a role at the V&A. I didn't think I stood a chance of getting it, but I'm going to apply now."

"Do it. Confidentially speaking, I know Aaron likes you more than some girl he fancies." Amber looked surprised and pleased. "Don't be surprised, you're lovely." Roy's hand beckoned her closer. "I don't tell many women that." She accepted his compliment. "Come, let's get a snack." Roy took Amber's arm and escorted her out.

Amber told Roy, "My father introduces me to lots of boys and none of them have Aaron's character and drive. He makes me tingle."

"I'll bet I know where you're tingling," Roy said as he walked her through the office corridor.

"You are so discreet and mysterious, in your oversize suit and hat." Again, Amber's accent warmed Roy. "But underneath, there's a dirty mind at work, no?" He just laughed and pulled her in by the shoulder and she liked him all the more.

"Aaron is also very sexy, no?" Roy kissed Amber on the top of her head. Outside, Bloomsbury traffic whizzed and crisscrossed the sunny streets.

Roy told her, "I'm in the mood for a gay café. Do you mind?" She happily followed Roy to Soho in the West End.

CHAPTER SEVEN

Aaron sat back, took a breath and Dr Liebermann smiled at him. Liebermann was fifty-one, with expressive greenish-brown eyes and a Lenny Bernstein appearance. He was rather like a father Aaron might have had. When he wasn't helping patients, Dr Liebermann could be found playing leading characters in amateur dramatics, such as Tevye in *Fiddler on the Roof*, or Max Bialystock in the musical, *The Producers*, among many other performances. He took particular pride in Aaron because he wanted to help him.

Dr Daniel Liebermann converted his library into a consulting room. The three thousand books that covered the walls weren't there for decoration. His Hampstead home, in one of the most affluent areas in London, said everything about him he wanted to be made public. Houses like his in that Borough went for three million pounds, plus; and most of the residents were men that ran their own business. The mix of Atheists, Jewish, Christian and a growing Muslim presence in the area was significant if you knew how some Jewish people felt about the 'oil men' as some of the neighbours refer to them.

The light green and white room harkened back to another era and the red leather chaise always felt good under Aaron. He looked straight ahead, knowing Dr Liebermann was sitting to his left because he could smell his *Eau Sauvage* cologne. "So, you made love to her and didn't reach an orgasm. Why are you still doing that?"

"I can take care of myself," Aaron replied smugly.

"Masturbation is not love."

"I know, but no woman is going to turn me into her bitch."

"I thought we dealt with this?" He saw Aaron clench his fist.

"Things have been a bit crazy the last week: what with Amber and Miriam."

"Why did you go on a date with Miriam and go to bed with her since she means so little to you?"

"She wanted me to fuck her." Liebermann could see the smile on his lips.

"I think you're showing signs of the pattern we identified before."

"What? We've covered a lot of ground over four years."

"I'm talking about your family's treatment towards your mother and father." Aaron tried to deny there was still an issue, so he decided to adopt casual ease.

"Aaron, what would happen if I listened to your heart right now?" Aaron sat up angrily and looked at him, but Dr Liebermann looked so paternally Jewish, Aaron felt as if he'd been scolded by a Rabbi.

"Do you want me to get the stethoscope?" Aaron got up from the chaise and walked across the room. He looked at the photographs of Sigmund Freud and Carl Gustav Jung. In the framed picture of Jung, there was one of his famous quotes: 'Knowing your own darkness is the best method for dealing with the darkness of other people. In the framed image of Freud, there was another quote: Unexpressed emotions will never die. They are buried alive and will come forth later in uglier ways.'

Dr Liebermann said, "Tradition remains the obstruction to progress in our lives, Aaron." He turned and looked at Dr Liebermann; bit his lip and nodded his head. He tried again to calm down. Liebermann pointed at the red leather chaise and Aaron walked back and sat down.

"I hate it when you read me like an X-ray. You and Roy are the only two that know all about me."

"What about your mother?"

"No, she doesn't understand certain things about me." He reclined on the chaise and tried to relax once again.

"What doesn't she know?" Aaron didn't answer and it took him over a minute to look at his Analyst and indicate that he wanted to answer; but with every attempt he made, the words stuck in his mouth and he couldn't force the sentence out.

Dr Liebermann took Aaron's hand. "In your own time, just say it, just tell me. I'm listening to you, it's just you and me; speak, Aaron."

"I'm ashamed of them. I mean their whole Stamford Hill orthodoxy makes me feel like denouncing them, because of the pain they caused mum. They never even turned up for my father's funeral!" He got to his feet again. "What the fuck is that?!" he yelled and startled Dr Liebermann. Aaron tried to calm down by pushing the anger away as if it were a physical hunk of matter in the atmosphere.

"My sister, may she rest in peace, told me that my grandfather came to her school and asked if dad mistreated her or whether mum is miserable with him."

"How much contact do you have with your grandparents?"

"None: they're an offense to me. I watched mum calm dad and only once did he hit the roof. Anyway! It's orthodox 'notions' that smashed and destroyed their lives. Why do we freak out over religion and race? Does it come down to a nice Jewish girl taking a Black man to her bed and maybe...spawning a primitive 'black' child?" He laughed at the absurdity and pushed the air out of his face.

"The Stamford Hill guys are mainly tradesmen; *my* father was a doctor! He saved people's lives, he was respected at Homerton and Bart's Hospital. I'm CIPD certified with an MA, but some bastard thinks my genes make me rubbish—please!"

"Do you remember what we discussed, a year ago, about displacement?"

Aaron replied: "No," but it wasn't true, he told Roy he didn't want to deal with it.

"It's when you unconsciously divert your sublimated rage, shame and urges away from a conscious level of dealing with them. You have a tendency to mask your antipathy by pathologizing the perpetrators." Daniel pointed at him. "Doing this makes you their victim."

Aaron scrutinised him carefully and walked back over to the chaise, but he wouldn't sit down. "Aaron listen, Miriam said all the wrong things on Mother's Day. She implied a lot about your identity and values, so you set out to teach her a lesson. You flipped her provoking seduction into your phallic mastery." Aaron smiled slyly and resumed his place on the red chaise.

"Amber's family tells her you're not good enough for her, so you plan to court her. You've sent her one love letter every day. That's bound to make her question her father's 'wisdom'. You saved her life and now you send her love letters. That's a profound mark on a young woman's psyche."

"You're making me out to be a real motherfucker." Dr Liebermann stood up and cast a shadow over Aaron's face, so he turned away.

"That Oedipal term and insult you just uttered; it has symbolic meaning." Aaron lay there, rather frightened of Dr Liebermann. When Aaron gave himself time to think through the inference and he heard it, he got to his feet, indignant and ready for a fight.

"That is so fucking disgusting! I've told you, that Freud shit is inverted Jewish blasphemy. What man wants to kiss or see his mother's cunt: fucking sick!"

"This is *your* taboo."

"No! Every man's! Well, not Hitler, he properly feasted on his mother."

"You think Hitler was a motherfucker?" he asked, always stimulated by Aaron's revisionist mentality.

"Yes," Aaron adamantly replied. "Adultery, terrorism, bigotry and child molestation are my boundaries."

"Why adultery first?"

"I wasn't ranking them. Please, enough about sex with mums." Aaron shuddered.

Dr Liebermann said, "I could tell you something, but I don't know if I should, considering where your head is right now."

"Liebermann, don't fucking do that," Aaron replied, pointing in his face.

"You came here because you're angry that your mum still sets up dates for you." Aaron nodded. "Well, there's a reason why you're acting like this."

"Look at you." Aaron eyeballed him, giving him an insubordinate once-over.

He eyed Liebermann's brown and black plaid shirt from Liberty's menswear, his cream-colored corduroy slacks, Argyll socks tasselled black penny loafers. Dr Liebermann was the picture of casual professionalism, but there were times, in fact, many of them, when he felt paternal towards Aaron. On one occasion Dr Liebermann took him to a gym for a physical and psychological evaluation and Aaron battered the heavy bag so brutally, he screamed out loud, brought the place to a standstill and then he passed out. Liebermann recorded that he felt as if his own son had collapsed helplessly before him and he felt dreadful.

"Alright, Doc, I'll bite, what is it now?"

Dr Liebermann did his best not to smile, because of all his patients, he enjoyed the challenge Aaron set him. So, he remembered his training and quietly spoke, "Your mother introduces you to women she likes. She trusts them and she knows they respect her. This kind of trust, by Donner's own admission, if I heard what you said, correctly indicates she won't be rejected if your wife becomes a loving daughter-in-law. Nor will Donna be neglected by you because you prefer your wife's company to hers."

"What's your point?"

"You have unconcluded sex with these women. You excite them, flaunt your perspicacity, take them to places that indicate you're serious. But these women have the qualities that remind you of Donna and so, even though Miriam is sexy, driven and ambitious; and the last person to squeeze you out of a penny because she wants to make her own fortune; she represents the strength that a mother possesses."

Aaron hurled himself off the couch, stood above Dr Liebermann and told him, "That's where you're wrong, doctor!" He punched the air. "I don't reject girls mum introduces me to because they're mother-figures like I'm secretly attracted to my own mother… how fucking disgusting is that! I don't want those kinds of women near me because they are never satisfied with life."

"What do you mean?"

"There's a kind of woman today I want no part of. Those creatures are carnivorous. Most of my former mates are trapped by them. Those blokes must get permission to live! Why should I be punished, or tolerate a retro feminist backlash because pre-colonial men robbed them? Those old geezers were slave masters, not me."

"Do you think most men today are powerless?"

"Yes. I want a wife who understands the meaning of happiness."

"What *is* the meaning of happiness?"

"Rejecting the State's brainwashing propaganda and cultivating our best instincts to help each other. Globalism and consumerism have changed our lives for the worst."

"Does your property and running your own business, as well as taking women to bed and having sex with them, but not reaching a climax make you feel powerful and happy?"

"Don't fucking turn on me."

Dr Liebermann's sudden silence made Aaron feel that he had offended Daniel, which upset him.

"What did you tell me when we made the breakthrough that helped control your alcohol consumption and the dependency you were going through with Donna's grief?"

"I said you're like a Rabbi to me and I need one."

Dr Liebermann walked away from him and went over to his desk and poured a glass of water. "I have 3,709 books in here. I've studied four principles of psychiatric and psychoanalytic treatments and what excites me if you want to know, Mr Rapchinski-Blackmon, is knowing I'm breaking through the rigidity of systemic thinking and then you try and bullshit me."

"I'm not!"

Dr Liebermann walked back to him as though he was a detective confronting a prime suspect. "If you're only going to reveal half-truths, we'll be here forever."

"What are you talking about?"

Through an explosion of Hebrew and Yiddish gestures and expressions, Liebermann yelled, "You can cook a chicken in a candle-lit oven, but it will take forever before it's done!" He stood right over Aaron and pointed at him. "And it won't taste good."

"More proverbs, are all Jews and Jamaicans addicted to them?"

"You're maybe the only misanthropic egomaniac miser I've ever treated."

"You accuse me of egomaniacal narcissism! My employees, my friends, grandparents and mum depend on me!" He grabbed Dr Liebermann by the shirt.

"I give!"

"Back off, because I can have you sectioned."

Aaron slapped him in the face. The two of them were stunned into silence for seconds. Aaron later told Roy he felt like he had hit his grandfather.

"Do you remember what happened when your father took the belt to you?"

"Fuck off!"

"I remember."

Aaron watched the look on Dr Liebermann's face. "No, fuck off! Get this in your history about me. As a teenager, I was a mess. I wasn't Black, I wasn't a Jew, I wasn't a hard-nut. I wanted to be something! I was ready to affiliate with a clique who'd validate my identity." Aaron took his worry beads out of his pocket and played with them. "Dad stopped me from doing that. He used to book time out to take me adventure hiking in the woods for weekends. Dad taught me ancient history and modern politics. Best of all, he explained how I made him proud. Dad always told Zara why he loved us." The memory hit him in the guts.

"I gave you those beads to stop you biting your nails, but you're going to break them if you tug anymore."

"Here, take them back." He thrust them at Dr Liebermann, and they fell on the floor. Aaron picked them up and went over to the window and stayed there.

"Your vision of love may not appeal to any woman because they want to feel you belong to them after you've said your vows. What are you offering Amber? What you define as your ideal relationship isn't much for any girl."

"Why are you turning on me? You took an oath to help people and—"

"I am helping you! You think it's normal to have sex and withhold, the way *you* do? To control one of the most sacred acts of human experience. You said at the start of the session that you'll respect Amber's virtue because her family thinks you're a pussy fixated gangsta trying to 'play' their daughter." Aaron turned around to look him in the eye. "They think I'm a *black*! I mean—worthless! They've put me where they think I belong. Amber doesn't see me that way, so I don't intend to get in her pants to show my love."

"You've just met her. Where is the tangible evidence of this love?"

"I was *meant* to save her life. There's a spirit to her and I feel it."

"Donna ignored Amber and expressed no feelings about her whatsoever."

"Liebermann, stay with me on this. Amber is everything mum isn't. That's exactly what I *like* about her. I am not attracted to facsimiles of my mother. I'm aroused by the physical opposite of my mother!"

73

"Haven't you slept with the women Donna's introduced you to?"

"Yes, that's how they commit."

"So, Donna *isn't* as pushy as you've said when she asks you about the women she introduces you to. *You're* hoodwinking your mum into believing the women she introduces to you are right for you."

Aaron demonstratively said, "I want mum to know I want a family."

"How many of the girls that you prefer have you introduced to Donna?"

"Three, but mum thinks they're nonentities. To her, Millennials are narcissistic lightweights who don't have the guts to tear the government apart if it leaves blood on their hands."

"What else?"

"Mum thinks vivacious women are leaders." Aaron flopped onto the chaise, exhausted. "But down deep, she knows turning suffering into survival is the path to happiness," he concluded hoarsely.

"Describe your ideal sort of woman. Pick a star that has the looks and qualities you admire."

"What are you doing?" Aaron asked, filled with suspicion.

"Asking you a question. Help me understand you, answer my question." Because his suspicion was aroused, he delayed his response to hear the silence and study his Analyst. Aaron went for a glass of water and then went back to the chaise and replied.

"I don't drool over some celebrity. My ideal concept of a woman is Amber."

"Considering Donna's idea of who's right for you, how will you get her to accept your choice over hers, to alleviate her fear of being abandoned?"

"That's my cross!" He tried to relax. "How much time do we have left?"

"There's time."

Aaron lay there and thought for two minutes. Dr Liebermann took lots of notes in shorthand and looked up at him.

"Mum shouldn't worry that I'll marry someone who'll cut her out of my life."

"No mother wants to lose her son to a wife who usurps her love." Aaron got to his feet and walked over to the image of Freud and pointed.

"What if she had a husband who gave her back the love she lost?"

Dr Liebermann looked a bit confused. "What are you saying?"

"If mum had another husband, then she'd be able to rebuild her love. Mum's magnificent. She's only fifty; plenty of men would love her."

"Why should Donna marry again?"

"Where is it written she shouldn't rebuild her life?"

"What would it give her?"

"Only Roy and I really understand her," Aaron said impatiently. "Behind her diva persona, she's a very humble woman. Mum needs to be loved. She needs a second chance to revive her life!" He triumphantly pointed at Freud and then turned to Dr Liebermann confidently.

"You think your mother would take less interest in who you married if she remarried?"

"Yes."

"She's your mother, why would she care less about you, if she remarried?"

"You're very old-fashioned; it's all your Freudian leanings. Mum hasn't had...intimate love since dad was killed. They used to go at it all the time."

"How do you know that?"

"I know," he replied which sent a spark through Dr Liebermann.

With grave apprehension, Dr Liebermann asked, "Did you ever see them?"

"I've never been 'traumatised' by the *primal scene*. Freud had no valid concept of Afro-sexual psychology. My dad was sexually liberated and a fucking great bloke: mum's said so." Aaron laughed out loud. "Dad took me and Roy weekend combat training in the woods. Once I caught him wanking when he thought me and Roy were canoeing while he was back at camp cooking for us."

Few patients were so honest with Liebermann. "You saw that?" Aaron nodded. "Did that excite you?"

"Oh, you dirty Freudian!" Despite himself, Dr Lieberman laughed.

"Dad told me he stripped off to empower himself with nature and conjure up the elements to visualise his wife—that doctor, is love!"

In Aaron's face, Dr Liebermann saw Aaron's pure devotion. It wasn't sexual. For a brief moment, Dr Liebermann recalled his own joy as a youngster, seeing the names of two Jewish guys, Jerry Siegel and Joe Shuster, as the creators of Superman. Because of Jerry and Joe's social acculturation, their ego, id and superego made Superman an American WASP. At the age of twelve, Daniel Liebermann wanted to become a psychiatrist to understand why two humble Jews couldn't see themselves as heroic. Therefore, Liebermann wanted to liberate Jews from 'the state's' indoctrination.

"When your father realised you caught him like that, wasn't that awkward?"

"Nah! He was naked with a fucking great hard-on; yeah—but that's when I realised, I *am* my father's son. And he is the man who's created me and mum is the woman who gave birth to me." Aaron held his head high, shining. "On the night I became a man, with my first girl, I *couldn't* speak." Liebermann watched and listened attentively. "I used the force of my father's spirit to mentally tell her I'm humane, not a brainless prick who wanted to defile her. Being sexually excited and romantically aroused is natural. Dad's naked worship wasn't dirty, and I wasn't *traumatised*. That kind of shit is for weak men who are unclean."

Aaron stood up and pointed at Dr Liebermann. "I can and I will help my mother remarry."

"Watch you don't outsmart yourself in running people's lives."

"Jews, Muslims, Royalty and gentry have arranged their kid's marriages for centuries! I mean, Jane Austen's whole Christian Capitalist social-climbing bullshit stories are about marriages that are arranged. I can rewrite that shit. I interview people for jobs all the time. I know how to select candidates."

Smiling defiantly, Aaron unsuccessfully adopted a casual manner and told Dr Liebermann. "I'll consider prospects, screen them. Find out everything, I have contacts that can do a background check on the suitable ones. I'll shortlist them and then!" He laughed. "I'll talk to mum and get her to meet them, date them and she can choose whoever she likes." Daniel watched Aaron swagger and pose.

"Great session, Liebermann! Sorry about the slap." Aaron flexed his shoulders and quickly adjusted his groin. "You can charge whatever you like for that, I'll pay for it. Bye!" And then he left.

Daniel Liebermann watched him exit and he took a minute to settle his thoughts. "He *could* pull it off."

CHAPTER EIGHT

Roy was talking to Aaron and their friends, at a table in the corner of *Ipso Facto*; the new 'happening' Café Bar on the Aldwych side of Covent Garden. They were on the roof of the building, so the city spread out around them in the dusty blue spring evening where the lights of landmarks and new high-rise business cluttered the skyline of Central London. Roy, Lance and Pierre were as smartly dressed as any three successful young executives could be. Lance was in a Prince of Wales grey suit; Pierre in a high fashion two-piece from an experimental designer, which revealed Pierre was as much a man of fashion as he was an architect who had designed several famous 'pop-up' buildings in London and Paris.

Bolstered by confidence and knowledge, Aaron looked at Roy and his two business buddies who were all friends since their time at King's College. "Amber should be here any minute now."

The bar was filled with London's 'highflyers' whose lives were dominated by their work because they'd been indoctrinated with online mythology. Even without taking a survey, I knew they believed life without social media affirmation was the road to a meaningless existence. By millennium standards, there wasn't an ugly boy or girl in the place, but two-thirds of *Ipso Facto* was made up of patrons who only spoke about themselves, which was so unlike the political era of the 1980s when I was a graduate about town.

I couldn't help but notice how sexy Roy looked, despite the fact he was hiding inside a zoot suit that covered up his body. But his face and the smile that continually showed me how much he enjoyed being with people, radiated from him. As always, he occupied the background because the star was and always would be Aaron for him, which made Roy all the more enigmatic to me.

Aaron told his friends in his best posh tone of voice. "Amber is pure elegance: her speech, her walk and thoughts. I don't want to tame any shrew, which is why she's so beautiful. Plus, she knows how Coco Chanel remade her reputation after she collaborated with the Nazis. And how fashion works as the Emperor's new clothes: even how John Galliano received absolution for his anti-Semitism by the fashion industry."

Pierre said, "Ask me to define a neo-Nazi, mangina and I'll cite Galliano."

"Amber was so fucking angry about that!" He rambled on for the next thirty minutes and Pierre and Lance recounted scenes from their failed relationships.

Amber arrived in a pink-white organza dress that shimmered, and her silver strappy sandals stood her in elegant grace. Absolutely everyone watched her because she was wearing a tiara and long sparkly earrings. She held onto a small silver clutch bag and Aaron gazed at her. She smiled and everything in sight sort of froze like a snapshot flashed in all our minds, within the bar. I came to my senses faster than the others because of the sexual energy that flashed between them. Whatever Grace Kelly and Elizabeth Taylor had on-screen, Amber had something more, I'd call it God-blessed. She simply existed within a feminine grace.

I had no idea of time, but Roy took my arm and led me away and we left them. We didn't say goodbye, we just left the Café and walked towards Holborn. The darkening streets were lit with car headlights as we walked past drunks and rebels making a lot of noise. Roy asked me, "How is the book coming?"

"Very fast! Every time I see Aaron, there's more to write about. He's really caught up with this girl."

"Yes, I told you, Aaron gave me a blow-by-blow account of his session with his analyst. Aaron's never been like this with any girl. She has erotic purity, doesn't she?"

"Bloody hell, Roy! That's why it takes the two of us to write this book. I couldn't have expressed it better. She does have a spirit that lights something inside us. Did you see the look between them?"

"I felt her connection with him." He pushed his trilby hat back and I couldn't take my eyes off his face. I could hear the sound of traffic and people coming and going, but his Jamaican face with all his British intelligence rooted me to the spot. I kissed him right then and there because he was just too fucking sexy to resist. Right there in the middle of the street, he grabbed me and his hard body under the suit filled my frame. His kiss lifted me out of my underpants, and I could feel he was on the rise, which gave me pins and needles.

When he pulled back from the kiss, he smacked my face. "Don't do that again, Dr M. Sophisticated Black men are beyond the limit."

I was confused, but he smiled at me the way that young soul boys teased the crowd and made you want more of them. Seriously, Roy is top-notch, and I'd have given up a year of my life to get him in bed and make him fucking crazy. He's got a body-rocking under his clothes that make porn stars look unreal. Last year, we shared a hotel room for David and Michael's wedding, and I saw him naked and I still can't forget how naturally sexy he is.

"You're the only Black man I've met in London I can confide in Eugene. You remind me of the family I've never had. If we get it on and I lose our truth because lovers *aren't* cool, I couldn't stand that."

"Roy, you need a man who's more than a family. You need a champion. You're everything I look for but never find in men today."

He took my hand, balled it up and kissed my fist. "I can't risk losing you." The look on his face was beguiling and I suddenly felt super cool in my sneakers, jeans, T-shirt and leather bomber jacket. "Eugene, that look is leading me into temptation." Here's a fact. When you're in your early sixties and feel half your age, a man like Roy makes you glad you're still in working order.

I watched the gentle smile come through his bright brown face and I didn't want to ruin our friendship either, so I stepped back and then my thoughts rushed all over the place until finally, I said, "Considering what happened back there between Aaron and Amber, does Miriam even stand a chance?"

Roy missed several beats before he replied, "There's another side to Aaron you haven't seen." We began walking towards Bloomsbury Square. "As ethereal and lovely as Amber is, Aaron will never marry anyone Donna really doesn't like. And Miriam has the kind of sexual character and independence that suits Aaron."

"He'd choose Miriam over that incredible girl who struck everyone in the Café like lightning?"

"Aaron won't marry any woman Donna doesn't like. Besides, Miriam's obvious sexuality is a perfect match for Aaron's hidden sexual nature."

"What do you mean?"

"I can't say without betraying a confidence."

"Then how can we write the book?"

Clearly, Roy was perturbed. He looked all around and I sensed he was on the verge of panic. I put my arm around his shoulder and he leaned in. A few people caught sight of us and one cyberpunk guy in black clothes sneered and called us 'fucking queers' as he walked past. Roy lunged at him and punched him in the face several times. He then landed a kick in the man's groin and screamed Jamaican obscenities which I'd heard my Barbadian father and Uncle used to Jamaicans to express their frustration with their powerless positions at work or in life. People cleared away because the violence was too real and too ugly.

I was so stunned because Roy is a guy that hides in plain sight, always in the background. Therefore, watching him come forth with all that fury made me sweat and breathe heavily. The flashing lights of a police car on the opposite side of the street came into view and people jumped up and down and ran out to flag the cops down. Roy shoved the guy over and dashed towards me and grabbed my clothes and we ran wildly through the street until we saw a cab and Roy stopped it. I took out my gold card and said: "Barbican, mate!" and gave him my address. We hustled away and sat back breathless.

"When we get to yours, take me to the bed and dramatize homo-eroticism for me." It took maybe eight seconds for me to get hard. He took my hand and placed it on his lap and I could feel what I'd imagined for ages. Outside the cab, London whizzed by because I was hyper and everything in my body was racing.

* * *

I woke up the next morning and saw Roy standing on the balcony, naked, hidden from public view by the brick and stone that surrounded everyone that lived in the Barbican luxury housing complex. The apartment was remodelled and decorated with a colour palette based on Maisons Jaoul in Paris, designed by the celebrated architect, Le Corbusier, but that was as nothing to me because last night I had the greatest sex of my life with the beautiful man standing outside my window.

His presence prevailed over all of Robert Mapplethorpe's images. I pulled myself up and put the pillow under my armpit so that I could take a long look at the body that was mine the night before. Amber was a true sight of feminine beauty, but nothing about her or Aaron compared to the autumn brown tightly muscled man whose backside was everything I never see in fine art. Rodin's *Age of Bronze* nude was wonderful! But Roy triumphed above that because he *was* God's creation and Roy's reconstruction through his self-definition. His arms and shoulders, his arse and legs were home to a man whose mind was as sexually explicit as it was refined by post-colonial knowledge and perceptiveness.

Roy turned around and there was the sexual glory I loved. He was framed by the glass wall looking out onto the City of London. Within that frame of urban architecture, his body contained the human complexity I search for. Only a few hours earlier, I saw how he came to attention even though he was now at ease. I got out of bed and went to him. He invited me to come forth and I walked out of the bedroom and through the sliding doors of the glass wall. I went to him and settled in his embrace. The smell of the morning and his skin penetrated my senses, which filled me with morning glory.

"Roy, before I become self-conscious and defensive, I gotta say last night was fucking amazing." Some people want to see monuments, mountains and lakes in the world. I'm easy to please because Roy stood out against the brutalist Barbican landscape. There's so much that resides in the mind and body of a Black man most people don't want to explore, but that is precisely what makes me who I am.

"Eugene, you know about my past relationships." He glanced at me plaintively. "Well, last night was unbelievable. For the first time, I don't feel a shred of guilt or infamy," he confessed, caressed me and I felt like crying, just out of happiness, because no man has ever told me that. Both of us were standing on a balcony stark naked and I didn't care who might be awake at six o'clock.

Nonetheless, I led him back inside the flat. He told me, "I can't believe you're over sixty, except 'that old school loving' you put on me dates you." He grabbed my erection and led me to the bathroom, where we showered together.

Later, I was making breakfast, but I kept looking away from the stove to watch him walk about; lithe and young, in his red socks and white underpants. He was a fantastic contrast to Habitat, Conran and Le Corbusier's vision of a home.

"This place is so 1960s design flashy, Dr M. It's like stepping back in time. The colour, the clean lines and it's cool. With all these windows, does it feel like a fishbowl?" He crossed the room and stood in the sunlight, which made him appear blazing brown, rather like an artist's muse, instead of pornographer's obsession.

"It's not mine. I'm just flat-sitting. His business is doing so well in Paris, he asked me to stay, but you need a £100,000 annual income to live here." Roy kept moving like he was making his way through a museum, taking in the sight of every detail. Granted, there was a lot to see because Lauderdale Tower and the Barbican reminds me of a model-village home, made real. It wasn't just the bright primary colours on the walls, the design of the furniture; or the bric-a-brac: it just felt like a display apartment rather than a home.

Later, in the middle of our Scandinavian breakfast, Roy put his fork down and stopped eating. I felt his unease as I stared at him. "What I haven't told you is that I love Aaron." I shuddered and clenched my teeth. The light in the kitchenette shifted towards the living room suddenly. I looked at him and I couldn't look away.

"It's not what I want. It just happened. But at the same time, Aaron's my best mate. I understand what Miriam sees in him. I don't think Amber's unearthed it. He's got incredible sexual power which he doesn't fully appreciate. In Ibiza, I watched him pull and fuck several girls. I told you about it." I nodded. "I love the force in him."

"Doesn't that make things rather difficult for Narj to compete with?"

"Yes! That's why we're close to breaking up and I don't want that. He relies on me to take care of him."

Spitefully, I said, "Michael De Farenzino was telling me just the other day, Narj's paintings are getting great press in Spain, and he went over big in Paris. As his agent, Michael would know if he's out-of-sorts. He's making an exhibition of *himself* at his shows. Japan was big for him, great reviews: he's picked up a lot of admiration recently." How subtle that was I didn't know, but I wanted to hurt him.

"That's why Donna is such a part of my life. She knows how hard I've worked to take care of Aaron and Narj, but I need someone to take care of me."

"I'm sorry things have been so difficult for you. I thought you were happy."

He got up and came to sit in my lap so I pushed the chair out and he sat. He rested beside me and for the first time in years, I felt needed. We must have made a strange sight in the apartment. Two Black men totally out of place in that apartment complex, sitting together in the middle of designer paradise but so far from heaven even though I wanted to find heaven on earth with him.

"Eugene, don't think I'm some kind of a skank like those nasty gay boys with Apps on their phones who place an order for a shag. Then an hour later, some prick comes over, so they can do it." He shivered and kissed my neck. "I'd never ever do that. I didn't get out of Jamaica to come to Britain to be everything I was accused of."

"What, baby?"

"A faggot. They called me dirty things." He suddenly pleaded, "I'm nice, I'm decent, ask Donna, I've been a help to her and Aaron. If I was a God-forsaken dirty man-whore, I'd kill myself. This book will show them how much I respect them and myself. I want to help Aaron to be the man his father wanted him to be. Humphrey helped me to be a man with dignity. I took care of his son and I want Donna and Aaron to understand how to resurrect Zara and Humphrey as a force of strength. If they discovered life in the spirit they mourn, Aaron and especially Donna could rise above the death inflicted on them."

"You've taken a lot on yourself. What if Aaron and Donna don't understand *your* vision? Or if they don't want it?"

"You don't know them, Eugene; they have an incredible capacity to love. That's why they took me in." It felt odd having him sit on my knee and tell me all this. I wanted to be his lover, but he made me feel like his dad.

"Roy, are you sure I can write the book the way you want?"

He stood up. "You're doing brilliantly!" I pulled back the chair and eyed him carefully. "I can feed you the information, but I can't write the way you do!" He gave me a glorious smile. "And here's the brilliance! You've captured my voice about the things I've told you so well. When I read the manuscript, it's like listening to my own thoughts. I mean, fucking hell, Eugene, that's what makes you a great writer. You hear me, but you explain Aaron so well."

I told him, vexed but excited, "There's a lot I don't know about Donna. I don't think I'm doing her justice. Of course, I pick up on Aaron and your dislike for Miriam, but I can't claim to understand the way she thinks."

"We'll get it in time; we're still on the first part of their lives," he replied, coaxing me with profound conviction. "As a journalist, believe me when I tell you people don't want to read about reality, they want realism! That's why the TV series 24 prepared Americans for Obama because they were introduced to their first African American President on that show through Dennis Haysbert. People depend on realism because reality is too tough to cope with."

"What about last night: you and me?" The smile that took over Roy's face brought a smile out of my guts onto my face.

Roy said, "You never know what a real man is until you meet him." He stepped closer. "Everything about you proves that." Roy placed my hands behind him. "You want it again?" His eyes felt like they were touching my vitals and the feel of his arse was like ripe breadfruit that filled my palms.

I pulled him onto the floor because the table was full. Then right there, on the Flokati luxury rug, I had him. He was no powerless recipient! He told me to fix him because only a man my age could cure his mess. What he brought out of me no other lover inspired in me. In case you don't know true greatness, let me tell you—it's having a former tearaway Jamaican boy turned British intellect make you feel like a hero and lover.

* * *

A few days later, in the tremendous hustle and bustle of Broadway Market in Hackney, people dodged each other as they weaved through the market stalls selling food and fashions. The cafés burst with Hackney Hipsters. Most of the men had groomed beards that made fashion statements. Their girlfriends dressed in everything you could find in second-hand shops and charity stores to affirm their 'shabby-chic'. The men, however, were consciously playing down their fashion, but they looked like characters in a Bertolt Brecht modern-day *Threepenny Opera*.

In this maze of plaid shirts, dyed cotton dresses and bric-a-brac fashion, Amber and Aaron stepped out of the *Dove Pub Restaurant* in pastel-coloured clothes. Aaron in a pair of white plimsolls, cream shorts, and blue T-shirt: Amber in a yellow cotton summer dress, flat sandals, and a green back-pack. Aaron took her arm and led her through the crowd, and they shone within the throng.

"So has your dad introduced you to anyone recently? It sounds like you have a flock of suitors at your door. Are you going with anyone now?"

Amber covered herself with a silk scarf and said, "You say, 'going with them'. Do you mean sexual liaisons?" she asked, concerned and possibly insulted.

Entreating her in French, Aaron replied, "You are not a coquette or a girl of the Demimonde. To come from a finishing school and end up as a bon-bon would be absurd, excuse my misuse of the phrase," he apologetically concluded.

"I accept your apology if only to hear you speak French. Your accent is a bit English, but I can help you with that."

"Well, it's better I speak French badly, than excel at French but can't speak a word of the language." The lascivious meaning in his words provoked her excitement seconds later, so she gasped and slapped his face, which shocked him.

People in the street were alarmed when she laughed loudly.

"Oh darling, forgive me." Amber tried to be conciliatory. "That's the dirtiest comment I ever heard, and I love it!" Aaron began laughing too, because she didn't have a heavy hand and he'd been punched in the face before now. He took her in his arms and kissed her. Some people whistled, but their kiss transported them beyond space and time in the middle of the market. When they pulled back, her nipples were erect and visible through her summer dress and his hard-on strained in front of his shorts as anyone could see. He grabbed her hand and dashed away, leading her to Regent's Canal, a few meters away, which was also crowded with Saturday out of borough visitors.

Amber told him, "If we start going out properly; I won't discard my virginity. Do you *still* want to go out with me?" Her pride was slightly undermined by her anxiety, he later confessed.

Aaron kissed her left hand and nodded yes, which pleased Amber.

CHAPTER NINE

Michael and David's house in Canonbury was one of the most beautiful homes I've ever been to. It combined an Egyptian style and Art Deco impressively. Their wealth and taste were visible throughout their exclusively designed home. The walls of frescos mapped a journey of the Bankolé and De Farenzino families from Italy, Africa and the Caribbean, to England. Above the frescos were enormous portraits of their children and family.

David said, "Eugene, you sound overwrought," as he mixed drinks for his husband and his brother. David and Solly have that Afro-Caribbean Black beauty I don't have. If I were the envious type, these are the only people I'd envy. The Bankolé's were the most famous Black British family in London. David was a twelve-time award-winning music producer and star-maker. And even though his brother, Solomon Jr, was no longer a premier football player, he was an icon in British culture, beloved by millions, because he was the greatest Black British footballer this country ever produced: therefore, the mass male population idolised him and women sent him their underwear.

Michael De Farenzino's marriage to David Bankolé was the unofficial event of 2016. He was over fifty and fit as fuck, which is why some people believed he 'won' David because David topped the 100 sexist gay men in England list in 2016.

However, I knew their marriage was based on the kind of love I'm searching for. I told them, "I'm helping Roy on a project. He appreciates my professional support." David crossed the luxurious room and handed drinks to Michael and me. "It's all hush-hush," I said and all three of them studied me carefully. "OK, but not a word." They all nodded. "Roy and I are writing a romantic novel about Aaron and Donna's quest to find love. They've been through *so* much." Michael and David knew them because David's mum was a very close friend of Donna's and Michael's ex-wife was Donna's best friend. David gave his brother Solly his drink and sat beside his husband.

"Roy wants the book to be a gift to show his admiration. He asked me to help him write it." I could see Solly contemplating for a moment or two.

David said, "TV broadcaster and novelist, but you're doing this for Roy?" Michael and Solly watched me so closely I could feel their thoughts. Michael got up and came and sat beside me.

Michael has enormous sex appeal, but more than anything else; he always reminded me of how pointless it was to hate white people. His decency and acceptance of life always left me with more questions than answers about him whenever we met. Michael asked. "Are you doing this for Roy, to impress him because he's in your heart?" His Italian English is so nice.

"I want to make Roy happy with this book." I couldn't say more. I *wanted* to speak the truth, but I couldn't tell them. I have no difficulty with the truth. I've never lied to myself. I find it hard to confide in people and tell them what I feel. I was in the closet for years.

David's younger brother, Solly, gave me a searching look and said, "When I met my wife, I knew every bimbo who sent me her knickers was the kind of light-headed bitch I should avoid."

Solly sat forward in the side chair and pointed at me. "A whole pack of sluts wanted me and they affected my judgment of women until I met Alice. Something is affecting your honesty, Eugene." The atmosphere turned strangely solemn. So much so, David scrutinised me and watched his brother thoughtfully.

Again, Solly pointed at me. "Eugene, you're a man, with guts; speak the truth." Solly's intensity raised my level of discomfort.

Under pressure, I said, "Yes, OK, I think the world of Roy."

"Do you love him?" Michael asked, dissatisfied with my answer. I considered my reply before I spoke, but all at once, the three men pointed at me accusingly.

Solly told me, "Don't even lie, because you're busted!" The full force of Solly's Black existential instincts made me feel exposed.

David said, "The truth is plastered all over your face, mate!"

With his distinct Roman vibrato, Michael also stated, "Men of our generation, we fought for free speech; speak." David stood perfectly still pointing at me.

"I do admire Roy, not just because he's sexy, but he has great ambition and incredible loyalty."

"You are not a politician," Michael interjected. "Eugene, speak the truth."

David said to me: "I've done my fair share of fending off questions. Stop spinning."

Michael added, "Before I married David, I was swamped with sadness. Now, every day, I'm happy. I don't care about people's judgment. That is the meaning of love to me: liberation from fear!"

I studied the three happily married men and I knew I wanted to hear something of the kind from Aaron about Amber, or discover that Miriam was more than Roy and Aaron imagined. I also knew the three of them were advising me. "What do you want me to tell you: that I touch myself all the time thinking about Roy?" I stated. "This book has brought us together. But I'll remind you, Narj is his boyfriend—"

"Get rid of the lover!" Michael declared as though he was planning a hit.

"Oh, how?" I asked.

"I can arrange it." We eyed Michael sitting there in all his butch glory. "He enjoys men who praise his work and consider him the first great Indian artist." An ominous grin appeared. "He's had a few men in his bed on tour. If Roy knew…"

"You're terrible!"

Michael smiled ruthlessly. "Nothing is permanent: except I will love my husband and my children no matter what becomes of me after death."

"No tricks! I want Roy to come to me. But I need to know what makes Aaron and Donna tick. Roy's a fountain of information, but I need to see them for myself. As a source, Roy's great, but I must discover certain facts for myself."

"Here's what I'll do," Solly told me. "Would you like to come to my place in the South Pacific?"

"Bankolé Island! Fuck me, I'd love it!" Shit! I sounded like a queen. I was breathless because I knew the place by reputation. It was an Archipelago. Solly had bought and built it and it was now a resort for the very rich and famous.

With underlined sardonic irony, Solly told me, "If Roy means so much to you, we'll put the two of you together. I'll invite Aaron and Donna to the Island to join mum and our families. Do you like it?" he asked, conspiratorially.

I said, "The logistics—" and David said 'bollocks!' His brother and his husband mutually agreed with him.

"Why are you helping me?"

"Eugene," Michael tenderly began. "Bigots wanted us killed because David and I love each other. Your film and news coverage saved our lives." David went to Michael, and they snuggled together as happily as any married couple could.

"Our family never forgets a kindness, and we always remember insults."

Solly interjected, "Let me do this for you." I nodded, gratefully, knowing the power and wealth the two families had.

Solly got to his feet and began planning, "I'll charter a plane and when we get to Fiji, we'll get the boat out to Bankolé Island."

"Tell us about everyone involved, not just Aaron and Donna," Michael said. I moved in closer. I could see their fascination and bewilderment as I unfolded the events up to my last meeting with Roy.

CHAPTER TEN

Ten days later, at the beginning of September, I stood by the cliffs and looked out as far as my eyes could see from Bankolé Island. If I'd been transported back in time to an ancient Greek Island, it might have looked like this azure sparkling sunlit sanctuary. The scale of the Indigo Ocean was epic, and Bankolé Island was hidden by the dazzling sun. If the native tribes of its forefathers came back from where death had taken them to their homeland, their life spirit couldn't have been more aromatic to me. I walked around the cliffs and hills that rose up from the dock below to see what the Bankolés used their money to create.

David's father Solomon was a QC and his cases had made new laws in Britain. Solly's mother Cynthia owned *Bankolés* the 2-star Michelin restaurant near Regent's Park, frequented by CEOs, stars and upper-class patrons. David and Michael owned the Actors Agency that represented over two-thirds of Black actors in Britain: and Solly had millions as a result of being picked to play for a Brazilian team where he became a world star player.

Clearly, by building this nature paradise as the exclusive resort in the South Pacific Archipelago near Fiji made the Bankolé family a fortune and even more fame. I'd never seen a seascape more translucent. We've all imagined places like this, but the reality is better. The sight, sound, and smell of the aquamarine waters on the east side of the Island made me feel as though where I was standing was timeless.

I watched Amber and her friend run off the dock and up the stone steps that led into the resort, smiling and laughing at the luscious scenery. Both girls began spinning like ballerinas, captured by the atmosphere because everything we could see was unspoiled. Amber's unrestrained joy caught Aaron's eye and then I saw that Miriam came to an abrupt halt when she eyed Aaron watching Amber. Miriam took on a hoity manner and walked away like Delilah in her flowing dress. As people entered the resort's concourse with its scattered bungalows and buildings, each face looked pensive against the epic Fijian environment.

The following morning, I watched everyone enter the dining room and I played it cool. Aaron and Amber, Donna and Miriam, Roy and Narj; Solly, his wife and their five children were ecstatic about their vacation. Michael's son, daughter, ex-wife, Lola and her second husband Tony were also there. Grace: David's ex-wife and their son, Adrian was there too. Tony's brother Giovanni was there as well with his hubby, a strapping Scotsman named Gus. By inviting the Bankolé-De Farenzino family, it looked and felt less like what it really was: a chance for me to study and examine Aaron and Donna.

After breakfast, I went outside, and Bankolé Island sparkled in the South Pacific. The Island was about fifty miles from a major port. Again, I was aware that the aroma was unlike anything I've smelt, anywhere. The South Pacific mornings and evenings were blush blue-green and purple-pink. Solly had forty Lexan MR10 glass bungalows built that were state of the art. That is when I realised what impacted on me. There were no more than one hundred people on the Island. I'd been to several Islands in the Caribbean, but everything here was so different because it was so uninhabited, everyone in the epic landscape looked fearless.

After dinner on our first night, we all went to the cinema and watched a film about the construction, development and building of all the services on the Island. I was fascinated to know how safe and eco-friendly Bankolé Island was in case of tsunamis or hurricanes.

The bungalows were divided into bedrooms, bathrooms, lounge rooms and kitchens. Almost everything inside the Lexan MR10 bungalows was handmade from wood: the floors, wall coverings and furniture, each with their own facilities. But breakfast, lunch and dinner were available in cafeterias serving vegetarian, vegan and seafood dishes along with the most varied range of menus I've ever seen.

There were also meditation rooms, retreat cabins and four screening rooms where different kinds of film and media screenings were held. The design of the place was done by Scandinavians, locals and African architects who knew how to conserve sea and beach properties to withstand the elements that battered the West and East African coasts. It reminded me of communes in the Hippie era.

The primary difference, however, was that guests had to pay a fortune to stay on Bankolé Island. The natural setting was paradise, but the living conditions were outstanding because Solly had employed leisure and tourism staff to keep the guests satisfied. Solly had found and brought philosophers, psychologists, and political theorists to come to Bankolé Island to research and work.

I discovered through David and Michael's advice, Solly bought into the idea of 'encounter groups' so people could think about how they wanted to live and what they should best do with their wealth, in addition to how to invest their money so that they would feel good about themselves.

Everyone who came to the Island did so to find 'enlightenment.' That is why men and women who were Buddhists, people who understood the principles of Confucius and disillusioned academics who were trying to create a working principle of gender equality came to Bankolé Island after they had met with Solly and David. The scholars were from all over Africa, the Caribbean and Asia.

Throughout the ten days on the Island, I was able to observe everyone discreetly. From time to time I saw Donna casually suggest walks Aaron and Miriam should take together and he did so. Donna looked pleased and Miriam appreciated it. Aaron was polite and hospitable the way men are when they have to follow the rules of Tradition within their religious Order. Amber and her friend Helena spent most of their time secretly talking about whatever interested them. However, I noticed that whenever Aaron approached Amber and engaged in conversation with her, she glowed as if she had caught the sunlight or moonlight.

For all of Aaron's efforts to be casual, it couldn't have been more evident that being near Amber brought out an unconscious masculine tenderness in him. One particular evening, Roy and Aaron sat opposite Amber and her best friend. Helena was a natural beauty who resembled the 1970s famous French actress Dominique Sanda in her golden years.

The heads of the families were seated; dining in the grand room with its Plexiglas vault ceilings that made the sky a showcase.

Amber was wearing a simple white cotton dress and Aaron was in a blue T-shirt and shorts. Among all the faces at the table, theirs were the two that shone most distinctly. They didn't exchange a word; they simply glanced and shared furtive looks, while Miriam recounted an adventure she had while on a business trip to Mexico. Miriam's low-cut jade green satin dress was enough to keep guests looking over at her. Without question, she had old fashion glamor; rather like a 1960s television personality. Everyone noticed her, except Aaron.

To my surprise, Aaron and Roy were at ease in nature's environment. Aaron never mentioned missing the city or anything to do with millennium life. Miriam missed staying in touch with her family, but Aaron and Roy were nature boys in khaki shorts and sneakers; hiking, swimming, water-skiing, and playing football. Almost all the women preferred to relax, but Amber and Helena were extremely fit girls who gladly participated in the sports Roy and Aaron engaged in, except for football.

I saw Roy as I had never seen him: he was a fit and competitive young man who wasn't afraid to go toe-to-toe with Solly. This made Donna and Cynthia cheer both of them on. Miriam said she couldn't see the point or feel any excitement for 'soccer'. Donna explained why she shouldn't call it 'soccer'. Miriam conceded because she didn't give a shit about football as Brits loved it.

Where Miriam did shine and hold the spotlight was in her smooth and stylish skill as a raconteur. She told us about her work as a men's fashion stylist. With the help of her graduate friends at The New School in New York, she invented **40-60**, a brand that revolutionised menswear for fellas in that age range. Her target was men in the mid-west and her styles had successfully transformed the fat and messy guys into smart guys; and in the process made an indelible name for herself.

The following evening, Miriam kept everyone at our long table thrilled with a recitation of a wedding she attended that was plagued with accidents and mishaps. It featured a ruined wedding dress, the death of a relative and the birth of a child in the church during the ceremony. Aaron loved every word of it and he laughed himself into an uproar. He periodically asked questions that elicit dry and witty responses from Miriam. Her star was as bright as it could have been.

The next evening Amber did not appear for dinner and the day after that she was nowhere to be seen. Roy told me that Aaron was concerned and baffled. Helena text Roy to tell him Amber wanted to leave, and he told Aaron. The following morning Aaron went to Helena and Amber's bungalow.

When Helena invited him in, he stood in front of Amber and took off his sandal and handed it to her. "If I've been a stupid fool, feel free to beat me if you want." He got down on his knees in front of her and lowered his head. She stared at him and exhaled. She then dropped the sandal and kissed the top of his head, ruffled his curls and grabbed a handful and yanked it, which made him cry out.

"Aaron, if you are easily amused, then leave me alone." He got to his feet and lifted Amber and kissed her tummy, then held her there.

* * *

That evening we were all gathered in the screening room when Donna stood before us and announced, "I've agreed to show you some footage of my 25th wedding anniversary. Most of us here were at the anniversary, but my friend Miriam has never seen my daughter or my husband."

Aaron looked a bit tense. "Mummy, are you sure—"

"Sweetheart, it's fine; the past doesn't go away by not looking at it."

Donna sat in the front row with Lola on her right, holding her hand as she sat next to her husband, Tony. Cynthia was to her left, holding Donna's hand, while her husband Solomon, sat beside her. We all sat in different rows around the screening room, and a short period of muttering among different couples led to the silence as the lights went down.

The film began with Donna searching through the faces. The colour film footage was rich. Donna wore a beautiful silver satin and lace dress and Humphrey, a tall, strapping figure of a man was in a silver-grey suit. He was one of those ginger brown skin men, who clearly looked like he'd battled life and wouldn't back away from a fight. I'd score him a 10/10 on sex appeal and his body language was convivial and inclusive.

"Miriam! Wasn't he the business? So many women wanted him, but they had to play with themselves because he never played with them." I was sure Miriam wasn't comfortable with Donna's comment, but Aaron and Roy looked across at each other and flicked their eyebrows.

Onscreen, imbued with pride, Humphrey eyed his parents Harold and Violet. There were 100 guests and the most distinctive thing about them was their difference. They weren't just Black and European; their age difference was plain to see. A microphone was handed from person to person paying tribute to Donna and Humphrey for all their work and friendship. Their friends were Jewish, Black Muslim and definitely from different class backgrounds. The affirmations and compliments raised thanks and comments from Humphrey and Donna.

Humphrey said, "I can't hear any more praise without my son and daughter up here because they taught me more than I know." He looked for them and Zara moved away from her Spanish looking boyfriend and Aaron let go of his Caribbean girlfriend's hand. She wanted to follow him but he told her to wait. They join their parents and four photographers immediately moved around them, taking pictures. The range of faces looked like something out of a street mosaic that you find in local community art. Humphrey's joy at having Zara beside him was unmistakable. Aaron kissed his dad's head and went to his mother.

Harold got hold of the microphone. "Humphrey, Donna; I couldn't wish for more! Son, your brothers and sisters are here, and I know they love you like me and your mother do." His four brothers and sisters jumped up and down in the crowd. "I tell you, there is no politician or national hero in England better than you!" That drew Zara and Aaron closer to their father and Donna kissed the crowd.

Humphrey gave his father the nod. Then with a distinct received accent, which rumbled with baritone warmth, Humphrey said, "Dad. All of you here. I remarried Donna so that Zara and Aaron could see that love doesn't evaporate, it really gets better. I want to say a few words about love and hate." Zara, Aaron and Donna eyed him closely and whoever the team of filmmakers were, moved around the church hall, capturing the faces of their family and friends.

"As a GP, I've seen the damage of hatred and that's why I've never subscribed to it. When I met this teenage beauty, the love I felt changed our lives. I've never betrayed this woman because she is my wife and, yes—my life."

Donna gestured and her best friends' elation was self-evident. "In *The Godfather*, that classic modern myth of love and hate, Don Vito Corleone adopts a second son who proved to be wise. That wasn't the inspiration I needed; I knew Roy needed us as much as we need him. So, my friends, let's get my love child up here!" Humphrey's comment got a great response from their guests and people in the screening room. Michael and David whistled, so Roy said, "shut up!"

I watched Roy on screen with his alternative family and I've never seen him happier. Humphrey said, "Roy's had to put up with a lot of shit because he loves that man," he concluded, pointing at Brian standing in front of JJ and Carlos.

Everyone looked at the three of them. "Hate can ruin people's lives, but my wife and kids and you Roy, are fighters so we battle injustice wherever it's rooted." Humphrey reminded me of Afro-Caribbean Preachers and his ability to reach out and engage people took me back to my own Church in Ladbroke Grove as a boy.

Michael's son Roberto and his team of staff made the film. He knew his job because the way it was filmed was really impactful, as a wave of people came towards Humphrey as if he was 'the man'. Roberto underscored the scene with the instrumental version of The Edwin Hawkins' song, *Oh Happy Day*. I looked at everyone in the screening room and they were absolutely spellbound.

Donna calmed her guests down and indicated that she wanted to tell them something. "My father's hatred blinded him to my husband and our kids. From this church hall in Hackney, I point in the direction of Stamford Hill and say to my father... 'Papa, can you hear me?'"

Not everyone in the church hall got the Streisand reference. Everyone in the screening room did. "I reject your prejudice and hatred! So, to hell with you!" In the screening room, Solomon and Michael clapped spontaneously and all of us turned to them.

From different areas of the screening room, Lola and Roy said, "Testify girl!" Lola snapped her fingers and Roy snapped back to her. Up on the screen, different people took the microphone and showered them all with praise.

Amber turned towards Donna and she must have watched her for a full sixty seconds, thinking something very intense as she shifted between Donna now and then, on screen. I think it was seeing how self-possessed and assured Donna was beside Humphrey, Zara and Aaron that made her look so vital. Roy had compared her to Jane Fonda, but to me, Donna was the kind of woman I imagine as Earth Mother.

Zara's Spanish-looking boyfriend put his arms around her, and Aaron's Caribbean girlfriend moved closer to him and whispered something. Watching everyone's happy faces on screen as Donna and Humphrey moved throughout the church hall among their friends called up memories of my parents.

When I looked back up on the screen, Humphrey was dancing with Zara and Donna was dancing with Aaron. Roy was dancing with Brian, and Carlos and JJ danced together. I've been covering politics and culture for thirty years but the reality of respect and love between these people felt powerful, just watching them.

The film jumped to later that evening where Donna and Humphrey began flamenco dancing and I can honestly say, the way they moved together, clapping and tapping their feet to the music was unlike anything I've ever used in any of my programs because their Hispanic and Caribbean fusion lifted their dance. The players sat in the background as Donna in a scarlet dress and Humphrey in black suit danced in short leaps, spins and arabesques that were punctuated by screams and cries from them and the Andalusian players. I've never seen a Black man move like that, and I've seen Carlos Acosta dance. I've seen porn that wasn't as sexy as them together. This made me think, what was his flaw? I mean Humphrey was a sexy as an impending orgasm, a trusted doctor, loved by many and he was a son who'd outshone his father, so what could be wrong with him. I doubt Aaron or Roy would ever tell me.

Donna told Miriam, "For ten years he studied flamenco, look at him, he's fifty-one and he moves like a thirty-year-old. It was our favourite hobby."

"You're pretty good yourself!" Helena hushed them and they shut up. Zara and Aaron joined them and that was the sublime moment. Both of them could dance flamenco proficiently. I didn't see them as Jewish, Caribbean, Brit or mixed race; they were a confluence of human beings. The wedding party roared loudly.

Aaron got up and quickly ducked out of the screening room. I haven't lived this long by ignoring my instincts. Something was wrong and I felt compelled to go after him and so I did. Outside in the evening's starry night, he doubled over struggling to breathe. He looked like he was in pain. I put my hand on his back and he looked up at me and his lion eyes were definitely teary.

"What is it, do you need help?"

"Me and Zara were so close...real friends, not big brother and little sister. Daddy taught us everything important. But grandpa's mentality taught us how dangerous religion is. 9/11 is like shit compared to what grandpa did. None of his family liked what he did. And when...when daddy and Zara were killed, grandpa never even came to mum. How fucking sick is that religious dogma? Dad used to get so angry about Jewish laws, but Uncle Saul taught him the Talmud.

"Before that, he refused to make me Jewish, but Saul and mummy's friends changed him, so I became a *Jewish* Christian..." Aaron laughed at himself. "That's my cross you know, being a Black Jew." He took deep breaths to calm himself. We walked further away from the building and out towards the seafront. The sky looked like planets had come closer to the Pacific sky.

"How was it, seeing your father again?"

"Mate, I see him all the time; awake, asleep...Amber reminds me of Zara in certain ways, that's why dad's always in my head. I know he'd have liked her."

"Would he have liked Miriam?"

He laughed for a while, and I waited for him to share his thoughts with me as we walked. "What's Roy told you?" His question hit me like a sudden cramp.

"What do you mean?"

"You fancy Roy and if you've made a play for him, he'll have ducked that by talking about things he likes. Queer theory, the occult, photo-journalism, especially *Look* and *Life* magazines, me and mum." I acted blasé to hide my response.

"We've discussed those things. But since I don't know you and your mum well, we talk about writing. He's an aspiring novelist, I'm an established one."

"Don't pretend." I said nothing. "You fancy him so don't get put off by Narj. You're much more his type really." I played innocent. "Sophisticated and sexy."

"No wonder you like Amber: she's posh, very sophisticated and sexy."

He flashed a smile. "You see it, don't you, everyone must! She's incredible!"

* * *

For all our days in the sun, three specific days stood out in my mind. The first occasion was the day we went swimming in the Pacific rather than the pools around the resort. Service staff pitched two changing rooms on the beach: one for ladies, the other one for men. That way, we didn't have to make our way back to the bungalows for anything.

Surrounded by the eldest to the youngest men in our entourage, ranging from David and Solly's sixty-eight-year-old father who had an imposing presence, even in his Bermuda shorts; down to David's young son, as lithe as most young skateboarders in their baggies are: Aaron was a commanding presence. The defused light inside the bivouac showed me the differences between the Italian, Caribbean, and African men.

At the same time, because most of the De Farenzinos were mixed race, Roy claimed his own distinction since he was a brown skin Jamaican, and Aaron stood out because he was a dark skin Jew. All the men were in various states of dress and undress, preparing for the South Sea blazing sun. Aaron had on red swimming trunks, and he dug his feet in as Roy vigor- ously covered him in sun cream and Aaron rubbed some kind of product through his dishevelled curly hair. Curiously, Aaron was very casual when Roy rubbed skin protection on him: there wasn't a hint of homoeroticism between them. They reminded me of images I'd seen of coal miners showering after work.

Aaron left the tent and I followed him out to the beach. The sand, sea and sky were naturally simple and dazzling. In the near azure distance, Amber was wearing an oyster-coloured bathing suit that covered her up and Miriam was wearing a strappy black Lycra bikini that showed off her ample breasts and her bottom. Miriam was standing by the edge of the surf and Amber was in the sea, sparkling wet. I saw that Aaron got a boner looking out at the women before him. They weren't far away so they must have seen the state he was in. The question was which one of them excited him that much.

He took evasive action in a manner I have to say was smart and quick. He did a handstand and walked on his palms along the golden beach until he was far enough away to stand on his feet and dash back to the tent. In the epic land and seascape, Amber and Miriam went off in their own direction and I followed Miriam because I had to know more about her to honestly write about her.

I played it straight and she happily told me as much about herself, as I didn't know because she needed attention and none of the married men in the entourage paid her the sexual compliments she wanted. I was surprised how much she revealed about herself because I was willing to spend the day with her and be her audience, but the beauty of the Island was majestic and mysterious.

Miriam confessed to me that she didn't have the easiest time with men due to men's carnivorous sexual desires and their inability to trust women. According to Miriam, the battle of sexes boiled down to money and freedom. Men wanted the freedom to hold onto their adolescence, which allowed them to 'behave like dorks and not be held accountable because they usually say they're naïve when it comes to women's issues'. Betty Friedan was her heroine. On three different occasions, Miriam contrasted her experience with the history of second-wave feminism and as a consequence of women's liberation from men's control.

I didn't tell her I'm gay, but due to the fact my career in Black British history pre-dated my career as a writer, I was able to align my knowledge with my mother's history of injustice towards Black women. Feminist discourse became the foundation of our empathetic chats because everything I told her about my mother's search for love, which ended badly, struck a chord with her.

Miriam and I became so 'pally' over the first four days, she eventually told me how much she disliked Roy because he's gay. It took enormous self-control not to tell her to shut her bigoted mouth, but I didn't. I shifted my attention to Amber and Helena, who were self-contained. They both asked how I knew the families, so I explained that Roy and I are journalists and his connection with Aaron's family, as well as the fact David was a great friend of mine brought us all together.

What amazed me was that neither Amber nor Helena asked about Miriam, even though everyone knew I spent time with her. Helena wanted to know more about Roy and so I told her; and by the second day with them, Helena said to me.

"You love him." It wasn't a question and there was no point in denying it. I asked her how she knew and she said she loved Amber; therefore, Roy fascinated her because she saw Aaron and Roy as the male version of her and Amber.

One morning as we walked around the Island, surrounded by the incredible tranquillity of the South Pacific, Helena told me about the depth of friendship she had with Amber because they shared their childhood and her anxiety about losing her. So, I told her about my love for Roy and the fact I'm too old for him. Helena was so emotionally compassionate towards me. I experienced the kind of platonic love towards a woman, only a gay man and woman can nurture.

Later that day, when we took a speedboat out to sea, I was impressed with how well Amber and Helena handled the boat. Amber told me; over the years, they spent countless vacations on lakes in Switzerland and Northern Italy and I enjoyed the drama of bobbing on the ocean at high speed. During our time together, the two feisty girls communicated in Italian or wordlessly.

I ask what they thought of everyone, and their response was courteous. When I mentioned Miriam, Amber said: "She's not a woman, she's a cunt! A cheap, vulgar American! I could run her over and drive off!" Helena turned away from the wheel as we danced on top of the puffed-up waves and we both saw and felt the sparks emanate from Amber and seriously, I felt a visceral shock!

In an open tent on the beach, Amber and Helena spent time with Michael and David's kids learning and discussing the meaning of Hipster life in Hackney. That afternoon, I accompanied Roy and Donna for a walk and we found Amber and Helena gathered together with Fabio, Adrian and Maria. Amber and Helena discussed their understanding of Hipster lifestyle regarding curating spaces through bricolage, underpinned by an entrepreneurial escape from corporatisation.

They spoke of a spirit of communal collaboration: sourcing products and then manufactured goods by way of Artisans' reclaiming their authenticity. Amber and Helena's Continental style and syntax fascinated all of us because their finishing school was not a world that Michael or David's kids knew. Despite the fact I didn't know Donna well; I knew she was impressed with the girls' sophistication and Amber's intelligent and elusive nature.

Donna asked what was taught at their finishing school, so Helena detailed the everyday life of the girls they grew up with. When Amber said the only thing that made it worthwhile was that she was taught to be the best wife any man could have; that was the thread that compelled Donna to listen attentively.

"Your boyfriends must be delighted with you," Donna said.

Helena burst out laughing. "Her father does not permit boyfriends. He allows suitors. Boys' filthy ideas never touch our lives."

Amber nodded. When that point sunk in, Donna asked Amber if she could give up a career to be a wife and mother.

Again, Helena laughed. "She is an heiress. Her parents and my father have provided for her. And God forbid, if I die before I have really lived, I have left my inheritance to her; my father is...how you say discreetly in English? Very Rich!" That word made the two girls laugh! The way Amber laced her fingers together to rest her chin and smile, was daintier than anything I'd seen a woman do in years.

As time drew towards the final days of the vacation, I sensed that couples must have been making love. Lola and Tony reeked of sex. Not to be outdone by his ex-wife, Michael and David had their own heat that warmed Solly and his wife and it wasn't long before almost everyone else lit their wick from the same fire.

Subsequently, I became aware of the others who weren't intimately engaged. Nevertheless, at the tender age of twenty-four, Amber outshone Miriam. She must have been radiating pheromones because Aaron, Fabio and Adrian were drawn to her.

That evening Helena and Amber led the troop of guests around the east side of the Island and Helena recounted stories of the gods and goddesses of ancient myth. At nightfall, guests were given special hand torches so they could explore if they wanted to. Maybe I've seen too many European Art films, but as Helena led the way, carrying her torch held high, I felt as if I was in a Fellini movie with a circus of people in procession, dressed to the nines at the end of the earth.

Helena spoke about her life in Capri, at Lake Como and the people her father invited to his villa in Northern Italy: also, a palace he recently acquired in Eastern Europe and his country home in England. She also mentioned the moguls who were friends of her family. Walking us around the Island, you'd think she been there before. Solly and his wife Alice compared her comments with their own life and all of this left Miriam at the back of the troop. Nothing in her life acquainted her with European extravagance that was demonstrated in the South Pacific.

When Helena said, "Naturally, due to Amber's family political influence in Europe, I have hardly enjoyed any of my life without her there. Money is very nice, but the friendship of a pure and honourable girl is invaluable," Amber turned away and her modesty was captivating.

Four days before we were due to return, Roy, Aaron and Lola formed a closed circle around Donna, but of course, I wasn't invited in but later Roy told me everything I needed to know. I saw that Roy was a confidant to Donna because he was by her side for the best part of a day and when I asked about their conversation, he was evasive and untruthful. I've been in the business long enough to know when someone is padding their stories or denying facts. Call me besotted, but I didn't consider him untrustworthy. I believe Roy's loyalty to Donna and Aaron clouds his judgment. That is why I have to write the bulk of the novel to get to the truth.

The other day, what stood out in my mind was the day Helena and Amber finished playing tennis on one of the courts. Several guests holidaying on the Island formed an audience and we watched the game with great interest. There were ten people I recognised as mega-media stars, Pulitzer and Booker Prize winners who were a couple and a retired sportsman who was a dear friend of Solly's who enthusiastically watched the match. Amber and Helena were very athletic. They darted and moved about the court without any sign of exhaustion.

Amber dressed in white, and Helena wore a peach and lemon-coloured tennis dress. The cerulean blue sky was cloudless, and the breeze kept fanning us. By the last game of the third set, Amber won by a slim margin. She ran and jumped over the net and Helena had a lot to say to her as they spoke rapidly in Italian.

Miriam left her seat to congratulate Amber on the best game she'd ever seen, and Amber put up her hand and stopped her.

"Do not speak to me, you vile, dirty idiot!" Miriam couldn't move, and everyone and I mean everyone, didn't know how to respond. Should we laugh, gasp, object, what?

Miriam began to say, "I was just—" but Amber and Helena walked away from her. Amber went and got her gym bag, took out her sunglasses and stared at everyone before she covered her eyes. For a woman who could not have weighed more than 140lb, she stood there like an Amazonian virgin imbued with power, dominance, and spirit. She and Helena picked up their things and walked off like two rich girls who were high and mighty.

It was the first time I noticed that Narj turned his attention to something besides his relationship with Roy. Of course, I knew he was a handsome Sri Lankan guy I should have learnt more about, considering we spent days on an Island. He was the son of a wealthy family who paid him to stay away due to the fact he was 'queer' and a disgrace to the family, but I didn't care and wasn't interested in him, so as far as I was concerned, the son of a bitch didn't exist.

Amber and Helena were the subjects of conversation among all of us that evening, but they didn't spend the night with us. They were nowhere to be seen. Miriam was still somewhat shaken by the encounter, so Donna and Aaron spent most of the evening with her. I don't imagine Amber thought that would be the result of her rebuff, but it turned out that way.

The Bankolés invited me to their bungalow to spend the evening. This is when I learnt that Solomon Sr. was the true head of the family, because he was a QC barrister from one of the great families of Nigeria. Even though his youngest son, Solomon Jr. was a British icon due to his football legacy, NGO reputation and his Island, Solomon ruled David and Solly, and their mother. Cynthia governed their father. They wanted their children to carry on their 'mission' to be the great Black British family.

The fact that David and Michael had mixed race children from their former marriages, all added to the legacy of the De Farenzinos expanding the Bankolé dynasty.

My favourite day of all was the evening we went to the amphitheatre and Donna and Aaron sat on a couple of stools in the middle of the stage and sang Simon and Garfunkel's *Old Friend and*

Bookends. Donna's loose hair in the breeze lightly danced over her kaftan as she played Spanish style guitar and sang and then Aaron joined her. In his khakis, vest, and sandals, both of them could have existed before Christ and after an apocalypse.

We were all there, the heads of the families and their sons and daughters, as well as friends. Donna thanked the Bankolés, modestly. But when Aaron took the guitar and played, Donna sang *Both Sides Now*, by Joni Mitchell. Against the expansive seascape and the Island's fusion of ancient topography and futurist design, everyone in the amphitheatre looked like survivors of tyranny.

Donna wasn't a 'singer'; she was a woman with a beautiful voice who moved us all. After the song, Roy got up and went down to the circular stage to embrace her. He was tearful and yielding, so she held him as a mother would.

I understood his tears because he told me about his dreadful childhood and his brutal parents. The sky at dusk couldn't have been more suited to the moment, particularly since the Island's aroma of citrus, jasmine and mystery filled my nostrils and sharpened my senses to everything and everyone around me. Donna kissed Roy on the lips as she spoke to him and then Aaron did the same and the two of them put their arms around Roy. Donna and Aaron's kiss unsettled Miriam for whatever reason: I couldn't read her face.

It was one of the few evenings that Miriam didn't dress up, she sat still like a woman who'd washed her face, knowing she could face life without a mask. To me, Miriam never looked better than she did right there sitting with guests on the Island. I didn't know her well enough to read her mind, but something made her gaze up to the sky, lost in thought.

Amber and Helena were on the opposite side of the theatre and from the look on Amber's face, she was listening attentively to Helena, who was confiding in her. I knew guests re-staged Greek and Roman plays there, because it was documented in the Island brochure, but I did not think I was going to feel like an orphan, with a strong desire to have my parents beside me, until I sat there in the open-air theatre with the atmosphere of truth and need hanging in the air.

Just before we were due to leave, Michael spent the afternoon with me. To a great extent, he was the kind of guy I used to fancy when I was in my twenties and thirties, but I've changed. We walked around the north side of the Island and he asked me if I had discovered what I needed to know. I asked him to tell me more about Donna since she was his ex-wife's best friend and he told me everything that was missing.

He asked if the vacation had given me a chance to work through my feelings about Roy and I told him. "Roy has Narj. I can't meddle in that. I'd feel like a shit." From the look on his face, I knew he understood me. "Are you and David still over the moon?"

"He's a Godsend; I love him more every day." I kept looking at him and don't ask me why but tears came down my face. I was so happy for them. Michael placed his hand on my neck and slowly, we both smiled knowingly.

The morning we were due to leave, Solly asked everyone if they enjoyed their vacation. He also posed a question I asked him to put to the guests. "If we were the last people on earth, how would we survive on this Island? How would we create a new generation?"

Everyone's answers told me more about the way each of them thought and it gave me the insight I didn't have before. Now I knew there was nothing about them I couldn't honestly write about. Solly, David and Michael frequently invited me to their home to discuss world politics when we got back. Along with their father, David and Solly believed the world we live in offers very little in the way of personal freedom to Afro-Asians because we are living an alienated existence in a world controlled by corporations.

They frequently discussed their belief in love and happiness and through all the answers friends and family gave, I learnt how much Miriam valued her place in society because her ideas had changed American men's image of themselves in search of youth and power. No one could dismiss Miriam as irrelevant, because her views about men's fashion offered NYC graduates internship at her business studio.

Likewise, Amber and Helena profoundly understood the meaning of friendship and it created a bond between them as deep as my respect and friendship with Michael. Subsequently, throughout the ten days—politics, humanities, nationalism, identity, money, history, science, imperialism, 'New Ageism' and love had all been the subject of conversation—and now I looked forward to writing about Aaron and Donna and what they wanted out of life, based on their allegiances and desires.

Book Two

FATHERLY

CHAPTER ELEVEN

Donna and Aaron stood in line behind couples waiting to be announced when they entered the Banquet Hall at the four-star hotel in the heart of London's West End. She had not attended the Wholesalers' Annual Ball since Humphrey died. It took the trip to Bankolé Island, her therapist, Aaron, Humphrey's parents; and her best friends Lola and Cynthia to encourage her, but she felt alright that evening.

Donna said to Aaron, "Who knew so many people would be here?"

"Does it feel like a reunion of sorts, mum?" Her loving face showed how distinctly she responded to Aaron's instincts as she pushed his blow-dried hair away from his eyes.

"How did you get so sharp?" He winked at her, and she hit him playfully. They were two couples away from the entrance where they'd be announced.

"Are you sure I look good?" Donna asked him. "These overseas buyers haven't seen me in ages."

"Mummy, you make a man feel big." His salacious look didn't escape her.

"When you get that look, I see your father." He took her hand. "My dress is just right, yeah?"

"You're in a black satin gown with this whatchamacallit shielding your boobs from direct eye contact. You're very ladylike."

"I'm wearing a lace bodice, silly! Oh, we're up next. Stand up straight." They moved to the entrance, where the room was filled with white linen-draped circular tables, covered with crockery and crystal, flowers and decorations. Most guests were over the age of forty, dressed in an array of horrible bright frocks, with the occasional well-dressed couple in evening gown and tuxedo.

"I was right to wear my hair down; these old gals have their hair up. Oh my God, look at that disaster over there; she looks like her 12-year-old dressed her."

"Stop! I feel a vulgar laugh coming on." Aaron handed over the invitations and they were announced. The lighting in the hall was warm and the space above their heads smelt tasty.

"Mr and Mrs Blackmon!" People looked their way and Donna began strutting. Her dark ginger hair swung as Aaron led her to greet people. Aaron did an immediate 180° scan of the room. Some of the best Jewish wholesalers in the country, foreign sellers, along with Christian capitalists who pretended there were no issues or distrusts between them milled about. As people waved, Donna offered her felicitations as if she really was a star.

"Marcus and Linda Hellman are coming towards us, smile, I like them." Donna held out her arm and her long black satin evening glove was a sign she was formal and flirtatious. Linda was a grinning, heavily made-up, aging woman.

"Donna! It's great to see you," Linda said. "You look like a million! When they said Mr and Mrs Blackmon, I thought you'd remarried."

"No, for heaven's sake, this is my son, not my husband."

"Young man, it must be all of eight years since I've seen you. Adam—right?" Linda's yellow smile didn't impress Aaron.

"No, Aaron." Marcus clicked his fingers and shook his head.

"Right, right! You're all grown up now." Marcus had a full head of silver hair and burnt dry skin due to over tanning. Donna asked where they'd been.

Linda leaned in and replied, "The Maldives! Beautiful, relaxing; everything: food, service, weather, a dream." She poked Donna in the shoulder. "I couldn't do Florida one more year, I'm as sick of the place as I am of his sister, oy!"

Marcus shrugged and replied, "She's an unhappy person with wayward kids, can I help it?" A lot of people eyed Donna because they hadn't seen her in years.

Hershel Schrader approached her with a pep in his step and a loving smile on his face. He was the kind of man every small claims' client would give a great testimonial about. He worked hard for them and never padded his bill. Donna saw Hershel and moved to welcome him with open arms. In her heels, she was taller than him, but Hershel was a soulful man, so he looked like he was going to bring the world into his open arms. They greeted each other warmly and spoke in Spanish for a minute. His thin grey moustache made him look rather dashing.

Donna turned to Aaron and gestured to Linda and Marcus. "This is Hershel, a great friend from back in the 1980s. We both have Spanish heritage."

Hershel said, "Excuse me cutting you out of the conversation, but Donna and I have strong Spanish ties." He reached out to shake hands. "I'm glad to know you. Hershel Schrader." His face was filled with joy and his green eyes distinguished him. If he had taken Don Quixote to heart, he certainly looked like he took it seriously.

"Do you have a card?" Marcus asked.

Hershel took one out of his jacket pocket and as he did, he studied Aaron. "My God! Aaron, so like your father, I'd know you anywhere. Do you—"

Aaron gave his business card to Marcus. "Remember you, yes, Hershel. Dad told me to call you if I ever had difficulty with an obstreperous employee..."

"Well, that aside, at least you sued the bastard that took him from us. Donna wrote and told me. Now, look at you! And you, Donna, you look fabulous!"

"It's all because of him," she replied, pointing at Aaron. He led Donna further into the banquet hall as they said their temporary goodbyes.

"What table are you sitting at, Hershel?"

"Nineteen."

Donna's smile warmed him as she moved away and said, "We're at table twenty-one. See if you can move or come over to me." He nodded and moved on, walking like a retired military man out of uniform among the guests.

The swirl of Donna's three-yard black satin skirt and her black lace bodice caught everyone's eye. One sour-faced elderly woman eyed Donna and Aaron and said, "Who is that? She ought to be ashamed, parading that young husband around."

Her husband also watched Donna and Aaron disapprovingly. He always looked forward to the Ball because it was one of the few times, they got to socialise without constantly touting for business. Aaron knew some people came to the Ball in search of a partner and hopefully a marriage because in previous years Donna came back stuffed with gossip. Aaron agreed to accompany Donna to the Ball since it was an opportunity to put his task to work, but he hadn't fully figured out a plan.

Donna stopped and greeted three couples and Aaron knew his best plan at the start of the evening was to observe and then seize the moment if it came. "Mum, how many of these people do you reckon are unhappy, but just stay together for the money and their business?"

"About half of them," she said, walking through the crowd of overdressed guests. Aaron chuckled. "What?"

"Nothing...nothing." He continued chuckling and it distracted her.

"What?" He could see he had Donna's attention.

"You're probably the only single lady here, who is totally liberated and free. Most of the people here have almost nothing except their business." Donna broke her stride.

"Don't be so judgemental. Not everyone here is in loveless marriages. And I've told you, this event is kind of a coming-out ceremony for great people to meet."

"I've gone to several of these things in the recruitment sector. They're usually about one-night stands, where people can cheat."

"That's because your industry is run by disingenuous bastards. They tell endless lies to sell candidates. I hate that about your industry."

"But I don't—"

"Do that. Of course, you don't. Darling, there are nice people here." She lowered her voice. "Some of the best Jews in the country are here. So, you do some business, maybe even find a sweetheart, what's wrong with that?"

"Nothing, but neither you nor Hershel would remarry after all you've both been through; you've resigned yourself to a life of solitude."

"Don't write me off. You don't know what I'm capable of. I'm only fifty."

"Mum, sorry. I just figured—" She stopped and pointed at him disapprovingly. "Mum, Hershel's just aged so much since the death of his wife."

"What? And I'm going to age myself to death..."

"Mum, don't talk like that."

"You're annoying me." He looked innocent. "Why have you suddenly...no, why are you trying to piss me off? What's wrong with you?"

"Nothing." She pulled back and she really looked like a mother dealing with a recalcitrant son.

"I know what's eating you." Donna smiled as she regained her composure and took his arm and led him towards the numbered tables, looking for theirs.

"What's eating me?"

"You think this is the place where I can *introduce* you to a bride. And you'll end up in a dreadful marriage with only the kids to keep you together."

"Maybe we're too damaged for marriage." Donna looked furious.

On the other side of the Banquet Hall, several couples saw them and the look on Donna's face, as she spoke to Aaron with a wagging finger, said a great deal. A young couple spoke in hushed voices, but behind them, Miriam heard every word. He told his pretty wife.

"Looks like she still paying for marrying her toy boy."

Miriam said, "I know them." She had on a sequined ruby red dress, and she looked as self-possessed and wilful as Scarlett O'Hara facing her enemies.

"They're Mr and Mrs Blackmon." The man was a typical Finchley Jewish boy who understood life according to his local environment, rather than life's complexities.

"Yeah, you can see he's not one of us. What's she doing with him?"

Miriam sarcastically replied, "Obviously, more than *you* can imagine."

"Who are they?" Mr Finchley asked, watching Aaron disapprovingly.

Miriam gleefully said, "He's the kind of man a radical feminist would throw away her vibrator for. Then she'd wait for him to call her." Miriam eyed Mr Finchley as a man with nothing to offer, and his dyed blonde wife barely held her gaze.

"Gotta tell you," Miriam added, "that tux fits you as badly as your face fits kindness." His eyebrows danced around, and his wife's mouth tightened. She eyed Miriam's 1976 Halston vintage evening gown and she looked like she wanted to untie the halter back sash and wrap it around her neck.

"Who the hell do you think you are?" his wife asked.

"Someone who knows—that is a mother and her son, you bitches." They looked again and Miriam smirked with contempt for both of them. "Back home, we think you Brits are so refined: so much for appearances."

His wife said, "Darling, ignore her, she's another crude American."

"Yeah, well, at least I know to marry within my species: you've settled for this animal." Miriam walked away as only Miss TWA 1963 would, moving her ass full tilt walking through a bumpy jet.

Donna told Aaron, "Now get a grip. I haven't brought you here to marry you off to some Jewish Princess. We're here because I need to get back on my feet. I'm not about to die or live as a recluse. Go back and see your analyst. We're not 'damaged'. You've got a lot to live for."

"Marriage is a serious business."

"Especially if it expands your life for the better."

"Could you remarry?"

She gently pushed him down into the seat by his shoulders and a man beside her stood up and pulled her chair out. She nodded at him. Donna placed her clutch purse on the table. "Not if you thought I was trying to push another father onto you or amuse myself in bed," she concluded in a hushed tone, glancing up to check no one heard her.

"You're not that type," Aaron replied in a near whisper.

"I have no intention of being a martyr."

"And I won't marry a martyr or a vixen," he told her through clenched teeth.

"Young man, if you don't behave, I'll...fucking throw a plate at you."

"Sorry—I just don't want marriage to ruin us." She turned to him. "Beasts and bitches feed on people like us today. If you can love someone else, I'll know there's still a chance for me."

"Your fear of marriage is because you don't trust women. It's become a disease with men today." Her comment startled and upset Aaron so intensely; he told Roy he felt a pain in his vitals wondering whether it was true. Aaron looked away and glanced around the Banquet Hall and then mentally took a nosedive.

"Oh, God, look who's coming."

Donna turned around and saw Miriam heading towards them, as people stopped her to compliment and chat with her. Donna said, "She told me you 'opened her up'. The smirk on her face told me she enjoyed it."

"If I gave her my life, she'd want my soul."

"What do you want?" Donna asked, frustrated by his petulance.

"A woman that understands the *meaning* of life."

Donna impatiently said, "Get a grip, she's five seconds away." Then she got up and smiled.

Miriam muted a scream. "Hey, Missy, look at you! You're a knockout!" Aaron stood up and she took a look at him. "My God! Does this man wear it well? The tuxedo is a perfect fit. If they can't find the new Bond, it's coz he's right here!"

"You look most becoming."

"That accent! Screw Hugh Grant. You're so posh, love it!" Miriam said, "A Master's degree, your own agency."

"I'm not rich and I'm certainly not posh. I'm a Black British Jew—trust me; that's not posh." Aaron walked around to the other side of the table and greeted the man who resembled a handsome BBC news presenter even though he was younger than most of the grey men on television.

Offering his hand, he said, "Aaron Rapchinski Blackmon, hi."

"Jerry Kawenouski, menswear, Belgium and the Netherlands, you?"

"Recruitment—I'm here with my mother," he said, pointing at Donna.

"No, she looks too young to be your mum. My mother looks like Baby Jane. She's dedicated her life to aging. Your mother is charming." Aaron pointed to an empty seat and Jerry sat down. The look he gave Donna was saucy without being lecherous. Donna turned to Miriam for a private chat.

"Mum's as funny as Elaine May, too." Jerry was puzzled. "You don't know her? How old are you, Jerry?" Jerry told him forty-eight. "You should know her. She worked with Mike Nichols. Their *Mother and Son* sketch is ten times funnier than Woody Allen and I say that, with a lot of love in my heart for him."

"Who else do you like?"

"Lenny Bruce, hate Seinfeld, love Sacha Baron Cohen! Mel Brooks, Billy Crystal. But Sacha kills me with his whole Ali G wannabe Black man persona."

"Why?"

"Because I is Black too, you know. My pops was Jamaican."

Donna turned quickly and told him, "Oy mister, stop that immediately. We're out." Aaron laughed and blew her a kiss.

"What was that?" Miriam asked Donna, amused, but confused.

"When he was a teen, he used to impersonate Ali G, a comedian, Borat. He's a Jewish guy who had or still has an obsession with British Jamaican youth culture. Aaron copied him, but his sister told him it made him look like a dumb white boy playing 'Black'. Zara could talk him out of making a fool of himself."

Miriam said, "I'd prefer a nerdy teenager who turned into an actual man than a fake guy who turned out to be a real kid." Jerry heard her and gave Miriam a nod.

Jerry turned his eyes to Donna and their flirt didn't miss Aaron or Miriam's attention.

Miriam said, "Where the hell are the drinks?" but she saw a waiter and held up her hand and he came over to them.

"We're dry here. Trust me, these men prefer their ladies wet." Aaron burst out laughing and then held up his hand and Miriam gave him a high-five.

Donna pulled Miriam in closer and whispered. A few minutes later, their drinks arrived and the looky looks between Jerry and Donna silently spoke volumes. Although I have only my imagination to fill in the blanks, Cynthia did tell Michael, in order for Miriam to understand her better, Donna was frank with her. So, their conversation included many confidences which Miriam responded to.

Miriam confessed, "I'm thankful for your friendship. Aaron's acting cool but I've felt the fire in him."

"His father taught him a lot about dignity and sex to stop him watching porn and getting dumb ideas about women."

"In New York, men's brains are soaked in porn. Aaron has manners, and...skills." Donna understood perfectly.

"He must get that from his dad. We had no barriers- racial politics, religion, or cunnilingus, we explored everything together." Donna's gesture revealed their confidentiality as she continued, "My mother would have freaked if I told her about it."

Miriam looked great, rather like Anne Hathaway as she tried to stop laughing.

Despite what Roy says, from what I could see, she wasn't anything like a Bond villain.

"It won't be easy calling you mom, but you're so fabulous I can get used to it." Among all the guests in the Banquet Hall, Donna was proud of her difference.

Donna leaned in to ask Miriam. "If I remarried, what would you think?"

Miriam abruptly stopped walking. "This is why Britain needs Jews." She took Donna's hand. "Take back your life, lady; yes!" she sincerely said. "Can Aaron deal with it?"

"Aaron isn't a child who needs me; he's a man that cares about me. On Bankolé Island, we talked. If I detested a woman he was seeing, he'd drop her."

Days later, Donna told Roy, she wanted Miriam to understand how devoted Aaron is. She also told Roy; Miriam enquired about her close friendship with him.

Roy asked if she told Miriam how his father in Jamaica died and Donna assured him that she'd never tell anyone.

* * *

On the other side of the hotel, in the Ballroom, Aaron was talking to the DJ and the assistant event manager. "...my mum's first social since we lost my dad. I just want to raise mum's spirit. It's been four years since she's been to one of these. Please play this CD, it's got Sinatra, Streisand and Bublé. I understand the band will be playing live, but you can warm up the room with dance music."

The DJ was one of those guys who had failed high school because he thought he was going to be a musician in a band. Although he wasn't handsome enough to be the frontman for the band, he felt he could be the bass-man. However, his ego was too big for a group, so, he had ended up as a DJ.

Observing Aaron's begging eyes and hopeful gaze broke the DJ's arrogance. Aaron took out a roll and peeled off £200, one hundred each for both of them. "I've picked a perfect mix; we're

talking twenty minutes of classics. There are only four tracks on it.
Help me to make my mum happy, please." Aaron's pleading face
made the 'ultra-cool' DJ capitulate. "Thanks, guys."

CHAPTER TWELVE

Throughout dinner, Aaron arranged for the event photographer to discreetly take pictures of Donna from a distance, capturing spontaneous moments of their party at the table of eight, as people came and went offering their greetings and goodwill to Donna. Jerry, the very image of a mature playboy, was most attentive and Hershel came over and stayed for twenty minutes; pulling up a chair to share the table. Miriam periodically eyed Aaron because she seemed suspicious. Their table was busier than the others due to Miriam's American magnetism.

Miriam looked away from the others, turned to Aaron and asked, "Having a good time?"

"Not exactly; this isn't my idea of fun."

"What hits that spot?

Mum's been talking to you about me again. "Video games with my mates."

"You're kidding me: but you're thirty!" People at the table looked over and her derision spoke to each of them in different ways. She hated the fact that she sounded shrill. Later that evening, Aaron told Roy just how much he loathed her for rebuffing him like that. Donna eyed the two of them and Aaron lowered his voice.

"If I asked you to leave early and head back to your hotel, would you go?" Miriam got up and led Aaron towards the ballroom onto the dance floor.

"I have to take my mum home, but I can join you later?"

"No." Miriam calmed herself. "Keep it in your pants." She plastered a smile on her face and left him on the dance floor, then proudly mingled, showing people she was a smart, sociable businesswoman for the rest of the evening. Meanwhile, Aaron focused on possible suitors. He went back to the table and escorted Donna around, so she could speak to anyone she wanted to and he danced with her.

* * *

Later on, Aaron, Hershel and Jerry were standing on line in the ultra-modern men's room waiting to relieve themselves. Aaron said to both of them, "Your interest in my family hasn't escaped my attention."

Jerry replied, "What? You're the papa we have to seek permission—"

"Don't finish that sentence, if you know what's good for you."

Jerry and Hershel felt his threat. They also knew a warning when they heard it.

Aaron told them, "Naturally, I want to hear more because we know what we're talking about; although if you mention a name while we're standing in here, I'll deny you any consideration." They stood quietly and waited. Before long, they came up to the urinals and neither Jerry nor Hershel felt they could speak until they were spoken to.

Both men were confident and strong-willed, but they felt weakened by Aaron. All three men shed the excess of wine and lager and Aaron boastfully asked. "What do you think of the babe I'm with?"

Hershel replied, "Fantastic, what a figure!"

Jerry said, "She knows menswear. I had a long talk with her at dinner. She's one of those Americans who've learnt so much from the family business. She had her eye on you even when we were talking."

"I can do better." Aaron turned to Hershel and Jerry and his manhood wasn't just in his face and attitude. They saw his swagger and they knew they were dealing with a bighead who fancied himself as a tough guy. Aaron took a step back and flashed the men standing both sides of him. Jerry and Hershel were startled because Aaron had a dark side to him. And what he was doing showed that he had balls they didn't have. Each man staring saw Aaron's pride and his potency differently because his whiplash was as close to being assaulted as they'd ever been.

Aaron turned his back on them and went to wash his hands. Several other men wanted to smack him. He made them feel small and no matter how rich those well-to-do Jewish men were, they couldn't handle it.

The attendant gave Aaron's tuxedo a brush down as Aaron spoke. "Jerry, Hershel; come to me next Wednesday and I'll tell you whether it's alright to move forward. This is more than cheap thrills. We're talking about honour. I won't take it lightly if I hear anything that displeases me," he said, pointing heavenward. Jerry and Hershel knew better than to mention his mother's name in the men's room. Aaron gave the attendant a £5 tip and the old Greek fella bowed and thanked him.

"Bring me your profile. Convince me you are men of substance." Aaron didn't smile; he turned and walked out, leaving the men stunned.

* * *

In the busy streets of Shoreditch, Aaron walked around the car and opened the door. Donna was sitting next to Miriam and Aaron kissed her goodnight and told her to call in the morning. Miriam stepped out and Aaron escorted her to the hotel's reception. She got her room key and he walked her to the lift.

"Tonight, has been a pleasure, Miriam. You're great company and a beautiful dancer."

"What a contradiction you are," Miriam told him provocatively.

"What do you mean?" Aaron replied, pushing his sleek hair off his forehead.

"You recited poetry between my lips. No man has ever talked to me like that."

Her smile could have given any man a lift. "I liked it, especially when you danced me around in the moonlight. Now is when you should shine as a man." He was on the verge of making a move, so she pulled away. "Bye." She sensed his blood was up, so she wanted to leave him high and dry.

* * *

When Aaron returned home, Roy was in the living room watching *The Matrix*. The scene with Morpheus captured and tied to the chair was on screen. Aaron silently entered the room with predatory impulses darting through him due to the night he had

had. The red and green neon in the room tainted the atmosphere like an LA crime scene. Roy told me, he was sheltered in the sofa, and everything looked distorted.

Roy felt goose bumps rise across his body and then he looked over and saw Aaron standing there. He knew the look on Aaron's face, so he forced himself to keep calm. "Hey, mate; were there any prospects at the reception?" Aaron nodded, yes. "Are you OK?" Roy recognised the famished desire on Aaron's face, so he backed into the sofa in his red T-shirt, white shorts and woolly sports socks, but erotic sparks shot through him. Aaron looked as though he was possessed as he slowly moved forward.

Roy asked, "How was it: Donna have a good time?" Aaron ominously made his way over to the sofa, as if his doppelganger had taken possession of him.

"You look tired, Aaron. I'll go up now you're back." Roy turned off the television and tried to hide his panic. The concealed lighting intensified the unexpected macabre atmosphere. Roy knew Aaron sometimes 'changed'.

Consequently, his pulse quickened and he fell short of breath. Aaron's eyes locked on him and so Roy quickly moved to the door and got out of the room.

Ten minutes later, in Roy's bedroom, he sat perfectly still, staring at the door, waiting and waiting until he began to breathe heavily gripped by dread and desire. Two minutes of excruciating angst darted and washed over him when his bedroom door opened and Aaron came in, removed his cufflinks, unbuckled his belt and pulled out his shirt as he approached the bed.

"I called Amber on the way here. Her dad still thinks I'm just a 'black'. He doesn't want me to go out with her. I'm to be shunned; like my mother before me." Aaron opened his shirt and exposed the dark hair on his chest.

Cramp shot through Roy's foot. "Aaron, you know these thoughts are bad for you. It aggravates your—"

Distraught and desperate, Aaron said, "I saved her life and her father thinks I'm just a 'black'. What kind of animal has he pictured? At the reception tonight, loads of guys danced with mum—admired her. I got their business cards. I told four blokes; before they get ideas about dating mum, they have to talk to me. If the orthodoxy can pass judgment on us, I can judge them. Root out *their* bigotry," he concluded, thumping his protruding chest.

"Aaron, why are you *so* unhappy?"

"I don't really have friends I'm psyched with, except for you." Aaron stood there in his boxers.

"You're beyond me. Men don't interest you; can't touch you. It's just *me* that gets to you. Aren't you just a 'bad boy' who's straight?"

"No, I'm not. I'm polymorphous; you've known that since dad died." Roy told me, every unrestricted libidinous impulse in his collective unconscious sparked and ignited him, so they went fucking mad.

* * *

Roy and I were sitting in my living room at the table with our laptops open. I printed the pages I'd written so I crossed the room to get them. Roy had his hat pushed back and his shirtsleeves rolled up. The light in the distance of the Barbican shadowed London. Waiting for the pages, I looked over my shoulder and I wanted to punch him in the mouth. But I'm sixty-two, so I've lived through heaven and hell, therefore, a sexy thirty-year-old hot-rod like Roy wasn't going to fry my brains. I brought the pages over and gave it to him.

He read it and I said, "This is Amber and Aaron's love story, not your liaison with Aaron. That's a rather sordid indulgence. He loves *her*." The distress that washed over Roy's face was exactly what I was aiming for, so I went and poured myself a scotch.

CHAPTER THIRTEEN

Amber pushed her food around on the plate and then closely looked at everything in the dining room. She hated every item and every piece of furniture her eye came to rest on. She hated the conservative chintz and suburban normality of the place. The royal blue and magnolia interior drapes, nets, carpet and the lacquered cream and gold sideboard along with the dining room table made her sneer and purse her lips.

Her frustration and disdain for her family home and their conversation displayed itself in her eyes. Just watching her parents made Amber's blood boil. They sat at both ends of the table in their dinner clothes and all she could think of was, who else dressed for dinner every day and had to make conversation instead of honestly talking to each other about their daily life. The food was of the highest quality and when one of the servants brought her a bowl of sorbet to clear her palate between the fish and meat to come, she tightened her fists and stared at the bowl.

"Amber, eat. What's the matter with you?" her father said. She looked up at him and he was the very picture of a Jewish patriarchal forty-seven-year-old father, except he dressed in £4,000 bespoke suits and handmade shirts.

"You're becoming impossible, Amber!" her mother scolded. The twin set and pearls, Toni & Guy 'young' hairstyle and the overpowering smell of Miss Dior perfume got up Amber's nose; so, she mimed the words coming out of her mother's mouth bobbing her head around which made her look like a mocking puppet.

Helena stared at her, knowing Amber was upset. Unlike Amber's well-off parents, Helena's father was an industrialist who was worth millions, but much like Amber, both of their fathers were too busy to spend time with them. Helena looped her honey-brown hair behind her ear and glared at Amber.

"Well, young lady, are you going to answer your father?"

"I don't know." She looked at her father. "Were you saying anything important?"

"Insolence is an unbecoming trait that a young lady should avoid." Amber sat up and adjusted her Stella McCartney white 'lulu' dress.

"But I *am* a young lady. Aren't I, Helena? I went to finishing school in Switzerland." Amber got to her feet and curtsied.

"I've studied Leslie Caron and Audrey Hepburn. I'm a dancer, a charity children's hostess and a jewel to any man worthy of me." Her startling angry eyes glared at her father. "What are you, besides a fraud and a criminal?"

"I am a diplomat of the Luxembourg government. How can I be a criminal?"

"Do you care whether I live or die?" He gestured to indicate the absurdity of her question and looked awfully grand doing so. Her mother sighed, bewildered.

"Answer me!" Amber demanded like a lawyer cross-examining a prosecutor's witness.

"Of course, I care whether you live or die; such nonsense!"

"I'm going to call a rebuttal witness to expose your perjury."

"Amber Louise Shapiro. That is your father! Have you gone mad?"

"Jean, she is having a tantrum," her father rebuffed.

"Yes, I am mad." Helena wanted to laugh but didn't dare. "You stand up in Brussels and make declarations, give reports, talk policy about how to save the world, secure good international relations and all your other fraud activities!"

"I am not a fraud."

"You are. You *claim* to care about people. You say you *care* about me. Well, I was almost taken from you: killed! But a man saved my life!" She picked up the bowl of sorbet and threw it across the room and they flinched. "You don't consider it right to allow him into our stupid Wimbledon 'mansion'? You have the audacity to forbid me to see him!" She stepped away from the table and pointed in his face.

"Who the hell are you?" Her father didn't know what to do because this was the first time Amber had challenged his authority. "You want to be known…" Servants came into the room. "Get out of my sight!" Amber screamed and they looked at her mother. "If you're still here in two seconds, I'll throw everything on this table at you!" They dashed out. Helena's mind raced ahead because in the years she had known Amber, she had suspected that one day she would snap.

"I caught an episode of the *Sopranos* on TV. It almost made me vomit because you're that kind of racist pig. Tony Soprano's hate cripples him. His daughter goes out with a guy whose parents are Jewish and African American and Soprano sinks into depraved racial pathology." She threw three plates of food off the table and her father grabbed her. She slapped him in the face and her mother began praying.

"Racial hatred is evil," she said quietly. "Haven't you learnt that yet?" Her mother tried to shift her back and take her upstairs, but Amber pulled away.

"Your generation talks about peace and then commit crimes that shame us. Aaron sends me letters about his life, he studied philosophy. He asks me philosophical questions. His mother was shunned and cast out of her family because she married a doctor; oh, sorry she married a 'black'! I have letters from Aaron, telling me how his family suffered and rebuilt their lives after that. I've met his mum. She's as lovely as any lady can be, but you don't want to know her because you're prejudiced or perhaps, you're just a racist."

"You have no right to talk to me like this."

Amber shoved her mother aside and lunged at her father, sticking her neck out. "I'll tell you what gives me the right to talk to you like this. You have moulded me into a demure, obedient, virgin, who has to get *your* approval to have an opinion. How I've never screamed until now is amazing! Over twenty years of doing what you've told me. Here's a newsflash! I want an apology from you. You'll do that by meeting Aaron and telling him thanks for saving my life."

Helena said, "Amber, he's an authoritarian *because* he's your father. You should have spoken of your feeling before. Calm down now! You'll make yourself ill."

Her father said, "There, your friend knows, she has respect."

Helena said, "No, Mr Shapiro, I don't respect the fact Amber has had to live in fear of speaking out and submerging her identity."

Amber told him, "We're not in session; this is what's going to happen. I'm going over to Helena's and I'm not coming back into the house until you invite Aaron and you take a moment to see he's the man I want to marry."

Her mother said, "His father and his mother were shunned by their family. Are they destitute?" Amber threw her arms up.

"Aaron and his mother live in two beautiful houses. Aaron owns his own business."

Amber turned as she walked away from her parents. "Oh, and who are you? You're the grandchildren of a Russian anarchist and a French Resistance leader. Let me remind you both, we're not royalty; we're Jews."

"And suppose I say I don't care to be dictated to by my own daughter."

"Then I leave this house and never come back." Her father rushed at her and Amber flung her arms out to shield herself.

"If you hit me, I'll have you arrested!" He froze, astounded by a woman he once knew as his little girl.

"I am the man in this house!" he shouted loudly.

"And I am a woman. I am not your child!" Amber screamed at the top of her voice. "You couldn't find me a better husband. Aaron, he's been tested. He has to live every day of his life, coping with prejudice and racial hate." Her gestures exposed her dismay. "But he still finds a place in his heart to send me love letters every day. A letter Papa, not a text; not an email: handwritten letters to me, every day." she told her father, gripping his arms.

"I know you like old fashion ways and traditional values. Well, thank your lucky stars because instead of your superficial match-making, I've seen this man's heroism and romanticism." She swung around to her mother and said, "He's lovely."

"And if I forbid you to marry?" Her father demanded.

"Then I'll tell people you work for you are not to be trusted. People I went to school with are now in positions of power. They'll listen to me."

In Hebrew, her mother accused her of treachery.

"I will meet this boy—" her father said.

"He's not a boy! He's a man, he's thirty!"

Her father closed in on her. "I will have him investigated. I'll find out what he hasn't told you."

Amber pointed in his face and quietly said, "If you try and marry me off, I'll ruin this family." Helena tingled and Jean looked startled.

"What can you do?" Her mother asked.

"I'll destroy the man you make me marry." Her mother was shocked at the determination and the force of her 'little girl'.

"I will ridicule his masculinity, mock his conversation, laugh at him in bed and make him impotent. He'll dread the thought of me."

Amber forced a smile and remembered her heroines, Anne Boleyn and her daughter Queen Elizabeth. Amber studied the Tudors and developed an admiration for them. She also thought of her comic book heroine, Wonder Woman, who she adored as a child. For years, she kept quiet and obeyed her father but Aaron's letters had convinced her he was the perfect man for her.

"If you decide to marry me off, there will be no grandchildren. Aaron's mother has lived a full life from what he's told me. I want to build on what she's given him and bring us peace and joy. We can all be happy, providing *you* change."

"There are other ways to deal with you."

"Yes, you can kill me."

Helena and Jean, cried, "No!"

"Papa, do you know the meaning of abuse of power?" She turned to Helena. "Help me put some things into a bag. I want to stay with you for a few days; may I?"

"Of course. Goodbye, Mr Shapiro. Jean." Helena followed Amber out of the living room and Amber's parents clung to each other.

* * *

At Helena's flat in Knightsbridge, they came through the door of her place on Basil Street. She lived on the third floor and they were tired of carrying their own stuff when they entered her flat. The best thing about the place was her address. It was well furnished by shops locally. They dragged the bags in and fell on the floor, laughing. It was late and they just needed to have herb tea and rest.

An hour later, Amber came out of the bathroom in her pink pyjamas with her face washed, looking like an adolescent woman.

She went into the bedroom and hopped onto the bed beside Helena, and she handed Amber a bowl of peaches in brandy. Amber said, "Oh, wow; remember when we first discovered these?"

"2006, at school. We were barely sophisticated, but we thought we were." Helena gave her a dessert spoon and they ate in silence, until they stopped and began making love.

* * *

A week later, Roy and I walked around the Barbican Centre complex and he kept giving me updates and theorising about what everyone's actions meant. The Barbican is a maze of disproportionate buildings, spread out like a labyrinth in brick, stone, glass and concrete. You need to earn over £100k a year to live here. To some extent, it reminded me of the Marina City in Chicago or something oddly retro in a futurist landscape. Everywhere we walked, buildings jutted, curved, sored upward or spread open to reveal ponds and fountains, among the brown and rust-coloured buildings that made up the apartments, shops and social spaces, like Barbican Hall. I somehow felt trapped in the middle of all the fuss.

"Helena called me. We went for drinks and she told me about the bust-up Amber had with her parents because Aaron is so upset about not seeing her."

Dressed in a lightweight zoot-suit, Roy casually strolled along with his trilby and sunglasses covering his face. "Do you mind?" I indicated to him. "Talking to you with your face covered by your hat and glasses is getting in the way."

"Oh, sorry." He removed his dark glasses and took off his hat. I quickly thought about him in bed with Aaron, but the beta-blocker I took was working so I stayed calm.

"What?" I asked him.

"You've got a peculiar smile on your face."

"It's sweltering. Anyway—according to Helena, Amber is losing her cool. She loves Aaron and I can tell that's shaking Helena's tree."

"How've you got so close so quickly?"

"I'm an openly gay man. People trust me because I'm not a liar. I'm on telly every week and she is going mad because she feels unloved when she has so much to offer a loved one."

"What exactly has she told you?"

"Besides what I've written in the chapters about the confrontation with her parents; we talked about unrequited love and really, she's one hell of a nice person. She's rather like you. In love with someone she can never marry, even though they have a life of friendship, sealed with occasional sex."

"My sex life isn't fixated on Aaron."

I wanted to grab him and hit him! Shake him or scream out in the Barbican, *You're shagging a straight bloke who uses you as his bitch!* But I dug deep and smiled.

"It's difficult to make you understand, Eugene. When Aaron and I get together, we share the most supreme and extraordinary love people don't talk about." Those words made him sublime and changed his appearance.

"Isn't he simply feeding where he can?"

A grave look passed over Roy's face when he leaned forward and told me. "We're not 'shagging'. Aaron's the epitome of butch sensitivity, especially when his body and soul turn hetero-flexible. He gives himself to me."

"So, he didn't fuck you the other night?"

Dear God! I actually said that?

"I can't talk about that," Roy quietly replied.

Eugene Martins don't blow it. Wait, is he trying to spare my feelings? For fuck sake, Eugene! You're on telly! People trust you. You've got a PhD. Get-a-grip! You've lived through poverty, the AIDS crisis and blatant racism.

"Roy, what happened with you two when he returned from the ball?"

"In this world of PC fakes, me and Aaron are tight." Roy stopped and took several breaths. "We've grown from boyz to men. I'd kill for him. One time at Uni, an Arab who believed his money and his version of manhood was the first and last word, tried to mess me up." Roy gritted his teeth. "Aaron dropped him with two punches!" The sneer in Roy's smile was no joke. "We're not just mates, we're spirits bound in flesh!"

All at once, I was reminded of the difference between people born in the Caribbean and Britain. I backed off to dispel the tension. Eventually, he regained his calm and said, "I *can* tell you the morning after the Ball I helped Aaron write a love letter to Amber. He loves her, believe me."

"Helena told me; Amber read the letter to her. Helena was torn apart because she knows she can't win Amber over. They make love, possibly the way you guys do; but she calmly told me, Amber's heart belongs to him. It wasn't easy for Helena to say that, believe me."

"How did a lesbian reach that level of trust with you, so quickly?"

"Watch your manners please. She's not some lesbian. I told her, loving you was equally painful for me." I don't know whether the clouds rushed by or the breeze turned cold, but I felt numb and I couldn't control myself.

"Eugene, you know my relationships have failed because...I don't know if I'm capable of having one." He questioningly looked at me. "You actually love me?"

How could he doubt it? Why didn't he know it?

"Yes, ever since you told me that your parents were poisoning you, but since it took too long to die, your dad started beating you up."

As dark-skinned as he is, Roy turned pale. I saw that he struggled to breathe and his eyes widened as his mouth tightened.

"He...he. He was kicking me in the face when I begged God to strike him down and he dropped dead from a heart attack." Roy's face went blank. "Those guys came to kill me afterward because they decided I was an Obeah queer."

I was overcome again watching him. Maybe it's because he's an erotic man-child. Perhaps it's because the 'Brutalism' of the Barbican isn't its architecture: its human brutality that unnerves me. And in the communal gardens of the Barbican, I sensed the bombing and death of its past and the beauty of what my life could be in the future. Maybe I'm too old fashion and need romantic love to keep me alive.

"Roy, you escaped to England as a thirteen-year-old and made a man of yourself. I love how you devoted yourself to learning. And the fact that Donna loves and confides in you tells me so much."

"You love me because of that?"

"And the fact you're modest and a bit crazy." He slowly smiled at me and I started to get some feeling back in my feet.

"Eugene, will you give me some time to think?"

"Yes. I mean, we have a book to write."

Judiciously, he nodded. "So, do we leave this part in concerning how you feel about me?"

"No, it's their love story."

"But I'm involved."

"It's realism, not reality. Every novel needs editing." He stared at me, quizzically for maybe half a minute.

He said, "I admire your discipline. Not to mention the way you handle me." I stared at him and I could feel a real sense of happiness fill my mind and body.

"Oh...you're getting a stiffy right now, aren't you?"

No wonder Caribbeans say, Jamaicans are the Nigerians of the Caribbean! Arrogant little bastard! I laughed out loud and people around the Barbican eyed us. I jerked my head and he followed me back to the apartment because we had another chapter to start.

CHAPTER FOURTEEN

The flashy cars, exclusive stores and brand boutiques glimmered in the summer evening light. Amber's hand felt small and comforted in Aaron's large palm. They swayed slightly as they walk through Knightsbridge, past Harrods. Roy and Narjan walked closely together and Narjan felt very special because of the conversation he had with Roy the night before last. Helena felt very good walking next to Aaron's Uncle Saul.

Throughout dinner, he'd kept Helena in stitches and she liked the way he occasionally put his hand on her shoulder to tell her something. Helena knew he wasn't making advances because he spoke so well of his wife and children. She also liked the memories he shared about Humphrey because if Aaron had spoken about his father, she would have questioned the veracity of his claims.

The six of them walked through the street, sometimes in a row, sometimes in threes and occasionally they broke in two's, to share a confidence with each other. Dinner was Helena's treat and Saul was impressed with her sophistication. Roy told me Helena's beauty that night rested on her intellectual prowess. Over dinner she explained Benetton and Olivetti's corporate mistakes and how her father's corporation has learnt from their errors and how she is building the women's Brands for her father's company.

Saul was particularly captivated with Amber because she was elegant and warm. Whenever she shared a remark in German, or Hebrew, depending on the context of the discussion, he felt she was proud of her Jewish heritage and would not engage in self-demeaning 'banter' because he knew many people who were like that.

Knightsbridge is a swanky place that did not take kindly to vulgarisms. It is a Borough of aristocrats, the high and mighty so to say. Narjan stood out because he was in white sneakers, jeans and a T-shirt. Aaron took out his mobile and began visually recording the group walking through the street.

Amber asked, "What are you doing, you crazy man?"

"You look so incredible in that purple dress and those shoes..."

"Helena, didn't I tell you he was something! This dress is a Tom Ford, and Helena is wearing a Prada. Take a bow Miss Carduluci." Aaron turned his mobile towards Helena.

Aaron said, "I'm wearing my heart on my sleeve!"

Saul shoved his fist in the air and said, "Nice Bubala! Good comeback. Your father would be proud of you!"

"What about you two?" Aaron asked and Roy stopped, took Narjan in his arms and kissed him which delighted Narjan. Helena looked at Amber and pulled a face to mark her approval because it was everything she couldn't do. Saul was rather taken aback.

"When did you discover you were...gay?" Saul asked.

Roy turned to him and said, "At twelve, I was homosexual. But when Humphrey took Aaron and me out into the wild to get in touch with our inner warrior, I became *gay*."

"Humphrey knew you were gay? He never told me."

"Of course not; Donna didn't tell you either because I asked them not to."

In Hebrew, Saul told Helena and Amber, "If Humphrey was Jewish, I'd have known. Can you imagine keeping such a secret from the family?" Saul asked, knowing the answer.

Helena replied, "I can imagine keeping it to yourself, but if you told anyone else, that story would have legs! Within a week, everyone would know!"

With great sincerity, Saul told Helena, "I think that's what makes your generation so interesting. You're full of secrets, plots and strategies." Saul grabbed Aaron around the neck. "And you mister, are a master of reinvention; planning to get your mother remarried. A son matchmaking for his mama. Oy! I never heard of such a thing." He went off on a Yiddish invective about tradition.

Aaron told them, "We were at the annual ball and there were lots of men interested in mum. I'm not having them invade our lives and disrespect her or try and play Papa to *me*. I'm going to screen and background check them all because who knows what they're into."

Saul told him, "I didn't say it was wrong, it's just different: really different. I wonder what your grandmother will say when she hears this."

"Don't tell on him," Amber pleaded.

Helena said, "My father and I flout conventions all the time. It's how we've made our dynasty and our money."

"It's a brilliant idea," Narjan told them. "In Sri Lanka, marriage is constantly arranged and so often they work out well. Aaron is simply taking a proactive approach to ensure the security and happiness of his mother."

His Tamil Nadu and English accent were very lyrical. Saul watched the way Narjan walked and he could see Narj led from the hip, which feminised his movement, even though he wasn't distinctly effeminate. However, his long black hair blew about in the breeze, but his eyes never shifted when he spoke. "Also," Narj continued: "I think it proves something important. Aaron is ahead of the rites of passage." Narjan left Roy and walked beside Saul.

Narjan said, "I respect the fact Aaron wants to prolong his mother's life not through medication but through happiness."

Saul turned around and told Aaron, "In my day, such conversations would never be heard. But I love you for asking my opinion because your father and I were so close."

"Were you?" Amber asked.

"I taught Humphrey about Jewish culture."

Narjan said, "But we're talking as though you guys are different species. You and Aaron's father were simply Judaeo-Christian. You both share a heterosexual kinship and paternalism—"

"Oh no, my friend," Amber said strongly. "My father has never made friends with Black people. I'm not saying he's definitely racist. In Luxembourg, Black people don't instil a sense of fear in us through immigration. And at school in Switzerland diversity didn't threaten our identity because there were only two Black girls from political families. My father plays the liberal, but he is 100% pro Jewish." Her dress blew up and the gathered ruffled chiffon and the silk sash tied around her waist billowed in the breeze, so Aaron wolf-whistled.

Saul asked, "Is your dad more politician than fatherly?"

"He's never been brutal to me; he simply expects me to obey his 'wisdom'." She remembered good and bad times with her parents and Saul and Aaron saw the tension in her face. Amber said, "His political pontifications obfuscate the truth about life." Aaron looked at her on the mobile screen and then looked at her in person. He realised there was a depth to her that he hadn't connected with as yet.

Saul told her, "You're an eloquent speaker. You'd make a good politician yourself."

"I don't need to assuage my conscience because I'm living a dirty life like them," Amber stated and Aaron recalled one of the conversations they had about political Eurocrats. "Politicians' are a pack of liars. Indeed, almost everyone I've ever met is a liar." Her emphasis took the men aback. "Except you," she told Helena. Then the two of them embraced and skipped off down the street like beauties in a ballet.

Narjan said, "It's too bad I didn't spend more time with you both on Bankolé Island but we had things to deal with." He eyed Roy and quietly told him. "People might think Amber's a Pollyanna but she has intellectual and emotional substance.

Women hold almost no fascination for me, but she is something, both of them in fact." Roy took his hand reassuringly.

Aaron didn't ask himself why he was suddenly aroused by the sight of Amber cavorting through the streets of Knightsbridge, but he watched her with a growing awareness of her mystique and transparency.

Aaron rushed down the street and ran in front of Amber. The smile on his face told Helena that her days were numbered, but something strange happened. Instead of her usual disinterest in men's sexual urges, she was moved by Aaron's face, which reminded her of faces she'd seen in her studies of the Harlem Renaissance.

* * *

Helena and I were getting slightly pissed in the *Oscar Wilde Bar* at *Café Royal* on Regent Street. I've never been there but the way the staff greeted Helena told me she was a regular in the ornate if not lavish decadence of the crystal, mirror, bronze and red leather rococo surrounding. She was impeccably dressed in some creation from Paris and I felt a touch shabby in my post-apocalypse gear. I know about the good life from what I've read and people I've met, but intimate cocktails with the wealthy are a different matter.

Helena told me, "On the Island, it was very nice to be with them, Aaron has nice friends, so interesting, so diverse; it's exciting to me: Amber also." She signalled discreetly and a waiter came. She ordered another bottle of champagne and he left. "I thought of you when I was watching Amber with Aaron. Roy is..." She mentally searched her English, and said, "...involved with Narjan. Narjan told me his parents pay him to keep away from the family." The look on her face was twisted by absolute astonishment. "Papa would never do something like that to me, even though my brothers don't know."

"Not even the slightest suspicion?" I asked concerned for her.

"No, they are involved with their wives and children. They are nice but like most Italian men...self-absorbed, except when their balls pull their heart," she concluded with a flick of her wrist.

I freely told her, "You're marvellous!"

"And you are very...high-minded. I'm watching your television program each week; I love your premise: 21st century neo-modernism in practice. You find all these Afro-Asian, Arabian and Caribbean artists and explain how they challenge the status quo. It should be on the BBC and not just Sky television."

"The Beeb have young Reggie Yeats and David Olusoga. I'm a different kind of BBC. And my diverse audience love my shows. It's why my viewing figures are higher than all the others. What does Amber think of the show?"

"She could talk for hours about it. She has a great passion for curating and discovering new arts." She took a chocolate from her bag and offered one to me.

"Not at my age, I have to watch everything I put in my body. If I get fat, I'm done for. Gay men hate fat blokes...sorry, old, fat blokes."

"The gays in London have built their own enclosures with the stupid rules I've read about. But I think Michael De Farenzino could teach us all a lot about freedom. I plan to introduce him to my father. They will get on like allies."

"I admire him: Michael and David are my best friends."

"Michael told me your documentary help to protect him, so I went online and I watched it: very nice." Helena suddenly exuded an air of mystery. "You have found courage over these last few years." I knew she sensed something, so I agreed. "Is that how you are dealing with Roy and his boyfriend? I'm trying to find courage myself; you understand me?" I said yes. "It's horrid when someone you love is involved with a nice person. But when there is hate, that's different. Amber would happily put a knife in Miriam." Because we were on the same wavelength, we shared our woes in the opulence of the *Café Royal*.

Three champagne cocktails later, Helena's open body language and words told me she had genuine magnetism. She wasn't a common celebrity with a six-month presence. Helena is an heiress with class due to her dignified heritage.

"Every day, Amber receives love letters from him. Aaron tells her his sacred emotions." She seemed unnerved when she said that. "I have met all kinds of men who are horrible for any woman and heroic to so many men that imitate them as lovers. These types of men love themselves so much. I detest it!" She stared at me and I could feel her distress. She grabbed her wrist and massaged and moved her fingers freely.

"I dressed Amber in her Oscar de la Renta the night Aaron took her to *Quaglino's* for dinner." Emotional turmoil overtook Helena. "Never, ever before has she looked so much like her own woman." She gestured discreetly and a man came over to us. She whispered to him and he left to bring us more of whatever she liked.

"I walked Amber down to the car and her shoes and her perfume announced a lady was coming: you understand me?" A tiny smile on Helena's face made her so beautiful to me.

"Yes, Amber *is* unique."

Helena lunged towards me suddenly and plaintively said: "Isn't she." She had her wits about her, so she didn't spill or gush. "Papa and her father spared no expense to be sure we learnt elegance, but we chose Hollywood Stars. The icons of the 1920s-1950s mesmerised us as girls. Aaron sees that in her, but like Marlene Dietrich and Audrey Hepburn, she isn't impressed with aristocrats. Aaron is a powerful, sensitive man."

That gave her poise. Concerned and worried for her, I asked, "Are you alright?"

"You have strong instincts, feminine instincts in a way, if I can say that without offending your masculinity."

"My masculinity hasn't been offended since I kicked out my former lover. He was a simple prick." She sat up and tossed her head back and laughed well. Her hair, smile and her dress all looked so debutante chic. She told me something in Italian and then she realised she'd have to say it in English.

"Cazzo! It's a lifelong obsession for men." I wasn't sure what she was saying, so she called me closer with her index finger. "Penis, cock...men love it." I laughed, because I couldn't tell her that I lived in a priapic state longing for Roy.

"Strange; I can speak of this to you. My life has been surrounded by girls and women. Men had no place in our lives growing up. Now Amber spends nights telling me about Aaron. When she came home from *Quaglino's*, she told me, unlike other men her father introduced her to, Aaron, lets her speak and he pays attention. For their next date, she took him to *Langan's Brasserie*. We told our parents we don't 'second date' a suitor if they are gross." Whatever passed over my face made her poke me in the shoulder and say. "A man took me to dinner in Milan and while we were eating, I saw the food going around in his mouth like dirty socks and underpants in a washing machine." I just choked and then laughed out loud and couldn't stop!

I said, "Men with bad manners leave me numb. I mean the most handsome guy can turn ugly if you catch him picking his nose." We spent half an hour swapping notes on things we've seen dirty bastards do.

"It is for these reasons why I can't stand a man to put his hands on me." I bowed. "And the female body is fantastic to me." I understood.

By eight o'clock, our confidentiality meant I told her a fair amount about myself. She asked me about unhappy relationships and I told her about my ex.

"Come on Chéri, his name; he's a famous fashion designer, you say...tell me." I leaned in and caught myself in the gilded mirror and I saw the expression of transgressive glee on my own face, and I felt that Oscar would have approved. I told her his name. "Oh! Such a great designer; but a worthless man: how typical."

"I'm over him. Roy is ten times better."

"The same with Aaron: he is alive in Amber's mind. You wouldn't know this, but he takes her out all the time. We'd need a montage that you get in films for me to tell you the places he's taken her and every time she comes home, she can't stop talking. He writes beautiful love letters and explains his Black Jewish family background, with so many pictures. He is unafraid of his emotions. And he doesn't believe he can 'heal' a woman's psyche from his penis." I was totally puzzled. "Oh, you don't know this?" Camille Paglia couldn't have trumped Helena's mockery. "Women are incomplete because we need penis." The irritated look of boredom showed her at her best.

"What women do you admire?"

"My mother, she was a revolutionary feminist; it's why Papa loves her. I've never belonged to a Movement, I admire pioneers. Post-war Italian women are amazing to me. They built lives out of the rubble of war. Growing up, Anita Roddick was my idol and Oprah is a brilliant dialectic. Because of them, I work for my father, and he lets me do business based on my feminist-intersection of international business studies. In two years, I've made millions for him." She smiled proudly and brightly. "I am President of Women's Social Interests." I felt so proud of her, I kissed her wrist. She flung her hands across her chest, beaming like a Pre-Raphaelite.

"You are nothing like the men I have met. I *have* to say I like you because that seldom happens. In my work, men resent me—and I don't care! But you like me, I feel it."

I simply gestured and she said, "My God, look at your face; so nice!" I might have blushed.

"You and your friends are exactly the kind of people Amber and I wanted to meet so we chose to live in London rather than Paris. We admire bohemians. Aaron is like that. One evening, Amber told me Aaron is self-conscious about his class. We have met millionaires' sons, who are trashy. She respects Aaron. But the minute Aaron tries to get her in bed, it's over." I asked why. "She's a virgin. Her marriage depends on her purity." That stopped me from asking about their love life. "From everything she tells me. Non è un coglione."

"Helena, what does... 'Non è un coglione,' mean?"

"It's to say. Aaron is not a jerk. Most men are driven by capital and conquest." She shuddered. "I think men struggle to repress their sexual impulses, while women struggle to liberate their sexual instincts."

My God, this woman had plenty to say and so much of it was simply that brilliant. I must use that in the book!

"You're a beautiful heiress, you make millions—what do you want to become?"

"Aspirations and destiny make this difficult to answer. What do you want to become Eugene?"

"The best Black British author of this millennium. There aren't many Black men who are successful authors in Britain. I'd also like to find the happiness I've searched for. So, I'd buy a place and live with my boyfriend."

"Roy?"

"He's not my boyfriend." She heard me. "But what about you? When Amber marries..." I could see that the thought troubled her, so she took her time to answer.

"I think I would adopt a child and raise my daughter in Italy. I'd move to Milan and create marvellous things for Papa's company."

"What does your father do?"

"We're the most successful Jewish Education Specialist Service in Europe. I launched the Women's Progress Department when I went to work for him after my MBA. Now it's running well, making a lot of money."

"You must be so proud to earn a living instead of living off your dad."

"Eugene! It's my greatest achievement!" She had to calm herself. "So far."

"So—no love interest?"

"I've never dated a girl. My family..." She shook her hand. "But a daughter would bring me incredible joy. And if I'm loved that would be wonderful."

"You're exciting enough."

"Yes maybe. There is some incredible high society dyke decadence..." I must have looked shocked or something. "Gay men know so little about us."

"I'm listening." She proceeded to shock me in the *Oscar Wilde Bar*. I was certain he'd have been thrilled to be with us. Helena spoke and didn't stop surprising me with lurid and lascivious tails of decadent, rich girls who loved thrills.

I also knew that I liked Helena more than any other woman I'd met in the last ten years.

CHAPTER FIFTEEN

Aaron introduced Amber to his staff two days later. She scanned around the no-frills office and saw whiteboards on the walls with the names of the staff and as she did, the staff eyed her. Amber's pink and grey suit, and her elaborate fire opal six strand necklace impressed all the women. Aaron's office manager, Margot, loved her fire opal bracelet, and the way Amber clasped a pair of pink soft leather gloves. The men knew nothing about fashion, but they knew Amber was more stylish than any girl they went out with. Aaron's staff had an entrepreneur identity, therefore Amber stood out as a 21st century debutant.

The girls saw the Audrey Hepburn elegance of her and the boys saw Amber as the beautiful French girl they remembered from *Amélie*. One of the girls in the office couldn't stop herself. She was a 'plain' but beautiful person that people liked, but didn't fancy. She told Amber, "I love your suit."

"Oh, thank you!" Amber moved in closer and whispered, "Every girl knows good legs can be as effective as wearing the pants." Amber's body and her smile somehow made the women feel great about being 'girls' dealing with the 'boys' in the office, who were always competitive. The men eyed Aaron with envy at winning a woman of Amber's class. Aaron took Amber to his techie corner of the office where he was in the position to monitor and address everyone face to face. In front of him, Aaron had many devices at his disposal.

Some of the staff were still qualifying leads on the phone, asking the typical recruitment questions to discern if the candidate on the other end of the phone had a personality to sit alongside the interesting CVs that the staff found online.

As Amber walked around and took in the sight of the place, she could see there was none of Aaron's personality in the office.

It could have been any office anywhere. The computers, the bland walls and the furniture said nothing except, there is nothing in the place to distract staff. Consequently, people sat at their desks, got on the phone and gathered information and then use their intelligence to close deals.

Aaron called her to his corner and pointed to the screen. Because he was facing the staff, no one could see his screen. She looked at the faces of middle-aged men and saw every Jewish facsimile of her entire family and friends.

She sat beside him. Amber scrolled past one hundred and twenty faces and her fingers danced over the keyboard. She studied the information that showed the ten social media websites where the men had posted their profiles. "I think you should log out; Aaron and we'll continue this selection at your home. I need to talk to you about these..."

"Candidates?" he said, and she looked at the members of staff in front of them getting on with their work. She nodded and then looked at the whiteboards on the wall with all the sales figures of the staff and the companies they did business with.

"So, recruitment is not about the candidates' careers and personality, what line of work they're best for, but more about selling to the companies? I see lots of company names up on the boards but no candidates' names." Aaron sat on his desk with his back towards the staff.

"The staff all work with specific firms and build relationships with them. They find out what employers are looking for in a new employee and then these consultants go online and find CVs that match the job specification. They then call up people and go through a series of set questions. I have to establish how serious the candidate is about finding work and if they have the skills, experience and personality to fit the firm and the culture of the working environment." Amber paid the closest attention to what he was saying.

"Remember the things we examined when you came in before? I take them through psychometric evaluations; 1-2-1 career analysis. Ascertain what life skills and personality traits they have that enable them to work in any industry because they have an extrovert, competitive, creative, leadership personality, or methodical research practice skills. Then I *sell* my employers the candidates."

"So, your philosophy and psychology degrees enable you to understand the companies' ideals and their worldview. And then analyse what makes candidates' tick and their behaviour which suit specific company cultures."

He smiled at Amber and that told her she'd got it right, so she clasped her hands together and swivelled in the chair, which made him get up and kiss her. The staff behind them looked over. Amber's joy warmed the women's hearts, and the three men stuck their index finger into their encircled fists.

With the exception of Margot, who was forty, the average age of the men was twenty-eight and the women were twenty-six to twenty-seven. Two of the men and one girl got up and went to make coffee. The L-shaped office had an alcove area, out of sight of the main office space. Ejay, the Black guy, and Gary, a white bloke, adopted a macho front and shared comments on what they saw. Fern, an English woman from a middle-class background in Bristol, listened to them and responded in a scolding tone of voice, coloured by her Bristolian accent.

"No wonder you plonkers are alone. That's not some hot totty he's got there. She's a young lady; can't you tell?"

Gary, a typical London working-class lad, said, "How'd you know?"

"She has pink leather gloves and Mary-Jane shoes, that's no slag. And he doesn't go out with slags. No, she's got Continental style; you can hear it in her voice!"

"She does have a sexy accent, give her that," the Black guy concurred.

Gary added. "Yeah, and that walk of hers is deadly sweet." They minced around, swishing left and right. When Aaron appeared, they stopped. Aaron was not misled by their image as nice lads, with plenty of banter; he'd gone to the pub with them often enough to know their social politics was lacking and their sexual cravings exceeded their reach. All of them had steady girlfriends and 'a bit on the side'.

"Boss, good on you there, she's lovely! How long's it been?" Ejay asked. He was the kind of show-off that excelled at sales because he was flashy, and girls loved him because he played the 'suited and booted' city salesman to the hilt.

"Get on with your work," Aaron told him with a sly smile.

"Come on boss, we're Hackney 'fellas', Spurs lads. Don't be an Arsenal!"

"Don't you call me Arsenal, you cunt, get back to work." They all laughed, and the lads got their coffee and left.

Fern smacked his arm. "She is really lovely." He pulled funny faces and leaned in.

"She gets me up in the morning feeling so great! I text her and she texts—"

"Don't say she 'gets you up in the morning', you know what those dirty sods are like." He just chuckled. "I can feel the difference in you, your face is all lit up."

"She's very chic, isn't she?"

"Aye, but not too rich for your blood." He walked out of the office alcove and saw Amber huddled between the women studying their screens and they pointed out things to her. She gestured to confirm she comprehended what they said.

Margot, who resembled Deborah Kerr, came over to him.

"Where's she from? She has a delightful voice and she's very elegant."

"She's from Luxembourg."

Margot watched Amber with the other women. "It must be quite dark there now."

"Sorry, what?" Aaron asked in an apprehensive tone of voice.

"She has such light and spirit. Luxembourg's a very small country and I think you've stolen the light from them." Overcome by Margot's consideration, Aaron walked away smiling and went to Amber. He took her hand and she looked up to him. He told Roy he could hear his heartbeat in his ears and became conscious of his own existence. The look on his face didn't escape anyone. Amber took his hand and kissed his fingers, which made him blush. She could also see something happening to him, but she didn't know him well enough to describe his feeling.

Right then, Amber fully realised that she loved him, due to the fact she was certain he was bold and humane. This subject was a question Helena and Amber discussed endlessly over the years according to what she wrote in a letter to Aaron.

Amber clasped her hands together and asked the staff. "Why don't you let me treat you to cocktails after work?" They looked at her happily and nodded. She gazed at Aaron and flickered with élan, so she led him to the door then all seven members of staff watched them go.

Outside, in the grey corridor she told him, "I am going to help your mother. We'll go through the men's dating profiles and see if they're right or wrong. You say the men at the ball gave you their cards. Give them to me. Helena's father has connections worldwide..."

"I've got a few contacts myself. Roy's at the News Agency and I've placed staff in industries all over London. I can find out stuff."

"Whatever you wish; I just want to help you get what you want, darling."

"Give me a kiss."

She lightly touched his neck and kissed him. When she pulled back, with a smile, her words settled inside Aaron's mind and body.

* * *

I was alone in the Barbican listening to Roy's WhatsApp recorded message to me. Roy said. Back at their house in Hackney, Aaron explained how intensely he felt about Amber's impact on his staff. Roy described Aaron's expression, but I could imagine it. What I did not imagine was Roy telling Aaron he was going to break up with Narj. I removed the earphones, got up to stretch and get some air.

I stepped out onto the balcony and Roy's words came back to me: he was going to break-up with Narj.

The magic hour light over London was striking. I looked over the Barbican site because the lilac sky on the horizon with its spiky cityscape was eerie. My neighbour, Thijs and his wife Beatrice, stepped out onto their balcony. They're a Dutch and English couple. He was a middle-aged, shaggy-haired, sophisticated man who worked for an engineering firm. Beatrice was an Ophthalmologist. She also made pottery and successfully sold it online and she had a taste for Hobbs fashion.

Whenever I saw her, she always looked smart. Our balcony partition was open.

"Oh, Dr Martins, good evening," Beatrice said. We exchanged pleasantries because they were nice people. "I can hardly wait for your next episode," she continued. "The last program on female sexual identity during the Caribbean Plantocracy was such an eye-opener for me."

"Coming from an eye specialist, I find that paradoxical." She laughed easily and then Thijs invited me to dinner if I was free the following weekend.

"We're having a Brando weekend: *The Godfather*, *On the Waterfront*, *Streetcar* and *Last Tango in Paris*. Please bring your partner." I said, 'Partner?' "Yes, that dashing Be-Bop guy you're always smiling with." I was glad most white people can't see me blush. A lie seemed so convoluted, but I tried anyway.

"He's a very good friend of mine," I stated flatly.

"Who you're in love with," Thijs replied categorically.

I took a moment. "Yes." Joy sprang up in me and I burst out laughing.

"You were such a hermit and so sombre throughout the winter but since you've been seeing your Be-Bop guy, whenever I see you around the Barbican, you're always joyful. I was the same way myself after I met Beatrice." I simply nodded. "We'd be so happy if you'd have dinner with us." His wife nodded.

"I'll be there: and I'll ask my friend, Roy, thank you."

The following weekend we joined them for dinner and Roy was charming. To confound how they saw him, Roy turned up in a 1960s Mod mohair 3-piece slim fit burgundy suit, white shirt and polished black monk shoes.

Roy's Jamaican Rude Boy meets Mods look changed the way he acted all night. He was the youngest person in the room and he brimmed with vitality. Everything he said after we watched *A Streetcar Named Desire* was filled with critical insight, wit and sensitivity. The two other married couples were fascinated by him because I was sure they seldom meet eloquent educated Black men who are heartfelt and soulful. Our poetry is the stuff of popular music from Nat King Cole and Otis Redding to Pharrell Williams.

Beatrice and Thijs had loads of questions for us because we were the special guests at their dinner, so Roy and I spent ages answering non-invasive but inquiring questions none the less about our work and the Bankolé's because we were often seen with them. Since the Dutch don't have the same level of pretence as Brits, Thijs said.

"I don't think I have ever seen two Black guys who are so openly in love. Do you feel like champions Roy?" Their urbane, well-dressed friends who had jobs at Google and KPMG lived the good life, fell silent waiting for Roy's answer.

"The only cause I've ever championed is fighting Brexit and bringing down this rotten government. There are people I love. They're usually liberated women and extraordinary men." Then Roy kissed me—in front of them!

When I opened my eyes, I was breathless and prickling. People around us smiled and made comments but I didn't hear them until Thijs said, "And the age difference makes no difference, does it? I say this because of Beatrice and me."

Roy replied, "I've never loved boys. The good doctor here is the perfect blend of progressive masculinity and 'Ancient Greek Love'." Roy stood up, gave me a saucy look and then went over to the open window and stepped onto the balcony. First, they looked at me and then they watched him standing there.

This was the first time I'd ever seen Roy shift from the background to the foreground where *he* was the focus. I suddenly understood Aaron as I hadn't before. Our loved ones are extensions of our ego. Amber is beautiful and intelligent. At Aaron's office, people envied and admired him because he loves and is loved by Amber. Beatrice and Thijs think more of me, not just because of my television program; I know Roy makes a difference to the man they think I am. Their smile also told me how genuine they are. When Roy came back in, he sat next to me and held my hand as I talked to the guests.

* * *

Aaron went to his parents' home, entered the house and said, "Hi mum!" and took off his jacket in the hallway. "I bought you cake from *Richoux* in Piccadilly." He walked towards the kitchen. "The manager told me to bring you back for lunch because they love you." Aaron fell silent and became tight when he saw Miriam. The dining area looked more like a country kitchen than a modern one. He looked at both of them and then Miriam put a catalogue to one side. She looked cool, beautiful, and confidently at ease.

"Have you become my mother's companion and confidant?" he asked in a rather posh way. He walked around the table and gave Donna a kiss. The walls had posters of recipes from around the world with multinational families smiling, which gave Donna's kitchen an intimate, yet personal worldview.

Donna said, "I'm not gonna let her stumble around London when she's been my front line in New York." Donna looked fantastic in a pair of jeans and a pink cardigan. Her hourglass figure showed because she was also on a yoga fitness kick.

Aaron said, "Yes, of course. How are sales looking, Miriam?"

"We're meeting a fashion agent next week. Everything's sweet."

"Speaking of which, here are some cakes: feel free to take what you like Miriam." His sarcasm didn't escape Donna's attention.

"Aaron!" He looked at Donna. "Go to your room, I'll be up in a minute." He went to the fridge, got a beer, took a glass from the cabinet and left quietly.

* * *

Donna came into his room and there were photos all over the wall with Aaron, Humphrey, Zara and herself. There were also photographs of Humphrey's family. Donna was the only non-Black face in the pictures.

"Why are you so hostile to Miriam?" she asked compassionately.

"We've had this conversation before. Listen; remember when I said I'd date Miriam if you considered seeing a few new people—guys. At the ball, lots of guys wanted to get to know you better." Donna was confused and alert. "Jerry called me; he wants to take you out on a date."

Perplexed, Donna asked, "Why did he call you?"

Aaron stood tall. "To ask my permission."

Flabbergasted, Donna laughed loudly! "We're not living in a Shtetl! This isn't 1817, Russia or Poland. It's Hackney in 2018. 'Ask your permission'; bloody hell!"

"Mum, the world is full of creeps. It's my responsibility to protect you."

"What are you really up to?"

"Nothing: except I want to see you happy and alive again; the *real* you!"

Donna took his face in her hands. "No one is always happy."

"Mum, I am screening candidates, investigating them. Roy said I didn't know my arse from my elbow about considering suitors for you, so he's coming by tomorrow to ask your consideration." She understood. "I'm calling in favours to check that these blokes are 100% decent. No dirty upstart is coming anywhere near you."

"In the name of God, you *are* the limit!" She laughed. "I love it."

"When I vet them, analyse them, test them; will you meet them and decide if you like them? If you do, I'll go out with Miriam and give her a real chance. I know you're matchmaking because, well... tradition—"

"I defied tradition and had the sexiest marriage and the best kids, ever!"

"OK, it's a deal! I'll give Miriam a real chance and you'll tell me who you'd prefer to see from my list of screened candidates."

"If you're not your father's son, I don't know what."

"Know it! Roy said he was going to give me a beating if I didn't talk to you."

"I love him." She went to leave the room. "Oh, what did your analyst say?"

"Liebermann questions all of my intentions. Sometimes I want to punch him around the room and other times I'm so grateful he's a well-adjusted Jew, who understands my history. What about yours?"

"She's a fucking bitch! I nearly tore her face off during a session. She made me feel like I had a morbid fascination for forbidden passions."

"What?"

"Primitive sexual acts," Donna said rather embarrassed. "I told her she didn't know romance from rape." Donna tried to supress a smile.

"Go on, just say it."

"I said, if she had a throbbing boogie on her dance card, she'd know the difference between a man and a prick."

"Mummy, I just love you!" He high-fived her.

"Mama don't take *no* mess!" Donna replied with a funky dance move. "Bigots always imagine a black beast instead of a light-skin Jamaican Brit. That's why I never let your dad go to the States. Every time I've been there on business, the cops' obsession with killing Black people terrifies me. I'd make Humphrey swear he'd never set foot on that soil. Of course, now it's worse." Aaron acknowledged it. "You must *never* go there. You're not white enough to conceal you're Black..."

"Mum, I'm not ashamed of our family." Donna grabbed him by the chin.

"Swear to me! Swear you'll never, ever, go to the United States of murder for *any* reason!"

"I swear it," he said and everything about Donna's body language was tense and threatening.

"And you. Now you swear you'll go on a few dates after I've screened the suitors and given you their profiles after I've done a full background check. There are tons of liars and perv's out there. I'll put them through psychometrics, run a criminal check on them, of course, medical check too. And build a dossier. Then you can choose whoever you like, and I'll shortlist them and you can make the final choice, yourself."

"Alright. I'll do it since I can pick and choose *and* reject anyone I don't like." She turned and looked at Humphrey and Zara, and all the family pictures.

"Isn't Miriam going back to the States?"

"No, she's moving here. Her father's British-born, so he's talking to the Home Office about his rights. Miriam was born here too and taken to America as a baby, hasn't she mentioned it?" He shook his head. "Well, now you've agreed to date rather than shag her, you'll get to know her. You'll see how nice she is. She's no little girl, she's a woman who can keep up with you." Donna left the room, pleased they had spoken honestly, but Aaron became pensive.

"Amber—" He took out his mobile, unlocked it and found the picture of her arrival at *Ipso Facto*; in a pink-white organza dress that shimmered and her silver strappy sandals that stood her in elegant grace. "Amber—"

CHAPTER SIXTEEN

In Aaron and Roy's living room, they were standing and inspecting a gallery of men's faces projected onto a wall. There was a diverse range of guys, aged from forty-five to fifty-five. Aaron looked at the faces and read their dating profiles. With a bottle of beer in his fist, Roy pointed at one guy. "Look at that one!"

"Couldn't he get a professional photographer to take his photo?"

"Was Donna shocked when you told her you're screening suitors?"

"In a way. I had to agree to date Miriam, to get mum to see the suitors I'm vetting for her." They stared at each other, but Roy couldn't read him.

"More trouble." Aaron was puzzled. "Miriam *and* Amber! How will you control that? Miriam's sharp…"

Aaron's mobile rang and he took the call.

"Amber, hi, how's—" He listened to her for 2½ minutes. "OK. I'll confirm." Roy eyed him questioningly. "Her father wants to see me at their home." Aaron went and poured himself a brandy from the bar on the other side of the room.

"Do you think he's planning to try and scandalise you to Amber?"

"I'm not a criminal or runaway dad. He can't touch me."

"In my work, cous', I always say, expect the unexpected." When they were intimate, Roy always called him cous for cousin.

"You think he'll disrespect me so that Amber will think I'm shit or a pussy?"

"I can't imagine Amber thinking you're anything of the kind."

"I'll meet him. But not on his patch like it's his home game. I'll make him come to me, but I don't want him in our house. I'll take him somewhere. A place so exclusive he might not be able to get in himself." He looked at Roy and the smile that came out of him had a mystique that would have bewitched Casanova. Roy got tingles down his spine.

"Could you get me a meeting with Solly?"

"I'd have to see David, but it shouldn't be tough."

"Can you call him; I mean now and parlay a drink?"

"Yes."

"Get him on the phone. Tell him—tell him anything." Aaron took a moment to think and then he stopped.

"Wait, forget it. I'm asking, or should I say using you to get what I want." He put the drink down. "This is what I hate." Roy eyed him. Whatever privacy existed between them, which Roy wouldn't tell me, took over.

"In spite of everything dad taught me and everything I've learnt, there are times over-ambition can trigger the beast in us. I was just flirting to get what I want. Miriam comes on to me to get what she wants. I'm not a cunt!"

"You stopped yourself. What are you thinking, what plan have you got?"

"Amber's dad thinks I'm some East End mongrel. Wouldn't it be a hoot if he met Aaron the businessman and 21st century 'gentlemen' with influential friends? That presumptuous twat probably thinks he's 'it'. Loads of people can vouch for me, from Uni, and in business. Plus, our anti-Brexit campaign shows we care. Amber's dad's a politician, that doesn't make him a saint." Roy's mind began plotting.

"Mate, invite me to the dinner. I'll introduce him to the Bankolé's, show him what great dining is like at their exclusive restaurant. Let's not forget, David's dad is as famous in law, as Solly is in football and media. And if that wasn't rich enough, Michael and David manage film stars. Bernard's just some diplomat I've never heard of." Aaron became increasingly excited.

Roy said, "Let Amber's dad meet Donna, she's beautiful." Aaron grew more excited. "Eugene and his programs about marginalisation have taught me, do not make yourself a victim."

"Cous, you're so good to me." Aaron looked up at the projected faces on the wall. They concentrated for a time and then Aaron grabbed Roy.

"You're always a better friend to me than I am to you."

"I left a dreadful life behind me when I started Uni and became a man; thanks to your father." Roy's blood was boiling. "I will always be loyal to our family."

"Cous, if I said, you're morphing into something incredibly sexy right now, would you think I was trying to get in your pants?"

"Yes, but I'm no longer yours." Aaron looked confused.

Roy stepped back and told him. "Whether it's on the pitch or on screen, there ain't a man can touch you! But I've lied and cheated on two men for you: enough now."

"I know what you've given me. It's why I can't live without our friendship."

When Roy told me all about their conversation, it made me wish I could have seen the looks that passed between them. Roy met me for a drink after work and told me about this exchange, but I really wish I was a spirit rather than a ghost in the room when that was said because I wanted to ask Roy: *Were you thinking of me when you told him that?*

* * *

Donna glanced around the restaurant and marvelled at what Cynthia, the proprietress, had done in raising the level of elegance and style. I had been to *Bankolé* restaurant twice before with my ex and I consider it better than *Balthazar*, in Covent Garden, serving French cuisine, or *The Ivy*, where the food was alright, and celebrities were all wrong. Donna sat with Aaron on her right and Jerry on her left. Among the elegantly dressed diners, Roy could see Donna felt grand and proud of Aaron because he kept the small talk sparkling for an hour about, sports, arts, employment, Brexit and his last trip to Israel.

David and Solly's mum, Cynthia, periodically looked over and Donna gave her a nod whenever she wanted the waiters to return with further courses and wine. As usual, the clientele that night was made up of VIPs, CEOs and the bourgeoisie. Many of them came to the restaurant not only because the food was first class, but if they had the chance to meet Solly Bankolé they chanced it. Cynthia's sons and her son-in-law, Michael, contributed to entertaining Amber's parents, Jean and Bernard.

As a diplomat, Bernard ordinarily felt like the top man; but Solly was worth over £100 million. Solly was also impeccably turned out which defied Eurocentric notions of Black masculinity because nothing about him echoed hip-hop mythology. Amber's parents, Jean and Bernard were aware of David and Michael's presence.

Roy told me; Bernard studied their intimacy. Amber looked like an aristocrat's daughter, in her pastel green organza sweetheart dress and Alice hairband. What made her look so radiant was the joy that lit her face.

Impressed by the restaurant, Jean studied the surroundings. The walls displayed frescos of various coastlines of Caribbean islands and above everyone's heads the wall was covered with Chinese wild silk in a turquoise colour. The tablecloths were sunset pink and the velvety dining chairs were covered lapis lazuli blue. Without any 'West Indian props', the entire restaurant's lighting conjured up a mood of the Caribbean at sunset. Cynthia took a tip from Michael and added the ambient sound of the Caribbean Sea, which shifted between different levels of the sea's surf movement to soothe the diners.

Aaron's charm-offensive was working effectively. Upon their arrival, Aaron saw aggression in Bernard's tight face. Jean tried to keep a smile on her face, but she couldn't hide her true feelings for long. Her angst made lines and creases in the corners of her mouth and beside her eyes, which resulted in ticks. She wasn't an unattractive woman by any means, but the energy that emanated from her was hostile.

Donna kept glancing at Amber and she had to admit her refined elegance and good looks were very becoming. She noticed how intensely Aaron eyed Amber, which made her realise how little Aaron felt for Miriam. The waiters kept coming with different morsels of colourful Caribbean food and Bernard and Jean couldn't resist taking more as one plate was taken away and another platter of aromatic food was offered to them.

"These dishes are too delicious for words," Bernard told everyone at the table. Solly's wife, Alice, told Jean how important it was to get off a diet and eat what weight watchers deny themselves. Alice was a picture of fertile African beauty. The two women shared confidences about their love of food and the difficulty in traveling with their husbands for work. Jean was enthralled to share confidences with the wife of such a famous man.

Bernard also found it exciting to confide in Jerry, because as two well-travelled Jewish men, he liked the stories of cultural kinship Jerry spoke to him about. By the time they were onto their eighth dish, this time, a sirloin steak cooked with various Caribbean vegetables, the food was so mouth-watering Bernard began laughing and sharing jokes with everyone.

Aaron glanced at Roy and they silently agreed they had disarmed Bernard, but they knew he had to be a tough nut because he was used to dealing with politicians and Roy distrusted all of them. As Bernard spoke freely about his travels and people he liked, Amber noticed how different her father was in the company of well-heeled strangers. She had seen him at ease with Helena's father, who had more money than Bernard could ever dream of having. However, Amber watched her dad trying to charm Solly.

"That goal you scored—" Bernard began and named the game, the country, the date and the outcome. Amber had written and told Aaron she considered her father to be as colourless as vodka, which he drank with a passion, and she could now imagine him with his mistress, whom her mother told her about five years earlier. What astounded Amber was the fact that Bernard was gregarious. Her impression of him, based on ten years of following his 'guidance', was that of a strong-willed patriarch, who was overbearing.

Jerry felt a close affinity to Bernard because they were European Jewish men approximately the same age. Although Bernard was more handsome, neither of them felt threatened, so Jerry and Donna's conversation about trade laws and business; and Bernard's knowledge of money-saving strategies fuelled Bernard's growing comfort level with Jerry and Donna.

A man sheepishly came over to their table. He was a fan of Solly's. "Hello, sorry to bother you, Solly. My son would be so thrilled. Could I have your autograph?"

"No," Solly told him. The overweight man looked genuinely hurt. He was in his mid-forties and use to getting his own way, so he was offended at being refused. "But I will take a photo-graph with you. I don't provide strangers with samples of my signature to duplicate, or who knows what that would lead to," Solly told him. Bernard and Jerry understood the point he made.

The man said, "Oh, right, yeah—that's great."

Solly stood up and the man got his mobile and took a selfie with his arm around Solly's shoulder. People in the sold-out restaurant smiled at them because they wish they had asked first. Looking at the picture, the man was chuffed. He went back to his wife, beaming, and the other diners kept watching him.

Solly took his seat and Jean asked, "Does that happen a lot?"

"All the time, but when the public takes to you and you need their backing for various projects or events, you have a responsibility to them and yourself."

"Even though I'm not interested in football," Amber said; "I think your charity for boys, worldwide, is fantastic."

"Isn't it, dear?" Bernard interjected.

"A handsome, successful man like you must be a role model to underprivileged boys worldwide. How many followers do you have on Twitter?" Bernard asked.

"Over forty million." Jean was flabbergasted when she repeated the number.

Solly pointed at Michael. "David and Michael have millions as well because they're the most famous 'interracial gay couple' in Italy, Britain and—"

Again, Bernard jumped in. "I was impressed with your father's handling of the case, David. I was impressed that you prosecuted those 'Grimy' horrid rappers who called for your death: what monsters." Bernard's accent prevented Aaron from reading the subtext in the things Bernard said.

Aaron asked Bernard, "You don't have issues with gay people or Black people in mixed relationships?" Silence fell across the table and Amber looked at her father. David, Michael, Solly, Alice, Donna and Jerry, all eyed him; but it was Roy who pierced Bernard with an accusing stare that took the warmth out of him. Everyone looked as though they had been caught in a flashbulb moment that contained photographic evidence.

"I have nothing against you, Aaron. I admit I've done a little checking."

Donna eyed Bernard accusingly. "Because there must be something wrong with him?"

Bernard told her, with a wry smile, "Jerry mentioned your son interviewed him before Aaron allowed Jerry to go out with you. I find that extraordinary! But at the same time, I respect Aaron wants to protect you from unsavoury people."

Bernard rested his hand on the back of Jerry's hand when he concluded, "I also have to protect my daughter."

"It makes no difference to you that my dad was Black British?"

"No," Bernard replied in full command of his political and diplomatic guile. "Your father was a successful doctor. You have a lot to be proud of."

Frustrated by the fact Bernard had gathered so much information, Aaron wanted a fight. "What did your investigation uncover about me?" That question didn't make anyone feel more comfortable. Jean adjusted her lovely evening dress and covered her neck.

Bernard helped himself to wine and now he looked triumphant, but Amber disliked the conceit that covered her father's face. "You run your own business. You own your own home and you are active alumni of King's College, University of London."

The Germanic accent and tone of Bernard's voice needled Aaron. "What?" Aaron asked. "None of your powerful diplomatic personnel were able to come up with any dirt?"

Michael knew things were getting tense. Donna happily watched Aaron pressure Bernard, but Alice wasn't comfortable. "You are not a criminal or scoundrel. You *have* had eleven girlfriends, but that is less than one a year, since you were fifteen, so you are harmless."

"How do you know that?" Donna asked.

Bernard simply said, "Facebook."

Donna told Bernard, "And considering all that you've said, Bernard, you haven't thanked my son for saving your daughter's life." Donna told everyone about the near-fatal incident that almost cost Amber her life.

"A drunk driver killed my daughter and my husband then tried to flee the scene." Jean covered her mouth and looked at Donna, offering her sympathy.

"I can understand your distress," Jean told Donna.

"Thank you, Jean. My parents couldn't give a damn. After all, what Orthodox household needs a Black man in the family?"

Bernard said, "What makes you think I am racist, if I may ask?"

Amber said, "Because I accused you, Papa. I know you. You don't care about Blacks. In Luxembourg and Switzerland, one hardly ever sees 'blacks'," Amber said, eyeballing her parents.

Bernard said, "I overindulge my daughter, as she is our only child. She imagines things." Amber was so furious, she looked at her father with violent intent.

Aaron stared at Bernard and said, "I asked you to dinner to tell you, I will not be bothering your daughter anymore." Amber was startled. "I have met you all and I have no intention of distressing my mother with the prospect of your approval in me or our family." More food and wine were brought to the table.

Aaron sat back and pointed at Bernard. "Your past is not unknown to me either, Bernard. You've led a politically transparent life without scandal, you're not imprudent: even though your mistress is a liability." Jean shuddered. "But you are much too ordinary for me to consider joining our families together."

Amber looked dejected. "Aaron…" she started to say. Jean looked at her daughter and Bernard glared at Aaron.

Bernard disdainfully replied, "You are typical of your generation of bastards: so external and no interior. Just a dressed-up beast." Jerry's eyes darted to everyone around the table.

Aaron told Bernard, "I demand that you get up from this table and step outside. I'm going to teach you a lesson. Do not make a fuss, or I will humiliate you here."

Michael turned to David who was a fighting man with courage to spare. Solly told them, "Break one glass in here and I'll sue you."

Aaron got up and waited for Bernard. "Are you a coward?" Donna took Jerry's hand and everyone at the table exchanged looks. So, Bernard stood up.

"Stay here, Jean. This is going to be ugly." Both men left the restaurant.

David told Michael, "Have we gone back to Regency London 1812?"

"This is absurd," Jean said. "Are they going out there to beat each other up or what? My husband is pushing fifty, much older than your son. Go out there and control your son." Jerry felt terrible and asked himself a dozen questions about Aaron's aggressiveness.

Amber said to everyone at the table, "This can't be happening."

Roy turned to each one of them. "Has it occurred to you; they just might want to hurl insults at each other?" Jerry was unconvinced. "If not, every now and then in life, you have to take a beating." That is when the families could see they had attracted attention because the diners looked puzzled.

Jean got up and quickly went to the door. She stepped outside, but all she could see was traffic and London's thrill-seekers on the streets half-drunk and overdressed for Saturday night. She stepped back inside and returned to their table worried and upset. As she sat down, she told Amber, "This is all your fault."

Amber told her mother, "If you say one more thing to me, I will tell you something that will ruin your life." That intrigued Donna. David and Solly then shared a few words.

Michael pulled his husband towards him, away from Solly and whispered. David listened closely then kissed him. Jean flinched at the sight of them and Donna saw it. Roy jerked his head at David, then got up.

"Ladies," Michael said and followed. "David, Roy, give me a minute." The three men got up and bowed out.

Out in Regent's Park, Aaron boldly stood face to face with Bernard. The darkened park was vacant. The wind in the trees caught their ear, but the empty space was filled with visible impressions of people in the distance and trees that strangely looked like aliens risen from the earth. "People tell me I should bow down and kiss your arse, but I'm not going to."

Bernard unbuttoned his waistcoat. "I have no such expectations."

"Amber is a lovely girl who touches my heart. But not even for her will I bring my mother one day of misery by marrying into your family. If you have problems with Black people, gays, or anyone, because you politicians have ruined the world we live in, keep your daughter and marry her off to a moron. I know how that works; my mother also introduces me to fools."

"It's interesting that you investigated me, but you know nothing about me!"

Bernard said. "I also see you have taken on the role of man of the house: good for you! You insist Jerry and other men must seek your permission to meet your mother. Amber told me what your grandfather did to your mother." He shook his head. "I believe in Human Rights, why didn't you mention that? You judge me incorrectly, so if you are not interested in my family, fuck you!"

"Fine, marry Amber off to some twit without a spine or a brute who'll ruin her." Bernard punched him in the gut and followed up with a combination of punches that pushed Aaron back and eventually knocked him sideways and he keeled over.

At precisely the same moment, Roy, David and Michael were in a stockroom filled with dry goods and condiments on stainless steel shelves all around them. Michael said, "What are you doing? Tonight, has your signature on it."

Roy replied, "I haven't fucking done anything."

"Lies!" Michael said.

David told him, "Since you haven't done anything—do something. You sacrificed JJ's son for Aaron because you're obsessed with him. Get off Aaron's dick and take care of your own business." Roy was about to object. "Shut the fuck up," David replied.

Michael told him, "You lie to Narj, you lie to Aaron, and you play with Eugene. He is my friend. I don't like what you're emotionally doing to him."

"I haven't done anything to the man."

Defiantly, Michael said, "Look in my face and tell me you haven't been to bed with Eugene. Tell me you don't know he loves you. Tell me you aren't a cock-tease. Eugene holds you in high esteem. But you fawn over Aaron who clearly should marry Amber. But you live in a fantasy dream about Aaron.

"That's not true."

Michael pushed his face close to Roy's. "With God watching you, tell me you are in love with Narj." Roy turned from Michael and David and pushed forward to leave but Michael grabbed him.

"You want to be a man? I mean a man who steps in to bring comfort to his family. Stop observing life and take part in it. You don't have a brother or father to help you, but you do have a man who can be both. Eugene is as right for you as Aaron is for Amber. Going by what I saw on the Island, Aaron is as wrong for you, as Miriam is for him."

"Didn't you just hear Aaron reject Amber and her family?" David tried to speak. "Donna picked Miriam for a reason: she knows her own son. He and Amber *seem* right, but unless they both change radically, it won't last."

Michael grabbed Roy's face. "Let me tell you something. I have four kids. This has trained me to stay alert." Roy became even more anxious. "You are doing what your generation does best: blur the lines. I speak to you about your behaviour and you bamboozle me with another tale, one that we are interested in because we care about Donna and Aaron. But I asked you about *your* relationship."

"If you must know, I am breaking up with Narj. And Aaron can never be my man because he's bad for me. And I realise Dr Martin *is* good for me."

"He's Eugene! Don't refer to him like he's just an acquaintance."

"Yes, Eugene—who wipes Narj out of my mind when he has me and overshadows the other men I've had."

"Naturally, *he's* a man," Michael said.

Roy said, "Hear this good, OK. You don't know Aaron and why Miriam is actually a good match for him because Donna knows her son. Plus, you don't know what's good for me because I'm not some British gay you can handle."

"And Eugene?" Michael demanded.

"As my ex-boyfriend's father use to tell me: 'don't busy yourself with what's not your business'." He pushed past them like a true defiant Jamaican.

When Michael met me for lunch and recounted all this, it differed from Roy's version.

Back in Regent's park, Bernard punched Aaron in the face and knocked him to the ground again and stood over him triumphantly. "I am a child of the real revolution, the 1960s and I learnt from the State regime what happens to weak Jews. That is why I am a man!" Aaron looked like a battered mess.

Aaron had taken four different beatings from his father for his rudeness and bad behaviour, however, looking at Bernard's smug face, forced him up onto his feet. Aaron crashed into Bernard, doubled his strength, then hit him, and Bernard staggered to one side.

"I am the son of Humphrey Blackmon and Donna Rapchinski and that makes me a Jew with Black power!" Aaron punched Bernard repeatedly. The force of each blow was deeply felt. The pain on Bernard's face showed it. With each punch, Aaron made him stagger and bounce until he knocked him on his arse and Bernard couldn't get off the grass.

Aaron stood over him. "I love Amber, but I won't live with bigotry. What my grandfather did to my mother by casting her out almost destroyed mum's faith but my dad saved her and—" he had tears in his eyes. "You will not bring any misery to my mother or rule me by Jewish tradition. It's the 21st century."

"You are full of hate and suspicion," Bernard told him, speaking through bloody lips. "It's good that I don't have to deal with your family. Your mother and your relatives are safe. Get out of our life."

"Gladly!" Aaron walked off and left Bernard there.

* * *

Aaron came to the entrance of the restaurant and everyone at the table looked at him. Amber immediately grabbed her purse and dashed to him. Diners watched her hurriedly leave and they could hear the rustle of her taffeta slip under her pastel green organza sweetheart dress. Because Amber's hair was tied back with her Alice hairband, she looked like a vulnerable young woman fleeing from danger. She took out her handkerchief and rushed to Aaron. He headed outside and she stopped him in the street. Roy charged through the door then stood back but watched and waited to offer help if needed.

"You're a mess, what happened?"

"Your father and I came to an agreement. I cannot see you anymore." She stopped walking and he walked on but then he stopped. "With all my letters and everything I've told you; you haven't written one letter to me to say you love me."

"Don't you know?"

"I feel my passion, but I'm not sure if your 'purity' will allow you to feel the same for me. Marriage isn't about the life we have in bed. It's managing the mess life throws at us. You're a beautiful, posh girl. But I won't trade my happiness to masquerade as a toff."

Amber looked distressed. "Fine! Go to the American tramp and waste your life. I wanted you to discover me. I do love you, but if you don't know it—Go!" She turned around and walked away but came face to face with her father. She saw that he was also a mess so she gave him her handkerchief. He took it and she opened her purse, took her phone and called her mother. Aaron saw Jean come out and join them. Bernard flagged a cab, they all got in and drove off.

CHAPTER SEVENTEEN

Miriam sat next to Aaron on the plane, and she took his hand as the jet rumbled and gathered speed for take-off. "Gotta say, you're the weirdest guy I know."

"Why?" In her white summer dress, Aaron genuinely liked Miriam's sexy and worldly look.

"I can usually figure guys out in no time. You're strange but in a good way. You turn up, apologised, offer me this little holiday in Lanzarote, I love it."

"My mate, Roy, said I've been unfair to you. I have. I know mum thinks you're fantastic and I trust both of them. I sometimes dig myself in—I'm rather stubborn." The twenty-year-old nice looking 'rave-boy' beside him gripped his fists a little scared on his first flight. The plane rumbled and rolled as it gathered speed to lift off. Most people were in their own world, but Miriam was a little anxious and Aaron knew it. He kept hold of her hand and after a time, her grip loosened and he knew she started to relax.

"Better?" he asked attentively.

"Yes. Since the age of terrorism, I haven't been the same. I used to fly all across America and overseas growing up, but 9/11 really changed my life." She took forty minutes telling him about people she knew who lost family and friends.

He told her, "If we don't get past the fear, we're really destroyed. I've flown to Australia, Jamaica, all over. Mum told us, terrorism means being afraid to live. I've watched her confront fears. Dad was fearless. This has given me a lot. What fears have you conquered?"

Miriam couldn't answer immediately because she needed to weigh up her pride, her needs and her ambition. Aaron didn't push her to answer. She pulled his jacket and he came closer to her so she could speak into his ear.

"I have trust issues because so many men are liars. I've dated a few, believe me."

"What did they do?"

"Men don't support my ambition." This made her angry once again. "But I'm not interested in being kept. I'm determined to be successful."

"You *are* successful. You've come to London as your own boss to build a business."

"Your mom's great. We've worked some deals, but this is big."

Shining with pride, Aaron said, "She started with nothing and built everything up."

"I know! At trade shows and when she comes to New York, she's been 100% on! My contacts love her. She's so British, which they love. She knows the UK market and she's got a knack for predicting trends."

Aaron was eyeing her and she said, "You're giving me the weirdest look, what is it?"

"You really respect my mum."

"Sure! I couldn't cope with what she's been through. When I first met your mom, all she talked about was Zara this, Humphrey that and my son. When she came back to work; afterwards...she kept singing your praises. And then she asked if I wanted to meet you." The cabin staff made their way past passengers offering bits and pieces. Most people on the flight were reading information about Lanzarote or listening to headphones.

Aaron told her, "I must have seemed bad-tempered when we first met—"

"Maybe I was too pushy. It's just Donna told me so many things about you, I wanted to find out for myself what kind of guy you are. And that little Princess did ruffle my feathers a bit." Aaron shifted slightly. "It's not often I meet a man that's established his own firm at twenty-five and made a success of it at thirty. How have you done that?"

Aaron heard Roy's voice in his ear. *You've got to give them a chance mate if you're thinking of marriage because Amber is lovely and Miriam might be. But you've shot her down before she's flown.*

"It's a long story..."

"This is quite a long flight," she replied with beguiling sassy ease.

"No, a..." Aaron thought about how much he wanted to hide. "I had a plan for the agency. I showed it to dad and he gave me advice and mum gave me more pointers." He turned around so that the aisle passenger couldn't see him. "I took my business plan to my alumni advisor, and we got someone to draft out the perfect business plan to show to banks. I did and they turned me down. Everyone turned me down, it was depressing. Anyway, the family didn't have enough money, but Roy's fella was stinking rich, his dad's a big name in the States. So, he bankrolled me because Roy asked him to."

"The business is split between you and Roy?" she asked confused.

"No, it's mine. But this guy loved Roy so much, he'd do anything for him, so Roy helped me out."

"Not many friends would bankroll a business and not have a stake in it."

"I know; that's why Roy's my best mate."

"And you share a house."

"Yeah, me and my grandparents got the money together for the sale. My sister designed the interior. Me and Roy have added our own stuff."

"He rents from you?"

"No, we've gone half and half on it."

"In New York, I can't think of anyone who'd get you money for business and buy a house together without being married." She could see her comment didn't interest him. "When you start a family, what will happen to your house and Roy then?"

"When he meets the right guy, he'll probably set up home with him. He's monogamous, he's no player."

"Wouldn't that change things with the two of you?"

"No, if I move, I'll sell to him, if he moves, he'll sell to me. That shouldn't change our friendship. *My* worry is the woman I marry has to be the type of person who's prepared to change. I can't abide a life that stands still. I'm not afraid of change, travel, meeting new challenges. That's how I've grown the business."

"How's your business going?"

"OK, what irritates me is that firms get fixed on types they want to employ. They prefer to fish from the same pool of Western Europe. I could make 40% more money if they'd listen. I understand people well because of my studies."

"Donna boasts about your honours and masters, plus HR management something..." He nodded. "In New York, talent like yours wouldn't go unheard if you were in business over there. A guy with your looks and talent would clean up in Manhattan. I say that because at my College, I met some schmucks, you'd wipe the floor with." Miriam laughed, but he didn't. She still felt she wasn't getting through to him.

"Donna told me that you and Amber's father stepped out and kicked ass." She laughed again. "In the States, people think you guys are all *Downton Abbey* or *Sherlock*. I'd have paid to see that reality." She leaned in and kissed him on the neck and the look he gave her brightened up her day.

* * *

I came home early from work with Eugene, to find Aaron in the kitchen cooking Caribbean food and dancing around in the kitchen. I was surprised because he wasn't due back for three days. He was in shorts, boots and a vest, looking like a shipwrecked adventurer, unshaven with his curly hair dishevelled.

"Mate, what are you doing here?" I shouted.

"I live here."

"You're back early. What happened?"

"Miriam's parents are here and she was desperate to see them, so we flew back. They rented a house for her up at Archway." He looked at Eugene. "Dr Martin, nice to see you. What brings you here?"

"We're working on a story. I have a commission for a new television series. *Cultural Differences*: it's a co-production between Roy's Agency and my network. Roy's head of research, he got the confirmation last week." Eugene threw me a look and I knew he was covering for us.

Aaron was totally at ease, so he gave me a hug and whispered, "Don't let him side-line you, Roy. You pitched and sold the idea to the agency, so get your credit, Cous." Then he stepped back and shook Eugene's hand.

Aaron went to the fridge and took out some beers and gave us one each and toasted. He then went back to the kitchen and continued cooking. When the flavour came out of the pot, the aroma hit Eugene powerfully.

Aaron said, "Curry goat and stew peas with breadfruit. I thought you'd like it, cous— Eugene, if you want, stay there's plenty."

"We were going to go out, but I'll stay if you tell me what it was like out there with Miriam."

Aaron pulled a face and then pointed to the dining table and Eugene and I went and sat down. I got up again to get the plates, cutlery and glasses. Fifteen minutes later, we were seated with the great food laid out. Eugene complimented Aaron on it and he gestured that it was nothing.

"Let me tell you about Miriam." I was keen to hear. "She was perfect. She totally agreed with me and did everything I wanted to do: raves, beach, booze, and food, everything. I gave her a DTF in bed and—" Eugene looked confused.

"Dick, tongue and fingers," I told Eugene.

Eugene asked, "How do you know what that is?"

Aaron told him, "We've been going to raves in Ibiza since we were boyz at Uni." I nodded.

A rascal's smile came over Aaron: the one that makes him ten times sexier than any 'hip-hop dude'. He said, "I've caught Roy having it off and he's seen me get it on loads of times. Remember that time when I caught Brian and he had hysterics?" Aaron laughed loudly about that because it was funny. "Anyway, Miriam was the perfect: Aphrodite meets Delilah. She tried to get me high on sex."

Eugene said, "That displeased you?"

"I've got a Masters in philosophy; she can't play me! No woman ever totally agrees with any man. But here's the thing. One night I had an amazing dream about Amber. I didn't know it, but it turned out that I was humming that old song by Don McLean— And I Love You So—all the next day."

I told him, "I don't know it."

Aaron got up and dashed out of the room. Eugene turned to me and said, "Keep him talking. Don't press him too hard. This is the first time I've heard him for myself." I agreed, but I felt a bit funny about Eugene being there.

Aaron came back with his acoustic guitar and pulled his chair out and tuned up. He played the song I never heard before but the lyrics, man oh man; they were absolutely wonderful.

As soon as he started singing, I was lost in his voice. In all the years I've known him I've never heard him take four minutes to tell me about a woman he's ever loved more, and we've spoken on the subject for years. Aaron put the guitar down and came back to the table and went back to dinner.

With concern and compassion Eugene said, "Roy told me that you and Amber fell out. Have you broken up? Or is Miriam, the new woman in your life and things, aren't working out?"

"Amber is joy and heart. *Thinking* about making love to Amber is better than 'doing it' with Miriam. I wrote letters to Amber about existentialism, comics, Tudor royals, Madonna and Oprah, they're all Amber's heroes. Miriam and her parents are nothing to me, nothing." He turned cold as he contemplated. "She won't turn me into Judas or play me as Jonathan Harker. I must get rid of Miriam but honour my mother. Whatever it takes, I must get Amber back." The light in his eyes vanished and a dark hue coloured his face as his expression turned grim.

CHAPTER EIGHTEEN

Donna was tussling with Jerry at her front door trying to get him to leave, but he was still making moves to persuade and entice her, even though she kept gesturing for him to leave. They'd been out earlier, so he was very well dressed and he took it for granted that she was now in the mood. "Jerry really, I'm not going to do anything like that. I can't."

"All this time and you don't like me?" he said, trying to kiss her intimately.

"I like you; I'm just not ready—"

"When? Your husband's been dead years already. Are you dead too?" He pushed himself into her and felt her breasts.

"Jerry, stop it!"

"You've made me hard." He pressed himself closer and she had to push him back."

Donna began to panic. "You won't have anything going on down there if I tell my son you're forcing yourself on me." A spark of fear dilated his pupils and his mouth trembled. It took about half a minute for him to cool off.

"Now leave, or this will be the last time I see you."

Jerry fixed his jacket and pushed his hair back to sort himself out. "Give your son my compliments. I'll call you." He opened the front door and headed out. Donna staggered back through the hallway and into the living room. She poured herself a glass of port and drank it. After a moment or two, she lifted her hand and watched it shaking, so she got the phone and dialled.

"Hi, mum, can I talk for a minute?" Violet listened. "I just had to deal with Jerry. He wanted to—he wanted. I asked him to leave, but he became—amorous and I had to throw him out." Violet asked a question. "No, I'm fine. Nothing happened. Can I come and see you; I need some advice?"

* * *

Two days later, Donna sat on a big side sofa, with her legs and feet tucked in. Her elderly therapist, Cassandra, whose silver and brown hair fell into ringlets catching the light, observed her. Donna had her scarf in her hand, which she twisted and tugged as she spoke in the comfort of the white chair. She kept her head lowered as she spoke and seldom looked up. "...and the minute I mentioned Aaron, Jerry cut it out. Seriously, I panicked. I like Jerry, but I'm not ready for that." Donna took a minute and tied the scarf around her hand.

The therapist said, "Although I didn't see you through the initial stages of your bereavement, I've studied your case and there are things I think we can work on because there's still a lot of residual trauma that's unsolved. And your relationship with your son *is* unusual."

"How?" Donna studied her therapist's face, body and attire in meticulous detail because she felt an increasing antipathy towards her.

"He's taken on the role of patriarch in your life."

"You listen to me you bitch! My son is a man and yes, he is the man of my family because he's my blood!"

"You see nothing wrong with him, approving men for you to go out with?"

Donna eyed Cassandra and spoke through her rage, "You live in your suburban Highgate Village seclusion and understand nothing about my life in Hackney, my relationship with my husband! You give me your 'guidance' based on a moral universe *you* occupy. I used to get drunk and stoned to get through the hours of death. My daughter was a woman I could talk to about anything. If she were alive, I wouldn't be here! I try to explain things to you because I can't talk to my mum about my desires; she's my husband's mother. But you sit there and judge me... Tell you what!" Donna got up, eyed the matronly therapist and said, "Go fuck yourself." Donna told Michael's ex-wife Lola that Cassandra's perception of her, reeked of orthodox judgment.

Later that evening, Donna was in the kitchen at Violet's house, helping her fry fish and make Jamaican carrot juice. A range of other dishes was seasoned and waiting to be cooked. It was a large kitchen and they were totally at ease, moving around each other and reaching for things and drinking. Ska music was playing because Harold was spinning tunes for Violet as he always did.

"...never going back to see her. I only went because I was— afraid to talk to you about something."

Violet said, "There's nothing you can't tell me?"

Donna placed the spiced floured fish into the frying pan. "I can't live without love for the rest of my life. You know I loved Humphrey—"

"You don't even have to say that. Humphrey was the happiest man in the family because of you and the kids. All three of you were the making of my son."

"I've slept alone and I'm crumbling without some romance and care. Aaron and I have talked about this a whole-heap-a-times." Violet watched the fish and turned it. She also saw Donna was close to tears.

"I've been afraid to think about another man. Aaron, God bless him, has seen my misery and said I should try to heal and think about my life now. So, when Jerry showed an interest, Aaron called him into his office and told him to bring bank statements and references from three women to confirm he was a gentleman. Then Aaron promised me he'd go out with Miriam."

"Lord have mercy!" Violet laughed good and loud.

"Aaron said he has no issues with me remarrying. I think he's trying to make sure he likes the man, even though I'd never force anyone onto him."

Violet said, "For sure he cares about your wellbeing." Donna took the fried fish out of the pan and Violet took the bottle of white wine and carefully poured it over the fish. They inhaled and then took the onions, yellow peppers and shredded carrots out of the oven and placed it on top of the fish. Violet took the liqueur and sherry and mixed it together while Donna took the pestle and mortar and ground the pimento and cloves.

In the other room, Harold could smell the food and cried out 'Yes!'

"Mum, I still have feelings. Humphrey and I made love all the time." Donna took some hazelnut oil from a cupboard and poured some into the small saucepan and then emptied the spices into it.

Violet said, "Zara told me, one time, she felt like going to bed with her boyfriend, but she wouldn't let him because she wanted to marry him. She told me she wanted to be like you."

Donna thought about that. "Amber told Aaron she wouldn't have premarital sex with him."

"Is that why he stopped seeing her?"

"No, he came to me and said, he'd been horrible to Miriam and he would be more honest with her and more like a gentleman. But she told me they've done it. She can't keep a secret. Her parents are over here. They're nice."

"What about him and Miriam?"

"She texted me from Lanzarote: she said he was doing everything she could want." Violet smiled. "Something's changed because now she has a light in her she didn't have before."

"Nice!"

"Thank God Roy keeps me in tune because there are times, I can't figure out my own son. Roy helps and I can tell him anything. He said my therapist was resentful of the fact I'm more alive than she is. He said I defy victimhood because my emerging passion is a force that is sustaining my life."

"What can he know about a woman?"

Donna lowered her voice. "He said his love for men connects him to the female sexual drive. He once told me—how to climax anally." Violet screamed and shortly afterwards, Harold rushed in and the two of them were in hysterics.

"Girl talk, get out, dad!" Harold shook his head and left them alone. "When I was sick and zonked out on meds, Roy once told me to recount the best night I ever had with Humphrey. I don't remember everything I told him but, the next day, my head was in a different place and even as he plait my hair, he kept singing. Prince Buster's *Wreck A Pum Pum and* Soul Sister *Wreck A Buddy*." Violet looked so shocked Donna laughed out loud. "He's got his London accent mastered now, but when he flashes back to Jamaica, he's bad."

Violet stated, "And he acts so placid and dignified whenever I see him."

"Don't let that fool you. Just the other day, he asked me to define female sexual arousal."

"But stop! He 'turning' or what?"

"Me-no-know!" Donna said like a pure Jamaican and they laughed heartily. "Hear this now... Yesterday Aaron came over and gave me the profile of five men he's screened. It's a full dossier on prospective suitors." Harold came in.

"Wha-a-go-wan inna, dis kitchen?" They turned to him, laughing.

Over a dinner of oxtail and beans, with roasted sweet potatoes and breadfruit; Donna told Harold what was happening and the dossier profiles were on the table. Harold pointed to the pictures. "Do you like any of these men?"

"Well, now we've read their profiles, two of them might be interesting guys."

Harold said, "All of the information in the file. Aaron's gone to a lot of trouble. And considering he idolised Humphrey, he's telling you plenty."

"I know!" Donna said. "If I spend the next year grieving, it will kill me. But *you're* my family."

Harold was glad to hear her say that because he loved Donna for everything, she did in making Humphrey the man he couldn't.

Harold took Violet's hand. "Be happy again." She grabbed their hands.

CHAPTER NINETEEN

Dr Liebermann's office door was open when Aaron came rushing in with his laptop, a portfolio, plus a box file under his arms, as well as a hold-all. Dressed in a T-shirt, shorts and trainers, he looked like a frat boy. "Sorry," he said, "my car broke down, I called the people and they've taken it and I had to get a cab to get here. My entire chill-out day has turned into a blocked toilet."

"You look like an urban nomad."

"Don't just stand there looking like the world's greatest authority on life and gentlemanly attire, give me a hand here." Daniel took his hands out of his baggy pants and quickly helped Aaron. He also took Aaron's iPad and box files, as Aaron put down the other bags, staggered over to a chair and flopped into it.

Daniel went to the fridge in the corner of the room. "I've got freshly squeezed orange juice; I must have squeezed twenty of them this morning. Would you like sparkling water with it?"

"Give me the juice." Daniel got glasses.

"Only today when we are going out on our physical therapy does the car breakdown—bitch!"

"Do you want to shift this to—"

"No, I need this. Plenty's going on." He took the tumbler of orange juice and gulped it. "Wow! Real oranges, I almost forgot what it's like, thanks, Liebermann."

"For heaven's sake, you can call me Daniel." Aaron nodded so Daniel crossed the room and went back to the desk to get his notepad. "What is all this you're carrying around?"

"Files on candidates for mum." Daniel asked what that meant and Aaron explained about the suitors' profiles and the background checks he and Roy's contacts are doing.

"It sounds like you're recruiting for MI5. You seem a bit overde-termined."

"No dog is coming anywhere near my mother. I'm screening everyone."

Aaron got up and quickly got his laptop to show him Donna's visual and text profile. Daniel watched and read everything.

"Donna looks much recovered. I like the video of her dancing at the party. And those photos of her cooking and in business meetings are good."

"All these candidates have passed the psychometric tests." Dr Liebermann began laughing. "What?"

"You bring a whole new meaning to 'protective'. What has Donna said?"

"She told me to keep double-checking. She said if it stops me from hating who she sees, even though this is not about that, then screen and interrogate them all I like. But I have to continue seeing Miriam because we made a deal and we have to stick to it. I give Miriam a chance and mum chooses three suitors and gives them a chance."

"You and your mother are probably the most curious people I know. I'm glad I'm not treating Donna. I'd have to flip from Sandra Bem to and Kate Millett."

"Do you think we're really fucked up and haven't made any progress?"

"Aaron, come on, are you kidding? You and Donna are possibly the greatest potential case study I've never done. You've both come through death impact, alcohol abuse, manic depression and deep rage!" Aaron looked relieved. "How is she doing with her new therapist?"

"Mum hates her. She needs someone more like you."

Daniel threw up his hands. "I cannot see both of you, I've told you before."

"I know, I'm just saying she needs someone who's an alchemist or anarchist. Traditional answers and standards are not for mum." Daniel thought about that for a little while.

"So, are we going to focus on you and Miriam, work and life balance, now?"

* * *

Dr Liebermann and Aaron went to Finchley Golf Club later that afternoon. The wide green landscape was a pleasure that calmed all of the members who were out in the open. The club was well known for its ever-growing clientele, mostly from Northwest London. Daniel and Aaron had changed into casuals, but Aaron looked far less comfortable than Dr Liebermann. Aaron took a swing and missed and then he had another try and hooked the ball. "I fuckin' hate this. It's too posh, so I'm no good at it."

"Aaron, you don't have to win at everything. This is relaxing."

"So, talk to me. I am listening." Daniel got into position and played a perfect shot. Aaron watched him and then he mirrored Daniel's body movements to get a better sense of the stroke and physical movement of the body. It amused Daniel. After the shot they began walking.

"The Lanzarote trip was alright." Aaron recounted their holiday events in specific detail to Dr Liebermann. "She never got on my nerves, not once. And she wasn't too clingy." He then explained further.

At the same time over at Donna's home, Miriam and her parents, along with Harold, Violet, Saul and his wife were playing poker. Miriam's parents looked like exactly who they were; respectable Jewish middle-class Americans of European heritage, who dressed befitting their age and status.

They were well into the game because there were several bottles of booze on the cabinet behind their table and all of them had glasses of vodka, rum and scotch near their hands. The room hummed with the sounds of *Sinatra at the Sands* with the Count Basie band. Also at the table were Donna's best friends, Cynthia and Solomon, Lola and her husband, Tony.

They could hear each other clearly, but the music added to the atmosphere Donna liked. Miriam's parents had taken her to Atlantic City every time she went over and they liked that a lot. No one at the table looked better than her because Donna had her hair done and the red blouse she had on was a constant reminder of her femininity. She also stood out because she had very good posture due to her Pilates class.

"What was the best part of the Lanzarote trip?" Donna asked Miriam. "You couldn't have spent all your time in the club dancing to rave music?"

"No, we spent a lot of time walking around the island and hanging out on the beach. We met a great couple. I never expected

Aaron to be so romantic. He read to me and acted out superheroes playing the characters and doing the voices; everything from *Dead Pool* to *Blade*." Donna told everyone funny stories about Aaron's childhood and his 'rave years' with Roy. As Miriam asked questions and recounted their days together, it became all the more evident to everyone that she had fallen for Aaron and that tapped into her sense of self-worth.

Beaming, Miriam told everyone, "One day, a couple we met were with us and I asked Aaron the question papa asked mom when they were dating."

Her father jumped right in! "I said to this darling girl: 'what makes you laugh'? She told me all her favourite stand-up guys and I told her mine. Every chance I got; I took her to wherever they were playing. The look of comfort and love between Miriam's parents was so discernible; Lola and Cynthia eyed their husbands and exchanged knowing glances.

Miriam told them, "I said, Seinfeld—"

"Aaron loathes him on a scale of hatred!" Donna laughed. "He's—"

"Crazy about Woody, Robin Williams, Mike and Elaine, yeah!" Miriam said.

Miriam's father asked, "Nichols and May?" Thanks to Bloomingdales, Miriam's parents were a far cry from a typical Miami couple: they were nicely turned-out. But their body language couldn't have been more telling of their heritage and what they identified with, as a preferred form of culture and expression. They were wonderfully exuberant with the finest displays of Jewish existential truth, unhindered by self-consciousness which their daughter just did not have.

Miriam said, "Aaron did a mother and son skit that made us fall to our knees." Violet and Harold chuckled and Donna proudly told Cynthia and Lola.

"I first heard Nichols and May when I was fifteen. I used to play their album for the kids: they loved them." Donna had a drink and then took on an American accent and mannerisms. She then began the sketch with the perfect tone, quoting the opening lines. 'Arthur, this is your mother, do you remember me?'."

When Donna finished doing the sketch, she had everyone in the room howling with laughter. They all needed to get refills and settle down. Everyone in the room had to tell a favourite parent and child joke or memory. The energy and heat in the room became so Vegas it felt like a throwback to 1962. The joy that transpired came out of universal family stories. They all 'got it' and found their conversation enlightening.

Miriam's mother said, "Do you know, this right here, this wouldn't be possible in New York," and without her saying more, Miriam's father nodded in agreement. Donna promised herself she wouldn't fly off into a rant on how much she detested current-day America, because she knew it would kill the afternoon light and plunge the evening she had planned into the darkness of her disdain.

"What do you mean?" Solomon asked. Cynthia and Lola gave him a look that made him prickle and so Solomon smiled because he knew he'd *hear* about it when he got home.

Miriam's father said, "New York is more neighbourhood bound. Hispanic, Jewish, Irish, you know." Donna heard Miriam's father deliberately leave out 'Black'.

Donna said, "We need ice and we're playing poker, not UN delegates—I've got some money to win. Lola, help me bring in some more stuff." Lola got up and Cynthia rushed to help. Harold knew they were bursting to talk, so he asked Miriam a question as the wives headed out of the room.

"What makes *you* laugh?" Solomon asked Miriam. Solomon loosened his light-coloured tie from his navy-coloured shirt. Saul took that as a cue and did the same and the other men followed suit.

"I'm crazy about Apatow stuff. I love his book! He's got my generation to a tee. *Knocked Up*, *Bridesmaids* and *Train Wreck* speak to me on every level."

Miriam spoke from her heart and Saul's wife loved her. When Miriam recounted how manic the maid-of-honour became in *Bridesmaids*, pointing out the critical moments of accelerated craziness she slipped into, Miriam tired herself out in all of twenty minutes and held the room captive, reciting. Her parents loved the sight of her and Donna felt the life in her throbbing as she recounted what happened in the movie and how and why she could relate to it.

"Sexual politics being what they are today," Miriam added. "It's still every woman's nightmare to live her life alone." Donna reached over and kissed her.

"You won't." She took Donna's hand and kissed it. They went back to the game of poker and Saul won. The next hand, they played Violet won. The hand after that they played Donna won.

"Finally!" Donna yelled.

"I know!" Miriam said. "I was starting to feel bad. You splashed out for all this food and drinks, the—"

"Your family are always good to me when I come to you."

"Well, you're like family, Donna, you know that," Miriam said.

"Yes, I do." Donna pulled in her winnings and then got up. "Food? We should take a break for a nosh." Tony got to his feet and gave Lola a great kiss.

Miriam's mother said to Tony, "You two are like newlyweds." He led Miriam's mother away from the table.

"I owe her my happiness," Tony said. Lola caressed his face and smacked his bum as he moved. Miriam's parents saw them as an interracial couple and they wanted to know more since they didn't know any white men who married Black women. Lola shared a few words in Brazilian with Tony, and he winked at her.

Miriam's mother said, "What's the story?" Lola mentally spoke to Tony and he nodded.

"My first husband, Michael, discovered he's gay: so now he's married to David, Cynthia's son." Solomon looked at Ralph and Sonya.

Sonya said, "What the fuck?" And the whole room broke into laughter. Miriam said, "Mum..." in a slightly shocked tone of voice.

* * *

Dr Liebermann stood there watching Aaron. Considering Aaron's background, he wasn't comfortable in the green wide-open space, in the white Christian wealth of the golf course.

"Doctor, I'm telling her my favourite comics and movies and everything I love and I just felt like I was entertaining her, instead of connecting with her. Picture it, the beautiful West African sunrise and sunset in the background."

"Did she connect with you?"

"Totally! She was laughing her tits off. But we weren't—" Aaron wrapped his hands around the air and danced the waltz and then a Mambo. His face lit up, smiling at a girl in his arms who wasn't there. "Not a drop of psychosomatic magic!" Dr Liebermann looked confused. "In bad weather, I get dry lips. If I *think* I've forgotten the lip balm, my lips dry up in seconds. When I find the Chapstick in my satchel, my lips go back to normal. When I kiss Amber—" His thoughts floated away and Dr Liebermann watched him and felt Aaron's spirit ascend. Aaron used the golf club as a wand to connect with the heavens, but he remained grounded.

"I told mum and Roy, I'd give her a chance, but I don't trust her. My heart doesn't sing. I don't yearn for her, ache for her, burn when I'm next to her."

"You're a romantic, Aaron. Love is doing the housework, the school run, the shit that makes you spit, but its everyday life."

"Don't tell me after four years of analysis; love is domesticity because as long as I can pay for a cleaner, I'm not doing that woman's work."

"Be sure you don't tell your girlfriend that domesticity is 'woman's work'."

"Take your fucking shot," Aaron told him. Daniel lined up and struck the ball exactly where it should go and then they moved on.

"Why is Miriam not the one?"

"I've listened to her, talked to her, laughed, danced and gone down on her: she's not the one!" Daniel laughed, tossed his club into the air and caught it.

"I've had patients who'd give a year's salary for what you're turning down." "They can fucking have her." Dr Liebermann became stern when he pointed to a spot on the green in front of him.

"Come here!" Aaron saw Dr Liebermann's change of mind and felt reprimanded; so, he didn't budge. "I won't tell you again, Aaron."

Aaron walked up to Dr Liebermann, pulling himself up to attention. "What?"

"I've gone through various methods and approaches with you over the years. Now I know this is best for you." He grabbed Aaron by the shoulders and shook him vigorously. "Your convolutions and defence are a denial tactic you must dispense with!"

When Dr Liebermann stopped shaking him; Aaron laughed so hard, he fell onto the ground, convulsing with laughter. Dr Liebermann threw his golf club to one side and flopped on the grass beside him and they laughed together. People in the distance saw them. They were confused, but the laughter stopped them from dashing over to check if they were hurt because clearly, they weren't.

"Bubala! What do you want?"

"Amber. But I promised mum I'd give Miriam a chance, but because of Roy, mum and dad, I know how to run my house, run my business and be a solid bloke." Aaron sat up. "Margot, my staff manager, has intelligence and decency I respect. Amber is like that only she's so hot! Miriam has none of that."

"Then tell Miriam goodbye and fix things with Amber."

"But Amber hasn't told me I'm the love of her life. It's one-sided." Aaron got to his feet and he held out his hand and Daniel took it, so Aaron pulled him up.

* * *

In Donna's living room, Miriam had all eyes on her. "In the clubs, Aaron dances something like this." She imitated rave dance moves. "But when one of his favourite dance numbers came on, he would move more like this." She danced in a more funky manner. "But some nights and on our last night, we danced on the beach more like this and then she waltzed around the room in between the furniture. She looked enchanted and most of the parents lilted as they watched her pick up the hem of her dress to dance.

"You're on the right track," Donna said and all the women agreed with her.

"Did he tell you that he loved you?" Harold asked. Miriam shook her head, no. Donna told Miriam's parents that Aaron was very 'bottled up', but Harold and Violet considered that to be an outright lie. Saul and his wife knew it wasn't true and Solomon felt everything was wrong because Miriam was trying too hard.

Solomon said, "It's important to let things happen, Miriam. My son tried to make things happen with his son's mother and that only turned out well because they had my grandson." Cynthia took his hand as Solomon continued. "Tony was in love with Lola for years, but he waited and let things take its natural course and then Michael changed." Lola gave Donna the eye to indicate Solomon was making decrees and they shared a smile that only best friends own.

Solomon stated, "When two people are right for each other, if they don't overwork situations, things work out. I've prosecuted hundreds of people who want it all. You're an accomplished woman; an ambitious man will see that. You've got plenty going on; relax."

Donna told Roy when she saw him the following day for lunch, she felt greatly comforted by her friends and Roy reminded her that everyone she knew was 'big hitters' when it came to taking care of her. She happily told Roy everything about the evening she shared with Miriam's family and her friends and later he recounted to me what he'd been told by all of them.

I'm not supposed to have any feelings one way or the other, but I felt everyone at Donna's family party, with the exception of Solomon were feeding on hope and fantasy. I also had to ask myself, couldn't Miriam sense there was something missing in the depth of Aaron's love? But even as I wrote up what people told me, I knew even I couldn't sense whether Roy loved me or not.

CHAPTER TWENTY

Amber stood at the counter of Forbidden Planet's bustling bright megastore and continued to ask. "You see, the man I'm buying for, he's a comic devotee. So, I want only the best; money isn't an issue. I want *Black Panther, Luke Cage*, and *Falcon*." Eighty comic fans were milling about the busy megastore.

The grungy thirty-year-old salesman in a cult black T-shirt with the image of *Alien* on the front said, "Is he a Black guy identifying with heroes, or a GenZ white guy into superheroes' equality?" He watched Amber assess the question and waited because looking at her pleased him. She was wearing a jersey, long-sleeved jumpsuit and strappy high heel sandals.

"He's a Black guy who's cool about comics, rave culture and LGBT friendly. Loves Prince and Garage, Grime, but listens to Aretha and Amy Winehouse. He's very *Star Wars* revival," she concluded with a magnificent smile.

"He sounds dreamy," he replied sarcastically.

"Don't be an unkind Brit. He's beautiful." Her voice and her face were so luminous the salesman tapped her arm and escorted her to the glass cabinets in the megastore and pointed to rear comics and explained what's what.

An hour later, he looked at her and told her all three comics came to £5,000. She took off her lightweight backpack and took out her purse. He pushed his slightly greasy long blonde hair out of his face and watched her. She handed over her high-value Coutts World Silk Card, which was a birthday gift from Helena. He took the card and input the information.

"Is this a birthday present for him?"

"No, it's just a little something." She smiled to herself. "I love him."

That night in her luxurious bedroom filled with feminine décor that Helena had chosen for the Knightsbridge flat, Amber wrote to Aaron.

Darling Aaron,

Every day I think of you with love in my heart. Knowing your passion for comics, which psychologically and culturally speak to you, please accept these as a gift of my love to you.

I'm also sending you WONDER WOMAN because she's my fantasy idol. Read about her creation in the 1940s and her transformation in the 1970s. My real-life idol is your mother because she's the kind of woman I'd like to become.

I can't share your mum's sorrows and recovery, but I can share her son if she lets me.

I mustn't go on because you'll think I'm a silly girl. I'm not really; I'm simply a woman who loves your words (in letters, rather than horrible text messages), your thoughts and your compassion. It reassures me that you're the type of man whose arms I'll always be safe in.
With sincere love,
Amber.

* * *

At Aaron's office the following day, a driver, Ilya, came in from reception. He was handsome, rakish, and full of himself because he was one of Helena's security guards. The staff watched him closely because he was dressed in a white silk suit. Ilya gave Aaron a red box, bowed and then left.

Aaron looked at the red silk box tied up with a gold ribbon. He opened it and there was a photograph of Amber, as a sixteen-year-old, dressed as Princess Leia with her hair tied into buns. Helena was beside her as Senator Padmé Amidala, former Queen. There was also another photo of Amber in Paris outside a fashion house carrying bags in both hands.

When Aaron stopped gazing at the photos, he took out the comics and gasped at each one of them because he knew the rarity and value of them. He then read her letter, but he didn't notice that his staff were watching him as he stared into the box and looked at the comic book of *Wonder Woman*. Margot came over to him and he showed her the letter as he remained spellbound. Joy took hold of him and he got his mobile and called Amber.

"Darling…" He couldn't restrain himself, so he dashed outside the office and into the hallway. "Darling, I've got your present. I'm coming over to you now." He listened and then nodded, then made his way back to his office. He grabbed his jacket and Margot gave him back the letter as he dashed out the door. Margot eyed the staff and told them to get back to work! They resumed their calls and continued to input data on their PCs.

* * *

Amber walked Aaron through the galleries of the Victoria and Albert Museum where she now worked. In her grey suit with a full pleated kick-skirt, the sight of her elegance and poise as she walked and gestured thrilled Aaron. His admiration was principally due to the fact she wasn't simply a pretty girl wearing nice clothes. Now he saw her as a woman who dressed to assert her character rather than making fashion statements.

"Before I spout on about the presents you sent to me, well done on landing this job."

"I read everything you put into your employability portfolio about employers' and great candidates' and then I used it to get through the selection and interview assessments. When I got the offer, I wanted to celebrate with you, but—you know. We were 'separated'."

"So, you're a…"

"Interpretation Editor. I work on many print and online texts to do with the V&A." They strolled through the Furniture Gallery, which displayed styles and designs in Western culture over hundreds of years. The wide variety of Art of the Ages caught Aaron's eye as he walked past the cabinets and free-standing exhibits, which shifted in colour constantly.

"I'm working with a lovely Indian girl. She has an arranged marriage and she knew the man was right after two months. She's getting married next week. She has no angst: no reservations about the family she's marrying into." Aaron stopped walking and turned to her.

"I am not the girl most men think I am. That delicate and naïve waif has nothing to do with my identity. I love Fleetwood Mac and

The Who because the chaos of the personalities appeals to me. Time passes and those players can't stay out of each other's lives."

"Are you a secret Rock Chick?"

"No, but I love the way your eyes flicker when you ask me that. You'll see, in time I will be so brave." She began walking and he followed her. "Anaïs Nin, do you know of her?"

"*Spy in the House of Love* and her *Diary…*"

"You seldom disappoint. Yes. Between her and Madonna, I feel they are a part of me. I am a woman of mystery. I don't want to be classified."

"Has something happen between you and your parents about suitable guys?"

"Yes, I can and will marry the right man. I never thought the 'right man' was there." She stopped walking and turned to him again. "You changed that."

"Amber, I know you're the one!" he said, exalted. "Not even Susan Faludi could tell me more about you than what I love already. I think you have greatness in you. You're going to become important and even though I don't know how yet, I know you're unique. I just want to be with you until God takes me!"

"So, you still want to go out with me?" He moved to grab her and she stopped him. "Let me talk to Helena because I've talked to her and listened to countless musicals thinking about you."

"Why musicals?"

"Silly, don't you know all of humankind's greatest hopes and dreams are in musicals and operas? It's the place that allows us to confess." He stared at her and began crying. She moved closer and kissed his eyes and then he took her face in the palms of his hands.

"Aaron, this is why I know our children will thank me for marrying you."

"How can you be so sure of me?"

"Everything you do defies bigotry. Millions of girls want to control men: I don't! I don't want us to use one another. I want us to need each other," she told him with her hands open and her head lifted, so Aaron felt compelled to kiss her.

* * *

Donna and Miriam were in a board meeting with ten men from the Czech Republic, Romania, Poland and Slovakia who were buyers for major retailers and their own business. Miriam and Donna hired a meeting room in a West London hotel and the men sat calmly in the 'standard' nicely decorated plush room. In the rooms upstairs, Donna and Miriam had samples of their men's clothing collections. After the free lunch and booze, the bulky men felt happy.

At each end of the conference table, Miriam and Donna had presentation screen projectors and laptops which they presented from. They felt self-assured dressed in different off-white trouser suits as they came to the close of business.

Donna said, "Gentlemen, the days when men walked around your cities looking like vagrants is over." Donna let twenty images of Eastern European men in scruffy clothes flash up on the screen.

"It's time to put a stop to this. You are in the position as buyers to change things." Donna let Miriam take over at her end of the room so that the men looked in her direction at the opposite end.

"Our American designers have come up with a new look that we are calling a 'revitalised style' for men who take their virility and power seriously. These are your people!" Fifty images of men in landmark locations in the Czech Republic, Romania, Poland and Slovakia, walking through the landscape of all the cities flashed up. The buyers took a great deal of pleasure in seeing their countrymen in business suits, casuals and weekend attire that was colourful; ranging from pastels to primary colours for tennis, golf, and evenings heading to classical concerts, which they were seen doing in all the cities.

"This is who a woman wants to marry." The men turned their head to Donna, who projected a photo of a handsome man, aged thirty-five and exceptionally well dressed, offering a woman an engagement ring outside St. Mary's Church, Gdańsk in Poland.

"This is who a woman wants to date," Donna continued, by projecting another picture. In the photo, a young graduate shaking the hand of a nurse looked very appealing. They looked healthy, happy and prosperous. Miriam paid for the shoot and Donna did all the location scouting, found the models and got the photographic crew together.

Donna said, "Of course, some women prefer lovers: married men who understand the rules when it comes to liaisons." A photo of a man, aged fifty who had a gift of champagne and roses in his hand, was caught taking off the wedding band of his lover.

His silk navy-blue suit was designed to slim his portly shape and make him look smart and naughty standing in front of the welcoming woman.

"We have the exclusive rights to these new designers' collection," Donna told them.

"These clothes are ready for manufacturing in London," Miriam added. "My colleague, Donna has twenty years of production experience in Great Titchfield Street, the centre of the fashion manufacturing and my family have been in the Garment District, in Manhattan since 1925.

A fifty-year-old ruddy-faced Romanian said, "Your proposal is interesting—"

Donna stated, "It's not 'interesting', it's great. I'm offering you a men's line for all ages; from talented new designers in London and New York to transform men's appeal in your countries. These clothes are going to give your men a lift and I mean, where it counts." Each of the men in the heated boardroom watched the women at work.

Miriam walked around the back of the chairs swinging her hips. "The Anglo American isn't the last word in hip masculinity. Look at this man." Donna projected several images of Aaron and Roy over the last ten years. "They are the future of equality in fashion. Men and women admire and desire these guys. They represent everything today's youth stands for. A shot of Aaron dressed in cool gear in Lanzarote projected on Donna's side of the room. "Women look at this man in two ways: a lover and a husband: why? He's women's sexual fantasy. Politicians have power, but those shmucks are as cold as stale piss. This man is a peacock. When he displays what he's got he makes women hot." All of the men watched Miriam looking at Aaron.

"Youth isn't just age, it's a mental attitude. It's how you include rather than exclude people. It's how you dress yourself to exert your pride. Europe once dominated the world, so why not remind your countrymen; in the 21st century, they don't need to envy everyone else." Miriam was full of herself and the men couldn't get over her, even though half of them wanted to.

Donna said, "Can you imagine what's going to happen when your guys get their hands on these mid-price clothes and start walking tall? They won't have to go abroad to find love—"

"OK!" A buyer said, "I will buy the Autumn/Winter collection for now—"

"No," Donna cut in.

Miriam raised her voice, slightly. "You buy for the Autumn/ Winter and Spring/Summer. We've spent ages with the designers and we are not treating them like rubbish." All of the men locked their eyes onto Miriam. "There's no bartering at this stage. The designers have researched your region for two years and designed for your market. Take it or not," Miriam concluded.

Miriam made a call on her mobile and a few minutes later, her father and another man came into the room. Photos of Aaron from the previous year, walking across the Szechenyi chain bridge in Budapest in a full length hooded faux fur showed him covered in a grey wolf's coat. Donna kept looking at him and she compelled the men to look up also.

Miriam's father, Ralph, came into the boardroom with another guy. "My daughter and my partner, Donna, told us they'd need an agent to offer your suppliers' services and guarantee, so they hired us to answer all questions on supplies, marketing and deliveries. This is my British agent, Bill Stewart."

In their 'old-world' groomed manner, Ralph and Bill's Jewish and Protestant pairing looked like a partnership to 'cover all bases'.

Ralph said, "It is my responsibility to provide sales forecasts to Miriam and Donna each month. Bill has to map out a marketing and sales plan based on Eastern European buying trends. Cultural imperatives impacting online fashion debates, and Eastern European economic shifts. These things must be studied. Bill has a sales marketing research team of men who report to him and once Bill has analysed the research, he reports to Donna." Miriam and Donna had done their due diligence.

At the beach on Bankolé Island, Donna charmed the Bankolé-De Farenzinos and guests into a shoot. "These were taken recently on a visit to an exclusive resort," Donna said, "Only the wealthiest people worldwide can go here. Nevertheless, in our mid-price clothes, no one felt or looked out of place." The buyers were impressed with the presentation.

Additionally, once the Eastern European buyers saw that Donna and Miriam controlled both men, they adjusted to a financial commitment because it was evident that both women were sound and financially focused. The buyers also realised Donna and Miriam had anticipated the men's objections and as a result of strategic thinking, they had backup plans to close the deal advantageously for all stakeholders. Miriam looked up at the image of Aaron and her smile confirmed her strength in her faith.

CHAPTER TWENTY-ONE

Aaron and Amber were in his office boardroom going through profiles and selecting men out of the hierarchy of faces on the projected whiteboard. The faces in front of them range between Mediterranean-looking men, Black men from South America, the Caribbean and North Africa.

Amber was sitting in a swivel chair in her white zip-up jumpsuit and black lace-up Edwardian ladies' boots. She looked like a sixties icon. Aaron pointed to the profiles and Amber's facial expressions and gestures prompted Aaron to shortlist candidates.

"These are the men who passed the psychometric tests I use here for my executive job seekers when I'm assessing their personality profile and work skills. You wouldn't believe the number of men who've failed the matchmaking questions I've had written up. Let me tell you, strength, kindness and ingenuity are scarce."

"Not to mention attractive," Amber replied pointing at a photo of a man on the wall. "That one looks like he survived a zombie attack. Get rid of him." Aaron deleted him. Amber pointed at the man on the far left. "We agreed that guy said nothing about his children and that tells *me* he's either unfeeling or stupid." Aaron deleted that man from the group. Amber rubbed her hands together and they nodded.

He walked away from the laptop and went and kissed her. Her smile had everything a man hopes to see in his girlfriend's eyes. Aaron returned to the whiteboard and fixed his suit and adjusted himself. She knew he was having a hard time.

They continued and eliminated thirty-three other men. Amber got up to go to the ladies' room. Aaron told her, "You know what I love about the way you look today?"

"No," she replied adorably.

"Everything!"

"Princess Leia meets Audrey. It almost makes me feel like *your* heroine."

"Heroine is a good word for you. Can you save me from myself?" he asked, prompting her to tease him.

"Have you read, *He's Just Not That Into You?*"

"Yes," Aaron sneered. "The book is about a bunch of insecure American narcissists." Amber discreetly got up and furtively sidled around the boardroom. I would later discover other women who refined Amber's seduction.

"I love the fact you're not an emotional coward." Aaron liked the look on her face. "Many of the boys I've seen have told me how good they are in private, if you know what I mean. But you have never spoken of your privates." Aaron had never seen her look so flirtatious, but it was her expression that forced him to laugh.

"If only I was joking. One boy told me he had a horse and cart in his pants." Try as hard as she could, she couldn't hold back her laughter.

When she finally stopped laughing, he was still in full throttle, stamping his foot. I later discovered Amber had endless stories about the boys her family introduced her to.

Aaron said, "Well, those *boys* are obviously a joke. A man doesn't need a ponytail: he needs a romantic psyche and if he's a full member in gratification, a woman will trust him." Aaron's cheeky smile revealed his dimples.

"As a full member, do you have privileges?" She found exactly the right tone of voice.

"Yes, they allow me to meet a woman's needs, indefinitely."

"Eve spoiled things, but maybe paradise is waiting for you and me."

"I have no intention of remarrying so there's a lot for me to learn." His heart raced when he said, "The more you teach me is the more I'll grow. So, I imagine after many years of marriage, I'll have a really big head." *Roy told me that Aaron quivered with delight when he recounted what he said.*

She said, "There's talking and then there's social intercourse; I don't know which one I like more with you." She backed off to exit, but before she went out the door, she turned back and said, "Boys use to scare me with the things they said. It's funny how a *man* can change that." Her glowing eyes left him wanting. He turned away from her, walked towards the flip chart and readjusted himself with joy and pain tearing through him.

Several minutes later, Margot came into the boardroom and gestured for him to come immediately. They dashed down the corridor and into his office. He found Amber face to face with Miriam as the staff watched both women.

Miriam stood poised in front of Amber like the perfect flight attendant in a storm. "Tell this stupid girl to back off." Miriam looked at Amber as though she was an annoying teenage salesgirl. The staff sensed an oncoming fight, so no one picked up a phone or looked away. The 'girls' in the office were on Amber's side because the night she took them out for cocktails and picked up the tap was one of the best they'd had in ages. The 'guys' liked the sight of Miriam because she could get a rise out of any man; she was a man's kind of woman, while Amber was definitely a girl's woman.

"You dirty American idiot!" The German intonation in Amber's voice was pronounced when she rebuked Miriam. "Stay away from him, you swine!"

"Oh, excuse me Princess lightweight go fuck yourself."

"You remind me of something you find in the toilet!"

"You better shut up or..." Amber lunged into Miriam and shoved her back which knocked Miriam off her high heels, but she grabbed a guy to stop herself from falling over. As she did that, Amber rushed in and slapped Miriam in the face.

"I never want to see your face again unless you're in a coffin!"

Miriam was about to attack her, but Aaron jumped in and placed himself between the two women. "Oh, wow," Miriam said. "You love this, don't you: me and her fighting over you?"

"No, I don't. Go home, Miriam." She stared at him and the staff watched all three of them.

Miriam abruptly grabbed Aaron and gestured to demand an exit to the door. "Do not follow me, or I'll rip your tits!" she told Amber. "You, outside!" she told Aaron with her finger danger-ously close to his eye. He turned to Amber and gave her a look that told her he was in charge.

In the corridor, Miriam spoke to Aaron with hushed anger in her voice. "You want to throw away your life on a girl that can't see what type of man you are."

"What type of man am I?"

"The best man I've ever met. You're ambitious and tough. You'd do so much better in New York where you'd make millions getting Hispanic and Black guys employed."

"You think?"

"You understand their difficulty and you'd sell them big time. People would do business with you because they'd never think you're black. You could get one over on everybody and make a shitload of money in the bargain. I know people and we all know there's talent coming out of Colleges who need a man like you. With your British accent and Mediterranean looks—"

"But I am a Brit. I couldn't live there."

"Yes, you could, my father and I can sponsor you and if we married, there isn't anything I wouldn't do. Your mom and I just closed a deal. She'll be back and forth in New York, so with you there, she could put her people to work in London and you'd see her all the time."

"Amber..."

Miriam wouldn't let him finish the sentence. "Is a child bride, you can't take her seriously."

"I like—"

"That's her angle: all sweet and light, the European Jewish Princess. Have you fucked her yet?"

"Don't talk like that."

"She can't cope with you. She'll grit her teeth and make you feel like a beast forcing yourself on her. I know the type. Is that what you want? Or would you like to come home for a cocktail and a kiss on your balls when I get in from work?"

"That's something for me to think about. Listen, go home and I'll see you later. Let me deal with Amber. I can't tell Amber that her sexual modesty turns me off. I have to let her know I realise what's best for me now." Miriam pulled him out of the hall and into the kitchen where they were alone. It was a typically upmarket office kitchen for the companies in the building to share.

Miriam caressed his crotch and gave him a kiss. As she did, she put all her passion into the kiss, but Aaron had his eyes open as he watched her. Gary, his second-best biller, poked his head around the door and Aaron eyeballed him and told him to leave. Aaron gently eased Miriam back and smiled as a scoundrel would.

"Go now. You'll hear from me." Miriam pulled back and he saw that she was excited as she glided out slowly. Aaron wiped his mouth with the back of his hand.

Back in the office, Amber was waiting when Aaron re-entered. "Give me a minute, darling," he asked. He went to his desk, took out a little varnished box and left the office. Seconds later, Gary got up and followed him. Margot and the girls looked at Amber reassuringly and Margot called her to the alcove to make herb tea.

In the men's room, Aaron was gargling and loudly spitting in the toilet. He rinsed and spat five times. Gary pulled faces and quietly made his way back out of the men's room. Aaron came out of the stall and went to the sink and washed his face. Afterward, he moisturised and fixed his hair. He took his mobile and called Roy and told him everything. "...expects me to leave mum to go to the murder capital where the cops can kill me and leave mum destitute. Total bitch! She thinks she can play me; I'm Humphrey Blackmon's son! Not some eunuch."

Aaron kissed his teeth and ruffled his curly hair as he listened to Roy. "Brother man, I'm gonna fix her. I'm calling mum now." He then cursed a blue streak in patois and vented some more. When another man came in, Aaron switched to English. Aaron rushed out of the loo, back down the corridor and out onto the street where he called Donna.

Aaron went back to his office and told his top biller, Ejay. "New client: he's got eight years BDM corporate. Ten years sales manager in charities and he's just left product development in PR after two years, now he's looking for NGOs. I think you should tell him about your company contacts in this sector. His name's Etienne Devereux, speaks five languages fluently."

"Fuck yeah! Get me his—" Margot gave Aaron the CV and Aaron winked at her. He gestured to Amber and she got up and went to him.

Aaron told Ejay, "I want him in front of your three best firms in four days. Call HR and speak to your recruiters. Etienne's the nicest gay guy a firm could have. Oh yeah, I don't want him to tell me again that you're homophobic. Staff can be legally fired for discrimination. If I hear any more of it, you'll be out that door; understand?" Fern and Margot discreetly watched and Gary took note, even though he was on a call. Ejay, recognised Aaron's warning. The other members of staff got on with their work, Aaron picked up his jacket, spoke to Margot and left shortly afterward.

Margot said, "You heard the man, bring the client into the office and call your contacts!" She fixed her suit and the staff went back to work.

Aaron and Amber scrambled into the taxi outside his office. "Beigel Bake, Brick Lane, emergency fast, mate." They watched London flash past them and the driver did as instructed to get them there. Amber noticed how much the scene changed from flashy to trashy as they travelled out of the West End and into the East End. As they bumped around the back of the cab, she periodically held him.

She said, "Sorry if I was loud and horrible with Miriam, but I—"

"I love you; you don't have to apologise for dealing with her."

"You love me, absolutely? You're sure?"

Aaron unfastened his seatbelt and moved over and kissed her. The taxi driver turned a corner to make his way to the City of London and Aaron rolled over and hit the side of the door. He laughed and the driver told him to buckle up and sit down.

"Why should I! You see this woman, she loves me!"

"Yeah, lovely and all that! Just sit still."

"You keep talking and you'll blow your tip!" Amber took his arm and they huddled together and watched London's landmarks flash past until they reached their destination.

They got out of the black cab and Aaron gave him money and took the change. Aaron waved a five-pound note. "Oops! Twat!" Amber laughed and they rushed into the deli.

Donna was there looking anxious and eager. Aaron dashed to her and gave her a kiss. "Hi, mum. First thing first! Amber is the one! I love her. Give her a chance because it's not like you to be unfair."

Amber said, "Aaron, you can't tell your mother what to think."

"Thank you, dear." Various customers from different racial backgrounds entered and left the deli as they stood talking.

"Maybe your mother doesn't like me because she dislikes my parents. Donna, if you don't like my parents, I understand. I don't like them either. I moved out because of it. I do love Aaron, though."

"Why do you love him?"

Amber coughed out laughter. "Because he's sophisticated. It could be the degrees or his therapy, but he has the right heart for me. He couldn't save his sister on the zebra crossing, but he saved me." Aaron turned his eyes to Amber. "He adores you. He's spent all his evenings, disqualifying men he thinks are unworthy of meeting you. He said—"

"Amber, you don't have to—" Aaron interjected.

Donna said, "Aaron, shut up."

"He sends me love letters speaking about the virtues of what love means to him, based on his experience with you and his sister. He understands feminism because he hates bigots. His past girlfriends, including Miriam, are usually too...greedy and bossy, or self-centred to understand what he values. I only respect men with compassion and love for women."

"What do you want for yourself?"

"I want *you* to help me to be a great mother. I want children and my family to understand the meaning of compassion. The world we live in doesn't believe in acts of kindness. Politicians with their Brexit and racism are so revolting. The political climate is too totalitarian. I don't want that in my house. I want my mother to have faith in my judgment, I want my husband to defend me against tyranny and unite my life with his."

"You're really in love with her, Aaron?"

"Yes," and he offered no further explanation. He turned away from Donna and ordered, "One salt beef on rye, one on pumpernickel and..." He looked at Amber. "How do you like it?"

"Oh...sourdough if they have it, otherwise salt beef bagel with hot mustard." When their orders were done, Aaron left the shop and walked through the streets of London's East End. It was packed, loud, dirty, unfashionable and showed its past. The Jewish tradesmen and shopkeepers were there and so were the new generation of Asian restaurant owners.

"That coat must have cost a fortune!" Donna said to Amber because she recognised it from the London Fashion Week shows.

Amber's haute couture peach-coloured leather coat had enough material in it to make a cape and the gold silk lining shimmered around her when she turned in two circles in the grubby street.

"It was a gift from Helena. She inherited her first million the other day. I love beautiful things, so she gave me this." Amber was a marked contrast to the scruffy East End market stall traders and the grubby walls that vista down the street.

"Nice friend," Donna said.

Aaron concurred and told her, "Helena's really nice, mum. You know, Amber, when you're happy you sound really French and when you're pissed off, you sound German."

"Oh darling, don't tease me, it's true," she concluded and slipped her hands through Aaron and Donna's arms. She looked like a girl who could have swung between the 'grown-ups' arms, but she wobbled her head from side to side and Donna smiled because Amber was so happy.

"I just love London! It's unlike anywhere I've lived in Europe."

"Your finishing school..."

"That's my past. Helena is letting me stay with her until I find my own place." Even though the streets and the area were run down, Amber didn't look at it or behave as if she was slumming. Dressed as she was, she certainly didn't look like she belonged there.

Donna said, "After living at a finishing school, parents in the Diplomatic service and a mother who shops in the Côte d'Azur, Biarritz and Tokyo—" Amber interrupted Donna. "Those are just places. It's packed with people that have money and no social conscience. Solly Bankolé has more money than my family, but look at what he does with it. He helps and promotes equality. It's what I love about Aaron. He's studied hundreds of suitors, who claim to be wonderful."

"How?" Donna asked.

"As a journalist, Roy has resources and I've placed people in various roles and corporate industries. I've called in some favours. So, I've eliminated the liars and fakes who are trying to meet you."

"Tell Roy, I want to see him and Narjan for Sunday dinner next week."

Amber said, "You see! This is what I love about both of you."

Donna cut in and said, "Amber, can you give us a moment?" She nodded and walked on.

"Why her and not Miriam? You said you discovered Miriam is filth. What the fuck is that about?"

"Miriam is lying to you, to herself and me. She aims to run my life and manage yours. Sex is all she has to offer and I won't marry for a shag."

"Haven't you gone to bed with…" She pointed at Amber.

"No, Amber's never been to bed with a man, her virtue is a part of her dowry to her husband. I love that. She's no Jewish Princess or material girl; she's got brains. She's an expert on Art and Tudor history: loves comics and knows its evolution. And she listens." He gave Donna a perceptive look. "I have an Aaron and Eve situation with Miss America. She plans to lead me into a life of sin."

"That's not the woman I know her to be."

"Let me put it this way. I'd never tell you: marry someone you don't like."

"How can you be sure I'll like any of the suitors you've chosen?"

"I can't. Some of the candidates are good on paper, but I'm still running health checks, criminal background and paternity. If you don't like these guys, drop them and we'll keep looking." Donna stopped walking and gave him a searching stare.

"What?" Aaron asked.

"You make my matchmaking and all matchmakers seem like amateurs."

"No filthy fucking dog is coming anywhere near you! I'll tear him apart!"

Donna smiled. "You would—wouldn't you?"

"Dr Liebermann told me; dad's spirit is alive in me. He's reaching out through me to protect you. I don't think that's super-stitious rubbish, do you?"

"No, it's just strange that a psychiatrist talks about the super-natural rather than cold scientific facts." In the background, men were busy selling from their stalls.

All their merchandise was just a bit tatty, from the fruit and veg to the wigs.

"Liebermann's a really incredible man; I like him."

"I *am* interested in meeting these guys you've screened."

"How's it going with Jerry? You've not mentioned him in a while."

"Err no; he's not right for me." Aaron was about to ask why, but knew he didn't have the right to cross-examine his mother.

"You can meet the first candidate next week. Are you clear any particular evening?"

"Any night."

"I'll tell them you're fully booked, but we'll move things around. You're never *available*. You're always in demand. If you learn that they've lied about anything, we'll cut them off. You're not Ms. Pussy Galore; you're a businesswoman, with natural grace. And if they so much as leave skid marks in their pants, they're out of the running."

"How are you going to check all this?"

"Hello! I'm going to their house. Can you imagine how telling that will be when they come out to meet you and I insist on going to their place?"

Aaron started laughing and Donna joined in. They began to stagger around, holding each other up and laughing loudly, heading towards Shoreditch in Hackney that was packed with rough and deliberately scruffy cafés, artisan small businesses and people who looked like they were sent back from a 1972 counterculture festival of sex, rock 'n' roll and anti-capitalist demonstrations.

"About Miriam, I'm prepared to expose her for who she really is."

Donna knew he had discovered something terrible so she couldn't speak.

"I'm not saying she isn't a good businesswoman. I'm saying she's bad for *me*."

Donna pulled him closer. "Have I really misjudged her?"

"As an ambitious businesswoman, no: but I will not be governed by Misandry."

Donna didn't understand. "Misogyny is about men who hate and use women. Misandry is about women who hate and use men." She thought about it for a time and then gestured in respect of her son.

"If *you* don't govern me and use emotional blackmail to control me, do you think I'd allow some woman to run my life? Make fake claims against me and abuse me, not to mention, give me permission to think for myself. I swear on my life and my father's grave, I will not capitulate to that for anything."

"You think she'd do that?"

"I suspect her of everything dishonest." Donna looked troubled and a bit upset. "That is one of the reasons why I love Amber. She is incapable of being Miriam."

"Darling, tell me; what has Miriam done?"

"Right now, I only suspect her. But I'm going to prove it."

A few meters away, Amber walked in circles taking in the sites, sounds and sights. Amber ran back to be with them and Aaron put his arm around both women and strutted through the street.

Roy told me; Aaron was concerned because he could see that Donna was terribly worried.

CHAPTER TWENTY-TWO

Roy walked through the architectural angularity of my Barbican apartment. In his birthday suit, he never looked better. We turned all the lights off so that the lights in the streets outside the windows would create the vibe we felt. So much had happened in such a short time. I got up and stopped him in the middle of the room and I was glad the night hid the flaws of my body. I was once a strapping young man, but I was no longer as muscular as I use to be. And he was so full of himself because he was at a peak, aged thirty.

The shadows of the interior loomed large in the room and the silhouettes of our bodies stretched up the walls. Thank God I wasn't fat. My shadow cast a giant phallus on the wall. Roy pointed at it and we had a cockfight through the shadows, which made us laugh. After a while, we stopped and lay on the floor and listened to George Michael's album, *Older* that was playing softly.

I quietly said, "You were so upset when you arrived: better now?"

"Break-ups are never easy. I've been going out with him for ages. I don't know what I'd do if we weren't working on this. But I'm glad you care about me."

"You know I don't *just* care about you." He embraced me tightly.

"I can tell from the chapters that you respect my friends and me. I like the way you've transcribed things I've told you. Aaron tells me more and more every day." He suddenly became a bit jittery and I could feel his heart rate increase.

"What, darling?"

"Donna loves me and shares intimate secrets. I feel funny talking to you about that."

"I won't be indiscreet or salacious about her." He hugged me tighter.

"She does look great these days, knowing things are changing: and Aaron just shines with pride because of Amber."

"How did he look the Sunday he set-up the dinner to expose Miriam?" Roy sat up and told me everything. His mental recollection was dramatised through his expressions. I could barely concentrate because he looked so sexy, naked in the shadows. As always, his face told me everything I couldn't see because I wasn't there. But that's how it always was. He'd meet me and recount what happened and his voice took on the characteristics of the person he was referring to. Roy could also act out who did what. Each time he left the apartment, after any of our sessions, I always had his presence and vibe in my head, guiding me on how to write.

As the novel progressed, I remembered that night in Bloomsbury Square when he said, 'lovers aren't cool'. He virtually warned me that if we became an item, we'd lose our friendship, so, I tried my best to keep it cool even though I wanted him emotionally and sexually. I wanted to take him to a city on holiday and walk with him as couples do. Write and plan how we could co-work together; or share a home and cook and clean our house together.

Roy was animated recounting facts to me, but he stopped and touched my hair. "I can't wait to read how you write this. It's not enough that you're cyber sexy—with your silver Afro and future-retro clothes: you can translate my words into a novel."

He gazed at me and I loved him so dearly, I wished my mum was alive so I could tell her, because she always cared about my happiness and worried for me. I had no family to confide in and explain how much love I felt, but I could tell David and Michael because they are family to me. Even Solly treats me like a relative.

The following day, Roy and I walked around the gardens of the Barbican, with its small water fountains, sculptures, elevated walk-ways, and its nooks and crannies. It was a bright overcast day, but as Roy spoke and I kept the voice recorder app on my mobile going, I watched his face as he recounted the Sunday dinner that brought the two families together.

"Roy, *you* should write this chapter because you were there and you felt it."

"But I'm a journalist; you're the prize-winning novelist—"

"You've told me that you want to write that book about LGBT politics and the lives of gay men worldwide, haven't you?"

"Yes, but—"

"Forget but. Don't just edit what I've been writing, start writing with me again. It will be great practice and experience for you."

"But I'm not inclined to romance."

"Yes, you are, even though things didn't work out with Narj or Brian. You have to learn to nurture emotional truth." He looked at me for the longest time.

"You're not just a big cock, are you?" he said, like a precocious brat.

"Behave yourself." The impish smile on his face was truly saucy. "You know, I always think of Black heroes throughout history without a nod, but you are some kind of beautiful."

As there is a God in heaven, I loved him all the more, right then and there.

I told him flippantly, "Sometimes, you're so young."

"And sometimes you're so sexy. You really love me?"

"Yes." I couldn't stop gazing at him.

"Even though I killed my father and caused the death—"

I grabbed his arm and stared at the changing expression on his face. "Your mother and father tried to murder you!" I was still disgusted by the fact. "They were poisoning you every day, so it would look like a prolonged illness."

"Yes but..."

"Your father had a heart attack while he was kicking you in the guts because he couldn't wait for you to die." My throat dried just uttering those words.

"So, you don't think I'm an evil Satanist that—"

I kissed him, to calm him. "You're lovely. Those boys who came after you—all those Obeah accusations were their 'get out of jail' defence."

"Three people died, so they accused me of—"

I categorically said, "Three murderers who failed to kill you died, Roy."

He calmed down and then rose from despair and became bright and sanguine.

"Take me to the Barbican's Conservatory. You said you would. I want you to love me up among the foliage and—".

"And get arrested! See my name in the tabloids as a corrupter of youth."

"I'm thirty, not thirteen." I smacked his backside.

"Let me call Michael and David. I'd love to be with them so they can see us. And later, make love to you in their house." I heard myself so I shut up.

Roy smiled provocatively. "Yeah! Call them. Besides, I've got a score to settle."

"You mean the time you guys were in the food cupboard—"

He cringed. "David told you!"

"Michael and I are comrades. We're not like you, thirty-something guys."

"You don't look a day over...forty-nine." It was one of the few times I didn't mind being teased because I really hate people making fun of me.

I cautiously asked, "Do I make love like other men you've known?"

"No, I never feel strange with you. Sometimes with..." His abrupt halt felt like whiplash. "Eugene, in bed, what I feel with you is remarkable. You're great."

"Sometimes, I wonder if today's LGBTs are better than my generation. But I like being old-fashioned." He touched the back of my neck and I felt it in my balls.

"Come; let's go back so you can write about the dinner and what happened. Then we'll go to Michael and David, high on what we're doing." He smiled at me with such joy.

* * *

I knew the violent explosion was going to go off in less than half-hour and my nerves were on edge throughout the entire time. I sat beside Narj at Donna's dinner table. Considering it was Sunday lunch, which was always sacred, the air was solemn as Miriam sat beside her parents at the dinner table. They were also rather stiff and tongue-tied. Donna and Aaron shared so many conspiratorial looks, I wondered if Miriam realised or felt that she was caught in a trap about to be sprung. Donna's well-furnished dining room felt like it was closing in on me: and Aaron and Donna's fake affability fooled them but not me.

Miriam and her parents couldn't know it but Aaron was overdressed; he never wore suits to Sunday dinner and Donna seldom wore dresses like the matronly frock she was wearing. I wondered if she had just bought it, because I'd never seen her in anything like a granny dress, with her hair done up in a bun. To my surprise, Donna didn't do a Caribbean Sunday meal: she did a pot roast with vegetables. She knew how to cook Caribbean food extremely well because Humphrey's family taught her and Donna perfected her own dishes over the years.

When the table was cleared of the first course, I noticed the tension and bemused pleasure that settled on Aaron's face as Donna brought in and served out the second course. We began eating when Aaron quietly stated.

"I hate to say this, but I have to…" That was a lie, Aaron enjoyed exposing hypocrites and liars.

"On Friday, there was a situation at the office with Amber, Miriam and I. I had to go away on business urgently that afternoon, so this is the first chance we've had to deal with what happened." Miriam turned to her parents and Ralph and Sonya nodded. They ate, complimented the food and sensed nothing, but as I said before, I grew up in a violent home and I knew when trouble was coming.

My father gave me no warning; he'd just lash out at me. My mother was different, she'd give me the silent treatment and then she'd beat me as if I was a burglar. She'd lash out like she was wielding a baseball bat or a machete—God, she was terrifying.

Aaron said to Ralph, "I'm sure Miriam has told you about Amber: I met her earlier in the year. Miriam sees no future for Amber and me; so she spoke to me about the prospects of my life with you and her." Aaron's contrived posh accent unsettled me because his acting was so convincing. "Miriam brought up things I hadn't considered. We need to talk, especially since mum and your family have recently won some significant new business."

Miriam looked calm and pleased and I thought—you idiots; you're walking into a trap! You're going to incriminate and dig yourself in deeper. Donna smiled at Miriam's parents and Miriam turned to her.

Miriam said, "I told Aaron; Amber is too naïve for him: he needs a vivacious woman to inspire him. You've got that, Donna, and I've been told I'm like that."

"You are, sweetheart," Ralph said and then he took Sonya's hand. They both looked like people in one of Woody Allen's nostalgic comedies.

Miriam said, "On vacation, it was plain to me; Aaron's very ambitious and committed to trying to get minorities employed. We spent a day talking about his political views because of his background. You know what I mean." Sonya and Ralph nodded. "Anyway, I told Aaron, if he really wanted to make big money, he should think of running his business in Manhattan, now you'll be coming over so often Donna." Miriam's parent's expressions told me they had given it some thought and they agreed with Miriam's logic. But Aaron moving to America and leaving Donna by herself: I don't think so! I took Narjan's hand and kissed it, but I didn't know why.

Miriam assured Donna, "We'd sponsor him, I mean I told Aaron, mom and dad would gladly do it."

Donna eyed Miriam's parents and they agreed. "People will flock to Aaron because he's smart and looks great. He told me he's not making enough money here in London."

Donna stated, "How much is enough? He's got a solid business."

"Donna, he has to bust his ass to convince narrow-minded employers about the talent they constantly turn away because like lots of highfaluting sons of bitches that run this country, they think they know it all!" Donna's face hardened and I could see strength and fury take hold of her. I'd seen it before.

Aaron told Donna, "I wouldn't just go there; Miriam and I would get married."

Donna blinked involuntarily so many times; I thought she was having a 'something'. Miriam said, "We're good for each other in a lot of ways, Donna. I know I come on strong, but I do that with people I love." Sonya agreed: I could see it in her genial smile.

Ralph said, "In the thirties, my father was introduced to his wife by her family right here in London. They married, had me, left London and lived happily together for sixty-one years. And before Papa died, he introduced me to this woman," he told Donna, taking Sonya's hand. "She was perfect for me and in our thirty-five years together, I learnt to love her more than I ever dreamed."

Aaron hadn't told Donna what he knew about Miriam. He wanted Donna to discover Miriam's duplicity herself. The bomb was ticking and none of them knew it, even though Donna was becoming increasingly agitated, but she didn't have that killer look, as yet.

"Aaron and I could do great things together." Miriam threw him a looked that was loaded with sex, but the cold stare from Aaron told me he was ready.

"His passion for social…" She searched for the word and finally turned to him. "Sweetheart, you mentioned it several times when we went away."

"Social transformation through political equality."

"So eloquent," Ralph said.

"Isn't he, dad, and look at him, is he gorgeous or what? I love this guy!"

"Yes, he is," Donna replied.

Miriam passionately continued, "I can see him in New York doing business; employment business with all the people typical agencies can't be bothered with. These are crazy days, under the current Administration. Clients would come to Aaron because of his background: Jewish, Caribbean, intellectual; British! My God, the accent alone, plus his qualifications and business savvy. When companies see him," she said to Donna; "they're going to a guy who looks Mediterranean and sounds British. They'll see ambition and money! They'll know, no two-bit punk is ever gonna run a number on Aaron, with his British intelligence."

Ralph said, "Tell her the other thing, sweetheart." Miriam thought for a moment and then her face lit up!

"Right! Yes! Donna, this is *so* cool. I thought; firms in America are always looking for great British talent for certain executive roles!" Miriam almost leapt to her feet. "Aaron could take a year building clients' to supply New York firms with top executives here that want to work Stateside."

Ralph said, "What do you think of these ideas and prospects, Aaron?"

Donna said to Miriam. "Marry you, leave and go to New York?"

Ralph replied, "Of course, we'll be so busy with our Eastern European venture, Donna, we'll be in each other's lives all the time if you can stand it?"

Sonya said, "Donna, you told us, last time, sitting still was driving you crazy, after what you've been through. This can be a win-win!"

Aaron casually said, "Isn't citizenship hard to come by in the States, these days?"

"We'd be married. I'm an American citizen and British-born subject. That works for Boris Johnson. Papa's a British-born American. European Jews have been going to America since the 1800s."

Aaron said, "When the authorities look at me, don't you think they'll see more than a Jew?"

Miriam laughed. "You're no darker than Meghan the Duchess. Look at you, no one would know!"

"Except the fucking cops who'd gun down my son!!" Donna screamed as she punched Miriam right in the face. Ralph and Sonya tried to pull Donna away and she landed two face breaking punches; then turned back to Miriam and began chanting her rage with every blow she pounded into Miriam's face as she dragged her off the chair, screaming: "No fucking cop is going to shoot my son because that bigot thinks he's got the right to kill Black men!"

Donna shoved Miriam onto the ground. Aaron stood back, watching without making any attempt to stop Donna. Narjan was in shock! Miriam's parents made another attempt to stop Donna, but she lurched at both of them and shoved them back. I looked up at Aaron and I could see that wicked spark in his eyes. Miriam's parents made another dive towards Donna, but she clawed at Ralph's neck, then kicked Sonya in the guts. Donna grabbed the food on the table and threw it onto Miriam. "My son isn't going to your homicidal nation!"

Donna was like a crazed woman in a horror film. "You cannot have my son! You will not rob me!" Aaron went and pulled her aside. He had to use his strength to get her out of the room and then he came back. The Sunday meal was scattered all over Miriam as she covered her face, crying, unable to get off the floor.

"Is your mom fucking crazy or something?" Ralph asked.

"No, sometimes she just gets real Black!" Aaron said and everything froze.

Donna came back and cursed a streak of Jamaican profanities and finished up pointing at Aaron and telling him, "Get these cunt rags outta my yard!" To put it mildly, there was no oxygen in the room after she said that.

Narj insisted we leave and ten minutes later, I was walking him towards Stoke Newington Church Street. Talk about an ethnic stream of people. Black, Asian, Eastern European and Orthodox Jews were all around the street, it was like aliens had returned a bunch of hostages they kidnapped on a world tour.

Narj angrily told me, "There's no excuse for that kind of violence and behaviour. She was like..." He searched for words and came up with; 'savage'. "You tell me how incredible they are and you devote yourself to them but look at how high and mighty they are—disgraceful!"

"Your parents pay you to stay out of Sri Lanka so your homosexuality does not stain their name. Even with your burgeoning fame, they still disown you." He was embarrassed. "You take their money every month. You accept that insult. Donna and Aaron would never spit on me like that!"

Narj said, "Stop screaming at me." People on the street were looking at us and I didn't give a shit. In Hackney, anything can happen on the street, be it nice or nasty.

"I'll fucking shout at you!" he yelled in my face. "You don't want to see the bad side of me, so shut up!"

I got in his face and said, "I know you've been sucking up to collectors on your exhibition tour." His guilt covered his face in shame.

"It's alright. Because you've become a whore, it forced me to become a gentleman. So, I found a man to be loving with. True, I detest you because you're a coward! But that doesn't matter now." I never saw Narj look so stunned and hurt. I loved it! "Now, walk to the bank and get your thirty pieces of silver; you cheap pussy! I'm done with you!" I walked off and he called out to me, but I never turned back. I left him calling my name and ignored him.

Book Three

2018
SUITORS

CHAPTER TWENTY-THREE

At *Helena's* luxurious Knightsbridge flat, she was dressed, so she watched Amber get dressed. Helena decided to wear her slinky Jean Harlow ivory-coloured satin gown. It showed off her athletic body in all its glory. Her Italian features were a perfectly refined portrait of a woman who was not frail. Her family's money refined every practical skill she needed to preserve her identity and passion.

In Helena's fresh and feminine white, pink and blue bedroom, decorated with the finest Harrods had to offer, she took a look at Amber dressed in her Issey Miyake black and rust slinky trouser suit and her boots.

"Oh, Cherie! That is it, you look wonderful!" Helena picked up the lipstick and reapplied for her. "You just need a bag: my Dior with the pink scarf!" Amber wasn't sure. "It's perfect. To hide in plain sight without a trace of evidence!" Helena laughed and Amber drew her in and they kissed intimately.

"I would have bought tickets to see Donna beat the living hell out of Miriam." Amber froze for a few seconds and then she laughed out loud. "Punched her and threw food onto her." She gestured in a manner to indicate delight and insanity. "He discarded Miriam like all blood-sucking vamps deserve. Do you think he'll break-up with me if I tell him about us?"

"He lives with a gay man. He knows better. Also, he's cultivated a wonderful group of friends. Michael and his husband, David, have nothing but praise for him."

Anxiously, Amber said, "If I tell him about us, will he think I'm a liar or a fake? He's not homophobic. But I don't want him to turn on me."

"My instincts are good about men; they have to be, you know how much I detest them handling me."

Amber declared, "He's everything I never expected in a man."

They walked into the lavish Georgian style living room and found the bags from L'Occitane and took out the fragrances. Helena rolled her eyes and exhaled.

"Monique!"

A minute later, her maid arrived. Helena was tired of Monique since she found a boyfriend in London. Monique's blue dress did nothing for her and when she curtsied, something about her seemed obsequious, which annoyed Helena.

Helena told her in French, "I expect to see this apartment cleaned up when I get back and please make me, onion soup, without cheese. I want boiled eggs, get the gluten-free bread and mulled wine." Monique curtsied and left the room.

With incredulous delight, Amber said, "I'm trying to marry into a family where the son beats up my father and his mother beats up his girlfriend." They thought about it and burst out laughing.

"You're going beyond defying your dad. You're overturning him."

"Please don't say I'm turning into a Carrie Bradshaw bitch."

"I'd have stopped you before you became that absurd. Unlike her, you don't deny men their masculinity, you renounce misogyny. It started the night you stood up to your father and left his house to come here." Amber nodded. "You are fearless. *You* are courting Aaron now. Don't get the jitters. If he didn't love you, he'd ask for a sexual reward for being a feminist." Her sneer narrowed her eyes with utter contempt for men like that.

Amber told her, "He hasn't said how 'good *he* is' for keeping it in his pants."

"If he ever says that, tell me and I will go to his house and spit in his face."

Amber caressed her. "You would, wouldn't you."

"Pricks bring out the butch in me."

Amber took her by the shoulders and said, "I know!" and embraced Helena wholeheartedly.

"Do you know how much I—"

"Yes, I do. I love you even more than that." They simply stood there and absorbed time and claimed the moment.

"No-one is going to stop me from marrying him. What's it like for you, knowing I want to give him children?"

Helena braced herself. "I know we'll have to—stop. But that doesn't mean we have to separate." She came to tears so quickly it moved Amber. "There's more to life than secrets."

Amber said, "You defy classification: no 'Stem' or 'glamour dyke'. You're great. I mean Queen Elizabeth and Anne Boleyn amazing." Helena embraced her because she still saw the girl of twelve, she fell in love with years ago.

"We've always been a bit different. On Bankolé Island, I saw how you looked at Aaron."

"Is all this too much for you, darling? Should I get out of here?"

"No!" Helena covered her mouth and stared at her. "A man won't come between us."

Later, Helena told me how frightening that moment was, so I told her what it felt like when my first boyfriend dumped me.

"Aaron and his crowd are beautiful people; I saw that on the Island. I understand your attraction to him. He's sexually clandestine. He obviously desires women and yet I think he adores being desired by men. His love letters reveal an uncanny female sensual manliness. I totally understand your passion for him."

"You understand me as no one else does." Amber kissed her lovingly. "You understand I cannot commit adultery."

"Yes," Helena replied and took a few steps backwards. She called Monique and she came in shortly.

"Call for my car." Ten minutes later, Amber and Helena made their way down the stairs and out of the front door. Her chauffeur, who her father had hired to protect her, held the door of the white Rolls-Royce open and they got in. His countenance reminded you of Luca Brasi in *The Godfather*.

"Enrico, take her to *Galvin La Chapelle's* first and then we'll go to Mayfair." He got in, started the car and they made their way through Knightsbridge traffic.

"Papa is going to love David's husband, Michael. He is so full of Roman spirit and his daughter is fascinating. When I met her, she told me of her turmoil about Michael's divorce from her mother and his marriage to David. I'm taking them to Mortons and we might pop into Annabel's since it's on the other side of the Square."

"Enjoy tonight. Mine might be just as lively, Aaron told me *La Chapelle* is one of his favourite restaurants. And he said now we're 'Miriam-free', he has so much to tell me."

Helena said, "That has a hint of orange blossom to it."

Amber laughed and clapped, so both of them embraced which also brought a great smile to Enrico's face.

At nine o'clock, I walked with Helena through Mount Street Gardens Park in Mayfair out onto North Audley Street, heading for the cocktail bar. I told her. "I feel very humble that you're able to confide in me, Helena." 'The beautiful people' of Mayfair came and went around us.

"I think it's because you are honest. I mean, I am also fascinated by how you deal with Roy: loving him as you do—knowing he has such strong feelings for Aaron. They are lovers from time to time, yes?"

I felt like an acupuncture needle stuck me in a tender spot and I flinched. "Why do you think that?" The streets of Mayfair felt like nowhere else in London.

"My feelings for Amber reflect your feelings for Roy because he loves Aaron. If I am wrong, forgive me, but I only feel this energy for a man who is simpatico with me. My father has this quality, that is why he knows me as my mother and brothers do not. You ache with love as I do."

"Yes."

"They are lovers, sometimes?" Because of her Italian accent that sounded more like a statement than a question, but she was asking rather than stating. *I suddenly felt that Helena was working on me: that our friendship was handled more by her than me. I had to lie.*

"Roy doesn't tell me everything. He's shy and discreet; you must have seen."

"Yes, when he was on the Island, he avoided us all, staying with his boyfriend. But I sensed no romance when I saw them together. But Aaron is very demonstrative and his masculinity reminds me of Italian guy's machismo."

"Well, Roy broke up with Narj because he feels my love is better for him." Helena came to an abrupt halt and she yelled with joy. She sputtered to me in Italian, but I didn't understand a word of it.

She yelled, "Why aren't you dancing and screaming?"

I jumped up and down repeatedly and I must have looked like an overage infant having a tantrum. But even as I was trying to distract her and remove the thought of Roy and Aaron's sexual involvement, I was unexpectedly so glad that Roy dumped Narj. On top of that, Roy made me happy because he didn't need to be entertained as if he has ADD. I've watched him write and research stories and then sit with me and watch all 309 minutes of Bergman's *Fanny and Alexander*. He came to the apartment one Sunday and spent the day with me.

That was the first time I wished we lived together. I wanted to spend more Sundays like that. Do a bit of work, watch a film, stop for dinner and then go back and finish the film and talk about it when it was over.

Then out of nowhere, I had tears in my eyes and Helena put her hand on my face. "What is it, my friend?"

"I really love Roy. All I need is for something to happen to bring us together."

She was comforting me when Michael and Maria came up the street and he began shouting, 'Yes, yes, yes! The group is coming together'. Michael saw me and then stopped talking. Helena started nattering in Italian and the three of them really got going. Michael put his arm around me and walked me away from Maria and Helena.

"Eugene, what is it, my friend? Please, you tell me?"

I looked over my shoulder and walked faster to keep a distance between Helena and Maria. "I was talking about Roy because Helena twigged that there's something between him and Aaron..."

"She knows about the novel?" Michael asked, concerned.

I shook my head. "She's gay, too. So, she senses there's something between Aaron and Roy similar to Amber and her."

Flabbergasted, Michael asked, "She's lesbian with Amber?"

If he said that 'Martians are landing!', he couldn't have sounded more shocked.

We lengthened our stride and as we walked on, he shouted that we'd meet them at Mortons in Berkeley Square.

"All this intrigue, to write a book; is it helping you get Roy?"

"He's dumped Narj."

"Fantastico!" He put his arm over my shoulder. "Bring him to our house for a long weekend. You can make a man of him under my roof. Roy is weak; we can change him when he sees how married men who love each other behave."

"Even I don't know that properly."

"I learnt it from my husband," Michael happily replied.

"I want so much to be happy," I confessed, distraught and relieved to speak.

Once again, Michael's friendship alleviated my anxiety.

* * *

A few days later, Amber casually gestured and strolled around the John Madejski Garden at the V&A museum on the shiny summer's day where she worked. The red brick, bronze and grandeur of the garden area, with people sitting around the oval pool, contented with the exhibitions inside, but a little tired, cast a distinct atmosphere of bourgeois leisure because East Enders were rear visitors.

As always, Amber was beautifully dressed and Aaron was also dressed well. His curly mop-top haircut forced her to occasionally play with his curls, which he definitely liked. "...and this is why I love my job here. They are impressed with me so early in my post."

"Don't be afraid to share your ideas. Companies usually fire people with no ideas or inspiration. Your knowledge and passion for art are dazzling. Let them see that." She took his arm and they walked quietly for a time looking at their Victorian surroundings.

"Last night I cooked tonight's dinner. It's a Caribbean classic fish dish I think you'll like because of your taste for fish and salads. I even bought the DVD *Working Girl* so after we watch it, you can take it home with you since it's your favourite film."

"And do we have a double bill with your favourite film too?"

"It's a shared top spot of *Ted* and *Infernal Affairs* and I thought we should watch it on another night. Let me make this your night."

"I am going to return the compliment darling..."

"Babe, I'm reading the expensive comics you gifted me. That's plenty." He eyed her and his joy wrote itself large across his face and body.

"I promise you, when I'm yours, this..." she circled his face in mid-air with her index finger, "emotion will be the beginning of your climax." He definitely liked what she said. "Will Roy be there tonight?"

"No, he's got some press thing he's going to with Eugene."

"And how does your mother feel about the profiles we've given her?"

"She's studying them. She's also talking to my grandparents and her best friends, Cynthia and Lola. She's got the ten files."

"But is she excited? I want her to be as keen as I am. If you hadn't saved my life and I was selecting you from profiles, I'd have still picked you. Your views on Genet and Jean-Paul Sartre tell me how you choose to live. I never want you to settle for tradition over self-determination. I have only come to this realisation myself." He was going to answer her. "Oh, and then there was the day I saw you in swimwear on Bankolé Island." She added more, but in French, so she sounded as elegant as she looked. No other woman he could think of possessed such a tempting gaze.

They resumed their stroll. "I want you and Helena to conduct the penultimate screening of the guys mum chooses, because I don't fully understand their lifestyle. You and Helena are upper class, so you'll know fact from fiction."

"Helena will be happy to help. Since you introduced her to the Bankolés and Michael..."

"They're closer to Roy than me."

"And you both share your lives," she insisted, "like Helena and me. My friends are also hers. Anyway, darling; I am happy you asked for my help."

"This is exactly the kind of trust I didn't have with Miriam."

"That's because she's *only* a cunt." Aaron bust out laughing and lifted her in the air and put her down. Visitors in the garden looked over at them. "I just love you more and more." She took his arm and led him.

"Salope! Le jour ne viendra pas où je penserai avec mon vagin." Aaron thought it out and translated it in English. "Slut! The day won't come when you'll think with your vagina." She nodded. He kissed the back of her neck and they walked off.

CHAPTER TWENTY-FOUR

Driving to London Fields in Hackney, Roy made his way through traffic and listened to Aaron. "So, I don't even know what I'll be dealing with when I meet all of Amber's friends on Friday night. I'm taking time off work when I can't afford to…"

"Margot can manage everything…"

"Can she print up some money in the kitchen because that's what I'm gonna need before I ask Amber to marry me. I'm not a bitch that lives off her money? It was difficult enough I asked you to help and you did what you did for me."

"Brian gave me the money because he could afford it. Besides, we needed our home and you needed the business."

"Yeah, and what did you get for it?"

"Plenty."

"No, I got my business and our home." Roy drove through Kingsland High Street. The Greek restaurants, Turkish shops, Caribbean take away and Hipsters on the streets were ever-present. In the night light, it seemed the generation of over fifties had retired and given up the streets to the under thirties of European immigrants. There were also the 'white boyz' caught up in their best Hackney pose. Roy looked at everyone, while people crossed the street.

"I'm not in a financial position to get married." His mobile rang and Aaron took the call. "Mum, yeah, hi—no." He put the phone on speaker.

"Aaron, can you swing by because I'm here with your gran and I've decided on the seven guys I want to meet. Your dossier is incredibly detailed. Harold told me it's like reading a police investigation report."

"I'm in the car with Roy. We were heading home but—"

"Donna, I'm turning around and I'll be in Stokey in ten minutes. Can you rustle up some dinner?" Roy U-turned and headed up to Stoke Newington.

Donna said, "Roy, I'll tell mum and we'll have food ready when you guys get here."

"Donna, you're an angel, I soon come."

"And thanks for your notes about Pedro, Roy! And Aaron, text me Helena's number; I want to thank her for opening their house to us. Boys, I'm really excited about meeting these 'suitors'. Harold and Violet have their favourites, but I'm in charge of this! To hell with *Love Island*, this is so much classier!" When Donna laughed, Aaron and Roy joined in and high-fived as Roy drove to meet her.

* * *

We pulled up in front of a grand country house in Ascot and then Roy and Aaron got out, in their casual clothes and got their bags. Two servants took their other bags and Roy and Aaron followed behind them. Aaron and Roy looked like fish out of water because the grand English country home was a long way from Hackney. Aaron and Roy were met by the Butler. I drove off and at various points in the day, Roy WhatsApp me; providing lavish descriptions of the Georgian house and its luxurious interior. Roy took the place in his stride because his ex, Brian, had taken him to grand places in South America and the States some years earlier.

Brian's parents, JJ and Carlos knew lots of people and they had so much money Roy adjusted to it; however, the Georgian excess weighed on Aaron.

They were shown to their room: a large bedroom with two four-poster beds and elegant furniture. The 15-foot-high windows and its tapestry drapes, with a view into the gardens, were beyond words, according to Aaron. Roy could see Aaron was out of sorts and so he crossed the varnished floor to comfort him.

Aaron said, "I've got the suitors here for tomorrow and somehow it all seems so…snobbish. I mean, who the fuck am I? A guy from Hackney. This Jane Austen toff's Mansion is too bloody much. I know my place, so let's get out of here."

"You're Aaron Lorenzo Blackmon; and I made a pledge to your father to use my Jamaican strength and British aspiration to take care of you. I'm here."

"But—" He couldn't speak.

"Aaron, those suitors must be checked. We can't put Donna at risk. And Helena has offered her family's home to help. Let them be your friends."

"Cous, be my friend."

* * *

There was no way I could tell Eugene how panic-stricken Aaron became and as usual, that is when he turned to me for help. Aaron kissed me and we caught fire in seconds and locked the door! He tenderly begged me; in the way he always did. If only it was just about him being aroused and the feelings he instils in me, we could agree we occasionally had sex. He staggered my senses! He threw off his clothes and pulled off mine.

He said, 'show me again I'm Black like you, inside out'. I had him and the pornographic poetry of his every word told me what to do. He loves me. That's why he surrenders to me and the power and glory of him mean we didn't have to justify it.

* * *

Aaron and Roy walked into the primrose and bluebell coloured reception room where they were greeted by Massimo, Helena's father, his wife, and four sons. Then Helena and Amber entered the room. Amber's summer dress was beige, and Helena's summer dress was cream. They resembled the European elite because that was who they are. All the brothers and their wives had an air of indifference as they spoke in different languages, exchanging pleasantries. Aaron was properly dressed in a linen suit he bought a few years back, but it was a bit snug. Roy was well-dressed and he conjured up various images of the Black male as an erotic spectacle in contrast to the wealthy Europeans one sees in paintings.

Whereas the characters in *Downton Abbey* were country folk of British stock, Helena's father, Massimo, was a Jewish French Italian in his sixties. His industrial software empire had made him richer than Princes. As a *bella figura* devotee, he approached Helena with a trusting smile and his stout physique was imposing. His silver-grey hair and tanned face cast him in line as one of the 21st century's self-made noblemen. His survivor family mentality was the force behind his nature and temperament. Helena told me; nothing was more important to him than his family. And from his body language, his deep affection for his only daughter was obvious.

Aaron went to Amber and touched his cheek against hers. "This house, it's nice," he whispered. "It feels like we've entered *Dangerous Liaisons*." She caressed his face with one hand.

"It's only a building with things in it: you're the trophy my darling. It's why Massimo is dying to meet you. Helena and I told him you're wonderful." Amber took his hand and Roy gave her a lingering look. The family's attention was held, as Aaron and Amber stood slightly away from the others on the Persian rug. There were grand portraits above their heads of Massimo's relatives across generations.

Massimo approached Aaron and he stood to attention and took a breath. Massimo looked a bit like Vittorio De Sica. "Welcome to my home and my family. I am Massimo Carduluci! Aaron Rapchinski-Blackmon, correct?"

"Yes!" Aaron bowed his head. "Allow me to introduce my best friend, Roy Burton." Roy came forward and smiled, which pleased Massimo and his family.

"We are to be joined by some of my daughter and Amber's friends a bit later and then the suitors for your mother." Massimo laughed and clapped his hands! "When Helena told me what you are doing, it made an instant impression on me!" he said gesturing out like an opera singer. "I love unconventional people!" His voice brought forth scattered sounds of Europe from the past and present in Aaron's ears.

Massimo threw his arm over Aaron's shoulder and led him towards his wife, his sons and their wives, introducing each one by name and adding how many sons and daughters they had.

Massimo's four sons were clearly related to each other because they shared identical gestures. They emanated Italian pride and beauty. There wasn't an ugly husband or wife among them. When Massimo led Aaron back to his wife, Aaron could tell she looked confused. Massimo led him away towards a table with champagne glasses. "My wife has Alzheimer's. It's terrible for all of us, particularly her. Helena has become..." He strained his face. "She is everything to me, now she manages social things for me. I could never run the company without her."

"What type of work do you do?"

"We create and manufacture software. Apps for education, management in education and some playtime apps for children... for learning, you know."

"That's wonderful!"

"There are other companies out there, but our specialism in Jewish history and education is very strong, very..."

Massimo mentally searched for the word, so he asked his family the meaning of an Italian word and Amber said, "Inclusive, Uncle Massimo!"

He touched his temple and nodded. "Yes!" He patted Aaron's upper arm and then held his bicep. "Very good: you are not like these string-bean English boys; there is a real man inside you." His tone of voice was filled with joshing bon vivant.

He offered Aaron a glass of champagne, which Aaron accepted.

"Amber tells me your mother is a beautiful person. She has also confessed her love for you. Amber deserves happiness: congratulations on winning her heart. Her father and I are friends and I'm pleased to know he is impressed with you."

Aaron was hesitant because he didn't know how much Massimo knew about their fight. "I understand you called him out for a beating!" Massimo gasped with laughter!

Across the room, his family cast their eyes towards him, as he pulled himself upright and mentioned the fight between Aaron and Bernard as the cause for his outburst. The family nodded and then carried on talking. Roy escorted Helena to another side of the room and asked questions.

Massimo continued, "When Amber and Bernard told me about this, I said bravo! Amber needs a strong man, but very different from her father. *You* are different!" Aaron felt encouraged all at once.

"I dislike being managed. My father used to advise me; I loved his guidance. But I dislike outsiders trying to manage me." Massimo made a sound at the back of his throat.

On the other side of the room, Amber observed him with Massimo. Helena's eldest brother's wife, Candice, came over to her. The jewels around her neck and the vintage Givenchy canta-loupe pink cocktail dress said everything essential about her. "You look pleased with yourself, Amber. Well done! A real knight in armour; he's very handsome." Amber was not as rich as them but her style was pure elegance.

"He's not handsome," but she insisted that he was. "Aaron is a beautiful man.

He has a heart and he isn't afraid to show me. I don't envy any woman who's stuck with a knight in shiny armour." Helena's sister-in-law was definitely puzzled. Amber said, "Candice, a man in armour, locks us out and locks himself in. Really? A tin man without a heart, haven't you seen *The Wizard of Oz*?"

"No," she replied, looking at her flawless ten-carat diamond ring.

"Uncle Massimo! Why is it important to watch musicals?"

Massimo replied in Italian and then continued in English. "Because all of mankind's deepest desires are explored in opera and musicals," he began; recalling the summer in Nice, where Amber as an eighteen-year-old preciously 'enlightened them'.

But Aaron interjected. "And the greatest secrets and longings are revealed in the characters' songs," he concluded. Amber was so proud, so pleased and overjoyed that Aaron had taken note of a previous conversation they had all night.

She looked up to Aaron and her face beamed. She gave him a *frisson*, which brought out a smile in him that made him appear rock star sexy. Amber began to pick and fix his curly hair. Her hand fingered his big curls so lovingly, Helena felt genuinely helpless. According to Roy, it all felt like a sudden blackout.

A minute later, a young woman and her husband were brought into the room without any need for an introduction because they ran to each other, as Helena and Amber affectionately embraced her. Her husband went and shook Massimo's sons' hands. All of his sons knew they had legal and secular power over their wives but their wives governed their everyday lives. However, a female's breach of their authority could cost her almost everything.

Helena and Amber chuckled and cooed and then Amber took Nova to meet Aaron. Nova was a golden blonde who was the pride of her Belgian parent's lives because she had married well. Her parents were research doctors for a major international pharmaceutical firm.

"Aaron, this is Nova, she was the 'good girl' at school, we were the bad girls," Amber said and pulled Helena closer and the three 'girls' joyfully spoke to him at the same time.

"Are the others here yet?" Nova asked. Helena said no. "Good, we'll have time." Nova waved to everyone and went out into the gardens, taking glasses of champagne. Roy told me Aaron was overwhelmed by these wealthy Europeans.

Later on, Helena and Aaron walked through the gardens and past the tennis court. Massimo was engrossed in what Aaron was telling him. "...equal ops policies aren't being adhered to. Unemployment ruins men. A job is the substance of so many people's lives. That's why I don't want mum to have to deal with some guy's struggles. She's earned the right to be happy." Helena's respect for Aaron grew because she had met so many poseurs, but she told me he was so confident.

Massimo said, "I am sure I will like your mother when I meet her. I applaud Helena for inviting these suitors here. I can see through fakes and my family's business sense is sharp. I rely on Helena's judgment because she introduces me to ideas and opportunities. Especially now her mother is...less able." Roy said Massimo's adoration for Helena filled his spirit.

"Anything, Papa, anything you need." Helena's love for him was also undeniable. In the manicured gardens with its flowers and a tennis court, father and daughter looked casually grand.

"Pray, you have a daughter, Aaron. Girls are so much more life to a man than a son." Aaron patted Massimo's back and walked through the grounds. "When will you ask for Amber's hand?"

Aaron told Roy that he felt the shockwave that seemed to pass through Helena. Helena saw Amber across the way, so she excused herself, went to Amber, who escorted her towards the marquee where the family was frolicking inside.

"Helena and Amber are not like sisters; they are more like..." Massimo gave it serious consideration. "Imagine what women become when men are sent off to war. If Helena loses Amber to you because you refuse to give Amber a life of her own, it would be tragic. I explained this to Bernard. The girls must have a life, something like what we as men develop through business, sport, passions..."

"Passions?"

"With some men, it's Baccarat; for others its horses and Maserati's. You will know, of course, there some men who love women: expensive and erotic females who get into a man's blood and drain him."

Aaron quickly interjected, "I don't do that." Massimo stopped him.

"When a man has everything, including the extras and then he robs his wife of her life, this is dreadful. A woman cannot live under her husband's decree. I am not talking about feminism; I am referring to humanism..."

"Massimo, I've studied Simone de Beauvoir and Judith Butler..."

"We will talk more about this. But remember, in a man's world, we need each other and ladies need their girlfriends, to stay alive as women."

"I agree. I'd never stop Amber or any woman from sustaining her life through women they depend on."

"Clearly, you have brains and good breeding. Bernard told me Amber has become incensed." Massimo became melancholy then sanguine. "Amber has never fought her parents. Loving you has changed her." Aaron didn't equate honesty and kindness with millionaires but Massimo made him think.

"Thanks. I've been asking myself a lot of questions about our future." Aaron looked over his shoulder and weighed up the cost of speaking truthfully. "My way of life is nothing like this," he said, gesturing towards the stately grounds.

"Aaron. I have asked my sons before." Massimo stopped walking and the shadows on the marquee behind him showed people dancing, jumping about, moving while drinking as the band on drums, brass, woodwinds and violins played. There must have been fifty people inside and their signs of life were full of joy.

"Suppose you don't ask Amber to change, but instead *you* change. You adapt to a lifestyle Amber life and loves. Can you do that?" Massimo could see Aaron's mind sparking through his eyes. He took Aaron's hand. "Tomorrow; after we inspect the suitors, tell me then." Aaron nodded.

"Helena paid you a great compliment: that is why I open my house to you."

Curious, Aaron asked with a smile. "What did she say?"

"She told me that she likes you."

"Oh, nice." Aaron didn't know Helena well enough to understand the true meaning of what she said, but my respect towards Helena deepened. But now that Massimo met Aaron, he was less worried that Aaron would take control of Amber's life, as so many husbands do. Massimo told him to go and join the crowd inside the marquee. As he went forth, Helena waved at him as she approached her father and he told her about their conversation. Earlier, Helena called and asked me to come down. She said she'd send a car and I told her I'd be there.

***

At two o'clock in the morning, Amber got out of her bed and slipped in with Helena, under the sheets. She snuggled up close and Helena turned around and faced her. There were two replica pre-Raphaelite paintings at both ends of the spacious room that were illuminated by candles in glass-covered shields. On the west wall hung a replica of John Everett Millais' *Ophelia* and on the east wall hung Dante Gabriel Rossetti's, *Lady Lilith*. In the shadowy light, they loomed large in the room where the candlelight flickered on the taffeta curtains, the gilded decorations and an elaborate chandelier.

"There's nothing for you to worry about. Papa had a good talk with Aaron and Papa said some of the things I told him."

"Aaron hasn't asked to marry me, so we're dreaming and scheming for no reason."

"You must prepare yourself because he will ask." Helena embraced her, and Amber placed her lips between Helena's cleavage and began kissing her.

"Helena, I know this isn't easy for you." Helena pulled back and recalled the spirit that brought them together sexually for the first time when they were fifteen. Helena said, "In the past, I've found it easy to hate the boys your father introduced you to on our holidays, or when we'd go and visit his friends and there would be the Romeo for you to play Juliet."

"But I always told you it wouldn't work out because I loved you."

"I was so blinded by jealousy I could only think of how to injure them." Amber giggled and pulled Helena close to her.

"You won't hurt Aaron, will you?"

"Never."

"Remember the letter Aaron sent, explaining how he'd pioneer employability programs for Black guys and SMB firms. Every boy dad has presented, has only told me how he's going to run my life to fulfil his ego. I told Aaron I want to establish a Jewish Modern

Arts Gallery and he asked how he can help." She became serious and clearly determined.

Helena said, "You're not who you once were."

"What am I now?" Amber asked her, pushing back Helena's hair.

"Audacious."

"Tomorrow, the suitors will be here."

"This is also your chance to be sure you can live with him. 99% of men lie, so find out if they want to put you on this wish list." Amber took Helena's hands. "Expect to see Carmen, Scarlet O'Hara and other Femme Fatales. I will mark their words and judge them. Donna's happiness is important to me too."

"Do you remember at school, when you played Anne Boleyn and Elizabeth? And the time we went to the party as Wonder Woman and Cat Woman. Those boys were incandescent and scared of us. You *can* be amazing."

"I want Aaron and Donna to see I have learnt from great women how to become la nouvelle femme. I will not ever become pretty ugly because my face is good and my mind is horrid."

"Mio caro, I watched you stand up to your father."

"Oui. Maintenant je me sens sexy." They gazed and slowly reached for each other and made sensational love.

The only reason Helena told me this at the *Oscar Wilde Lounge* was that she needed to prove she wasn't pathetic. In exchange I confessed intimate facts about Roy and me. Only an analyst could tell me why I told a woman about the sex and love I shared with a man. Nonetheless, I felt intensely for Helena.

The day I arrived, I watched Aaron and Roy eye Amber and Helena, seated beside the Carduluci family in the lavish drawing-room. The atmosphere was alive with anticipation about the suitors. I also sensed people wanted to be amused and diverted. The hazy warm sunlight lit and shaded the drawing-room and the family were like something out of Luchino Visconti's period drama films. They all looked pampered and privileged because they behaved like they were regal, when in fact they were a 20th century wealthy family, but according to Helena her father's family had a distinguished name.

Some of Amber and Helena's school friends who had close ties to the family were seated among them with their boyfriends. They were a clan of approximately twenty people. I had been friends with the Bankolé De Farenzinos long enough to know what a wealthy family looked like and I definitely knew the Carduluci family were establishing an Italian Jewish dynasty. The entire image of the family was offset by Helena and Amber because they were distinctly post-feminist chic. Their manner gave them an edge that none of the other people had. Not only did they embody sexual power, particularly that day, but they were women who worked and it gave them a distinctive persona, unlike the other married women in the family who didn't work.

Over in the corner of the lavish drawing room, a woman played the harp and a man played the Steinway grand piano. They filled the silence with Claude Debussy's compositions and as they played *Clair De Lune*, it wasn't obtrusive. Aaron got up and faced the Carduluci family. In a navy-blue suit from his tailors in Shoreditch, a white cotton shirt, and suede loafers, he was full of confidence.

"I'll make this quick. These men who claim to be fair and noble might be trying to trick my mum. Massimo told me about your mum. Suppose someone was trying to take advantage of her and you were all that stood between her safety and her mistreatment. That's how I feel." I noticed how Aaron got to them immediately. Their faces suddenly looked disturbed and conflicted: every last one of them.

"I am not posh, but you are. I have a Masters degree and my own business.

I'm smart enough to know when I need help. I don't know what Fakakta habits these guys have, so help me separate the mensch from the meshuggenehs."

He eyed everyone in the room. "I'm relying on your judgment as amazing Jews to tell me if any of these schmucks are trying to shtup my mother." Everyone laughed. So, like a good stand-up, Aaron gave them time to recover.

"My mum's happiness depends on your know-how and my instincts. Help me." Money and class set them apart but his speech locked them into him.

"Observed them. Score them out of 10 on everything you see and sense. Check your mobiles now. I've put you all into a WhatsApp Group so we will all be alert of everything when you text or voice message." They all looked and found it. "Mobiles are so ubiquitous these days, they're innocuous. These guys will never know you're rating them."

Helena made a quick call on her mobile and soon the drawing-room doors opened. "Fellas!" Aaron said. They all looked at him. "Thank you." Her family shifted in all directions and some servants came in and an exchange of looks passed between Helena and Amber and then the rest of her family.

Servants brought the men in one after the other. The family watched as the first man, Yves entered and stood his ground. He was a very well-tailored man, with good looks and an Alain Delon air about him. Then came a slightly stooped, older man, Joshua, who was done up in his best suit. He looked rather like Harvey Keitel. He was followed by Pedro, a strapping Black guy any woman would give her panties to. He oozed cool charm in a white suit and black shirt, which made his brown face gleam with a smile. I saw that the family glanced between each other.

Behind him was George, a stockbroker. He looked like he was born in a Savile Row suit and grew up in a London penthouse. He was a bit older than the others, but clearly, money kept him well. His bright blue eyes and light tan reinforced the belief he only lived in Mayfair and Antibes. I spotted Helena's sisters exchanging comments about him. George reminded me too much of Jeremy Irons who I didn't like much.

Behind him came Omar, a rather startling man, dressed in loud designer regalia. He was from the Democratic Republic of the Congo: actually, let me just say it—he was a 'Congo Dandy'. I glanced at Roy and he looked like he was in shock! I looked around the room and the sight of people's faces showed how gobsmacked they were. Aaron looked ready to get off his arse and fling the man out of the room.

Another man, Oliver, was brought in. He looked North African. But I lost focus because I couldn't look away from Omar since he was a walking disaster. He was possibly five shades darker than me and his pearly whites and gold teeth could blind a dentist!

The final man, Estevao, was led in. Roy hadn't told me anything about him. He only mentioned Pedro because he's the bloke Roy picked as the most likely to impress Donna. Estevao was a Julio Iglesias look-alike, but I felt nothing radiate from him.

Standing in front of everyone, the seven men looked at us all. Aaron stood up and told them, "You've been chosen out of 100 contenders. You've written essays, gone through psychometrics, accepted a criminal background inspection, health checks, personal references; and I'm currently waiting for credit check reports, so don't get too comfortable if you're a broke bitch."

The men looked perturbed, except for Joseph, Yves and Pedro. "The lady in question will be here tomorrow. Over the weekend, we want to get to know you and we'll end the weekend with a game of cricket at the Solomon Bankolé Sports Ground."

Omar said: "Yes baby!" and Aaron eyeballed him violently. Aaron clocked him and the look on his face hovered between rage and distress.

CHAPTER TWENTY-FIVE

Amber strode into Massimo's Regency *Salon* in an ivory-coloured, silk strapless gown that was tied at the waist with a red silk sash that fell to the hem. Her skin, make-up and hair cast a dramatic contrast to the simplicity of the gown and her red shoes. She had a fan in her left hand and used it to punctuate things she said.

Aaron was delighted by the sight of her because once again he was seeing her differently. He had on a tux, as did the other men who followed them into the *Salon*. Roy, on the other hand, had on a white dinner jacket, black bowtie and silk black evening trousers. Walking in, Roy admired the three ornate chandeliers that hung from the high turquoise ceiling in the vast and sumptuous *Salon*.

Yves, one of the suave suitors and a strong contender for Donna, escorted Amber into the *Salon* as she replied, "What kind of woman am I; you ask?" She strode across the *Salon* like a theatrical star. "I'm a bohemian. I live to cultivate experiences that will transform my life and inspire my husband!"

Yves worked for Air France as an IT Analyst. He claimed to love life's artistic possibilities, but he was frustrated with the life he was living and wanted to meet a woman who would awaken him from his sleepwalking existence.

Yves said, "Today, there are not really bohemian's as we have come to understand them in France; since 1830. Are you prepared to starve for the love of Art?" he asked Amber. Helena told me the family knew Amber could show off.

Amber replied, "Remember, meaning evolves, for heaven's sake; haven't you read Roland Barthes? Don't you think Baudelaire or Gramsci would contest that your emphatic argument is in itself the ultimate testament to bourgeois hegemony?"

"I think he would be more generous and allow me an opinion," Yves, replied. Aaron watched Amber navigate the conversation and he was mesmerised by her rhetoric and command: as well as the playful tone in her accent.

Amber stood back and poked Yves in the chest with her fan. "Nonsense! Between *La Traviata* and *Carmen*, which do you prefer?" she asked accusingly.

"*La Traviata*," Yves replied. Amber pointed to another suitor, Joshua; the solicitor who specialised in real estate contracts. He was not the most handsome fellow, but his romantic compassion in all of the test questions scored high in his compatibility with Donna.

In the background, the whispers and glances created what I can only call a thrilling atmosphere of complicity and exclusion. It felt like the husbands and wives finally found the amusement they'd been seeking for ages. "I am not an expert on opera," he replied. When he adjusted his tux, Aaron saw liver spots on the back of his hand. Oliver, who looked like he was dressed for an award ceremony, pushed his way into the conversation.

"Is Donna a devotee of opera? I'd take her anywhere to see *La Bohème*." Oliver looked vaguely like Terence Stamp in middle age.

Roy examined Oliver and leaned in and told Aaron, "Cocksucker." Aaron turned towards him, startled. "Him?" Aaron covered his mouth. Roy whispered, "If he's straight, then so am I."

Amber began singing *Glitter and be Gay* from Bernstein's *Candide*. Her coloratura voice and timing were good. Added to that, was her acting out the false destitution of the maiden. The family was perplexed by an element of Amber's character they had not perceived. Amber was flirtatious, silly, knowing and shameless all at once. For eight minutes, she owned everyone watching her. I saw Bernard and Massimo study her, unfamiliar with their beloved girl. Her style made Lady Gaga look absurd. Everyone in the *Salon* was captivated by Amber's voice and sinuous body, covered by her exquisite dress. Massimo's sons only thought of her as Helena's nice school friend, but watching her vocal coloratura vamp, I later discovered they considered her a tantalising minx.

When Amber stopped singing, Pedro asked, "Do you live the life of a bohemian, without any sense of judgment?" Amber looked at him closely and to an even greater extent, Yves was beguiled by her.

Pedro, the brown skin handsome man from Bermuda, was entirely at ease in his own skin. Some of the suitors were trying their best to make a good impression on Amber and Helena because Amber led them to believe, without her recommendation; they didn't stand a chance with Donna. For reasons of their own, some of the other suitors were happy to keep each other company; and gorge themselves. So, they ate and drank as much as they could.

Amber told everyone, "I believe the 21st century offers us lifestyle choices. I choose to live with my own style." Her finishing school elegance served her well.

Suddenly, Amber's cadence took on an English tone. "Haven't we all learnt from the 'Bloomsbury set'? I find it impossible to ignore the role of the imagination in English life. Paris and Italy say so much about Art, but when it comes to rebels who celebrate their identity; give me London in the sixties and Britain between the wars: such an inspiration! Don't you think so, Omar?" Amber stopped in her track and posed.

People turned to Omar, but everyone kept their distance from him. Aaron and Roy were still in shock at the sight of Omar because they both pegged him as a 'Congo Dandy'. Omar was dressed in a tangerine bright three-piece suit, with patent leather white shoes and gold buckle. He sported flowers in his lapel next to his sunshine yellow tie and white shirt. His hair gleamed with a gel that shaped his hair into a pompadour style. Massimo had seen too much of the world to be shocked, so he was surprised that he *was* stunned by Omar's poor taste. To some, Omar stood out in the room like a Vampire scorched by the sun. To Roy, Omar looked like people had dressed him up as some kind of figure, native islanders planned to sacrifice on a midnight pyre.

I looked around and I saw just about everyone texting secretly as though we were in a *Mission Impossible* environment and we were keeping tabs on live action. Because none of the photographs in his profile indicated who he really was, Aaron looked horrified. Consequently, Amber and Helena's friends and family took their lead from Aaron and watched Omar in stunned silence. I thought he looked wretched. I turned to the side and checked my phone but turned back to him.

Omar told Amber. "In Anglo-American countries, you guys don't really know what it is to be bohemian. In Africa, we are all bohemians. We cannot be decadent artists. Poverty is real." He was a handsome fellow, but his clothes were unsightly.

Amber said, "You really should leave; you're hurting my eyes. You're much too ridiculous for me to speak to. The lady I represent wants to meet a gentleman, not a clown, look at you. I'm close to laughing in your face!" Her accent was twice as damning as her words.

Omar told her, "Watch your mouth before I slap you!" Helena lunged forward and tore her fingers across his face, which left him bleeding. Her eyes were incandescent with rage. Her brothers took note, their wives took a step back and her father moved forwards.

Omar yelled, "Bitch, you're crazy!" with aggressive gestures flying. Helena's four brothers charged forward ready to tear him asunder. The stomping sound of their feet sent a shockwave through me!

Massimo told him, "Since you don't have your own transport, I can have my sons put you in a wheelchair if you want." Helena's youngest brother swore at Omar in Italian and his elder brother made a violent gesture at him. Massimo pointed at the door, but Omar stood his ground with pure hatred in his eyes towards Helena.

Amber said, "Take your eyes off her, you worthless dog." He glared at Amber now. "Would you like to live in poverty from now on? My father and I can arrange it." All of the suitors were clearly surprised by Amber but Yves' eyes were filled with disdain towards Omar. I heard a number of mobiles buzz. I then saw that Bernard was excited by the sight of his fearless daughter.

As though Amber heard someone call out to her, she looked among the guests. "Ruin him? Is that what someone said? Get me a phone." Omar shifted and Amber gave him the most contemptible look. "My friend at the British Home Office is going to be interested in you." She fanned him as if he smelt. If someone called me a poof I couldn't have been more insulted than the gesture she made.

"And what would your government find if they raided your office?"

If this was the naïve girl I first met, then something had gotten in her blood or Roy had failed to tell me a lot about her. Amber told Omar, "If you get out of my sight, I'll spare you." Bernard watched her triumphantly defeat Omar, as he turned and walked out quickly.

People were still looking at Amber and the back of Omar when she said, "Uncle Massimo. Yves tells us he's a wine connoisseur," which was all Massimo needed to hear before he escorted Yves over to the bar and forced him to taste five different wines.

Massimo expected a loquacious response and he got it. Yves positively shone and Helena brought over German, French, and Spanish friends of her father's and kept them talking.

Helena's ability to manage people was nothing short of 'natural'. She did everything in a spontaneous flurry. Considering what she told me about her work, this woman wasn't 'queer', she was unusual.

Amber surreptitiously told Aaron and Roy. "These suitors, who claim to be 'important', believe me, Helena and my Uncle Massimo will make rubbish of them if they are liars, then we'll know for sure who to introduce to your mother, darling." Bernard approached the three of them with his sexy mistress, who modelled herself on Bardot. Bernard said, "Miss Dalio, this is Aaron, Roy; and my daughter you already know. Amber, please give me a minute."

Amber leaned in and said, "One down, a few to go; excuse me." She left with her father and he grabbed two glasses of champagne from a footman and moved to a corner of the room and spoke in their native language. When I met Helena, later on, she told me the substance of their conversation.

Bernard said, "I think I've lost valuable time away from you. I am proud of the way you're conducting yourself. It is not simply that you are behaving like a strongminded adult. You've become a woman and I haven't realised it until now."

"Let's meet for lunch. Call me and we'll agree a day that's best for you."

"Are you so busy—"

She interrupted him. "Yes, I'm a curator. I'm at the V&A. I enjoy my work." Amber paused long enough to reveal her pride. "My schedule demands my time: but I'll make time for you."

"Are you helping Aaron, or is he helping you?"

"When people care for each other, there's no distinction," she replied in English. "I can tell you this. The day he asks me to marry him; you'll be the first to know. If he doesn't ask me: I'll never marry any man." The smile fell from her lips and her eyes were vehement, which clearly made him cautious.

"Your beau and I had a contretemps. He fought like a man and I like him. But you've inherited your mother's most exasperating trait: stubborn." Amber half smiled, knowing it was true and flicked her fan open.

"Let's hope that's the only failing of hers I have." She hit him on the arm with her fan. "Like you, I intend to live. Not as convention would dictate."

"I live according to many conventions."

"Yes, Miss Dalio proves that. Oh! I don't disapprove. Morality is for people who have nothing else. Because of you, I have embraced the life of a bohemian."

"Me?"

"Yes, Papa. You do not care about the consequences of your choices. You live to gratify masculine privilege. I don't blame you. Mother was foolish enough not to ask for anything; she wanted to be a wife. I am going to be more than that." She adjusted her dress. "If you want to continue this conversation, meet me in the morning for tennis after breakfast. *Don't* bring Miss Dalio." Amber turned and walked towards everyone.

One hour later, Amber was in Massimo's art gallery as he escorted Oliver, Yves and Pedro from painting to painting. Simply put, the room was opulent in a grand manner. Massimo said, "Some of these are mine and others are replicas, but I love them so. It's why I've bought replicas." He looked at them and Yves glanced around.

Oliver said, "The Pre-Raphaelites are all copies, aren't they?"

"Why do you say that?" Massimo asked, standing imposingly.

Pedro stepped forward. "I think you spend your money on more than things of the past. Your company has a market share on Education apps that are giving at least four corporations a run for its money. I know someone that works for that bloody awful American apps firm, newly based in the UK. But Carduluci International has branched out from education into leisure for pleasure, women's interests."

"Impressive, Pedro!" Massimo declared. "That is correct. The women's business is run by my daughter. She is a genius of invention and ideas."

Pedro replied and as he did, we noticed that he was relaxed and debonair. "My daughter, Rochelle, recently took me out. She uses your apps for so many things." Helena bowed her head. "If I may make a suggestion?" Aaron, Roy, and Amber listened to him. "Try to come up with something that helps women calm their nerves after work. Something that makes them feel gainful rather than spent. Rochelle and her friends are so wound-up and frantic after they get out of the office." Not only did he have a friendly voice, but he was also sexy in that President Obama, nonchalant manner.

Helena went and took his hand. "Sit next to me at dinner, we can talk."

Oliver said to Amber, "*You* should like the Pre-Raphaelites; they were very bohemian."

Roy confidentially told Aaron, "I think he'll be more like a 'girlfriend' to Donna."

"Yes, I'm seeing all the signs of a Queen, rather than a King," Aaron replied.

"I'll tell him something about my sex life later on. If I'm right, he'll want to know more. If he stops me, then I'll know at least he's on your team."

"Ick, I don't want him on my team," Aaron said. "Now that I see him, I know his voice will give mum the creeps. He sounds like a drag queen imitating a man."

"Anyone ever tell you, you're a real bitch at times?"

"Yes—you." Roy laughed without restraint. Amber turned around and Aaron pointed at Roy to exonerate himself and her smile clearly warmed him.

She turned back to Oliver and said, "The Pre-Raphaelites were very permissive."

"That is putting it discreetly," Massimo stated. "Rossetti and Morris shared his wife. And of course, the Bloomsbury set shared each other. Didn't Virginia Woolf have a husband and a girlfriend? And her sister's daughter wed her father's ex-boy-friend." Massimo's Italian grandeur made light of the statement.

Oliver delighted in saying, "Oh yes, the Bloomsbury crowd were a circle, who lived in London's Squares and loved in triangles." Oliver looked gleeful in his Aquascutum finery.

Oliver swayed as he walked through the gallery. He was highly educated and worked at a Russell Group university as a Business Development Gift Director, which Aaron knew was a job raising money for the university. On paper, he liked many of the things Donna loved. But now Aaron saw him, he could not imagine Donna kissing him and he didn't want him in the family.

Joshua, the avuncular guy who acted older than his age, was totally wrong, Aaron thought. Donna wouldn't go for him no matter how loyal and devoted he was.

Yves said, "The Bloomsbury set, sound more French than English. The Left Bank to this day is filled with Artists in a state of moral indecision. Brits are very set in their ways." There was no denying the Frenchman's charm.

"No, they're not," Amber playfully said. "In Hackney— some hipsters are in a quandary for life, far beyond life in the demi-monde, or post-war Existentialist!"

Pedro concurred, "This is true. Britain frequently produces subcultures that unite this country that was once racially divided. So, the Two-Tone movement, Rave Culture and Punk bring together Black and white people who overturn the idea of white separatism."

"How do you know so much about it?" Yves asked aggressively.

"Because Pépé, I served in the British Arms Forces. And if you want to learn how and what Britain really thinks of you, do a stint in the Royal Navy." Roy elbowed Aaron and they gestured comically at what they perceived as duelling cavaliers.

Roy whispered, "Some of the women in my office would finger themselves dreaming about Yves."

"Reckon he's a bit of a 'goer', yeah?"

"What is this, a *Monty Python* sketch? Cool your jets, mate." Aaron bumped into him and Roy bumped him back. They were larking about like a couple of lads. Massimo caught sight and stepped back into the room to speak to them.

"This is not a fun time before football," Massimo scolded. "Amber is using a series of very cleverly considered questions to trip or keep them. Pay attention, she is working hard for you."

Roy said, "Sorry, sometimes he sends me into a spin. He's always been an idiot."

"It's OK," Massimo said. "If you want my opinion, Pedro has perceptiveness and ease. Everything from Yves is spoken to make an impression."

"On What's App, George is the top man," Aaron said and Massimo nodded his head and grunted.

The rest of the evening was filled with an atmosphere of competition and testosterone between Pedro, Yves, and George. They threw hostile looks between each other like X-Men with supernatural powers.

Later that evening, when the house was still, I walked through the gardens and caught sight of the three of them in separate locations discussing how much they fancied Donna, and why each of them were ready to share their live with her.

* * *

In the morning, Roy made his way to my room and came in. I was awake and dictating events of the night before into my mobile. The house belonged to another century, so my green room was as large as any other guest room in the house and just as well furnished.

Roy headed towards me in his loose black silk pyjamas. "Fuck *Downton Abbey*, this place is real!" He dashed across the room and jumped onto the bed. He tickled me and I was a fidgeting mess. He got under the covers and kissed me; then emerged from the bedclothes with a cheeky grin.

"I kept my eyes on you," Roy said, "moving in the background. How did you get an invitation?"

"Helena sent a car for me. Watching Amber and Aaron together is tough for her. She has friends, but—get this. I'm her first man friend. She told me men are revolting pricks. But we've become friends because respect means something."

"That's wonderful! Glad good things are coming out of this. What did you make of Amber last night?"

He sat back and stared at me. "She is polymorphous and fascinating."

"Who knew she was such a chameleon? That dress! And the fan; mixing different languages and presenting that debutante verses woman-of-the-world persona to perfection. Aaron was astonished. And Amber and Helena definitely eliminated the wrong man."

I said, "This house is the perfect stage for her. This is who they are, how they live."

"It's not how Aaron lives. He's a bit intimidated by it all. When he gets nervous, I have to talk him through it."

"How is he now?"

"Solid." He kissed me. "And how are you, my man?"

"Thrilled to be here—this house! Helena told me Massimo spent millions redecorating it. A Jewish palace in the heart of the Goy-land, instead of England he calls it."

"I've seen better." I jumped onto him and pinned him down.

"Where?"

"Brian's dads' place in Seychelles."

"I can't offer you anything like that, can I."

"No, but whenever I'm with you, I always discover something. Wealth can be boring. It didn't keep Brian and me together. Amber's worth more than anything in this house and I'll tell you why," he said gleefully.

"I'm listening."

"She doesn't expect to be waited on hand and foot like some bitch."

"Aaron respects that?"

"He'd never live off somebody else's money." He suddenly fell silent.

I wondered what occurred to him or if he was lying to me, or worse—himself.

"Anyway, I just came for a catch-up.

I said. "You should know. I can't keep spying on my friends. It's disgusting."

He moved closer and caressed me. "You're doing something very important. You're documenting how we're defending a woman who is greater than my mother and her son who I made a promise to his father to protect."

"I'm invading their privacy. And speculating their thoughts and ideas with my fiction."

"When you write, you're inside my head from everything I tell you. Your fiction is better than my truth. We have an amazing future together."

Bloody hell, is he telling me what I think he is?

I took hold of him and made love to him in that grand room and all its splendour.

CHAPTER TWENTY-SIX

Aaron suggested a day of sport that would expose any lies the men may have put down in their application concerning their prowess. Roy told me about it and I suggested they invite the Bankolé-De Farenzinos because between them, they'd double-check the suitors, identify if they were fakes and advise Donna if needed. Just outside of Braintree, Solly and David had worked together to build a sports ground for teenagers. It was a costly venture that brought them both national praise because of the hi-tech set-up and the cultivated open fields sports ground.

The men's changing room was abuzz with broken conversations between Aaron and Roy talking to Solomon, Solly, David and Michael. Massimo's sons were excited to have the Bankolé's in their entourage. Every one of Massimo's sons admired Solly because of his football skills and Massimo was fascinated by David's husband. All of Donna's suitors considered it a special day to be able to play cricket with the rich and famous. The wooden benches and pinewood lockers bore the words: *"If money builds things, let people build character through good sportsmanship." David and Solomon Bankolé Jr.*

Pedro found it easy to talk to Solly. He told him about Bermuda and the popularity of cricket and the status Solly had in the minds of the youth in his home country. That was principally based on the fact that Solly was an international English football player, bought by a Brazilian club, where he shone as a striker who made the team stars on the global stage.

In the far corner of the changing room, Aaron saw Oliver sneak a peek at Roy when he took his pants off to get his protective cricket gear on. Roy didn't see it, but Yves saw that Aaron clocked it.

"Lances and horses might be next; to show our love for a lady!" Oliver said.

"For this lady, I'd get on that horse," George the stockbroker replied. "Her messages to me were lovely. She's incredibly beautiful."

Estevao replied. "Her letter to me confirms we are like-minded. I've met many foolish women. But Donna is a lady." From the look of both men, they didn't misrepresent themselves when they claimed they played squash in Maida Vale and weekend five-a-side football in Blackheath. They were healthy looking fit men in their fifties.

Michael struggled to fit into his 'protective box'. When Massimo saw the build on him, he told Michael, "Be careful you don't get your 'leg before wicket'." Michael answered him in Italian and both men laughed vociferously. In fact, all the men were in hysterics because of the jocular mood that prevailed.

Outside on the cricket ground, everything looked tranquil and ever so English. It was a green and gold day with bon vivant all around. Amber, Helena's her sisters-in-law, Candice, Lola and Cynthia mingled together on the green. Solly's club manager and the groundsmen could barely take their eyes off the women because they represented so many different kinds of European beauties. I was walking in the background, but Helena dashed over to me.

Massimo hired staff to cater and attend and so the preparation and visitors for the day's match all seemed rather grand to the Brummie club manager. Helena told Aaron the night before that, although her sisters looked ideal because the family network helped them to stay happy and healthy; she had next to nothing to talk to them about. Their conversations focused on their children, shopping, and their husbands; subsequently, Helena's relationships with her sisters-in-law were vapid.

Solly's wife, Alice, told Helena, "This cricket ground is a gift to London boys from our family." She went on to explain the founding principles of helping people overcome their dependency on mobile devices, by interacting with each other. Solly and his staff wanted kids to learn about each other's different cultures and bring inclusivity to communities across the counties. Amber became aware of how devoted Alice was to Solly and it made her think of the inter-dependence of marriage.

The array of fashion Helena's family wore was noticeable, that's why I was aware that Amber and Helena exhibited female Dandy attire. I'd say Amber drew on the persona of Diane Keaton and Helena championed Katherine Hepburn's style. Donna spent half the morning with Amber and Helena and they helped her dress to meet the men she was going to date.

As Helena walked me around the edges of the green, away from people, she told me, "Today I want you to meet my father. Yesterday was so mad..."

"I thought you both managed the suitors brilliantly. Not to mention how great you looked."

"This morning we gave Donna all the advice we know about fashion for this occasion. The clothes should make the statement and the woman should make the conversation."

I liked Helena more and more each time we met.

"I love the way you put things."

Smiling wonderfully, she said to me, "You see, this is why you fascinate me. You appreciate things. And you don't say it because you want to take me to bed."

"Please! I'm an old-fashioned, respectable gay man." She pulled me to her side and rubbed my shoulder.

"We got Donna a Giorgio Armani classic and a Vivienne Westwood vintage coat. I will get her now. You'll see how well she looks. Amber is obsessed with getting Donna to see she's resourceful, the way a good daughter-in-law should be. I haven't seen her fuss like this—ever! Certainly not with her mother. They are not simpatico. Amber wants so much for Donna to forget Miriam and want her."

"How can anyone refuse kindness when it's offered without conditions?"

"My father is going to like you so much. You speak the same language."

"Well, let the games begin. How do I look?"

"Young!" I opened my arms and Helena came to me.

* * *

Twenty minutes later, Amber and Helena escorted Donna onto the cricket field. Amber bought her a brown Hermes handbag and soft leather gloves. Donna's hair and make-up made her look very different. She appeared rather stately than friendly. Dressed as she was, Donna felt different about herself. She mentioned it but she didn't say exactly how. I knew staff at Condé Nast and Donna looked like one of the ladies that appear in their magazines.

The men were all brought to meet Donna and they lit up! Each one of them looked at her and whatever was going through their minds wrote itself in big smiles on their faces. Upright shoulders. Masculine grace in their cricket uniforms, greetings in several languages, and a bow from Yves. They went off to play and Donna was escorted away by Amber to sit in the front row to watch.

All of Helena's family and some of Amber's friends sat in the rows behind them.

Helena's staff at her father's firm, created an app that Amber downloaded onto Donna's iPad that showed the status and complete background on each man. From their birth certificate to their tax returns, along with their psychometrics evaluations, Donna could access their lives at the touch on a link. Bernard came over to Donna as the men were preparing to start the match. He looked casually elegant in a sports coat, with cravat, shirt and tailored slacks.

He told Donna, "We have come a long way since before at the restaurant. I hope today proves to be the start of something good for you." Donna had every reason to be happy, so she thanked him.

"We have to try harder, no? I believe your son is perfect for my daughter. Can we talk about that soon?" He sounded very French and his voice smoothed its way through her ears.

Donna asked, "What changed your mind about Aaron?"

Bernard said proudly, "She looks beautiful, no? She loves him. You are a woman who understands love. Let's talk about their marriage." His joyful smile made Donna realised he was good-looking, even though he wasn't her kind of guy.

"Call me." Donna took a card from her handbag and gave it to him.

"So English: ladies who give cards for business meetings. Amber has adopted the custom. Maybe she will become more English with a bit of a cha-cha because of your son." He gestured and left. Donna saw him head towards Miss Dalio. He fussed about and asked Miss Dalio to wait a moment and she pouted and went over to the Carduluci sisters.

Bernard rushed back to Donna and said, "Please, you give me a minute, very quick."

Donna nodded and they walked back into the clear green area. "I heard about the betrayal of Miriam. I have none of those racial ideas. You must know that."

"I'm glad you've told me, Bernard. My husband was a proud and great father. Aaron learnt a lot from both of us."

"I know this now."

With a yielding heart, Donna asked. "What changed your mind?"

"My daughter: I've never seen her so magnificent. A man's love can do this." When Donna recounted the exchange to Aaron that evening, she confessed she had judged him too quickly.

Bernard added, "You look completely wonderful today! Like a movie star at Deauville."

Donna accepted the compliment and Bernard bowed and left. Donna took the iPad out of her bag and checked the profiles. She became so engrossed; she was startled when Aaron came up to her. He looked dashing in his cricket whites.

"Mum—you look great."

"Do you think my hair and make-up make me look like I'm trying too hard? I wanted to go to Tony and Lola but the girls said try something unfamiliar?"

"You look very VIP." They took a seat and she slipped her coat over the back of the chair and sat elegantly and then took a pair of binoculars out of her bag.

"Amber told me to see and not be seen until I'm ready. Sweetheart, I had no idea she is this lovely." Donna looked around. "Fucking hell, they're in the money though, aren't they? That house!" He nodded vigorously and attempted to speak, but he knew she wanted to say more.

"In Helena's bedroom, they've got art on the wall, must be worth millions. She showed me lots of scarves that she 'keeps in her chiffonier'. I didn't know what the fuck that was until she took me over to this antique chest-of-drawers thing. Beautiful! She has a room where she stores her 'clothes of the past'. I was like—I give mine to a charity shop. She buys Amber loads of clothes, all because—get this! 'She'd rather *wear the money* than keep it in a vault'. Besides, she tells me, "*I don't have to think about investments until I'm thirty-five.*"

Donna rolled her eyes. "She and Amber make Miriam seem cheap. Amber asked me what you were like when you were in love with other girls. I told her she's the only one you've really loved."

"She's gorgeous, isn't she. I've never seen her badly dressed. And that accent and the way she uses language, even when she's speaking English."

"You look wonderful. And here you are courting without bonking. I knew it would take one hell of a girl to change you."

"Amber's polysemic!"

"What's that mean?"

"That she's gorgeous because there are so many facets and reading to her. Listen; are you ready to see these guys?" Donna nodded.

I approached them and Donna said, "I love the new TV series, Eugene. Roy came over and he made me watch it. Glad I did, really good. And I understand you've become friends with Helena and her family."

I said, "Yes. You look great, Donna."

"Has Roy mentioned about today? Not just the sports," she asked.

"Yes. I understand there are several men here who want to meet you."

Aaron corrected me. "No. Mum is considering whether to meet *them*."

"Pardon me. I'll get out the way then." I left them as quickly as I could. Aaron ran after me a few seconds later and took my arm. I tried to conceal my exasperation with him.

"I didn't mean to sound like a berk! Today is life-changing for mum." He explained the importance of the day and I acted like I knew none of it.

That was so bloody strange; it made me feel like a Stasi spy.

Donna loved cricket because it reminded her of the many days she and Humphrey spent with their friends. However, watching the match with potential suitors demonstrating their potential gave the proceedings a totally different level of energy. Donna sat with Lola and Cynthia on both sides of her. They made observant and critical comments about the men playing.

All around them, the Carduluci's watched and sent WhatsApp messages into the group chat. Massimo was the umpire at one end and Solomon was the other umpire at the other end of one of the innings and they took their roles seriously. However, since they knew they were working on eliminating candidates for the final choice of suitors, Massimo and Solomon enjoyed the game.

In their cricket whites, the men looked very 'proper' playing the game. I watched Donna scrutinising them through her binoculars and she constantly turned from Lola to Cynthia. If I was unsure of how close they were as friends, watching their body language assured me that they were 'sisters'. My mobile buzzed yet again and I read through the judgments and criticism the family and friends made. When I looked up and saw Donna, Lola and Cynthia reading the messages and quietly discussing their thoughts I knew I was missing an earful but I absolutely knew it was not my place to invade their privacy even to satisfy Roy.

Because George, went to Charterhouse Public School, he was an excellent team player. His voice reminded me of Nigel Hawthorne and he was an affable and breezy fellow. Everything about him screamed money and from the way he behaved towards Pedro, he understood the value of people's humanity. The text messages about him were 80% positive. The negatives referred to his gentile heritage and his family's colonial background in India.

I moseyed over to the ladies and decided to camp it up. I didn't want to pry into their lives but I needed material for the chapters so I had to get an in. I said to Donna. "I'd kidnap my favourite in the bunch, put him through the Stockholm syndrome and call his family for ransom money for us to live on."

"Which one do you like?" Donna asked me.

"Before I turn him into my fantasy lover, which one don't you want?"

Donna didn't even have to take another look. "Estevao."

"I don't want him either," Lola and Cynthia agreed.

Lola said, "I don't think that any of them could keep up with me. My husband keeps me in shape. Tony is more than money and style."

"True," Donna said because they'd obviously discussed it. "That's why I've got my eye on the bronze, silver and gold out there." Amber came to us and she caught the tail end.

"Which ones, mama?"

Donna became rather demure. She pulled Amber closer and whispered. Amber was impressed and got her mobile to check the latest scores. "He scores as one of the favourites." She showed us her iPad as Helena came over.

Donna said, "I bet he knows how to keep a woman happy every night." Lola nodded and Amber clutched her neck.

Amber anxiously asked, "My God, do they want it every night?"

Donna asked, "Hasn't your mother talked to you about this?"

Helena laughed. "Her mother doesn't talk about penis: Palestinians—yes. They get her blood boiling. Sex is the last thing Jean wants to hear about."

"Is she really like that, Amber?" Donna asked.

"My mother is very reserved, or as my father would say, 'frigid'."

"Who do you talk to about female matters?" Donna asked and Amber reached out and took Helena's hand.

Amber replied, "Of course, since we've never been with boys, we have only our perspective. But you know something?" The three women leaned in closer. "I imagine myself with Aaron: our wedding night. He won't be an animal."

Cynthia told her, "I've been married over forty years and believe me, only misogynists are beasts. A man that loves you, isn't like that. But you've got to teach him about the feminine mystique." Amber was intrigued.

Lola, who looked half Black half Gypsy with her reddish skin and full curly hair said, "My fanny and my husband speak the same language." I laughed out loud. "No lie! Tony is Brazilian, so I don't have to shave, he knows where it's at!"

Helena laughed and I've never seen her look more wonderful. I put my arm around her shoulder and she placed her cheek next to me.

I said, "Ladies, gay or not, no man is complete without a woman."

Donna grabbed me. "Since you're that smart, do the right thing. Give my Roy what he needs. He gets into a right old state at times. I saw it with Brian and Narj, but he's mad about you. He tries to keep you a secret but when he starts talking about you, he lights up."

"Nice." *That put a smile in my pants.* I pointed to the field. "What about them?"

"There's no contest. I've watched his videos, read his essays, his references are great. I want to see him naked," Donna stated.

"Which one have you chosen?" Amber asked. Donna put on her sunglasses and casually got up and walked away towards the playing area. Amber went after her and slipped her arm through Donna's. No one was able to share the secret or Amber's strategic plans.

At the end of the match, Amber stood beside Donna. All of the ladies formed a reception line on the green. It felt like 'the gentry meets the locals. Aaron brought all of the suitors over to meet Donna again, so she could compliment them. She held out her gloved hand and shook theirs. George, Yves, Pedro, and Joshua were deeply excited by the attention she showed them as Donna stopped and chatted. Donna's style and her beauty didn't escape any of their attention because they'd boasted to their friends, they were going to spend a weekend with an exceptional lady.

Donna's style brought a special smile to Yves' face. "The last time I saw a lady at a sports event that looked as fascinating as you, it was Ava Gardner at a bullfight. I had the picture on my bedroom wall next to A Bout de Souffle." He moved on and Aaron introduced Joshua. He kissed Donna's hand and she nodded her head at him. Friends of Michael and David's ushered by and Donna praised their game. At the end, George took his time staring at Donna with lustful eyes, so Massimo took Donna's hand and led her away.

Men watched Donna elegantly walk back towards a limo and Aaron took the iPad from Helena and he jerked his head, so she came to him. "Guys, please come this way." The cricket players were still greeting the ladies, but Aaron called three names and Helena pointed the way. The cluster of men moved aside to put their bats safely away.

Amber said, "Tea and cakes are this way. Please follow me." The men paid attention and did precisely what she told them. The three businessmen were used to women playing hostess, so they followed Amber's lead into an office on the other side of the sports ground.

Inside the office, Aaron and Amber sat with Joshua. "I want to thank you for your time and patience, Joshua. The compatibility between you and Donna isn't quite right. She asked me to tell you, she knows someone she thinks you will like." He looked disappointed. "If you're still keen to meet someone, Donna will arrange an introduction." He agreed and thanked them both. His timidity made no impression on them.

Three minutes later, Oliver came in. He was refined, kind and sincere." Aaron said, "Oliver, Donna told me you are the perfect friend, but not a boyfriend who could be her husband. I want to ask a deeply personal question. May I?"

"Alright." He was clearly upset.

"Are you ready to have a woman in your life? To be intimately committed to a woman and her family?"

"I know you think I'm some kind of a queen. I've never been very butch and I've never been with a man. I'm not so inclined. I love women and I'm ready for marriage, now."

"I wish you happiness in the future then, Oliver." They stared at each other for what seemed like a dreadful 60 seconds and then Oliver got up and left. Aaron told Roy he didn't believe what Oliver said and Roy told him, Oliver would head out to walk the dog at nights and end up in some man's clutches.

Five minutes later, Estevao, came in and said, "This woman is so grand, high and mighty. Her profile didn't show her as Lady Knowitall. I'm not interested in living with a woman who believes I must bow down to her, no matter how beautiful she is."

Aaron said, "It pleases me to say, you're not good enough for her. You're good on paper, but as a man, no. You're dismissed." Estevao, gave Aaron a filthy look. Roy told me Aaron wanted to punch him in the eye for looking at him like that. Estevao, called Aaron a cunt under his breath when he got up to leave.

* * *

That evening Donna sat in Massimo's *soirée Salon* and looked at everything. The excess of riches kept her eyes searching. I liked the way people looked at her and they were keen to share their thoughts. I could be mistaken, but I don't think so when I suggest Massimo's family and their friends seemed more thrilled to have something different to do than actually being a support group to Donna.

I could not discern an iota of genuine care. They started their day swimming for exercise and when I went to the indoor pool that morning, they looked at me like an intruder. No! like a foreign intruder. I haven't felt that Black in ages.

Paying close attention to them I sensed they were more engrossed in each other's comments, than in Donna taking their advice to heart. Everyone wanted to tell her what they thought, especially the husbands so they each aired their opinion on the grounds of class, cash and character. Their wives didn't miss the tiniest detail when it came to the men's characteristics and attitude.

Massimo said, "Donna, what is your decision? Yves is very cultured but I cannot see Aaron and Yves in your future. There are very interesting comments in the app about George and his rich life..."

Bernard sat forward and said, "George has money and position, but if I understand what Amber has told me about you, Donna, that's not what counts."

"One man stands out and the other one seems good." The Carduluci family were genuinely intrigued.

"Who do you prefer, mum?" Donna leaned in and told him. Aaron smiled and nodded quietly. He searched out Amber sitting with her school friend. All the husbands and wives in the room asked who it was. Donna told us and we all talked about it.

The former school friends chatted about the amount of food the men ate and 'that guy with bad teeth!'. That raised a gasp from them. Aaron took his mother's hand and led her out of the *Salon* as he excused himself. He was so pleased he looked relaxed and Donna proudly accompanied him.

Book Four

HUSBANDS

CHAPTER TWENTY-SEVEN

Donna walked through Regent's Park, with Sondheim's *A Little Night Music* score swirling through her mind. She felt light with Pedro, who comfortably held her arm. Her make-up and hair were done in a 1963 Cleopatra style.

In his black silk shirt and evening suit, Pedro looked very dashing. "I've read that Sondheim is a great composer, but seeing that, I know why now," he told her. "I loved it! I sensed that you felt the same?"

"Yes, love stories get my vote, especially when they're not trite or ludicrous. To this day, I can't understand the popularity of *Pretty Woman*, it's so...I hate it!" Couples in evening clothes shifted and passed by, heading out of the park.

Pedro continued, "Your list of 100 favourite films was fascinating to me. How did you come up with that selection test? It took me a week of mind searching to pick 100 of my favourite films."

"Well, it spoke to me! There were 70 films of yours, I agree with, 20, I've never heard of, 5 I didn't like and 5 I could argue with you about."

He said, "That's not so bad." Donna gestured as she glided through the park.

"I like the fact that you had ten Woody Allen films on your list: how can you not love *Manhattan*?"

"My son feels the same way. He, well both of us, love Woody. We've spent years watching his films. Those allegations. I'm unconvinced by Rosemary's baby. Do you believe the claims?"

"No. Same with Michael Jackson. But for a man his age and a father at that, he was really irresponsible. Eighty percent of America has the most psychotic perception of Black people. America, from what I've seen won't accept a Black man as a philanthropic humanitarian since they invest so much effort in framing Blacks as inhuman."

"Don't get me started. I will not allow my son to go to America."

"Really?"

"Are you kidding me? Look at the way they treat Obama and he was President! I won't have my son exposed to that treatment. I got into a real fight with someone about it." She stopped walking and had to catch her breath. Pedro looked at her face and her decorative eye make-up when Donna opened her eyes. She was slightly unsteady, but she did her utmost to regain her composure.

"Sorry, I— My son's a wonderful man." Donna kept breathing and half laughing and then took her Spanish fan out of her sequined evening bag. She fanned herself and continued walking through the park, away from the theatre, but the crowd was thick. "When your children become adults, you look up to, you know you've done your job right!"

"I feel that way about my daughter. There were so many questions you asked about our background. The 100 favourite films were a test, as I said. But the essay you asked for on *In what ways, if any, does equality shape our lives today? Discuss.* I really felt that I was back at school. Where did you get that title?"

Donna laughed. "That's a very long story; the point is you answered the question, not based on your opinion, but on issues in Globalism. It told me you were not some fake who claims to know what he's talking about and I'd be at risk of dealing with an idiot."

Pedro laughed and put his arm around her waist and then removed it a few seconds later. Donna put her arm around his waist and he loved it.

"My mind is racing, but I won't speak because I don't want you to think I'm a man who just comes out with pick-up lines and chat!"

"I was married to a real man and I know the difference."

"The man who represents you; he was so intense when he questioned me, I know why now. You're exceptional, not because of your elegance. I imagine your upbringing and tradition has made a great lady of you."

Right, the daughter of a Hasidic Jew, who was cast out of the family.

"Marriage and children were the makings of me," she told him.

"How many children do you have? You said that you have an adult son, but you just mentioned children, so how many?" Donna got stuck, so she tried to think her way out of it and became flustered.

"If I don't clear this up, it's going to get in the way. My husband and daughter were killed in a...accident. It nearly killed my son and me. So, I only have my son now." Strangers' smiling faces shone around them.

"I am sorry for your loss, really. If I lost my daughter, I'd—" He was so obviously rattled by the thought he couldn't hide it and Donna studied him even more closely. "My first marriage was a mess because we were too poor and desperate. It made a mess of my youth, but we had Rochelle and she is the greatest achievement in my life. If anything happened to her, I'd be destroyed. So, I'm really sorry for the family you've lost." Donna pulled him close as they walked and he felt special.

"Your perfume is so wonderful."

"Chanel No.5," Donna casually replied and walked towards the cloakroom so that she could get her beaded evening coat.

* * *

Pedro escorted Donna down the steps and into the art deco warm light of *Brasserie Zédel* in Piccadilly. The dining room was a luminous glow of the past and she felt she was stepping back into a bygone age of 1930s elegance. They stopped and waited as their reservation was confirmed and Donna kept mentally repeating *You have the right to be happy; you have the right to be happy.* "I love it here, my son brought me—" She waved it away and sashayed in. In the burgundy red and gold dining room, she really did make people glance and look at her from across the configuration of tables and low-level booths. In her hour-glass black and white dress, she felt that she was everything she used to be as a twenty-five-year-old with two beautiful children: a doctor for a husband and a house of their own.

They were seated in the middle of the room and the jazz band was over to their right playing Django Reinhardt tunes. Pedro looked pleased with himself as he told people around him, good evening. His manner, face and spirit made a gentleman of him far more than the clothes he was wearing.

The waiter in his white apron stood commandingly beside them. He was French and very Gallic. "Champagne?" Pedro asked her.

"No. A Cinzano Bianco, sparkling water, crushed ice and orange slices, please."

"I'll try that too. And bring me a Citron Pressé." Pedro was anxious to follow her lead and not overshadow a woman whose profile presentation he had liked the minute he saw it.

"The video of you talking with your friends, about life as you live it, having your clothes made by reproducing fashions you saw on the women you idolised: I was fascinated with you. The video was so relaxed and natural."

"Roberto De Farenzino made it; his father played cricket with you guys."

"Oh, yes."

"My friends told me to show people who I am."

"I loved how you included people in your neighbourhood. The guy who did the Q&A with you; I like the way he asked your friends and neighbours: how would you describe Donna? Someone said, 'a friend for life', 'down-to-earth', 'gutsy', 'passionate'. I liked that. But the Jamaican women who sat together and said: 'Donna's the greatest friend we've ever had'. A shiver went through me because of their voices and the look on their faces. Like they really knew the heart of you! That's why I wanted to meet you."

"I was lucky enough to meet them because of my son. His best friend introduced them to me during my period of mourning." Their drinks arrived and Donna sat back while they were served. She told herself to take command and stop being nervous. After they toasted, she enjoyed the light taste of the drink.

"I didn't finish telling you, so before it becomes a mess, let me straighten it out." He looked anxious and she leaned in and took his hand. "No, it's nothing horrible." His face showed he was relieved. "The man who interviewed you— that's my son."

For close to a minute, Pedro went back through everything and his face continually changed until a smile turned his face into a human-looking teddy bear.

"That explains so much. One night I was in his car and I thought I was going to meet you, but he said. 'We have to make a stop'. It was OK, but I noticed we were not driving into town." Donna eyed him with all the easy-going elegance she could muster, but the way he spoke to her had its own suspense in the cadence of his voice. "We were back in my Highgate neighbourhood and after a time, we were outside my apartment. He said to me. 'We're going in and you better not have any ideas beyond the line of decency'. I was nervous. I tried to make him explain, but he said, 'don't speak'. We got out of the car and went into my place. It was empty, nothing strange; just empty. I came home early from work, bathed, dressed to meet you and then left."

"He was checking to see if you had planned to manoeuvre me back to your place and have your way with me."

"Oh my God! No. No, no. I wouldn't do that. Wow!"

"I thought he was going too far as well, until he took one of the other guys back to his place and found, bondage gear. So, I told him—keep screening. You and two others passed all the tests." Pedro flopped back in his seat shaking his head.

"I know," she told him, "dating is something...if a woman doesn't protect herself, she might have to deal with those threats. But Aaron checked everyone out with more resources than I ever could."

"I got an email from a friend, at my former workplace, before I ran my own business. He said he'd received a letter for a reference. Not an email. He said the reference had to be handwritten."

"Aaron wanted to be sure you didn't write it. In your correspondence he had a sample of your handwriting. With the other guy, it wasn't just the bondage crap; he had cocaine. Then there was that Congo Dandy who turned up at Massimo's house!"

Pedro laughed so much; people look their way. "Oh, yeah, he was shocking. Some of the 'brothers' from the motherland leave me speechless! He told me with great pride. He has the stuff to cure white women's blues."

"Oh, vomit!" Pedro laughed at Donna's comment and she really liked the sound of his laughter and the expression that passed over his face.

"But I've chosen you, so tell me what's not on those pages."

"My daughter and I are very simpatico and I admire Rochelle's husband a lot. I'd like you to meet her. My first marriage was mired in youthful greed. We were so typical of poverty; we could have been on the *Jerry Springer* show. My father was a cab driver his whole life. He belittled himself to tourists that came to Bermuda, to keep food on the table and a roof over our heads. Of course, he wanted me to be bigger than him. The Royal Navy taught me everything I needed to learn about colonial power. At forty, I left, ready to run my own business. Say what you will about Britain, its institutions will make or break a man."

"Did you experience racism?"

"Racism is as much an institution as a personal choice. People decide to practice it, or they refused to practice it. No one did that to me, not because I am all-powerful and threatening. When somebody brings that to my face, I ask them. 'Does it make you feel important to be a maladjusted racist?' There was a guy in the Navy who was a racist. I told him once. 'God is watching you and you'll rot in hell for your sins'. Whenever I saw him, I'd say 'rot in hell'. He had me brought up, once. The brass asked me why I was 'insubordinate'. I said, 'if I called your wife and daughter a whore and your sons' queers, wouldn't you take offense at my conduct? I told them his racism affected me that way."

"What was their response to that?"

"They promoted me so that I was no longer answerable to that shit and I was placed in charge of the new recruits and gained the respect of everyone."

"After all those years in the Navy, what did you come away with?"

"A non-victim mentality. If a man wants to kick me, I hope he's wearing a bodysuit. I will strike back because God has blessed me with dignity."

"Humphrey would have liked you. Nobody could tell him he was a Nig…you know. Aaron's the same when it comes to bigotry."

"He's so light; he looks more Mediterranean, possibly North African."

"He's got my Andalusian and Israeli Jewish genes."

"I'm Bermudian and African, but our genes are now Portuguese due to my son-in-law and grandkids."

"Does it make a difference?"

"None; we're just from different parts of the planet." Donna liked the fact he answered her question, rather than tackled her question.

They ate and she was relieved that he had good table manners. Donna didn't hate many things but she'd seen some people eat and it was like watching a Kenwood mixer. The band moved on from Django Reinhardt to the American Songbook. After that, they returned to *la Chanson Française* the French classics made famous by Piaf, Charles Aznavour and Juliette Gréco.

Later, Donna and Pedro walked up The Mall, towards Buckingham Palace that was floodlit. As they walked up the wide boulevard, Donna held his hand and walked tall. "I've always loved *Desert Island Disk*," Pedro said, "When you're far out at sea and Britain seems like it's on another planet, *Desert Island Disks* is so comforting."

Donna asked. "Does it make us middle-aged or middle class since we love it?"

"It makes us classics," he confidently told her. "So, go on, tell me. I answered enough of *your* questions. What're your favourites?"

"Eight disks: Aretha Franklin's *Angel*. Barbara Streisand's *Woman in Love*. Stevie Wonder's *Ribbon in the Sky*. Marvin Gaye's *Sexual Healing*."

"Oh yeah," he responded.

"Peggy Lee's *Fever*. Duke Ellington's *Diminuendo and Crescendo in Blue*. Dusty Springfield's *Son of a Preacher Man*. Gershwin, *Rhapsody in Blue*. The book?" She gave herself time to whiz through her favourites. "*Frankenstein*. Luxury item... L'Occitane shea butter." Pedro liked her choice. "Now, you."

"OK. *Rhapsody On A Theme Of Paganini 18th Variation* by Rachmaninoff. *Smooth Operator*, by Sade. *You and I (Will Conquer the World)*, Stevie Wonder, I love it! *Summertime* by Ella Fitzgerald. *Born To Run* by Bruce Springsteen. Great stuff! *Star Wars* by John Williams. *Exodus* by Bob Marley. *What a Wonderful World* by Louie Armstrong. The book would be *Encyclopaedia Britannica*, I know it's allowed—someone before asked and it was approved. The luxury item would be a surfboard. The disk I'd save if they were going to be washed away would be, *You and I (Will Conquer the World)*. That song keeps me dreaming of a woman to love. Since I'd have read *Britannica*, a woman would stay with me because the last thing any woman needs is to be stuck with a moron for life."

"Oh, look at you, fucking hell...oh, I didn't mean to swear—"

"I grew up in the Navy, swearing is like a second language to me." They both delighted in each other as they strolled together. Wait, he took his mobile out and flicked around and then pressed the speaker.

"I love this and the time is right." The melody of *Dancing in the Dark* sung by Diana Krall played and he tucked the cover of his mobile into his top pocket and let the mobile hang there as her voice sang out. He offered his hand and then they danced in the wide-open regal street in shouting distance of Buckingham Palace which was brightly lit up. The slow delivery of Diana's voice comforted her greatly. People who saw them dancing in their evening clothes and heard the sound of music coming from them without seeing the mobile thought they were magical in their own way. They made a grand sight of themselves as they danced up The Mall.

As they danced, Donna felt wonderful because she'd never done anything of the kind. The bossa nova rhythm and Pedro's confident command of the beats guided his dance. "Does this make us very old-fashioned, dancing to standards and—"

"I'm fifty, which makes me far from old."

"I thought you were forty-nine," Donna said.

"No, I'm fifty, too."

"Hey, did you lie on your application?"

"No, I had a birthday recently. I'm fifty also, not fifty-two." Amused, she continued laughing and smacked his bum, which made him blush, much to her liking.

"We'll dance like this on the beach when I take you to meet Rochelle and my grandkids. You'll love Bermuda, the beaches are pink. I can picture you there in a white swimsuit walking in all your natural beauty."

The expression, 'waiting to exhale' always seem a bit ridiculous to her except when she did it. Diana Krall's voice soothed her deeply. The bossa nova rhythm gave him the room to sway without exerting himself next to her, nevertheless she felt his erection brush against her thigh and she flinched and he backed away. Laughter rose in her thorax.

"Pardon me," he said out of the side of his mouth like Groucho Marx. Donna's suppressed laughter broke through and popped like champagne into an effervescent shower of sounds popping in his ear. "You will love Bermuda!"

"It's an extravagance—"

"No," he interjected. "It's my gift because I am sure marriage to you would be the best years of my life."

Donna kissed him and quickly became aroused. She looked at him intermittently and the strength and heart of him deeply affected her. Never before had she danced in the street with people passing by, charmed by a couple that had music coming out of them, tucked away. Pedro kissed her easily as if he were taking impressions of her lips over and over again.

When Donna got back home, she undressed, cleansed her face, slipped into bed, listened to her Nat King Cole CD, and replayed the evening. With the mood in her soul, she called Roy. He was with me and so I heard the level of intimate confidentiality she shared with him. I wasn't surprised that she didn't want to speak to Aaron about how she felt sexually, but I was surprised how well Roy knew how to intimately converse with her. When he got up and left the room, I realised he wanted to retain their confidentiality and keep me out of their lives.

CHAPTER TWENTY-EIGHT

Eugene tickled me. We were in Brixton, having brunch with four of my friends. We meet once a month for a Black gay men's social over food and drink. They are always busy, so we agreed we make it a priority to stay in touch through the group social. Although it's superficial, we always look like a hip crew of good-looking young professionals who any man would want to date or hang out with. The fellas were very fashion-conscious and I was the only one who was retro-modern, so we fit in the place perfectly.

One of my friends stopped eating and said, "A fucking hunk is coming this way and he can come all over me if he wants."

I said, "You know you're borderline disgusting, don't you? Besides I've already got a sexy man." Eugene leaned in and touched his forehead against mine. All four men looked away from us with four different smiles on their faces, so I turned around and saw Aaron standing behind me. His unbuttoned white shirt, Star of David and Crucifix on his hairy chest and fists by his side made a sight of him, but his tense face and angry eyes gave off a truly hostile vibe. For whatever reason, he made me tight and anxious because I know him.

"I need to talk to you right now. I'm parked on double lines so…"

"You know my friends…"

"I could get towed." Whatever mess was going on in his head plastered itself all over his face. He kept his eyes on me until I got up and then he looked at the others. He said, "Next time, yeah… bye." He jerked his head and started out. I looked at Eugene and his eyes told me it was OK. I should just go, so I did.

When we got to the car, there was a ticket under the wipers and he looked at it and turned brutish with rage. "Fuck south

London!" He screamed so loudly everyone on the street turned their heads and found him.

Some guy in the crowd said, "Fuck you, motherfucker!"

"Kiss my shit!" Aaron raged out which stopped people in their stride. "You. Get in the car!" I got in and my anxiety worsened. What triggered him off? He got in and we drove.

"Aaron, what..."

"You wait. I just need to head north, cross the bridge and get back to where we belong, then I'll talk to you." He drove through Brixton, to Elephant & Castle as though we were in a Dodge 'Em car race. At times I thought I was going to hurl. He navigated the chaotic Elephant & Castle roundabout and I gripped the seat and watched him eat up the road until we approached London Bridge and he slowed down and made his way over the bridge and then into the City of London.

"Aaron, go to the *Scruffy Chic Café* in Shoreditch. I don't want to hear a word, because if you head home, I will get out of this car and you can deal with whatever shit this is—alone."

"Fine!" He drove through Bank and towards Liverpool Street.

"OK, we've left the South," I said, "so tell me?

"When did you break up with Narj?"

"A little while ago so what?" His face appeared to blow up into an enormous balloon of grotesque fury.

"I was talking to mum and she just mentioned it. That got me thinking; I've spent months talking to you about everything that's happening to me and what I feel about everything and you've been bottled-up and distant. You didn't even tell me you broke up with your boyfriend. You just say— 'I'm cool', 'it's good', 'oh the usual'. You've distanced yourself from me. We're growing apart. What have I done to make you push me out of your life: like you don't like me anymore?"

"Aaron, that's nonsense; besides your mother, there is no one else on the planet I love more than you." His jowls were pulsating and I could hear his teeth gnashing. His eyes were on the busy road, but he turned to me and the look on his face was scattered with confusion and despair.

"But you've been so weird. Not like you're ignoring me, because you've helped me with lots of stuff getting mum sorted and all that. I know you've used your contacts to check on the pricks that sent their profiles: but something's off." A guy cut in front of Aaron and he screamed raw obscenities at the man.

"Yeah, so you know I'm a hundred percent committed to the family." He drove in silence until we got to Shoreditch, which was grungy and packed as always. Aaron saw a guy pulling away and nipped into the parking space. When we got out, he fed the meter and he cursed south London once again.

Over coffee, he unloaded a raft of concerns about the fact I've been secretive and everything in his mind filled his face. "Aaron, I didn't tell you about Narj because you've been so caught up with Amber and what your future together might be and Donna and how you're trying to be a caring son…"

"I'm so caring except my best mate can't talk to me?" I didn't know how to dismiss what he was saying.

"Aaron, how many things can you deal with? You're worried about the business making more money. You're worried about your clients being rejected. You're worried about Amber's parents. I can't put more on your plate about Eugene and me, I mean Narj…" He grabbed my arm and stared into me.

"Wait, you're going out with Eugene?" I tried not to react. "You and him—" The entire Hipster crowd in the café turned to our table because Aaron's vibe was so violent, even though he wasn't shouting. He then mouthed the words: "Are you sleeping with him?" Because no sound came out, he looked like he was struck dumb. Mothers and their kids, dads and their mates basked in the bright light from the café window, pretending not to notice what was happening at our table, but they looked over and shared eyeball conversations with each other.

"Yes." He looked into the mind and heart of me and I grew increasingly upset. He became a quivering mess until tears came down his face. In among the packed café with its clutter and clatter of re-cycled paraphernalia and chalked up information on blackboards and whatever else that hung on the exposed brick walls; I felt the place closing in on me.

"Don't you love me anymore?"

"What are you talking about? You're on the verge of marrying Amber. You're straight. Eugene has nothing to do with us."

"He's the one you tell your secrets to now?" He wiped his eyes with the back of his hand.

"You're the love of my life, what are you talking about." A woman at the next table heard me and she looked sympathetically at him.

"Aaron, I don't love any man more than you." The woman nodded. She had to be single.

"Give me the keys, I'll drive us home."

"What's he got that I haven't? And he's so old."

"Oy, Eugene's not some has-been."

"Yeah, he's got his own programme on the telly, knows the rich and famous, moves in elite academic circles. Have I done something wrong?"

"Give me the keys." He gave me the car keys and tried to pull himself together, but he was so distraught his face couldn't hide any of it. We got up to leave and people pretended not to look at us, even though they were watching.

When we got home, I closed the door and Aaron staggered about, dipped forward and began shaking. I hadn't seen him like that in years. When he stood upright, his face cracked and tears poured out of him. *Oh, God!* He lurched forward and began sobbing and I felt like I'd been punched in the face.

"Roy, please don't leave me." I took hold of him and his entire body was shaking. He grabbed me and held me; then gripped me. "Daddy's gone; I can't be without you. I— you've found Eugene and now he—" But Aaron shook uncontrollably with sobs that burned my face.

"Baby, I'll never leave you, never." He cried and cried and wept until my heart gave out and I began crying too.

As distressed as I've ever seen him, he said, "Now, you've got Eugene, you don't need me."

"Darling, darling: darling! I need you—I always will."

"You can tell him everything. Talk about life as two Black men and I won't be able to. He'll take you to bed and everything you do will be more than we've done, but I love you as much as mum and Amber, but I won't have a man to help me anymore."

"You think I'd do you like that: after what you and your dad did for me." I wiped the tears away from his face and he kissed the tears on me. He was so pumped up and rigid: his arms, chest and tummy were tight.

"But you don't come to me anymore. For ages we've been growing apart. I know Amber..."

"Cous, listen to me. The only reason I'm not crazy is that you've got Amber and truth from my heart, cous; I really like her! She's lovely and exactly right for you. People might think she's just pretty and swishes around in nice clothes, but she's got guts and the kind of stuff Donna is made of: heart, decency, love. I know it, I know it!"

"I love her; she's more than I want in a way; except I need you." Then he started sobbing again. I rocked him and hushed him.

"I know you juiced Brian and got the money for me. And I know I didn't make things easy with Narj; but Eugene is everything I'm not, even though I love you more than he ever will." His sparkling eyes reaffirmed his words. "Maybe I'm hetero-flexible, as you've said. But I love you because you're more than all the brothers who rejected me when only dad could make me feel proud. You've *never* made me feel white—I can't lose you." He held me tight and I could feel him stiffen up.

"Love me; please, kiss me." He was so fully charged; he overwhelmed me and I took his hand.

* * *

We lay together on his bed and he wrapped himself around me with his arm behind my neck and his leg between my knees. He smelt wonderful and I played with his curls and kissed his face. The framed photos of his heroes were on his walls: Barack Obama, Sade, Lenny Kravitz, Craig David, Slash, Bob Marley, Halle Berry, Joshua Redman and Rebecca Walker. He pulled me closer and kissed my head.

"No one can tell me a love injection is immoral or bad for me." He fondled me. "I was so afraid you'd leave me; and I'd lose you. Earlier I wanted to die; even with love between me, mum and Amber." He turned to me and his eyes revealed a pure depth of consciousness. Eugene could phrase it better than me, but Aaron used his knowledge of philosophy and psychology to reach people. He knew I adored him, so he looked sacred lying in my arms.

I should have told him everything I've hidden from him. Growing up I felt unclean because of the accusations made against me. Sexual diversity brought out the worst in bigots. In Jamaica and here at school I was just queer. So, while my school

273

mates rejected me, I studied diligently and passed my exams. I didn't need to be in their gang. I got into university and they got into drugs and crime. Then when I discovered how friendless and alienated Aaron was, that became my opportunity to assert my friendship because up until I was fifteen, I hated almost everyone except my grandfather.

He whispered. "I haven't been that far out there since daddy and Zara." He abruptly stopped. "If Freud knew how incredible Afro sexuality is, I'd admire him, but I don't." He climbed onto me. The gold crucifix and his silver star of David rest in the hair between his full pectorals. "You quiet my soul." His voice was wonderful as he touched my face. "I saw Eugene eyeing you the night of the Prince party. I should be happy since you've come through attempts on your life and madness! I know how much you deserve love. You're incredibly kind. On top of that, you're fucking amazing." I had to smile. We caressed each other for a good length of time.

"Like most men of my faith, I overthink everything."

"Well, you were born Jewish, raised Baptist and you're hetero-flexible."

"Don't you love it?" We laughed. "We've got high but when you're inside me, the ancient Afrocentricity of *my* being comes alive!" His body tightened.

I pushed him back and climbed onto him. I didn't kiss him, I eyed him. That filled his flesh and bones. He always looked like someone in the Old Testament to me. Maybe I watched too many epics growing up but he was the apotheosis of religious past and political present.

Aaron told me, "When you look at me like this, I love the human animal I am. To hell with civilisation's dogma: that's why my heart, my body, my soul is yours."

"Amber won't like that."

"I know." He took a few deep breaths and became a bit teary. "Amber needs me and after everything daddy taught me, if I became an adulterer, I think he'd haunt me. Whatever has happened with you and Eugene, I'll bet he *needs* you. I won't steal your love. You haven't said it but I'll bet you love him." I closed my eyes and nodded and then looked him in the eye. "As long as you don't abandon me, I can be a devoted husband. I don't love you less than her and I definitely don't love her less than you." I kissed him and we rolled around in the sheets.

He said, "Whatever got hold of me this morning— Sometimes the boy in me gets scared. Except for Zara, mum and dad, no one loved me before you."

His tough face, full lips and curly hair made him so sweet.

"I was going to cut my wrists and bleed to death in the tub. But mummy—" I put my hand over his mouth.

"You'd have destroyed *all* our lives. Everyone who loves you." He nodded. "I'll never abandon you—you've blood marked me. So, take me. I've been unfaithful to Brian and Narj and now Eugene, but never unfaithful to you."

"Mate, when you 'played' Brian and got me the money and then you left him, I knew you were mine." He started trembling and looked me up and down. "If ever a man was gorgeous, you are," he told me.

"I don't want to hurt Amber. I don't want to risk Donna turning away from me. Eugene is my sanity. He's the rational way for me to live my life."

"Yes, that makes sense. So, tell me why with Amber's love and mum's devotion. Everything dad taught me about being a man, and the homophobia out there. Plus, the love Eugene offers you, why were you shaking and cussing rocking my arse so I wanted to live again?"

I don't know how long I thought about it, but I couldn't reply for quite a while. "You're a strange other part of me I have to keep alive." That made Aaron pulse between me. I eyed him and the surroundings went out of sight.

"Yes. I hear you. You're the Black part of me. The other side no one sees." Everything, since the death of his father flooded back in my mind and we made love again.

Nevertheless, that evening when we lay around drunk, I actually knew I committed a sin. Other people matter. Even though I was drunk, I told him to go to sleep in his room and think about Amber. I can't describe what it felt like to give ourselves to each other and then know someone else needed our love. I knew this could never end up in the novel. So even though I was drunk, I had to ask myself, what kind of lies would I tell Eugene?

* * *

I walked through the reception of Barbican Arts Hall and met Eugene. Everyone I laid eyes on looked so respectable and posh in comparison to the way I felt after the sexual addiction I was still coming down from. Addiction has a way of making you feel deeply ashamed because Aaron has sexually fed me for the longest time and it's sweeter than sin.

I bought Eugene a drink and took the time to explain what happened. As people mingled and headed into the concert hall, I studied his face as I tried to justify myself. "I'm telling you the truth because lying to you would mean I didn't respect you. Even though I've been in another man's bed. I want to be in yours."

"Roy, I have to admit, if you told me nothing happened the other day, I would have called this quits: the friendship, the book, all of this."

"Can you forgive me?" He looked off into the distance and I knew his judgment was coming so I anxiously waited. I recounted what was happening to Aaron and Donna.

"Don't you dare try emotional manipulation on me," he said, "I'm no silver daddy who'll tolerate anything to get in your pants." I felt condemned. Once again, I'd kicked another man who loved me.

"Eugene don't act your age. This is the 21st century. Sex isn't the monolith that defines our lives. I'm hoping to build a life with you."

"I'll give that serious thought. I should tell you that a two-timing slut is the kind of rapacious moron I utterly detest."

I thought I was going to cry so I couldn't move. I couldn't speak. I became hot and I felt bile rise in my throat and I couldn't swallow.

Eugene proudly told me. "In the 1970s, I shagged guys I liked and then in the 1980s, when all of our lives were at stake, I changed. Your generation of fuckers are a joke to me. You lot have reached this age without understanding the history of love as we fought for in the 1960s to the '90s." Eugene dropped my ticket on the ground and walked towards the auditorium.

I looked at it and then watched him leave me. I felt paralysed as I saw him vanish. All at once, I grabbed the ticket and made my way to him. The concert was on the film scores of Dimitri Tiomkin, Miklós Rózsa and Franz Waxman. I found my seat and then I silently asked him to make room for me. He did and I sat and listened to some great music.

I took Eugene's hand and kissed it. "Please forgive me," I begged but he didn't hear and at the end of the concert, he left me.

CHAPTER TWENTY-NINE

As usual, Helena and I met for dinner. We dined at *Morton's of Mayfair*. Over dinner she told me, she and Amber were walking through a department store in Knightsbridge, shopping for a gift to give to Massimo. People were rushing about the place with their kids seeking attention from their parents.

"That's the most incredible thing you've ever said," Amber replied. "I have no idea how Aaron would feel about being a sperm donor."

"I can't stop thinking about it." Helena took Amber's arm, but she could feel that Amber was tight. "If I had a child of my own, I can imagine making my life my own, without constantly needing you there. You know I couldn't have a man... fuck me," she said, knowing Amber's concerns about men's expectations. "I know you and Aaron are beginning to feel stronger about each other."

"How do you know that?" Amber asked inquisitively without sounding aggressive.

"Our conversations are now taken up with 75% of his life and family. I don't say it's wrong, I admire his mother. All the questions she needed answered before she decided on Pedro, made me feel useful as a woman helping someone anxious about men. I like the hamper from Fortnum & Mason she sent Papa and the Women's Day Spa gift card treatment she gave to me."

"She's caring and sincere," Amber stated.

"Yes, your life with them is going to be for the better. But my money isn't my whole life. You've been my life. I can only continue without you if I have something that will change my life too. Do you think Aaron would find it... outrageous?"

"Honestly, I don't know. We haven't discussed kids so he might be progressive. Maybe 'new age', or he could be... really orthodox patriarchal."

"Do you think he's more Jewish or Black?"

"Helena?" Amber came to a dead stop in the department store and Helena saw people staring because of Amber's tone of voice. Amber wouldn't move, so shoppers had to walk around her.

Amber whispered, "Are you more lesbian or Jewish?"

"Don't talk like that. You know my passion is strictly female." Helena tugged Amber and got her walking. "What are *you*? I loved the way you stressed that you're a bohemian, when you were at Papa's. You were incredibly sexy." A child and his mother bumped and crashed into Amber.

"Excuse me, lady," Amber said, "that boy is not allowed to crash land all over the place. If you can't manage your kids, use a condom. I shouldn't suffer because of you."

The upper-class woman was deeply embarrassed, so she ranted at Amber about children's rights to play and freedom of movement. To make her point, she took off her Dior sunglasses and waved it at Amber while defending her son, Christian, who she called a healthy boisterous child and accused Amber of being a child aggressor.

Amber snatched the sunglasses out of her hand, threw it on the floor and then stamped on it. "You are not entitled to abuse me because you cannot apologise when you are wrong! Your son was out of order and you are the adult: for heaven's sakes mummy!" Amber shook her head, bewildered.

"You broke my glasses; you owe me £150!"

"Oh! What is the English expression?" Amber searched for the phrase. "Oh, yes! Piss off you twat." Amber walked away and the woman grabbed her arm.

Helena spat on the woman's coat and said, "Suck cock and die, you stupid whore!" Frightened, the woman stepped back because Helena looked dangerous and borderline violent which struck fear into the mind of the woman.

Half an hour later, they strolled through another area of the department store.

"You and I having Aaron's children?" Helena comforted her. "Siblings, from the same man. My husband's child, is to be my girlfriend's daughter." Amber looked unsettled and tense.

"Convention is hardly our thing!" Helena said excitedly but she could see that Amber was turning the thought over in her mind.

"Let me ask Papa to talk to him. Aaron will listen differently, when he hears it from a man."

"Yes, he might," Amber replied anxiously.

"Papa said he listened attentively when he had a talk with Aaron. I tried to get Papa to tell me everything, but he wouldn't. He said, 'some things are private'. Papa tells me everything, usually."

"I think it's a sign he respects Aaron. My father said Aaron is fearless and compassionate." Amber's expression indicated she never expected to hear praise from her father. "Miss Dalio must be giving Papa life lessons now. Can you believe my father is thinking like a humane person, instead of a pompous politician? I had lunch with him and he behaved like a caring father. He said Aaron will take care of me because now I've become fascinating."

"It used to be you and I against them. Now you're strong."

"You speak like you're in mourning. We're not breaking up."

"Soon you won't need me." Helena was strangely aggressive and vulnerable.

"Miss Carduluci don't be absurd. I am a bohemian, not a poseur."

"Distinction, please?"

"I cultivate, I don't consume." Helena looked at her watch and then rushed. She linked arms with Amber. "I am not saying farewell to any of our life. You will be with me. If Aaron agrees to be a donor, that tells me more about him. Wow, both of us, having his children?" Helena grinned and vigorously shook her head. "But at the same time, it's strange." They walked in silence and Amber later told Aaron it was the first time it felt like Helena was taking something away from her.

* * *

After Eugene sent me his pages about the conversation between Amber and Helena, in Harrod's, I got fired up because the idea of Aaron being father to their children wasn't something I could have imagined. At work, I couldn't concentrate, I had to write about what Aaron told me when he went to Dr Liebermann.

Aaron sat with Dr Liebermann and told him. "I'll need to increase our sessions soon." Dr Liebermann loosened his tie and top button.

"You're strangely reticent today, what is it?"

Aaron nodded and studied him, from his tassel loafers, corduroy trousers, and tweed jacket to the crisp white shirt he had on. "Sometimes with you, I see Norman Mailer and other times I see Lenny Bernstein. Today you look different."

"Evasion." Daniel looked him straight in the eye without blinking. Aaron glanced over at the thousands of books, and then he pulled himself upright.

"I am going to Amber's father to ask permission for her hand in marriage."

"Mazel tov!" He pulled Aaron to his feet and embraced him.

"There's a problem."

"What problem? You're not even married yet."

"They might reject me. I'm not rich enough to sustain Amber's lifestyle. My business earned £280,000 net after bills and taxes, but it's not enough. It's these fucking goys who hire the wrong people 80% of the time. They don't see the talent in 'minorities' who work their socks off for a chance to build a career in the corporate sector." Dr Liebermann was about to speak. "There are unemployed talented people who aren't getting hired. I got into this business to...to make employers see talent. I offer career guidance to lots of companies. But they want those all-white Joe and Joanna Millennials because they think their online savvy is intelligence!"

"Aaron, listen to me. Amber's father won't reject you. He wants to see his daughter married."

"I have to tell Amber we'll wait a year; I have to make my business generate more money. Amber's entire family circle is posh and Amber's command of style! Fuck me, it's beautiful!" He laughed loudly. "She never dresses badly; her voice is music. She has ambition. I get so turned on with her I could—" He stopped abruptly.

"Could what?"

Aaron walked away but paused. He looked over his shoulder and saw that Dr Liebermann was still waiting for an answer. "Shoot my load," he flippantly replied.

Daniel earnestly said, "Finally, your passion is running smoothly."

"I want her, believe me, I want her."

"Aaron, we've made considerable progress over the years."

"I have, haven't I." Dr Liebermann concurred.

"And how is your mother?"

"She went out on her first date. Wait, look. Here she is." Aaron took out his mobile and showed him photos of Donna at the cricket ground, with the families from that day. Aaron showed one of Donna with him just before she went out on the date with Pedro. Dr Liebermann's face turned pale.

"Daniel, what is it? You've gone as white as a ghost."

Dr Liebermann needed to get his bearings to reply. "Blood sugar, maybe. Now listen, go over and speak to Amber's father, his generation and mine started life with much less than you have and we lived happily on it."

"That reminds me. Amber's Uncle asked me a fascinating question. He said instead of Amber having to adjust to my lifestyle, could I adjust to hers?"

Dr Liebermann grabbed his shoulders. "That's an offer very few men get in life. You're blessed with good luck. Can you live the way she and her family do?"

"I wouldn't be much of a man if I lived off my wife's money."

"But don't you see? You are being offered a marriage that will enable your new family to invest in you! You're not a man that sits on his arse and fails to think! Examine your prospects, son." Aaron acknowledged what he was told and then he left.

Alone, Daniel Liebermann went to a cabinet in the room and then drank from the bottle. He took Aaron's file off his desk and looked at pictures of him and Donna, whose face he touched. He placed several pictures of mother and son side by side and studied them.

CHAPTER THIRTY

A *week later*, Aaron drove up to Amber's father's house in Wimbledon and stopped his car. He turned to his grandfather, Harold. "I'm shaking inside, how do I look?" Harold didn't miss any detailed the Sunday we all went to him and Violet and he told us all what happened. I forgot that when Harold had a good story to tell, he made a meal of it. I took mental notes and it was easy to write it up because time and again, Harold spoke to me as if two Jamaican men could read behind the events of everything he recounted, with absolute glee over dinner and drinks.

Harold sat in the car and told Aaron. "Listen to me. You have everything to offer this girl. You're a decent man: prosperous, healthy, and ambitious. You don't have money worries, even though you've explained paying your staff and Amber's lifestyle will drain your reserves." Harold adjusted Aaron's tie, but he couldn't get it right, so he untied it and retied it right there in the car.

"Don't say anything negative about yourself to her parents; I don't care how rich they are. My son gave you balls and brains, plus bravura! You come from a long line of fighting men. Plus, your mother is fierce. Feel nice! You're a Jamaican Jew and that means you don't stand for no fuckeries! You hear me!"

Aaron's eyes shone and Harold could feel his grandson's emotions. Harold kissed his forehead. "Remember, you're a Blackmon." Aaron embraced Harold with all the love he felt and he still shook with nerves and excitement, but he pulled back and sat still so that he could take good deep breaths.

Inside, Bernard and Jean sat opposite Aaron and Harold. The room was a very comfortable and well-furnished living room, but it was nothing like Massimo's estate. It was modern but not particularly stylish. It could have been decorated in 1985 with the best of what that era had to offer. Jean loved it and that is why she sat upright in her grey skirt, twin-set and pearls. Bernard's non-descript suit and white shirt fit the life he lived at home and lacked the savoir-faire he projected when he was with Miss Dalio. Harold felt he was best dressed as he could be, escorting his grandson to his prospective father-in-law.

Bernard sat forward and put his cup and saucer down on the coffee table next to the Jewish Chronicle and Golfer. "I am happy to give my consent for your son to marry my daughter." Bernard didn't look at Jean when she began to speak, he simply raised his hand and she fell silent. "There will be no complications about this." Aaron looked at her and he could see she wanted to say something, but he knew with the subject of matrimony, the word of the father was law.

"My daughter's dowry is worthy of her. I needn't confirm that she is chaste: less than a month ago she gave me medical proof from her doctor. You can both read the report if you must."

Aaron said, "Knowing my obligation, I also have proof that I am untouched by debilitating conditions, be it in my blood, my sperm, or my mind. These are further reports." He took his zip-up leather business portfolio from the side of the chair and opened it and handed over the manila envelope.

"My grandson's business may take him overseas. Is your daughter free to travel worldwide or does she require special consideration or visa?"

"She is not affected by Brexit; she can live anywhere."

Aaron said, "I know your work takes you worldwide, Bernard, but I should tell you, Amber and I will never settle in the USA. If your work takes you in the States and you need to be close to her—"

"Why not America?" Bernard interjected, sitting back casually but alert.

"I'm at risk in America from the police. I can't pass for white."

"I don't understand," Jean said.

"For God's sakes, don't you know it's open season on Black people in America?" The look Bernard gave Jean exposed his deep contempt for her. "I will bear it in mind, Mr Blackmon. Amber is politically conscious."

Jean said, "She is not political, she is cultured. That is why we spent good money to bring her up as a lady. Not some ugly feminist who lacks maternal intelligence."

"Would you please go and bring the Scharzhofberger Riesling and the Montrachet Grand Cru," Bernard told her, disinterested in her statement.

"It's over £8,000 a bottle! It's vintage—"

"Shut up! Go and bring it." She got up. Harold glanced at Aaron and turned back to Bernard as Jean left the room.

Bernard said, "There is nothing I can do. I'm simply glad Amber is not like that. I should be honest, Mr Blackmon. I have a lovely girlfriend. We spend excellent time together so you will see her from time to time. I make no pretence about her being my secretary or PA; I adore her."

"And your wife?" Harold asked.

"Meaningless and dull. Convention will not restrain me. I am a man who's earned the right to be happy. This is why I am so glad to welcome Aaron into my family. You should know I spend a great deal of my time with my good friend, Massimo Carduluci, and his family. I don't lie to him about my girlfriend. He and all his people know Claudine Dalio and I are in love. Do I shock you, Aaron?"

"No, I'm more shocked that you're this honest."

"Why should I be ashamed? My wife is interested in 'traditional correctness'." He grimaced. "Who wants that?" he said as if he'd bit into a rotten apple. "Oh, let me give you some documents that layout Amber's dowry. It's over a million." He waited for them to respond and he was glad that Harold was impressed, but he saw Aaron wasn't.

"It doesn't please you, Aaron?"

"I'm not marrying her for her money. I love her."

"I believe you. I should add; Amber stands to inherit a great sum from her Uncle Massimo."

"I have no inheritance of that kind—"

"As yet," Harold interjected. "He stands to inherit from our family, we're endowed."

"As I'm sure our grandchildren will be. Now young man! I trust there are no existing entanglements to your impending marriage?"

Aaron was slightly caught off guard, but he knowingly lied when he said, "No." Bernard's admission of his mistress proved his unconventionality, but Aaron couldn't explain Roy.

Jean came back with a bottle of wine and glasses for them all. Harold saw they were small sherry glasses, so he forced himself not to laugh at Jean. However, Bernard gave her the dirtiest look. Aaron also knew the glasses were too small.

Bernard took the corkscrew, opened the bottle and said, "To my daughter's happiness and your prosperity!" He drank from the bottle, then passed it to Aaron, who took a swig and loved the taste. He passed it to Harold who drank it and really loved the wine. He then passed it to Jean. She held the bottle and then got one of the small glasses and poured a miniscule amount into the glass. They all watched her, bemused.

The next day, Aaron walked Amber through the exhibition of wedding dresses at the V&A. Amber walked confidently in a ruffled white skirt and black blouse. Aaron dug into his pocket and took out a box. Amber stopped walking and adjusted her clothes because it felt as if her blouse suddenly stuck to her body.

"Amber Louise Shapiro. I would like to make you happy for the rest of your life. Will you marry me?" He opened the box and there was a diamond engagement ring. She stared at the ring and looked at him. She looked back at the ring and then stared directly at him.

Amber said, "Do you remember, I once said to you, I want you to discover me?" He thought about it. "It was on an important night." He soon remembered.

"At the restaurant: no! Outside the restaurant when I took your parents to Bankolé's restaurant."

"Yes, then. Have you discovered who I am; what I am?" He thought about it as quickly as he could. "You haven't as yet. I love you, but I haven't told you everything about me." She began walking and he followed. "I'm not like the typical bride in waiting, who offers her virginity and a congenial family as everything a man could want." She stopped at a very famous wedding dress on display. "I want you to take a bit of time, to consider whether I am ideal. I have many friends I share my life with. And I don't want to push them aside to be a wife and mother who only exists in her beautiful palace, you know, the home. I want to keep my treasures."

"I don't want you to be a housewife. You're much too glamorous and independent for that!"

"I'm not glamorous..." He stood back and eyed her, dressed in the classic reproduction Yves Saint Laurent black and white dress from the French film, *Belle de Jour*.

"Are you bloody kidding me? I'm from Hackney: you're glamorous! And loquacious...who else would say: *The mind often taxes the body for the pleasures it craves.* When you said that, to one of the suitors we interviewed, I felt it in my balls—fucking hell! You're style, with *real* substance. Trust me, I've read philosophy, I know shit!"

"Darling, you're wonderful!" she confessed with French colouring her voice.

"Well, come then, take the ring, say the word."

She looked at the diamond once again. "Aaron Lorenzo, do as I tell you. Think back on what we've shared. Ask yourself if you know me and then come back and show me that you do." He held the little box up higher. "I can see it. But I want to own a gallery and be like no other Jewish woman. I would never ask you to dismiss Roy from your life because you were going to marry me. Women give up a lot, once they agree to a marriage." She resumed walking and he followed her.

"Aaron, I look at my mother—she wasn't always that...vacant. But she gave up everything to marry my father. I can't give up my friends to be a perfect wife." He was going to say more, but she kissed him and he felt her heart say 'yes'.

"Oh! By the way," she said as she walked away. "If I don't marry you, I will never marry any man. You're beautiful!" She made her way down a corridor and back to her office.

When Aaron arrived home, he went into the kitchen and Roy was making dinner. From the minute he saw Aaron's face, he was shocked. "What the fuck!" He stopped what he was doing. "Why not?" Aaron told him everything.

"She wants to marry you, but she can't give up what she's got, even though she hasn't got another boyfriend and her father gave his consent, so there isn't someone else waiting in the wings." Aaron picked up the Cockspur rum and drank from the bottle and handed it to Roy. They both shuffled about aimlessly. Roy wondered if Aaron would figure out that Helena was at the heart of the matter.

Aaron went to the fridge for a beer and took out a couple and tossed Roy a can. He drank and took his shirt off and flopped onto the dining room sofa. He stayed there for thirty minutes in serious contemplation. "Fuck me gently, it's Helena!" Roy told me, pretending he knew nothing about Helena made him feel horrible.

"Helena's never mentioned a bloke or any man she likes. She's gay!" Roy didn't register the right level of shock, so Aaron picked up on something, but Roy told me, due to the fact they'd never had secrets, Aaron didn't suspect him.

Aaron said, "Helena is gay and they've been involved. What do you think? Or am I crazy?" he asked, gesturing wildly, waiting for confirmation.

"That could explain a lot: but Amber and Helena, lovers—Like us?"

"Yeah, where's your fucking gaydar man? She's hiding in plain sight!" He drank and thought it through. "Where's Judith Butler when I need her for clarity because there's got to be a new classification for Helena and Amber. They went to school together. Wait! They've been intimate since they were girls!" Aaron searched the air for more clues.

"Wait!" Aaron got to his feet. "Massimo knows. He fucking does! He tried to tell me, but I didn't connect." Aaron explained everything Massimo told him.

Aaron said, "OK, I'm not speculating, they *are* a couple." Roy gestured, feigning surprise. "Amber said she won't marry any other man. But she doesn't want to erase Helena as if they've concluded a Sappho liaison!" They took the time to think.

Roy said, "Mate, we're doing this all wrong. Psychological and philosophical inquiry demands a dialogue. It's always interesting when you turn into a sexual detective."

"What do you mean?"

"At Uni, the stuff you asked me about gays' politics and psyche. Then in Ibiza, you clocked how the gay boys rolled and that opened a door for you."

He proudly stated, "You mean that I'm heteroflexible."

"I love it when you say that."

"I *am* sexually unlimited." Aaron went bug-eyed! "Amber is too. That's our alchemy!"

"That's probably why you can spend an hour telling me what kind of sex you think Amber's capable of. It's the only time I've ever been able to listen to that much about the labyrinth of the labia without gagging."

"If I remember correctly, didn't you write something about anal maelstrom?"

"About you, mate, yes." Their intimate gaze shared their history.

Aaron sat on the dining room chair across from him. "How are you today, I didn't ask you because you were dressing me, going through my lines with me."

"Eugene is talking me through the mess in my head. Seriously, cous. He's as right for me as doing my Masters and getting my job. We talk about life. Meet his sophisticated friends. What he's done, and what I am."

"You guys are solid, I'm telling you, man."

"How?" I got up and thought it through as he went to the fridge to get the sushi he had bought the night before.

"You never complain about him. As shy and secretive as you are, whenever you come back from seeing him, you look really happy."

Roy said, "Cous, call her now and get it sorted; find out if she's bound to Helena, in love with her...just sleeps with her, or what."

"Shut up! I'm not about to call the woman I love and demand answers from her like she's a sexual fraud, especially considering we're lovers!" He took his mobile, called Amber and waited.

"Darling, listen, when are you free, I need to tell you something important. It concerns what you told me to think about." He stalked back and forth as if he was caged in the room, with his hand down his pants. After a minute, he said, "Super!"

He hung up and told Roy. "Day after tomorrow, we're going over to Helena's and I'm going to tell her about us."

"Don't make me out to be a cunt, man." Aaron raised his eyebrows.

The following day after work, Aaron went to see Donna and she was in her office at home doing business with America on the phone. She turned Zara's room into a draped room of femininity. Aaron told Roy he could see that something about Donna had changed because her hair was tied back with a scarf into a pigtail with the ends of the scarf breezing about. She wasn't wearing much make-up and she looked alert, intense, and appeared younger and more energetic.

He happily watched her as she handled business. She talked about prices, deliveries, new lines of menswear, the feedback and sales figures from Poland and Hungary. She looked at the email and Aaron watched her download a file and read it. "Bart, listen to me! These sales figures are shit. Send me a realistic target and we'll talk."

Donna hung up and quickly leaned over and kissed Aaron. "All day, one thing after another; I spoke to your tailor and he put me in touch with some people who can deliver to Eastern Europe. So, Miriam and her fucking mother can eat shit. I found a way around them. You look great! How's Amber? Pedro is taking me out again tonight!"

"Slow down."

"Can't, too busy! I'm off to Bermuda!" she yelled, singing the word out. "Pedro can't wait to show me off. He's got over one hundred people working for him, did you know that? Daa, course, you did. You know what blood type he is," she said, referring to the dossier.

Aaron asked, "When are you going: for how long? What's the setup?"

"He's going to introduce me to his daughter and her husband."

"Did I do right, mum?"

"Yes. How's Roy and Eugene?"

"They're working on it, finding out if they're right. Roy hides a lot, but you should see his face when he talks about Eugene. His voice is cool, but his face is alive. Really bright!"

"Great!" She kissed him. "Tell Roy, I'll bring him back something super from Bermuda. How's Amber?"

"Her work has her out of London for now, but I'm going to ask her day after tomorrow." Donna smiled and he felt greatly comforted by his mother's love.

"Pedro is collecting me, so you don't have to drop me at the airport." He stood there and took it all in, fidgeted and then kissed her and moved to leave.

When I received the pages from Roy, once again I asked myself if it was worth continuing to write the book with him. I couldn't answer my own question so I went to the kitchen to cook dinner and while I did that, I took a mental survey of what was happening to all of them and the emotional truth of everyone involved, then it hit me.

I couldn't stop writing the book because I cared what happened to the women's lives. In all honesty, I cared less about Aaron but I knew why. However, the bond of life and death was more important than sex. My professionalism got the best of me, consequently, I emailed Roy and told him to keep sending me chapters.

CHAPTER THIRTY-ONE

Aaron and I went to Helena's place in Knightsbridge smartly dressed, to see Amber. Helena told Eugene about her flat, but it was twice as posh as I imagined. It was filled with Persian carpets, silk curtains and pastel feminine elegance. The living room was a *Tatler* magazine dream. Aaron stood in front of Amber and said to Helena, who was dressed in baggy slacks and a white shirt. "It's important we're all together. I need to tell you something." Amber looked at us questioningly, as casually dressed as I've ever seen her in jeans and a top. Madonna's greatest hits were playing and *Like A Prayer* ended and *Erotica* started.

"I've done as you asked, Amber. I believe I now understand your innate..." he searched for the word, "humanity. You and Helena have been mates since you were at school, aged twelve. Me and Roy have been mates since we were at Uni, aged eighteen. We're perfect mates."

Puzzled, Amber looked to Helena and back at him. "I know you love Helena and that her love for you is something you can't discard. I have the same thing." Aaron turned and came towards me, hugged me, and then kissed me.

When he broke his kiss with me, he turned to Amber. "Now you two. I know; I understand." Amber must have been asking her brain if her eyes deceived her.

She wasn't shocked or startled, she was surprised. Whereas Helena looked like she was dealing with a man who dared her to be herself. She turned to Amber, embraced and kissed her. After a certain time, I looked at Aaron because I wondered how long Helena was going to hold onto her and then I remembered how vocal and crazy Aaron and I were in bed. This prolonged kiss could have rattled another man but Aaron watched unshaken. When

Amber pulled back, Helena was defiantly thrilled to have shown him the love she has for Amber.

I watched Amber walk towards him and I couldn't take my eyes off her. She looked pensive but at the same time she seemed aggrieved. "You should have told me." He was about to speak when she stung him with a slap in his face.

"I was afraid you'd leave me if you didn't understand my love for Helena." Her consternation stripped her of power but not dignity. "Don't hide from me again. How many boyfriends have you had?"

"None: Roy's the only man I could ever imagine making love with."

Amber modestly asked, "You prefer women?"

"Yes. Do you?"

"No—Helena and I have been together because I love her. We are not sex companions."

Helena said, "Absolutely, no one has touched her, only me." I didn't know if she was boasting, but the Italian tone in her voice was filled with alacrity.

Anyway, we all kept looking at each other as though we were playing mind-games where we had to act out what we were thinking. With the hit *Erotica* playing, it was the strangest few minutes I've ever had.

"Your mother knows this?" Helena asked.

I said, "No, Donna doesn't know. Does your family know about you?"

"My father knows, not my other family; Bernard also discovered, by accident. He is terrified his little Princess will be a dyke."

"Please, Helena; I don't like that word, you know that darling."

"Bernard regularly insists a doctor confirms she is intact." Aaron was going to sound off but he stopped himself.

Amber asked, "Have you been sexing since you meet me?"

I said, "No!" immediately.

Aaron said, "Girls, ladies...Helena; darling. This isn't an inquisition. Our libidinal impulses are ignited by our devotion to one another." When he smiled, he defied a fixed identity. Neither Dorian Grey nor Dracula looked more seductive. That totally rattled Helena.

"Aaron, if you say to me, don't ever see Helena again—"

"Amber, I'd never say that: not ever. You still love her, don't you, Helena?" Helena did everything she could to remain proud, but I could see the emotional truth tear at her skin. Aaron spoke to her in Yiddish and Helena replied to him in the same language. Eventually, he embraced her and they spoke for a time until Amber moved to join them.

Suddenly I wanted Eugene. Time and again, I felt this isolation. Aaron was drawing them in like he'd mastered the Jedi mind-trick.

Helena stared at Aaron and said, "So, you are not gay, but you have sexual experience with Roy. And Amber is not gay, but she has sexual relations with me. What does that make us?"

Aaron said, "That makes us sexually disruptive—this is the 21st century. I've seen orthodox rules shatter people's lives. We're following our instincts and that's why emotional and erotic intimacy has bonded our friendships."

"So, you are not going to restrict Amber's freedom?" Helena asked him, knowing that his race and orthodoxy give him the authority to make demands.

"No."

Amber told him, "And this is why I want only you." Somehow, I was certain that statement was damaging to Helena.

"I love Amber for everything we've lived together. Can you live without Roy?"

I said, "I'm not in love with Aaron. I'm in love with Eugene."

"Without Roy and my analyst helping me through bereavement, I'd be a wreck but you're the woman who healed my heart, Amber."

Helena said, "If I asked Eugene to join us for drinks; would this bother you, Aaron?" He said no, casually and Helena said, "Suppose Amber needs me and Roy needs you, later on: sexually—what then?"

Amber said, "I think we should stay out of each other's beds. Husbands and wives shouldn't be in other people's beds."

"But what if—" Helena started to say and I got really mad.

"What are you doing?" I asked her, but I knew everything Eugene told me about her. This is the kind of emotional abuse I grew up with and couldn't accept. All three of them looked at me and the atmosphere turned chilly. Helena eyed me anxiously.

"This isn't about sex. *Any* interference by us is unconscionable." I could feel Helena's tension and Amber's relief.

"Great," Aaron took out the box and got on his knee. Helena caught her breath and Amber flushed.

"Amber Louise Shapiro. Will you marry me?"

Amber flushed. "Aaron Lorenzo Rapchinski, yes I will, Mr Blackmon."

He offered the ring, she put it on and I yelled, 'Mazel tov!" Amber screamed and grabbed Helena and kissed her and then she rushed into Aaron's arms and kissed him. Amber yelled. "Look at me in jeans and a T-shirt! Like a tomboy. My darling, let me get dressed."

"No, I want to call mum and let her talk to you. She said she'd give me a slap if I didn't call her if you accepted me." Aaron got his mobile out.

"No, no; I'm not wearing anything; I cannot talk to Donna like this."

"Relax!" He dialled. Amber jumped up! She began speaking rapidly in Italian and Helena replied in Italian. They must have exchanged a hundred words in seconds. They were rushing about grabbing and yelling at each other.

Aaron said, "Hello mum, my soon to be wife wants to talk to you." The girls heard Donna screaming on the phone, so Amber grabbed the mobile.

"Hello, mummy! Yes! Yes! He just asked me." She laughed. "The ring is on my hand! He is wonderful! I love him! Helena is here, wait."

"Donna!" Helena spoke to her in Spanish and they went on and on and shrieked down the phone. "I know! I am going to phone my father: she will call her parents too."

With all the euphoria, I sensed that Helena was downhearted even though she was hyping herself up. I could see the blues in her eyes because I had seen it in my own eyes on quite a few occasions.

After the call, Amber and Helena left the room and fifteen minutes later, Amber came back wearing a dress. She settled down and took a seat, but she was all fingers and nerves as she dialled.

"Hello, it's me. I have good news. Aaron asked me to marry him and I just accepted." Helena massaged her shoulders and patted her. As she listened, Amber became intensely emotional and

Aaron saw the change in her. "Yes, yes, Papa, I am very happy." She smiled and became a bit tearful. "I'm not shouting and screaming because I have been doing that for the last twenty minutes." She listened again. "Yes, put her on." She paused for a few seconds. "Yes, mother, a few minutes ago. Oh, the ring is beautiful!" She listened closely. I watched the loving care and attention Helena gave to her. "Yes, he is." She waved and Aaron came to the phone and took it.

"Yes, Bernard! I'm very pleased! I will. Call my office manager and I'll set that up." Helena got on her mobile and called her father. "I look forward to that, sir." Aaron handed the phone back to Amber. She continued, then switched to her native language and spoke quietly to her father until tears of joy came down her face. She then told him goodbye.

"Papa!" Helena began and continued in Italian. She waved Amber over to her and the sound of laughter filled the room as Massimo told her congratulations.

His voice swept her up and she began laughing. "Yes, he's listening, Uncle Massimo; we are all listening on speaker."

Massimo said, "Hello, my friend! Congratulations, I will tell my people to start expecting visits. I want to make a big thing! My lovely girl is getting married, that's wonderful!" He asked so many questions he tired us out and then brought us back to life as he put friends on the phone to congratulate Amber and Aaron. As the call was about to end, Helena took the phone and went into her bedroom.

* * *

Several days later, back at our home in Hackney, Aaron and I were totally captivated by everything Donna told us when she got back from her trip. She sat in the best chair and held court as we brought her food and drink so that she could relax and simply share her experience. Perhaps it was because she was at our house rather than hers, but the daylight streamed in through the living room windows and our life-size sculptures of C3PO, R2D2, Vader and Emma Peel from the *Avengers*, along with the Xbox and other toys looked adolescent with a real woman in the house. We were sitting at her feet on the floor looking up to her and listening.

Donna continued. "…His daughter was a really nice girl. She has two kids and her husband is Portuguese, nice bloke." She took another sip of her wine. "You still can't imagine what the place looked like. Bermuda has pink beaches and there are lots of tourists, but where he lives is about a mile away from his daughter's house. It's a well-to-do area of private houses. Executives and Civil Service people live there. He had me stay at his daughter's and if and when I wanted to, I could stay at his." A brilliant smile rose up on Donna's face.

"Pedro is very accommodating…" But she lost it then and began laughing until she pulled herself together.

"Let me guess," Aaron said. "The two of you made love?" Donna stood up and walked towards the window and looked out. In her summer dress, she was so womanly and mother of the earth. I've seen Spanish women in films by Pedro Almodóvar, who looked similar.

"It's been ages since I felt pampered by anyone else besides you guys, but you're my boys. Pedro took me out everywhere every night and it was nice to hear his life story through his daughter's love for him. And his son-in-law genuinely respects him, you can't fake that." Donna turned to us and stared for a while. "I love you boys for going through all that to find decent blokes."

Aaron seriously asked, "Do you like him, mum?"

"Yes, definitely: I sense he's working hard to please me and so I still don't know what he's like on an average day-to-day basis, but he's solid."

"Is there anything about him that troubles you, Donna?"

She sat back down and thought and then she said to me, "Are you absolutely sure about Eugene? Can you imagine your life with him?"

"Yes."

"My God, he's blushing," Donna said.

"Eugene remembers things I've told him and takes me to things I like. He introduced me to friends of his, some of the best academics around the country who discuss race and gender. Other novelists. They listened to me and praised me on my articles. We drank Sambuca and talked about a holiday together in Capri."

Just the memory of that weekend with Eugene's friends made me feel great.

"And he takes me to places I've said I want to go, like The London Eye and the Planetarium. He kissed me under the stars when we were there."

Donna said, "Ooh-la-la."

That made me feel weird, so I asked, "Are you making fun of me?"

"No, sweetheart." And Aaron said no also. She called me to her, so I went and sat in the one-seat sofa snug next to her and she whispered in my ear. I could see Aaron wanted to know what Donna told me when I burst out laughing and I returned to his side on the floor again.

"So, we did good, mum; with the shortlist?"

"Yes, Pedro is definitely a 9; because who knows where a 10 is, these days with men as iffy as they are. I'm going to have dinner with Yves: on the face of it, he's an 8; but I don't know how much more there is to him unless I go out with him. He mentioned a Paris weekend because he gets lots of flight deals working for the airline, but I've got a business to run so I can't be gallivanting all over the place."

She got up and gestured for our glasses. "But Pedro is very loving." We gave them to her and as she headed over to the cabinet, she said, "I had to laugh Aaron, when Pedro said, you told him to meet you and then you drove him back to his place to check his house was safe!" She screamed with laughter. "That, child of mine, was cheeky and very clever!"

Aaron was so pleased with himself he couldn't hide it. He looked up at his mum the way I never ever looked at my mother. Although Zara and Humphrey weren't with us anymore, sitting in my home with my preferred family and knowing I could invite Eugene over whenever I liked made me so happy, I can't remember when last I felt happier.

CHAPTER THIRTY-TWO

Aaron followed Bernard and Massimo around a new home in St John's Wood. It was a four-bedroom house with two receptions, dining and living room, with a conservatory and a large garden. Both men in their jeans, cashmere jumpers, suede loafers and man-bags, pointed out features to each other as they spoke to Aaron casually displaying their wealth of knowledge and power. The house was empty, so they were able to freely talk as they walked in and out of all the rooms.

Aaron said, "But you're talking about me helping Helena to get pregnant."

Massimo said, "You have said you don't judge her because she prefers the company of women. She is deeply saddened by the prospect of losing Amber. We are not talking about some lurid lesbian love affair. My daughter deeply loves Amber because they have shared their life. The prospect of being alone…"

Bernard said, "Amber told me that she is terribly worried about what their separation will do to Helena. Can you be happy, knowing your wife is grieving for the friend that has given her life meaning? What impressed me about you is your profound understanding of care for your mother."

Massimo added. "You show great sensitivity. That is why I was happy to help find the ideal person for your mother. Can you help your wife to support her—"

"—Girlfriend?" Aaron interjected.

Massimo said, "I am more understanding of Amber than your grandfather would be of Roy. If you haven't told your mother I imagine you don't want to tell your grandfather."

"Are you marrying my daughter to hide behind her?"

Massimo turned to his friend. "Don't say that Bernard." There was a dreadful silence.

"Are you a man or a homosexual?" Massimo asked.

"I am a man."

"Maybe you're confused and Amber and Helena offer you a half-life to be with Roy?" Bernard said.

"I am not confused," Aaron stated. "I love Amber. Nor am I confused about Roy's loyalty and friendship. My father's death tore me up and Roy stitched me back together. Why wouldn't I love him?"

"Does your mother also understand?" Bernard asked.

"Mum and I love him intimately. If you want to get slapped, violently; ask her about their confidentiality." Aaron noted their expressions as he outmanoeuvred their manipulation.

"My love for Roy does not include a third party in my wife's bedroom." Fear rose up in him. "Helena's child could disrupt our marriage. Women can be deeply jealous."

Bernard said, "Amber and Helena are closer than sisters. We know them better than their mothers or friends." That further unnerved Aaron.

They stopped talking and then guided Aaron through the rooms. It was a very homely house, even though there was nothing in it. Anyone with an imagination could picture a family in it. Aaron recognised the value of their ploy.

"Let's say, I help Helena get pregnant. What would happen then?"

Massimo inhaled. "I have a palazzo near Lake Como. Helena also has a house in Milan. The child would be raised there, by Helena and our people. She would run her department in the Milan office, which is the Company Headquarters. Even though she would move from London, back home. She will still be near her former school friends and yes, Amber would be able to go and see her."

Bernard said, "Helena knows she cannot live in your life, Aaron."

"What rights, if any, would I have?"

"It will be Helena's baby, not yours."

"Will I ever have a say in the child's life?"

"Time will answer that," Massimo replied.

"My mum would be gutted if she knew nothing about this. Or if she couldn't see the baby, not to mention the disturbing lies that go with concealing this."

"We want to be sure you don't feel that Helena and my family are invading your life or your own family with Amber when the time comes," Massimo told him.

"How do Helena's needs fulfil my life?" Because Aaron was frightened, he used a relaxation technique Dr Liebermann taught him.

Massimo put his hand up. "I know you are no fool or mercenary. I will give you one million pounds." Massimo put his arm around Aaron's back and led him to the conservatory that allowed them to look into the garden.

"Considering the problem you spoke to me about, with the clients who are too blind to work with you according to your commitment to equality: I would like to turn your firm into my HR service. Does that appeal to you?"

"I can't say. Hold on." Aaron's heart began racing. "The artificial insemination procedure, how do Helena and I get this done?"

"There's a clinic in Bern. You'd go there. Provide sperm and then Helena would follow and the doctors would work with her until she's pregnant."

"So, I'd have to bank several deposits."

"They need enough to be sure Helena is with child," Massimo said.

Bernard quickly said, "I think this could be a nice home for newlyweds to start a family. Amber told me, you have a nice home, but not enough room for children. And your friend Roy lives there, yes?"

"I am not giving my sperm to doctors in a Swiss clinic." Both men's faces dropped. "I appreciate that you guys have millions. But these are my balls and they're not for sale to any woman looking to fulfil her own ambitions."

Massimo said, "Do you remember what I asked you at my house?"

"Yes. 'Can I adopt my wife's lifestyle and not force her to adopt mine?' Yes, Massimo, I remember. I plan to make Amber very happy."

"If you make her break her friendship with Helena, this will not happen."

Bernard said, "Perhaps I should speak to your grandfather about this. If he is happy with your boyfriend, maybe he will be comfortable with you having children outside of your marriage. All things considered with your *disposition* and Amber's nature, at least we'll be sure there are grandchildren..."

"Excuse me," Aaron said without shouting even though he was distraught. "I'm not obliged to make Helena's dreams come true. I'm in love with Amber, not Helena. No disrespect. She's gay, I'm not. That means her disinterest in men should not include me."

"I can see misery ahead," Bernard said. The remark wasn't in the least advisory, it was intimidating. He continued, "The other boys who were interested in Amber, she swore to bring them misery and humiliation if she was forced to cut Helena out of her life. If Helena is left with nothing of her life with Amber, you will bring grief into your house that will destroy you. I've had to deal with this before. I don't want to hurt you, Aaron."

"Amber is a true bohemian," Massimo said casually. "She has invented a 21st century way of living she wants to bring to life. If you lose her, you can explain to your mother and grandfather you do not offer her the consideration you give to your boyfriend." Aaron stood motionless as if he had turned to stone, trapped by Bernard and Massimo's words.

CHAPTER THIRTY-THREE

At Dr Liebermann's, Aaron marched back and forth with heavy feet wearing out the carpet. "For me to explain fully, I have to tell you something intimate." Aaron sat down.

"When has that ever stopped us from talking."

"If I told you, I'm sexually unlimited, how do you read that?"

Dr Liebermann eyed him, referencing Aaron's stages of distress and recuperation.

"You might be referring to your predilections; so many people these days include dominance and submission in their pleasures."

Aaron stared back at him unresponsively and so Liebermann gave it another try. "Perhaps you include other girls for variety." Aaron still gave him nothing. So, Dr Liebermann cast his mind across their many sessions and he saw that Aaron's eyes willed him on. Aaron leaned forward with his elbows on his knees and rested his chin on his thumbs.

"Oh." Aaron stared at him wide-eyed. "Do you also find men attractive?"

The fact that he worded it that way instead of asking, 'are you attracted to men?' made him smile.

"I'm not attracted to men." Dr Liebermann nodded. "But I do love Roy. Yes, I love him."

Dr Liebermann sat perfectly still and let the thought run through his mind.

"I'm listening," Aaron said. Daniel's face constantly changed expressions. "I don't go to gay bars or watch gay porn or anything like that. And I don't steal sidelong looks at blokes when I go and play football, or hang around in the showers—you know, lurking. Roy and I share everything in our lives."

"What kind of sex do you have?"

"Equal." Dr Liebermann stared at him probingly. Aaron knew he didn't get it. "The self-oppressive 'top' and 'bottom' nonsense gay boys saddle themselves with is pure rubbish to me."

"Explain and answer my question." Aaron gave him a potted history of current LGBTQ practices as defined by the community.

"So, what are you?" Aaron sensed the emotional fluctuations Daniel had.

"Heteroflexible. I respond to human beauty. Roy is beautiful, not just because his physique is 'fit'. He understands my soul." Dr Liebermann was stunned by Aaron's nonchalance.

"Won't this affect your marriage?"

"No."

"Do you want him more than her?"

"No, I've wanked my balls dry thinking about Amber."

"As vivid as always! So, you want her and the life that goes with marriage."

"Amber loves me. And she has a girlfriend." Surprised, Daniel got up, went to the other side of the room, opened a cupboard, took out two glasses and a bottle of brandy and poured two drinks. He approached Aaron and gave him a glass.

"Cheers! In life, I've met many, many boring people. You can never be accused of that." Dr Liebermann's eyes made Aaron down the drink in one.

"Her girlfriend is putting the screws to me through her dad and Amber's father." Aaron told him everything as briefly as he could.

"Aaron, my life would be so much poorer without you. Come, let's go out for dinner; I want to hear all of this so we can find a way through for you."

"The session time's over."

Dr Liebermann put his pad down. "Forget that. We'll take all night if need be." Aaron sensed something in Dr Liebermann he couldn't explain, but he felt safe and relieved at the prospect of having extra time with him.

"Dinner's on me though, Daniel." Dr Liebermann shoved him towards the door. "Wow! Out of hours sessions and socialising." Dr Liebermann walloped Aaron across his backside.

Aaron told me he felt like he'd been disciplined.

"Ouch! Sorry daddy," Aaron joshed and happily got a move on.

* * *

Aaron took him to the restaurant, *Meat People*, and they enjoyed a grilled and roasted dinner with beer and wine. The atmosphere and style of the place was definitely French bistro. What Aaron liked was the buzz of the place with loads of people coming and going. Unlike Hackney's hipness, the patrons were 'Islington trendy', namely, middle-class aspiring people, as opposed to Hackney's aspiring working class. Over dinner, they continued talking and searching for solutions.

"Aaron, you and Amber are cut from the same cloth. That's one in a million. Now the girlfriend is acting up. Which isn't surprising: she stands to lose more than Roy does. He accepts you're heteroflexible. I love that expression by the way; never heard it before. But Helena most probably hoped Amber would remain as they were before you came along. What type of Sappho, lesbian, gay is she?"

"Helena's Italian, wealthy and good-looking. Her father and her uncle are threatening to tell mum and grandad."

Daniel gritted his teeth. "The balls on these money men! How dare they threaten to tell your grandpa! I bet they know about Blacks' essentialist hatred of homosexuality."

"I toughed it out with them, but they're heavy hitters."

"No one's going to lift a finger against you as long as I live," Daniel said, pointing to heaven. "Moguls are narcissists and mobsters are psychopaths; let me help you to deal with them. I know how to destabilise their egos."

Aaron told me he saw malevolence in Dr Liebermann's face he never suspected he was capable of. What gave Aaron pins and needles was the fact Liebermann knew he revealed something of himself that he wanted Aaron to see.

"I didn't know you were a bit wicked, but your face is a dead giveaway."

"I've dealt with lunatics and predators so I know how to protect myself. The thing to understand with her father and her uncle is that they are empire building.

They aren't wicked, they're greedy and they want everything they can get for their families: especially their daughters."

"The thing is. If I take the money:" Aaron lowered his voice. "Give them my sperm and move into that house; I won't be able to call my life my own."

"Yes, they're leading you into temptation."

"Yeah, if I were a Godless millennial without a backbone and decency."

"By our standards, you are at risk of being emasculated."

"They don't understand I've always been influenced by pagan and pious ideals. I embrace philosophies that cleanse me of subjugation because racial and sexual liberty lives in me," he professed. "I give myself to Roy because it creates existential physical harmony in my soul. When dad died; my Afro-sensibility collapsed. Roy saved me and then you restored me."

"So, being heteroflexible is more mental than sexual?"

"No, we have each other with gusto. But it's the other side of male violence. We're sensual, carefree, tender." The pride and joy he felt showed. "Sometimes I get frightened and I feel like I'm dying. That terrifies me. When we have each other, I reignite. Yes, it's a visceral high of incredible sexual pleasure. But more than that: my Afro-sensibility is restored. I'm not white, I'm not gay: I'm a once removed Spanish Black Jew. Even if I'm one of a kind; I'm me. I won't have those wealthy European Jewish families take my wife from me. Dad didn't give me these balls to give away and mum didn't teach me to be a Jew who runs away." Dr Liebermann patted Aaron's hand.

"I'm sure of that. Your mother is an intelligent beautiful woman. What she's come through and her ability to hold her dignity in spite of her father's cruelty." Daniel shook his head. "I wouldn't be surprised if your grandfather is an insomniac robbed of sleep so he can face God night after night and ask the question: 'Have I shamed myself through perverse cruelty to my daughter?' I couldn't live with myself if I ever did what he did! Kadokhes, Shtunk!" he concluded in Yiddish.

"You think a lot of my mother."

"Naturally! Look how you turned out!" He affectionately said, "she wouldn't like it if you made a eunuch of yourself just to get some 'dosh' out of them. She'd be proud if you aced them. You manoeuvred Miriam into a trap." Daniel smiled. "Together, we can bring these men to heel."

They ate quietly and Daniel immediately spotted when Aaron remembered something. "Bubala! Talk to me." Aaron leaned in closer.

"It's this business with bohemians Amber mentioned several times. Correct me if I'm wrong. The movement started in Paris in

1830..." Aaron then navigated his way through its French history and up to Britain in the post-war period. "The 'Bloomsbury Set' was the real turn around. Instead of starving artists in Paris, we switch to posh toffs in London swapping partners, shagging each other and their kids. But they had so much money they could indulge their vices."

"Your ability to recall and synthesize has always impressed me. Yes, correct."

"Amber said something once—phrased with her European voice, it sounded lovely. She said. *The mind often taxes the body for the pleasures it craves*'. How do you read that?" Daniel thought about it very carefully for a time.

"I believe she's referring to the seven deadly sins: pride, greed, lust, envy, gluttony, wrath and sloth. She is very cautious, even though her knowledge of desire and dread reveals a temptation. *Why* are you smiling at me like that, Aaron?"

"You're brilliant! I love you doc."

"Stop it. Listen. There is a way to handle the men. But let me ask you. How much do you think she loves you?"

That evening when Arron and I stayed up until three in the morning, I still saw how his face lit up as he recounted it to me.

"She works at the V&A. One night she invited me out to an Event with her boss and colleagues. We went to *Sexy Fish* in Berkeley Square: loads of posh people swanning about. Amber was head of our round table, beautifully dressed as always. She kept telling everyone how brilliant I am, me. *I* was the catch, like she isn't a diplomat's daughter raised in a Swiss Finishing School, with millionaire friends." *He was so thrilled he blushed.*

"Amber said: 'I think he trumps every man in town; isn't he marvellous!' Those toffs eyed me and I was like...yeah, cool." Then all at once, Aaron couldn't keep still and Daniel noticed that a few people eyed him.

"Aaron, I'll tell you how to deal with her family. Sons of bitches. But let's get out of here first." Aaron had no idea what was coming but he knew he had to do what Dr Liebermann asked.

After the meal, they left the restaurant and walked across Islington Green, over to Upper Street, avoiding drunks in fancy clothes, high heels and screaming into their mobiles. They strolled quietly and allowed their thoughts to take root. They walked past the shops, restaurants, and bars for a good stretch of the legs as the winding road was scattered with window displays and dark doorways. Daniel stopped for a minute so Aaron looked at him and Daniel took a breath.

"Based on everything you've told me... I love your mother. Her strength and heart have deeply affected me." Dr Liebermann held his head high and pushed his chest out. Aaron saw the vein in Daniel's temple pulsating.

"I sensed that you feel something for my mum."

"I wish I had the chance to show her I'm a decent man." Liebermann searched for the right words. "You gave those strangers a chance..." Aaron attempted to cut in.

"Let me finish." Liebermann's hand began to shake and he lost his words.

"Daniel, when I told you about not letting any fucking pricks near my mum; I felt a heavy vibe rise in you, during that session."

"I'm not some fucking prick." They walked on from the Church of St Mary the Virgin and Daniel led rather than followed Aaron.

Aaron gave him a searching look. "I know you're nothing like that. I also know nothing would make me happier than introducing you to mum."

"OK! There you go, yeah!" Daniel said almost bumping into someone. "I love who Donna has become. I cannot overstate her courage in recovering the way she has. Every time you tell me about her, I've felt closer to her."

"I'll introduce her to you. You don't even have to sit a psychometric test."

"Will she like me?" Aaron saw that Daniel was consumed by doubt. "That question has dogged me ever since you started screening people to meet her."

"She already respects what you've done for me."

"Was she very taken with the guy she went to Bermuda with?"

"He's a 9/10."

"A nine! Shit. And Pedro's younger than me and really handsome. I wish I'd never seen his face or heard your praise about him," he stated through clenched fists.

"Daniel, easy—You're a doctor and a mensch!" Daniel bumped into Aaron's shoulder and he bumped back into Daniel. "You're amazing, doc; mum will see that, especially with the way you've helped me."

Dr Liebermann contemplated and they walked silently for a time, until he stopped and told Aaron, "Withdraw your offer of marriage and let Amber deal with her family. You told me Amber's heroines; considering who she admires, Amber will vanquish both men."

"I don't understand."

"Women have power that men cannot attain. Men are terrified of weakness. Women are not. The love letters you've shown me. Amber wants you in her romantic and everyday life. She won't take kindly to anyone robbing her of the life she wants. Withdraw your offer of marriage and I'm telling you as a psychiatrist—Amber will make those men regret it."

"She might just think I'm a total lying bastard."

"Not if I know anything about women."

Rather worried, Aaron told him, "I'm trusting you to help me win the girl I love."

"And I'm relying on you to help your mum see I'd be the perfect husband." With a nod that is specific to Jewish men, they silently agreed to help each other.

When Aaron sat up all night and told me all this, I realised he was a bohemian in the true sense of the word.

* * *

I couldn't take my eyes off Roy as we came out into The Mall from the Institute of Contemporary Arts. Dressed in our finest, we all felt great, having just delivered our Papers to the Afrocentric Aesthetics Association where the BAME literati came to hear the 'Thoughts of the Day' concerning Black Identity politics. We were champions. Michael contacted me when they put out 'a call for papers' and I told Roy and so all four of us delivered to the delegates. Michael and David looked as pleased as punch as they stepped into the magenta evening with the royal boulevard leading up the road to Buckingham Palace and St James's Park. The night shimmered with autumn leaves and lights directly across the street from the ICA.

I was so proud of Roy; I put my arm around his shoulder as we crossed the street. He was obviously proud of himself because the energy boosted his 5ft 9" frame to a giant of a man mentally. The night air smelt ripe with Cointreau, greenery from the Park and something indefinable. Maybe it was all the cologne and perfume people wore, but I felt grand because in his linen suit and evening shirt, my man looked as sexy as he is smart.

I couldn't help but ask myself and then Michael: "We 'represented' tonight, didn't we? Based on everything we said and heard, what class do you think we belong to as Black Brits?" David was about to answer when Keith rushed up to us and appeared in my face. He was a piece of rubbish I knew a long time ago.

"Eugene! Loved the paper; yours too, Michael!" He was the very picture of aristocratic masculinity: entitled, married, self-important with some influential friends: and he sat on several Art Committee Boards. "I hardly see you these days," he said and gestured as if he was royal.

"Roy, your contribution is more than welcome. I read your column. I'd love to hear more about your ideas of 'Reconstituting Black Equality for Inclusion'. Do you really think this generation is playing at being Black in the gay community rather than actually being authentic?" He touched Roy's shoulder.

I yanked him around so that we were eye to eye and then I spat in his face!

"You so much as email him and I'll tear your balls off!" He screeched with my spit in his eye and gob running off his nose. Michael and David closed in and I jabbed Keith in the forehead. "I'll tell your wife how I fucked you and I'll give her the names of Black guys you've shagged behind her back. This is my man; you don't go near him."

He took out his handkerchief and wiped his face. "You'll regret this."

I punched him in the face as hard as I could. All of a sudden, I recited Grand Master Flash, *'Don't push me, cause I'm close to the edge'*. Never in my life have I ever used a rap song to articulate my feelings about anything, so, I don't know how that came out of my mouth, but it did, with violent intent. Whatever I looked like, he looked like he was going to shit his pants.

"I kept your emails from 2006-2007. Like so many pathological sex addicts, you leave a lot of damage. I'll reveal everything you did to me. I have all the evidence and it goes beyond you stalking me. I'll show your wife the kind of cock hungry slut you are and what you do with Black men, if you come anywhere near Roy, or me."

"Don't." he said, as his nose began bleeding and he used his hankie.

"Fine, fuck off." Keith nervously looked at Roy, David and Michael and then he left. The coming dark skies swallowed him into the night as he vanished in the park.

Roy took my arm and I eased away. "Michael, drop Roy home for me. I need some time." I kissed Roy goodnight and then David walked twenty yards with me.

"Come to us for breakfast, OK?"

"I knew he'd resurface, like some slag with herpes."

"Eugene, he can't hurt you anymore. This isn't 2008. You're the talent; you're the prize-winning academic whose work is studied in universities. Keith's just a hungry cum-slut who feeds on Black men. And like the other dogs of his breed, he's inhuman. You're not."

"Thanks Dave." I looked over at Roy and Michael was keeping him still. I nodded and then got a move on because I didn't want Roy to see me like that, especially after I agreed to continue seeing him. He came to me crying and couldn't stop. I had to take him back. However, I did tell him, I don't do open relationships. If he couldn't cope with that, he could finish this novel without me and I'd leave him alone. I was born in the fifties, so even in this day and age, love matters to me.

CHAPTER THIRTY-FOUR

Donna was in her garden surrounded by more than fifty flowerpots with different plants of all colours. Never had Donna looked more domestic at home, moving around the garden. She kept turning from the flowers to Aaron.

"Mum, it's good Yves has respect and Pedro clearly has had an emotional impact on you, but I know someone who loves you. No bullshit, no masquerade."

The intensity of Aaron's eyes and the smile made the hair on the back of Donna's neck stand up.

"What? Who?" She watched him until she felt connected to him.

"Dr Liebermann."

"Your doctor. What the—"

"It's happened because I kept saying how incredible you are. He told me he's never had a patient that praised their mother. What he's used to hearing is: 'if it wasn't for my mother…' Bitching like a cry-baby. Or, 'Dr Liebermann, my mother's wretchedness contaminates my life…' blah blah. But with me, I kept saying we're each other's lifeline." Donna was stunned. "Because of what I've said, he considers you to be magnificent and he loves you."

"You're not joking." Aaron shook his head and that smile, which was so like his father's covered his face. Donna was captured and held still.

"If this isn't some kind of psychiatric illness, I should meet him." Aaron nodded. "For fuck sakes, he loves me even though he's never met me?"

"Yes, mummy he really does." The light in Aaron's face moved her.

"I have to meet him. What's he *really* like?" Aaron's wondrous smile lifted her heart.

"He's a ten!"

Donna placed her hands on her face staring at him. "He fell in love without meeting me: if this were Cádiz, 1820, this wouldn't sound so strange. Are men these days that romantic?" She pondered her own question.

"Who knows, but I'll tell you this about him. He's got brains and heart. Oh yeah, and he's very intuitive." Aaron told her more about Dr Liebermann as Donna put soil into pots and tended the flowers. When he finished, she took her hands out of the earth and everything flowed through her mind.

"You are *such* a blessing to me, darling, no joke."

"One more thing," he said. Donna looked at him, intensely. "Roy and I are so tight; we've been mentally and physically intimate." Aaron eyed her, prompting Donna to speak. "Go on, mum, say it." She took his hand.

"I remember when that friend of mine, or should I say that *former* friend of mine called Roy a queer and you punched him: called him '*a man cunt*'." She shook her head again at the language he used. "The only reason daddy didn't slap you sideways was that he told me, you loved Roy. He said it might be sexual and if it was, we weren't going to go homophobic and beat you up." Aaron took her hand.

"I know you love him. And when we were manic on pills and booze and Roy came over and cooked, cleaned, washed my clothes, my underwear—helped me to bed. I saw that you loved him. You were crying and you hugged him and kissed him." She shook her head. "Besides: when he gave you all that money for your business without asking for anything back; that meant something."

"I love Amber and him in totally different ways." She pulled him closer. "I told Amber; and there is a problem." Donna's eyes inquired and probed him even further. His spirit and energy changed.

* * *

Donna asked Roy to bring me for the dinner invitation at Amber's. She was going to confront her about Helena and I didn't want to go; but writing this book I had to go. What was going to happen I didn't know but I felt dreadfully anxious.

313

Amber was in the kitchen at Helena's flat. It was a specially designed ultramodern white and stainless-steel kitchen-diner that had flat surfaces with soft close doors and cupboards. Amber looked like a performance artist, opening, and closing doors, moving left and right, cooking the dinner in the oven, on the stove and inside of the grill. Her all in one azure blue suit made her look like an ice skater with a decorative sequined pattern covering her bust and arms. Much to Aaron's delight, her athletic figure was fully displayed in the suit. Aaron was reminded of the film *Mon Oncle* by Jacque Tati where an idealised ultramodern family house, with its mechanical efficiency, is a disaster zone for Mr Hulot, but Amber knew how to navigate the kitchen as though she was a ballerina with props. She was cooking an elaborate meal for all of us.

Donna said, "Amber, I must ask, what *are* you cooking? It looks like nine different things."

With a glorious smile she said, "It's something special for you and a specific meal for me. I have to watch my figure. Some of the women in my family are fat. I have no intention of letting myself go."

Aaron told her, "I don't think there's an ounce of spare fat on you darling."

"Good!" She took rice crackers with smoked salmon from the fridge and went to a cupboard and got the Waterford crystal goblets. Donna and Aaron watched her semi-circle as she headed for another cupboard where she carefully carried a vessel that contained warmed Saké. The delicate Japanese object looked very special the way Amber carried it over to us at the table and then poured the drinks.

I said, "I feel very privileged to be invited to your home, Amber."

"This is not my home, Eugene. It's Helena's Pied-à-Terre, her mother gave her a wonderful house in Blackheath, after she graduated, but she rents it for a fortune and lives here because she works close by." We all took a sip and yet again, Aaron was impressed with her poise.

Donna said, "That's gorgeous!"

"Saké; the very best from Japan." We took another sip and quietly let the flavour take hold. "Darling, when we're married, I plan on hosting some fantastic dinner parties. As you see, I can cook. Wait until you taste dinner. At school, it was a core study: etiquette, food, wines, household management, communications in European social intercourse and current worldwide events. But let us not become preoccupied with customs," Amber told them.

Aaron said, "I'm glad you invited us all love, because something important has happened and I wanted my family to understand it." Amber was clearly anxious.

"Aaron, let me," Donna said.

"You're scaring me, Aaron."

I knew what was coming, but I was determined to do anything I could to help because I like Amber more than I can explain. Writing this book has given me months to think about her and the life she wants. Amber's desires were fragments of my own hopes during my twenties.

Donna told her in the most compassionate tone of voice I ever heard come out of her mouth. "I know you and Helena and Aaron and Roy have sexual relations that hold you together. But when Helena wants my son to be a sperm donor and father a child that we have no rights to see or help, that is too much."

Aaron said, "I'm going to your father to withdraw my offer of marriage and I want you to demand your right to marry me without turning our life into your family's possession. Massimo tried to blackmail me..."

"Stop, wait! What?" She looked like she'd been struck by lightning. "Aaron, you mustn't do this. I love you; you can't withdraw...reject me. I haven't done anything wrong."

Oh God, this is horrible! Roy asked me to help him write a book, not to suffer with them.

"Darling, don't cry," Aaron said. But she started and couldn't stop. Roy reached out to me and I knew how he felt.

Amber said, "I'm so sorry Aaron. Tell me, what are they doing?"

Donna took over, "Your family threatened to tell my father-in-law and me about Aaron and Roy because they want to buy my son's sperm for Helena—"

"Mummy, please stop!" Amber grabbed her ears and turned away from us all. She went over to the stove and turned everything off and then she leaned on a wall and cried her heart out.

Amber said, "I have tried to be good and they make me weak and silly: like an unfaithful girl who is disobedient and always has to be told off."

Donna asked, "What do you mean, unfaithful, Amber?"

Amber turned to us all. "A wilful girl who has no faith in her religion. No faith in her mother: and no faith in myself. Why must I be subservient? I don't need anyone's money or approval to be a woman!" She looked at each of us and declared, "I want to be myself. Not a simulacrum. You told me this word, Aaron and I looked it up because your letters are always so full of intelligence and love." I watched Aaron's face and he was crumbling and I mean losing it! "Don't hurt me. I have done nothing wrong."

When Aaron moved towards her and took her in his arms, I think that's when I knew beyond anything that Roy had told me; how much Aaron loved her.

"Amber, I won't have kids with anyone else. I won't put anyone else in our bed; I won't keep secrets that ruin our lives." She kept staring at him and he brushed her hair away from her face. "You're the only woman besides my sister and my mother that I've ever trusted and I won't live without you."

Donna kept nodding and so Roy went to her and I stood alone but bonded to these heartfelt people.

What was so difficult for me is that I couldn't cast Helena as the villain of the peace. How could I feel so close to a woman, who was so unlike me, yet care for her so much?

CHAPTER THIRTY-FIVE

Two days later, in Aaron's living room, Massimo and Bernard sat side by side. They had glasses of whiskey and they needed it because Donna had them on the spot and they both knew it. Aaron sat in a side chair watching. I sat next to Roy and Harold sat on the other side of the room watching all of us. Donna stood in a red dress with a black belt, in front of the two men.

"I won't ask you what you see in my son, I'll tell you what he is. He's free! He doesn't have to live in fear that he's out of his class. I'm sure you're used to buying whatever you want." She walked right up to the sofa and pointed at both of them.

"His children are not for sale." They looked untroubled.

Aaron said, "Bernard, we made an agreement, I wanted to marry Amber because I love her. I don't think you understand why. She's a truly kind person." Aaron got up and pointed to a seat and Donna sat down. "Roy, come here." He let go of my hand and went to him. "Are we a couple?" Roy said no. "Eugene, do you love this man?" I said yes. "Are you aware that Roy and I have been sexual?" I said yes. He turned to Harold. "Grandpa, did you know that?"

"Yes. Last week you told me these motherfuckers are trying to blackmail you. I know you guys have money. I'm not surprised, after all, you're prostitutes." Harold's contempt coloured his voice. The air turned rank and thick with hatred.

Aaron said, "My mother's father forbid her to marry my dad. Shall I tell you what's happened to him?" Bernard and Massimo definitely wanted to know. "He's gone insane. He prays to God for mercy, but there's no forgiveness for what he did. Bigotry is evil!" Aaron crowded them, which made them uncomfortable. "Wickedness will not go unpunished!" he shouted, pointing in their faces. "I reject the laws of orthodoxy. I also detest emasculat-

317

ing women who try and govern me!" he yelled so loudly, Massimo and Bernard flinched.

"Massimo, I liked you, why've you fucked that up?"

"Control yourself," Massimo said like a peacekeeper. Aaron grabbed Massimo's shirt and dragged him out of the sofa, which startled him. "I won't hit you; I've seen your sons and God only knows who else can show up here to cut my throat; brutalise my mother, or who knows what."

"What do you think I am?"

"I thought you were a grand Italian gentleman. Now I see you're just a fascist, Don Carduluci." Aaron said that as if he was referring to someone in *The Godfather*. Massimo's face twisted with rage and became bloodshot.

"I want no part of your family business, so go back and tell Amber I withdraw my offer of marriage."

Bernard said, "This is the wrong thing to do: Amber doesn't deserve this."

"Both of you have manufactured this godless filth!" No crime drama ever showed someone more indignant or threatening. "Live with your crime." Harold stood up and went to Aaron and then took his hand.

Donna said, "Tell Amber my heart hurts and I will miss her." Bernard was distraught. This time I didn't need Roy to describe it, I saw the pain for myself.

* * *

The day after, Helena arrived back at her flat. Amber had packed and sent her bags to a hotel. She'd also booked a cab. When Helena entered the living room, she noted that Amber was dressed in her trouser suit and seemed fit for business rather than relaxation. "Darling, hi! It's so good to get back home. Milan was great, fantastic business, but the flight was delayed and the trip was tedious." Helena's maid and her minder Enrico came in and put down some bags.

"Please leave us," Amber told him and the maid. They both left and Helena knew Amber's tone and posture meant something serious had happened. She took off her gloves and went over to the bar and poured herself a brandy.

"What is it?"

Amber looked around at the luxuries in the room. "This, all of this, is beyond me now. My father and I don't have this kind of wealth. I like it, but I don't need it. For the rest of your life, you will receive one million each year. You have things I love and it's wonderful that you share it with me. I like it." Amber walked up to Helena. "The only thing that's mine that I can't share is my husband: not at this stage or when we are married. There have been many assumptions about him. Let me straighten that out. Uncle Massimo and my father couldn't bend him to their will. He turned them down and rejects me if I'm going to turn him into a virtual male."

Helena tried to speak and Amber stopped her. "No, a moment please, Helena. 'A virtual male'—why must I marry a virtual male? I've shared everything I have with you. But darling, Aaron is the one thing I've acquired on my own virtue..." She mentally sorted through countless words. "I'm a humane person. Why shouldn't that be attractive to someone who wants to marry me?" Helena touched her arm and Amber removed her hand from her elbow.

"I cannot allow you to take him from me to satisfy your self-image. He's mine."

"I only wanted a child to unite us through him, so we'd—"

"No! I know you and Uncle Massimo get very angry when people don't do what you want. I won't stand by and let you punish Aaron; so, I'm leaving and you don't have to bother with him or me anymore."

"What do you mean?" Helena asked, unsettled.

"I'm going away. I don't want us to end badly." Amber walked away and Helena was suddenly panic-stricken.

"Amber, darling, don't be silly. Where are you going?" Amber left the room and Helena made a dash for the door and blocked the exit.

"Darling please. A Bette Davis and Joan Crawford catfight; I don't think so. I will call you tomorrow."

"Where are you going?"

"Wimbledon."

Helena had to settle herself. "Okay, listen. Go and speak to your father. I don't *have* to have a child."

"I know that. We only *have* to have what we need. I need Aaron's love because it's real. It isn't money, it isn't business. It isn't arranged. It's unconditional, except he won't marry me if we turn him into 'a virtual male'. He is a man."

"Talk to your father, I'll talk to Papa."

"Good!" Amber moved to leave, but Helena wouldn't move away from the door. Amber told Aaron that it was the first time in their lives she saw fear in Helena.

"Call me tomorrow." Amber nodded and reached out for the handle and she had to slowly move Helena's body to one side and make her way out.

* * *

Later that night, in Dr Liebermann's old-fashioned dining room, Aaron watched Daniel and his mother, Rosa. Aaron leaned in and spoke to Rosa earnestly. She was every bit the Jewish matriarch, in her pink twin-set with a rope of pearls around her neck and a smart cotton skirt. Her face wasn't aged with tyranny, the light in her hazel-coloured eyes showed her laugh lines and her mouth was a bit topsy-turvy due to her lifetime of asking questions. Her grey hair was decorously styled into a chignon with wisps of hair around her forehead that was most becoming.

"Rosa, my mother's a beautiful person. You'll see that when you meet her. She's been widowed and alone. I spend time with her, but a son isn't a husband." Rosa nodded. "Your son, Daniel; he not only takes care of me, but he's also taken a liking to my mum and I totally approve."

"He needs a wife," she said. "A mother isn't a substitute; I know. I was married to his father for years. Life with Daniel isn't the same. He should have had children, the wife he had, a shiksa, Oy!" She spat three times. "A cocktail waitress, with big bosoms: like decorations." Half smiling, she stated. "She gave him plenty of worries, but no children." The gestures she made with her hands told another story.

Aaron astutely said, "I can see happiness for Daniel and all of us because my mum is incredible, Rosa: enough suffering, yes."

Rosa asked. "Daniel; why have you said nothing to me about this lady: why should a stranger come to me like this?"

Daniel replied, "He wanted to know if *you* 'had issues.' He's very protective of his mother. He won't allow me to date her if you don't want another woman in your life."

"What? I'm not some old yenta." She gave Aaron a smile. "I don't run my son's life. He's his own man: I like that about him. Don't get me wrong, he's no prince."

Daniel joshed. "Just in case you were wondering how Jewish we are, now you know." Rosa dismissed his comment with gestures and sounds that might have been incomprehensible to gentiles, but anyone from their background would know.

"Sometimes, Danny gives me conniptions instead of grandchildren," Rosa confessed.

"Aggravating situations makes my mother verklempt! She can't stand it. And I don't like troublemakers."

"Danny, what's she like, the mother?" She asked to confirm Aaron's statement.

"She's a dish! Beautiful! Maternal, strong..." his thoughts wandered off and his mother studied him.

"You... come to us, you son of a dish!" She liked her joke.

Blissfully, Daniel said, "I say the same thing mama! I called him a son of a dish!"

"Well, you got your brains from me! Let's meet her. I'll call the family." Aaron asked if they were free on Sunday.

"We'll be here on Sunday," Daniel replied.

Aaron's mobile rang and he looked to check. "Excuse me; my fiancé." He got up from the table and stepped outside the dining room, into the hallway.

"Amber, yes, sweetheart, how are you? What happened?" He listened very closely without interrupting her.

"Text me the name and address of your hotel; I'm just sorting out something, I'll come over..." He listened to her.

"But you're at a hotel, not at your father's. What's Helena going to do when she sees you've packed your clothes and cleared out? And she discovers you're not at home." He listened once again.

"Oh! You *want* to make them suffer. Wow! Remind me not to piss you off!" He laughed. "You want to teach them a lesson—fuck yeah!" He chuckled and listened. "No love, I won't say a word to any of them if they call me. When can I see you? I'll go mad if I can't see you."

* * *

At the hotel, Amber scattered the bride magazines across the bed she brought with her and poured a glass of champagne in her small room. "Mon chéri, think about where we are to be married: send me locations. I will look into it. I also have an idea for the wedding. If your ideas are better than mine, I'll—"

Aaron said, "It's outrageous for *me* to call the shots. All I'll say is—we've got the rest of our lives, so let's keep some of the money to start our lives. That doesn't mean I want to rob you of a fantastic day." He listened for over two minutes and he loved everything she told him.

"Darling, if that's what you really want, then that's what we'll have."

She smiled. "I'm not bossing you around too much?" *The Philadelphia Story* was on her TV in the hotel room. "I'm glad I'm not, I detest devious women. Bye, my love." Amber then hung up and called Donna. "Hello mama, I just called him. I just told him what's happening." She listened closely.

"A year ago, I couldn't have handled Uncle Massimo and Papa. Today, I'm not in the mood to be governed by them." She listened closely, once again.

"Dr Liebermann is very interesting. I like his thinking." She went and poured herself another glass of champagne. "It's so important to have Jewish radicals on your list of contacts." She listened to Donna. "Unlike my mother, you inspire me. You defied your father. Everything my mother gave away, I will reclaim. Most of all, I'm so glad you want me in the family. My loyalty shouldn't have gone to the girl that has everything. It should be to the woman who needs everything a daughter can give." She listened for a time.

"Mama, don't cry, please. I'm so glad I will be your daughter. I *can* imagine what it means to you. I am going to prepare myself to claim my liberty from Papa and Uncle Massimo. I just have to get it right and I will." She said goodbye and hung up. Amber later told Aaron she was determined never again to be an imitation of a woman.

CHAPTER THIRTY-SIX

Several days later, Roy picked up Aaron's phone while they were faffing about the kitchen. Aaron was gathering things to escort Donna to meet Dr Liebermann. "It's Bernard."

Aaron said, "You take it." Roy got the call as Donna and Aaron stood still and listened on speakerphone.

"Hello. Yes, Bernard, it's me again. As I told you, Aaron left his mobile at home. He needed to charge it. I've looked at it and I don't see any messages from Amber in the text or phone." Aaron quietly sniggered. "She's sent you text messages to say she's fine and safe Bernard, so she's in no danger." Roy listened closely. "Listen you prick! You don't care whether *I live* or die. I'm just another servant you use. Your life bores me!" Roy cut him off and snorted at the mobile. Aaron and Donna were clearly upset.

"Mate, I'm sorry if—"

"Shut up. Mum, use your instincts tonight! You know what a good man is. You were married to one."

"What are you doing tonight, luv?" Donna asked, concerned about him.

"Something gay, and uncomplicated." When they left, he came over to me, but if I've learnt anything about Donna, Roy's outburst will play on her mind. To me, she possessed the kind of knowledge that her Caribbean and Jewish family would have taught her about discrepancies rather than ideals.

* * *

Aaron and Donna knocked and Dr Lieberman's housekeeper came to the door and welcomed them in. "Good evening! I'm Sheila; let me take your coat. Donna heard a Polish intonation in her voice. Sheila was a little pale with dark brown hair and a stout figure.

Donna took off her coat and gave it to Sheila. Donna's Gepur black lace dress with a silver lace jacket was exquisite, along with the suede slingback evening shoes she wore. Sheila led her across the foyer and knocked on the heavy wooden door. Someone on the other side opened the sliding double doors to reveal decorations that said 'Donna, welcome to the family'.

Before they arrived, Daniel told his family he didn't care what they thought of Donna, he liked her and so all of his brothers and sisters were dead set against Donna even though they hadn't met her. But they knew the type of easy women Daniel liked, so they weren't prepared for Donna.

The furniture, the candles, the Jewish artifacts, lighting and the decorations in the large room and in the foyer suddenly made Donna feel as if she had stepped back into her teenage years at home with her family when everyone loved her. All of the great Jewish faces in the room reminded her of days and nights of faith and family. Dr Liebermann's family was not Hasidic, but it made no difference to Donna.

As a girl, she was allowed to visit other Jewish families who weren't Hasidic, but faithful to their own Jewish beliefs. Her father considered Stamford Hill his whole world, but her Spanish mother wanted Donna to meet the most prosperous men so, she was escorted to other family's home by her brother or sisters. The Liebermann brothers and sisters responded to Donna's age, her elegance and the life that gave her presence authenticity. She was nothing like Daniel's previous young girlfriends which none of them approved of.

Dr Liebermann walked past his family of fourteen relatives. He looked like a Jazzman, but his Jewish pride marked him as Head of the family. His face instantly appealed to Donna because that morning, he had a groomed haircut and his brownish-green eyes and smiling lips warmed her. Daniel's orange shirt, two tone mohair blue-green suit and polished brogues appealed to her because everything he wore made her look at his kind and compassionate face.

"Dr Daniel Liebermann," he told her and not even the words, 'Bond, James Bond' reverberated in her like Daniel's voice, which brought about a *frisson* that rushed through her; she later told Roy. Daniel's voice, his authoritative and caring manner lingered in her flesh for the rest of the night.

Everyone in the room and all the symbols of Jewish celebration and hospitality caught her eye. "Call me Danny or Daniel, but not Dan." She agreed. Daniel took her arm and led her to his mother, his brothers and sisters.

"Welcome to my home, let me introduce you." His deep voice continued to resonate inside Donna as he quietly said, "After everything Aaron's told me about his life and your incredible love to keep him going, I've been hoping to meet you." The tiny hairs on Donna's neck stood up. I later heard from Michael that Donna spent three hours telling his ex-wife Lola the type of chemistry that sparked between them. Daniel discreetly spoke to her as though their heritage gave them ancient affinity.

"Over the past four years, I've heard Aaron sing your praises. I so seldom hear that, it fascinated me. You captured my imagination the way a man falls in love with a star because fans keep saying, 'she's great'." Donna was drawn in by Daniel's expressive greenish-brown eyes and his ebullient tone of voice.

"Before you think—it's too crazy for a psychiatrist to fall for a woman he's never met, just remember. Men have fallen in love with women they've never met for centuries: in literature, on screen, in myth, in art and music."

His statement set her mind racing. "Let me introduce you to my family." His mother stood upright. "This is my mum, Rosa, she keeps us moaning." Donna greeted her in Yiddish and Rosa was pleased to hear Donna's dialect. Dressed as she was, Rosa looked nothing like a typical widow holding onto her kids. Her dress was elegant and becoming. Rosa took Donna's arm as Daniel introduced the others who all had the same wavy chocolate brown hair colour which only varied according to his siblings' stage of grey.

"This is my younger brother, Sasha and his wife, Ingrid." Donna offered her felicitations. Sasha and Ingrid looked like intellectuals who lived with Jewish pride, so their faces were younger than their age. "This is my other brother, Nathan and his wife, Hilda."

They were a severe-looking couple with marital difficulties. They were still battling the role of the sexes because Hilda was a quasi-feminist, but she was also a wife who was scared of losing her husband. Subsequently, each one of their fights left stress marks on their faces.

"And here's my sister Ursula and her husband, the comedian, Zigor." He was a handsome, tall, skinny Hungarian guy and Ursula was a pretty, flirty chef who knew how to run a kitchen and manage the staff.

Aaron said, "Dr Liebermann, I'm starving, let's eat and mix, maybe then we'll remember everyone." Donna looked heavenward and rolled her eyes.

Out of the side of his mouth, Daniel told Donna. "Him; always talking back, seven-eight times you have to prove a point before he learns." He gestured, and Donna's body language responded in kind. Daniel added. "If he were a Yeshiveh bocher, my life would be easier; but not *nearly* so rich! He has a great mind. I have to study more than psychiatry to deal with him, but—my professional development would never be the same without him."

"Have you ever 'fallen' for a patient's wife or mother before?" Donna asked.

"Never!" Daniel turned his back to the family and told Donna. "Survival for us comes in many ways. When Aaron said that your family wouldn't accept his father, I was drawn to every case I've treated where someone has married outside of the faith and they've been abandoned; my soul has wept for them."

Rosa said, "Everyone, come, prayer." The family gathered and prayed and they spoke from the heart in Hebrew. The solemnity of their prayers seemed timeless because of the old fashion decor of the dining room.

Throughout their meal, Donna felt taken back in time and all the pleasures and joys of her youth lifted her soul from out of its protective shield, so she spoke to Daniel's family in Hebrew and Yiddish. The family was not fashion conscious. They were spirit focused and Donna sensed no signs of hostility between brothers and sisters, nor among the husbands and wives. The homeliness in the room, due to its décor and its religious custom, felt life-affirming to Donna.

The feast of hot and cold kosher food, wines and pastries sat on the sideboard were dishes of almost every colour looked appetising. Donna said, "Rosa, the blinz is so light."

"They're mine," Ursula told her, so she and Donna spoke for a while as if they were continuing a conversation, they started ten years earlier. Daniel was delighted by the sight of them.

Donna leaned over to Daniel and quietly asked. "Your brothers and sisters, are they always this relaxed?"

"I medicated and hypnotised them so they'd be on their best behaviour for you." Donna slapped his shoulder, laughing lightly and immediately apologised. He waved it away. "Just having you at my table—lovely; do what you like." He looked at her and his bright eyes searched her and told her, 'I want you'.

Donna said, "Loving a woman on screen is much easier than dealing with a real woman."

"I don't live in a fantasy world. I like my life and my loved ones to be real."

"Even with the headaches women bring?"

"I'm a doctor, I can handle it." His eyes wouldn't stop searching her and she kept scrutinising him to judge if he was genuine, yet at the same time, she told herself he was honest. The family ate, drank, and conversed with ease.

"Daniel, when you're not healing the sick, what do you do with yourself?"

"I go to jazz clubs: Ronnie Scots, the Vortex, Dalston Café and Camden. Also, the British Museum, I'm a member, there's plenty on. I do work for the synagogue, play a bit of tennis and of course, go to Wimbledon—"

"Wimbledon?" Donna exclaimed and flopped back in the chair.

Zigor shouted, "Donna, don't let that put you off. We've all learnt to ignore that side of him. To make up for his goyish hobbies, he bakes!"

Sacha yelled, "Proletariats' bake; with him, it's patisserie—he's so fancy!"

Ursula said: "It's sublimated sex, it's a wonder he stays trim!" Rosa and the women in the room were greatly amused by Ursula's remark.

Ingrid told them, "Shut up, he's lost weight since I saw him last."

Zigor said, "It must be the tennis that's keeping him fit." Zigor's comment made people laugh due to his Hungarian accent, lopsided good looks and kind eyes.

"You like tennis?" Donna asked.

Rosa laughed loudest. "He *loves* tennis!"

"He goes every year," Zigor said. "Wimbledon is like an obsessive ritual with him."

Daniel told them, "I'm single, I need my treats."

Donna said, "I like Wimbledon too. It's usually so expensive or booked, I don't go, but the BBC coverage is great."

"Would you like me to take you?"

She nodded and once again, her smiling face warmed him. "I'd love it."

"It's a date!" She felt strangely lyrical as though she wanted to walk and swing a basket of wildflowers she'd picked in the woods, she told Lola and Roy. "What else do you like?" Daniel asked her.

When Donna and Roy went to the Rio cinema the day after, she told Roy, *'You must know what it's like to want to go to bed with a man to find out if he's as sexy as he is smart.'*

"Decorating. My daughter and I spent hours talking about design."

Hilda asked, "Where's your daughter?"

Caught off guard, Donna braced herself because Hilda's simple question made her light-headed and she quivered as if she stood up too quickly. Donna's face drained of colour as she tried to speak. "On 4th March 2014, my husband and daughter were killed. An American official was drunk at the wheel; he ran down and killed my child and my husband. I got a call at ten past three from the hospital." Everyone watched her and stopped eating.

"I was in the supermarket when I got the call." Donna was immediately gripped by the memory. "I felt numb, as if I needed to scream, the way you know you want to sneeze, but it won't come out." Donna held her hands in the air and stopped, frozen as if she had pulled people out of thin air into her mind. Everyone watched her, trapped in her vision.

"Then I realised I *was* screaming." She looked anguished and the family was transfixed. "The manager rushed to me and stopped me from falling on the floor." She panted and remained silent, but Aaron was shaking as though he was having a spasm. Daniel saw that Donna was reliving her pain and grabbed and kissed her.

Lola told Michael, Donna confessed: 'Fear and shock forced its way to her vulva.' *When Michael told me that, I thought his ex-wife must have had a reason to confide in him. He confided in me and made me promise not to write it in the book so I won't.*

Exulted by his kiss, Daniel put his lips to her ear and told her, "The pain of death is fading away. The joy of your marriage is all that remains. All that remains. All that remains. Remember when you were a girl and you dreamt of your first kiss. You were pure and happy with nothing to fear, nothing. Reclaim the memory, it was a part of your beauty; sixteen years of age and so loving. So worthy." Daniel's soothing voice continued, "Let me give you that kiss. Ask me for it. Ask for your kiss."

Caught between a dream and desire, Donna said, "Kiss me." The family watched spellbound but not disquieted, because Donna and Daniel appeared to be more like a couple in an opera, enacted right in front of their eyes. The impact of their kiss was felt by everyone present. For Aaron, it felt like so many moments he knew from studying Erich Fromm on the subject of love. For Daniel's family they were caught by the memory of *Marnie*, a film Daniel was obsessed with. He made his family watch it so many times, they stopped visiting him. So, when Daniel kissed Donna, his family could virtually hear the score from *Marnie* as Donna settled into his arms, lovingly.

Daniel eased back from their embrace and Donna's eyes were still closed. Tears marked her face and Daniel looked over and saw that Aaron was crying and so he gestured for him to come closer. Aaron immediately went to him and the family moved out of the way so Aaron could sit beside him. Daniel held them both in each arm and he kissed Aaron on his head and Donna on the side of her face. Daniel's arms were full and everyone in his family saw something exhume from his dead soul. It wasn't until later that I would discover none of his family could define Daniel's needs. But Aaron felt an impetus take hold of him where he was conscious of being alive. No one said a word. All the faces of the fourteen members of the family acknowledged what was happening. They all knew Daniel's obsessions were realised by the two people he held in his arms.

Rosa's consenting eyes confirmed her thoughts with her family. Sacha stuck his neck out and his body language spoke clearly, indicating his silent—yes. Zigor and his wife held each other's hands and blinked in a manner that confirmed the family's blessing for his future with Donna. Every member of Daniel's family knew how much time he'd spent, living in his thoughts; preoccupied with his frustrations. They had all advised him to stop thinking and start living. Now they saw life in him.

Donna said, "Please, please... I'm sorry. We're having a nice time." Donna raised her head and said to them, "It's so wonderful to be here. When I lost my daughter and I went to my father, I wept and begged him to help me because Aaron needed help. But since I married outside our faith, Papa wouldn't forgive me. He didn't come to the funeral—his own granddaughter. His orthodoxy wouldn't allow him to help me. Aaron seemed to inherit my pain, but it changed him. This..." she looked around at them, "...with all of you; it's so nice. It's been so long. I needed this." Daniel was barely able to contain himself. Rosa saw his lips quivering.

Daniel said, "I want you here, Donna."

Aaron placed his hand on Daniel's face, so Daniel got to his feet and took them both in each arm. His brothers and sisters were relieved to see him with a beautiful Jewish woman in his arms at last. Nathan and his wife Hilda got up. Hilda went to Donna and took her away and Nathan took Daniel to one side and then out of the room. They had the same bright, enticing eyes, but Nathan looked more like the maternal Russian side of the family, while Daniel looked more like his German Liebermann grandparents.

Nathan pushed Daniel into the foyer.

"My God! What a woman! I'm telling you; enough of the shiksas and the easy sluts you like to park your dick in. For the first time since we were kids, I see you. You've brought your dream to life through people you've healed who need you." They continued in Yiddish. "What's her financial situation?"

"She runs her own business, earns a good living and her son is marrying money."

With a magnificent smiling face, Nathan said: "I like them!"

The house was a maze of interconnected rooms with doors in both corners of the rooms that led from the living room to the dining room, into the kitchen and out to the foyer. In the dining room, Aaron sat at the table and he was thinking about Amber. Daniel kept shaking him. "Bubala! Come, I have an after-dinner treat for your mum."

Aaron gazed vacantly for a time and then Daniel led him out of the room and took him upstairs to his bedroom. It was very masculine and the only modern room in the house. There were many pictures and posters of films that used psychoanalysis as the foundation of the story. Dominating the room was a massive poster of Hitchcock's *Marnie*. Aaron looked around.

"You're not infatuated with mum, you've given her a lot of thought, haven't you, Daniel?" There was no point in hiding anymore, so Daniel said yes and the look on his face indicated deep loneliness to Aaron. It was palpable through the spiritual energy that Aaron locked into; due to the relationship he had created in understanding clients who came to him for career counselling.

"Your mum is lovelier than I imagined. In my work, I have to imagine a great deal. Donna reminds me of everything I tried to forget, that's why my work has been so influential with patients. I've conquered my fantasies."

"Of what, Daniel?"

"Greatness. I wanted to be greater than anyone else in my field. Greatness is arrogance incarnate. Being good is what counts, that's being natural and sincere. I've helped people to change. I see your mum and she reminds me of what's real. That comes from outside my ego. Her struggles and yours show me who I am. You and your mother make me feel 'good' instead of *thinking* I'm great." *When Aaron told Roy about this conversation, Roy told me he sensed that Aaron was still contemplating the emotional state of Daniel's life.*

At the same time downstairs in the kitchen, Ursula told Donna, "This is one of the reasons why the whole life in Stamford Hill and the Hasidic tradition gives me haves," Ursula concluded in her girlish teenage voice, which was rather sweet.

Hilda asked Donna, "What faith was your husband?"

"Baptist."

Rosa entered the kitchen and Hilda said, "Mama!" Rosa came to her as quickly as she could. "Donna's parents freaked because her husband was Black; how crazy is that?" Until Donna told them Humphrey was Black British, they didn't know, so Ursula wanted to see what their mother thought. All of the women in the kitchen came over to Donna and Rosa with questions in their eyes.

Donna knew the questions they might have even though she'd been out of the faith for thirty years. "Yes, Humphrey was a doctor with a prac—"

"What were they worried about?" Rosa asked.

"You know..." Donna replied. Rosa slowly nodded because she saw no reason to pretend or give Donna a hard time. Her daughters concurred. Soon, they all gestured and sighed, knowing what they'd heard about 'blacks'. "This is him and my daughter." Donna pulled the gold chain until she fished the locket from between her bosom and it made her laugh trying to do it. "Usually, I don't have this problem." The women huddled around her, responded warmly and one of the sisters-in-law gave Donna a pat on the collarbone. Donna opened the locket and showed them, Zara and Humphrey.

"So handsome and so pretty," Ursula said.

Rosa looked at them closely and knowingly said, "Your father was worried they'd turn out sot black and see how fair she is. And your son is very handsome. Again, not the black phantom your father imagined." The women agreed with her.

With nonchalance, Donna said, "My son's engaged to be married. She's a lovely girl." They liked that. "The father is a diplomat; she's a virgin with a dowry of two million." They cooed at that. "She went to finishing school in Switzerland."

A wrinkled, aged woman on the edge of the family circle asked, "A shiksa?"

"No, French Jewish father: Luxembourg German Jewish mother." Rosa muttered in Yiddish and then laughed. "Shtoltz—such pride! Your father must be kicking himself. He thought you were gonna blacken the family reputation, but your son turns out gold; then he wins the hand of a European heiress and her Jewish father's a diplomat." They all laughed at the folly of ignorance.

Rosa asked, "What's she like?"

"She's like me, only younger." Knowing that was so many mothers' dream of a daughter-in-law, they all laughed loudly.

An elderly aunt asked Donna, "What does the fiancée look like?"

"Audrey Hepburn!" The roar of laughter from the kitchen reached all of the men's ears in the dining room.

"When's the wedding?" Ursula asked.

Donna leaned in. "Not before mine." The ladies threw their heads back, laughing.

In the dining room, Aaron told the men, "Oh yeah, that's mum. She has a way with people. When I was growing up, mum held court in the kitchen with the ladies-*not*-waiting: Married Black women are not 'ladies-in-waiting'. And dad would hold court in the living room with the men-who-knew-better." The men didn't understand him exactly. Aaron turned into a cocky 'preacher man' in front of the family and Daniel loved the way Aaron impressed and presented himself as a pundit.

"Some Black men have learnt from their wives; they better not try and act like they're 'king of the hill'. And Black women know they better not try and keep their men down." Aaron gave them a précis on Black masculinity they didn't know.

Back in the kitchen, Nathan's wife, Hilda, asked. "Donna, what do you think of Danny?" Her question was more analytical than conversational because of her marriage. Her life with Nathan had instilled insecurity in her over the years.

Donna asked with a humorous, inquisitive display. "Is he always so groomed and suave, or is he making an effort?"

"He's very high-brow," Hilda replied, "Jazz concerts, clubs, fancy dinners, Wimbledon, art events, Medical conferences around the EU: he's renowned."

Ursula said in her youthful voice even though she was far from ignorant or silly. "Yes, but when Danny isn't doing that, he bakes cakes, appears in shows, and composes music."

"He composes?" Donna asked, impressed and curious.

Hilda replied, "Yeah, it's no big thing, he plays for us. Not in public."

Rosa said, "His compositions are like jazz in the Shtetl. But when he sings and dances in the musical productions, he's a joy!"

"He sings?" Donna quickly responded.

"Oh, he loves to sing and dance," Ingrid told her. "With his love of musicals and Barbra Streisand, we thought there might be *something* there since I tried to fix him up with so many of my friends and nothing."

"He likes Barbra?" Donna asked with a smile on her face.

"He *loves* Barbra!" All of the women said and then gestured if not to imply then suggest the implication was 'nonsense'.

Rosa said, "Who spread that idea in the first place? Daniel has no interest in that direction. He used to be something of a playboy. But...age has a way of teaching us lessons, huh? So many women wanted my son, but they didn't have the faith. I'm talking about love. They see money; they see a doctor who dedicates his life to learning and healing and those...so-called 'ladies' couldn't stay the course," Rosa concluded with a brittle discord.

Donna asked, "Was he hurt by those failed relationships?"

"Mama would say yes," Ursula replied, "but I don't think so. He was married once, years ago."

"Her—she was a liar, a thief, a bitch and a catholic!" His mother stated.

"Danny got over that because he takes love seriously and that—thing thought more of his money than his heart," Hilda told Donna.

"I'm glad I've got money," Donna told them. "I'd hate you to think I'm a gold-digger."

"What kind of money, we talking?" Ursula asked. Rosa slapped the back of her had.

"Manners!" All her sisters tutted.

"I've lived long enough to know that isn't a question I'll answer even if the police are making enquiries. And besides, I've recently signed a mega deal with Eastern Europeans that will keep me in money for the next ten years."

"You've answered some of my prayers," Rosa said.

Hilda said. "More to the point, I see the way Danny looks at you." They all laughed out loud.

"He isn't easy to please, but Danny has big dreams. And he's great with kids, but the loneliness hangs on him," she said with long-suffering capitulation.

Hilda said, "Yeah, sometimes I watch him walk and it's like a man who's been told he has cancer, God forbid! I'm just saying. But this last year I've seen him change. Now he's like a plum, he's ready."

Donna told them, "I should eat him while he's ripe." They nodded and then howled with laughter.

CHAPTER THIRTY-SEVEN

Days later, Amber and Helena saw each other on the steps of the V&A Museum and Amber turned around in her white one-button trouser suit and walked in the opposite direction. Helena rushed towards her and brought Amber to a standstill.

In Italian, she asked Amber, "What did you just do? Why are you running away from me?" Amber began walking, but she had to mobilise her strength to deal with Helena's confusion and distress. "Amber, answer me, I must have called you seventy-five times. Your mother is beside herself and your father is so worried, he hasn't slept in days. Where have you been?"

"I don't have the skill to argue with you. My father is devoted to Uncle Massimo and my mother is like a Replicant from *Blade Runner*. I have lived in the shadow of my true self. Do you understand that? I'm not Miss Duality, two women trapped inside a fiction of my own fears. I don't know how to argue with you, darling." She lengthened her stride and Helena had to walk faster.

"Amber, you're not making sense."

Amber abruptly stopped walking and gave Helena an accusing stare that went straight to Helena's ego and splintered. "I've loved you; I still love you. But why should I share my husband when you don't want any 'intimate connections with a man'?" Amber's tone, along with her demeanour, was fully confrontational. "I am not accusing you. I understand your feelings. For the first time ever, I'm simply saying, I'm entitled to *my* life. No one is going to rob me." Amber felt herself pouting, so she forced herself to stop.

"But why have you gone into hiding? You lied to me the other day. I thought you were going home. Your mother calls me every hour!"

"Please, you stop now," Amber said unequivocally.

"This is childish, we're worried about you." Amber strutted away as though nothing could stop her, so Helena dashed after her and grabbed her.

"You and your father and my dad too, if you don't stop controlling me, I will kill myself. Think about living with that."

Helena was shocked and stood dead still as Amber walked away, flagged a cab, and got in. Helena watched it vanish into traffic.

Inside the cab, Amber tossed from left to right laughing before she took her mobile and called Aaron. "Darling, I am coming to your office, I'll be on the other side of the West End in…" She asked the driver how long it would take.

"I'm not clairvoyant, the traffic dictates these things," replied the skinny unattractive man.

"Be careful of your rudeness because I know someone who can make you regret it."

"Oh yeah, who's that?"

"Me, you ugly moron."

"Get out of my cab!"

"No! If you put me out, I'll call the police and get you in trouble. I'm a beautiful girl and you're a schmuck. Don't test me because I'm in a bad mood."

Aaron fell forward laughing and everyone in the office gave him strange looks. He listened to her for a time and then hung up. Margot came over to him.

"The 'Mrs' is on her way in. She just gave a cab driver a tongue lashing." He told her about the exchange.

"She's no pretty bimbo, don't let her get away."

"Fuck no!" His staff was still watching him. "Hello, people—clients and money! No deals, no meals!" They went back to their work.

Amber arrived at the office bearing gifts of hot drinks and pastry. All the staff made a fuss about who wanted what and happily thanked her. This time all of the guys instead of the girls noted in minute detail just how chic she was, dressed in her white Armani trouser suit, red cotton shirt and purple leather gloves. She stared at Aaron and he told Roy later that day, merely seeing her again made him feel better. She liked the look on his face because his pent-up feelings reminded her of the times she wanted to share a secret with Helena.

"How did things go with your mother and Dr Liebermann?"

"Extremely well, how are you? What's your hotel like? Have you spoken to your dad? Massimo called me five times yesterday."

"I called him and my mother from the cab to tell them to calm down. Helena came to my workplace. I reprimanded her about her conduct." Her eyes indicated she was referring to 'everything'.

"Come to the boardroom," Aaron said.

"Before we talk about solving problems, let me just sit with you and your staff because I know this work means a lot to you..."

"Work that pays me so we can fly around the world and dress like celebrities."

"I want to meet your mother's dressmaker friends. I don't need labels if I like the style, I'm happy to wear it. We're going to have such fun, living *within* our means," she told him and flicked her eyebrows.

He lowered his voice. "I don't want you to look like High Street girls. Right now, you look very...Vogue." She tossed her head back with a smile. She knew she aroused him and that excited her.

Margot crossed the office with Fern, the Bristolian recruitment consultant, and stood in front of Aaron. Margot told him, "Fern just got off the phone with the candidate who accepted the job offer."

"That's my girl! 'Counsel and Care' for our clients!" Margot rushed over to the gong and rang it. The staff cheered and Fern pulled funny faces. Aaron went over to the board and wrote figures under her name, as she raised her victorious hands in the air; and then Aaron wrote up the week's new total.

"We're on target now!" He told his staff.

Gary, the cockney lad, said, "Gold five to Red Leader... Stay on Target!" Amber swung around excited because she recognised *Star Wars* language.

She said in *Star Wars* lingo, "*Once you start down the right path, forever will it dominate your destiny.*"

Aaron screamed, "Yo! The Force is strong with this one! We have a new heroine: Princess Amber!" He lifted her high and his staff yelled. "Princess Amber, I'm yours to command."

"Marry me right after Rosh Hashanah," she said.

Beaming with energy, he said, "New Year: it is done!"

Amber continued in *Star Wars* lingo, "I've found the location and the dress. We will go to Luxembourg: there we will be married. I want to put an *end* to this conflict!" Her ability to speak *Star Wars* went through Aaron like sexual energy and everyone felt it.

"Now you have spoken, so it shall be done!" The staff around them cheered!

Margot's mobile rang and she took the call. "*100xSuccess Recruitment*, Margot speaking." She listened. "Tell me everything important they asked you in the interview, Lucy."

Amber said, "I know getting people employed so they can live is important to you. My job seems trivial in comparison."

"Don't you like it anymore?"

"Yes, I love the V&A, it's filled with a history of art and culture. I'm learning everything I need to know when I establish my Jewish modern art gallery. There's no way I could run my business without the V&A experience."

"Then it's not trivial. Without culture and history, life isn't worth living. That's why you're going to lead the way in curating your gallery."

"You *have* discovered—" Her mobile rang. She got it and showed Aaron that it was her mother.

"Will you speak to her now?" Amber rejected the call and took his hand. Walking through the hallway, Aaron asked. "What are we going to do about Helena? If I told Roy, he wasn't going to be my 'best man', he'd kick me in the teeth. You need Helena."

"This is my first fight with her. I don't know how to manage her. And she's not the kind of girl *one* manages." Aaron unlocked the boardroom and went in. The whiteboard still had targets for each member of staff and strategic goals on it they agreed to use for each candidate client they interviewed throughout the process.

"You sound very German again. You get like that when you're upset."

"I'm not upset," she replied, sounding upset. "She's been my joy in life, you know. But *she* has everything I don't. I won't share you." She walked away from him so that she was on the other side of the large boardroom table.

"You love Roy. He's very sexy. Will I have to compete with him?"

Aaron made his way around the table to her side and said, "No."

"I'm glad because I like him. He's not Diva gay. I can't cope with that."

"Helena *is* Diva gay."

"No, she's used to getting her own way. In my hotel room, I have made plans. Helena and Massimo will pay a 'tribute' to me. I will use the money to buy our home. Do I have your cooperation, Aaron?"

"Yes." She moved into him and gave him a kiss that lit his fuse and left him giddy. He told her, "I've seen a house in Albion Square, Hackney. It's two million and it's beautiful there. It's me and I'd like it to be us."

"Take me to this house. If I like it, I'll buy it." He was taken aback. "So many Jewish wives are powerless. I have learnt my lesson. That will never be me. People who insult me, like Uncle Massimo and Helena, are going to have to pay." She never looked more serious as she walked out of the room.

CHAPTER THIRTY-EIGHT

Daniel escorted Donna into the beautiful grounds of Wimbledon. Dressed in his green blazer, with flowers in the lapel, cream-colored trousers and a Harrods hamper, Donna loved the sight of him. It was a bright summer's day and Donna looked poised in a white and green polka dot dress and a floppy wide-brim hat. They looked like people the press should know. Strolling beside Daniel, Donna felt that she was his 'Lady Luck'.

Her mobile phone rang and she took it from her bag. "Mum, I'm calling to wish you a perfect day. Amber and I are going to view a house. I know the Wimbledon gates are open now."

"We're making our way to a spot where we'll have strawberries and cream," Donna replied. Her facetious tone amused Daniel because it was clear she was not a snob. "Dr Wonderful and I are looking forward to a scintillating day!" she replied, talking like Lucy Snodgrass, which made Amber convulse with laughter even though Daniel could only hear her on the phone.

"That's Amber, we're in a cab. We'll come by later or meet, whichever is better if you don't know what time you'll leave. Amber has a *punishing* day ahead and Helena and Massimo are going to know about it."

"Put her on." Aaron did so. "Amber, are you alright?" Amber told her she was going to deal with her family. Donna listened and took comfort from Amber's courage. "Amber, you told me you're 'La nouvelle femme'. Go and show them." Daniel kissed her neck.

* * *

At the end of the First Set, Daniel was fully involved in the game and whatever masquerade Donna thought he might have played was clearly shot to hell when he yelled at Ms Sharapova, "Give birth already!" because of her screams whenever she hit the ball. "I can't stand her," he told Donna and she saw the disdain on his face. Donna knew the look because she'd seen her house filled with West Indian cricket fans who chanted abuse at opposing teams on the television, filled with more colourful vulgarisms than she'd ever heard in her life.

Later that afternoon, she had the pleasure of watching Daniel abuse Nick Kyrgios because of his unsportsman behaviour. "That runt needs to be dropped into a barrel of shit, so he knows what nasty is really like. Play the game like a gentleman, this is Wimbledon!"

An Englishman in front of him said, "Can you please be quiet?"

Daniel looked down at him. "Can you please shove your head up your arse!" People were shocked because the confrontation was more like a football match.

"Since you don't know me, let me tell you this." The gentile middle-class spectators in their thirties and forties turned and strained their necks to get a look at the face-off. "I will kick your arse so hard you'll shit your pants!" One woman thought their face-off was totally incongruous because Wimbledon was a game for the 'best kind of people' as far as she was concerned. Some other spectators found the sight of two elegantly dressed 'gentlemen' one of the surprises they came to Wimbledon to witness.

The English gentleman said, "I'll have you thrown out."

Daniel said, "Shut up, you panty sniffing wanker!" His remark caused a commotion in his section. Donna took his arm and rubbed it, so Daniel sat back down.

"I love you," she told him and he spun around and consumed the sight of her. Donna's face was luminous with joy and Daniel shifted from aggression to adulation.

Later on, they sat on the green in the languid early summer evening. Daniel periodically stole glances at Donna between eating the strawberries and drinking champagne. He watched Wimbledon's crowd taking it easy and said to Donna while looking at the lush grounds and smart set mingling together.

"I've been coming here for over twenty years. I do most things by myself these days. I don't mind it." But Donna saw oblique melancholy in his face. "I sit myself down, have a brandy; bake a cake, or play with myself." He chuckled and then turned and looked Donna straight in the eyes. "I've sorted myself out now. I used to have a lot of faults, which I hid craftily. Boozy blondes, gambling, hanging out with amateur musicians, playing at making jazz—I love jazz. I hid that from the family. I took up community plays—musicals, *Fiddler*, *The Producers*, *Top Banana*; it was my way back to professionalism.

"I couldn't let my mother think I was a pussy hound with a propensity for cheap thrills. So, I spoke to my analyst and I worked my arse off to set myself right. It's been a struggle, but now I'm on track. I'm particularly proud of the way I've worked with Aaron. He's a hell of a guy."

"He has the deepest respect for you."

"I've listened to neurotic, pathological and vicious accusations hurled at women; and then I heard Aaron's praise for you. I'm also close to my mother. Everything he told me sparked my consciousness of how a woman survives evil, misfortune, lost love and bereavement." The intensity of Daniel's rich voice pulled her closer to him and the sound of Wimbledon encircled them.

"For all my fascination with Hitchcock's heroines, my fantasy; and the knowledge of the women the Nazis slaughtered, which still remain my nightmare: your son's praise of you forced me to consider the meaning of honour in love." There was no hiding the joy on Daniel's face.

"Daniel, will you marry me?" A great cheer from the crowd went up and Daniel's face changed all at once. The joy he felt made him appear younger. Donna's love wrote itself across her face. All at once they felt the love between them: it was tangible. Daniel was lost for words, so he kept looking at her asking himself countless questions.

"God! I thought I'd have to push myself to the limit to let you know I'm not some deviant who falls for a patient's mother. I planned to show you I am rational and bold. I know you've seen people Aaron has put through the mill and tested to make sure they're not pervy or poor—not to mention trashy and prejudiced: but us—how do you know?" he asked, pointing back and forth between them.

"You're imperfect. I love that. All the men I've met have tried to show me they're perfect. I'm far from that," she said resolutely.

"But I haven't proved myself as yet."

"Yes, you have. I've gone through early menopause and depression. My mind, spirit and vulva talk to me about you and us." He pulled her back and then he kissed her. There was another cheer from the crowd on the centre court for the match they didn't have tickets for. Eventually, Donna sat up.

"But I haven't given you back the faith your father took from you as yet. That was my greatest ambition; to—"

"You have. That dinner with your family has reawakened every Jewish part of me. Then you invited me back with Aaron and Amber; and played jazz. You look great with a saxophone in your hand. Watching you and listening to you, I felt conscious of my future rather than re-living my past. I couldn't sleep all night. My dry body felt fertile and sensual. I feel like you've performed a virtual operation on me," she told him, digging her fingers into her stomach. "My therapist couldn't understand how my father's damnation infected me like cancer. That's why I immediately knew you were giving me back my childhood." Her face was a wonder and he pulled off the ring from his right hand.

"This is my father's wedding ring. Take it until I get you an engagement ring." It was too big for her finger, so she took off her locket and put it on the chain and placed it between her breasts and then he kissed her cleavage.

"Your lips tell me a lot, Daniel. I think my lips will speak without me saying a word." Daniel flinched and she saw his eyes light up. "Dr Wonderful, we should marry very soon."

"Let's marry and honeymoon in the Holy Land."

"Yes, that way, I can make love to you: sacred love, that's fucking sexy!" She felt excited by just saying it and he felt amorous just hearing her say it.

CHAPTER THIRTY-NINE

Amber went to her father's stately office at the Embassy. Aaron had invited her to his office to meet Dr Liebermann after work and he offered her great advice. Then Donna took her to Lola and Tony's salon to do her hair and make-up and so; dressed in her trouser suit and a button-up shirt, she stood in the officious surroundings full of conviction as she faced Bernard and Massimo. They looked imposing in their expensive attire, and their uncompromising faces reminded her of men she studied that had the power to destructively change people's lives. They embodied high ranking political figures and belligerent financiers, which in fact was who they were.

"I've considered Aaron's withdrawal of marriage, so I've decided I will never marry." They both looked at each other. "Helena has shown me how natural it is to love a woman and so I won't shame our family. I will remove myself from your sight and our faith. I know me being a lesbian is going to be difficult for you, Papa, but if I walk away from my Jewish life, maybe one day I will find a woman. This world has changed—"

"No!" Bernard cried out. "To live like a faithless sexual wanton, please..."

"Papa, I would be the daughter you want if I was a wife and mother."

Bernard desperately turned to his friend. "Massimo—we cannot..."

With alacrity and cunning, Amber took her father's arm and said, "Why aren't you speaking to me instead of your rich friend?" she demanded, pointing in his face. "What is your obligation to him?"

Massimo said, "Amber, your father and I—"

"Silence! You took my father from me and your daughter has taken my husband from me," she stated flatly.

"We haven't," Massimo protested.

"You have defiled my mother. Tarnished my fiancé, abused his mother, and subjugated me. I am happy to get away from both of you." Her accusations and composure chilled them to the bone and left them indicted.

Amber told them, "With God on my side, I look you in the eyes and curse you with—"

"Amber!" Bernard yelled. "Stop. Uncle Massimo loves—"

"Don't lie to me." Amber turned to Massimo and searched his face. "Do you love me? Does Helena really love me, or have you twisted my brains?"

Massimo said, "I love and value your life darling."

Amber stepped forward and pointed at Massimo. "Then I demand you pay me a tribute for the unconscionable insult you have shown me." Bernard was confused.

"Cosa vuoi amore mio. What do you want, darling?" Massimo asked with a strained grin.

"Helena must pay for my wedding and honeymoon, and you will pay me three million pounds in a bank transfer before the close of business, tomorrow."

Massimo asked dryly as he lifted his eyebrow, "Why three million?"

"That is my business. And I have a lawyer," she replied unshaken. "Of course, you can keep the money you were going to leave me in your will. This may be the last time you see me. I can vanish. There are girls online who've offered me plenty. I doubt that either of you will want to see how a decadent lesbian makes the most of her life."

Bernard told her, "You must not consider that kind of life. I'm your father and I cannot lose you as if you're dead."

"You have allowed your friend's money to dictate our life. I have the guts to renounce Helena due to her demands, where she showed me that my life and my happiness come second to her pleasures and need. Shame on her," Amber said pitifully. "But you've colluded with your friend to shame a man that has honour, Papa. I told you I would marry Aaron or no one else. Your adultery with that woman is bad enough but planning to take Aaron's children and blackmailing Aaron on 'moral' grounds when you're

345

sexually *feeding* on Ms. Dalio." Amber backed away from him and Bernard moved closer to her. For the first time in his life, Bernard was afraid. Massimo saw it.

Amber pushed her fists into her waist and held her head high. "At Yom Kippur, is there any atonement you can make that will cleanse you both of this sin? What you've done and what you're asking for, violates human rights, Papa. I would ask you to prove you love me, but you have Ms Dalio and your friend here, so you don't need me. I'm free to be a lesbian..." Bernard grabbed Massimo.

"I don't ask you for favours, Massimo, I help you with things. Help me save my child," Bernard begged him.

Massimo was forced to say, "Helena and I will pay you tribute. Don't spite us." Amber eyed them and took out a card from her pocket.

"If the money isn't in my account tomorrow, *you* will be the one that robs my father of his daughter, because I'll be gone. Wealth doesn't give you the right to mistreat me. I'm not a stupid girl that likes dressing up. You're looking at a woman."

"Amber don't abandon your family. Please, darling—don't leave me."

Amber pointed at Massimo. "Look what you've done." She walked out on them.

* * *

Amber, Aaron, Roy, and I walked down the South Bank while people stopped to enjoy the summer evening. They were drinking wine, skateboarding, sightseeing, watching the boats on the River Thames and observing men busking to crowds of tourists as they do every night and day. As we walked under the sky that lit the Houses of Parliament, I told Amber, "You were courageous to stand up to your father and Massimo."

"My mother's weakness reminded me what it is to be a coward and Donna's courage reminded me what it is to be a woman." Aaron kissed her.

"My Uncle and father live by ultimatums because they usually issue them. I was prepared to break them because Papa would be gutted if he disgraced himself to me."

"But he's very selfish," Roy said, "does he really understand disgrace?"

"Don't be silly, of course he does. You couldn't know but he loves me very much."

Again, I was reminded of what Roy could not tell me about her.

"I know him! My mother's capitulation has taught me everything." She held out her left hand and looked at her engagement ring. "I knew if Uncle Massimo refused to help my father; that would break their friendship."

"Suppose he had said no to your dad?" Roy asked.

"Massimo needs Papa and he loves him like a brother. Their lives would change if Uncle betrayed that friendship. They are sometimes brutal with people but never with each other. I was prepared to ruin them if they continued to ruin me."

I said, "They got the message."

"Yes, the money is in my account," she replied triumphantly. "Darling you've never told me how many children you want. We now have a house to bring them up. I've decided to call it, *La mason bohème!*" She laughed delightfully. "I bought it cash as a reminder; I am not a powerless woman any man can control. People think I'm an Ingénue. I let them think that because a woman's secret weapon is surprise."

Aaron said, "I thought it was intelligence."

"I've had a lawyer for three years because intelligence requires power. Now he is taking steps to buy my house: cash. Darling, our new home in Albion Square." She was suddenly thrilled! She grabbed Aaron. "We will hold our *soirées* where they'll be everyday happiness."

No matter what Roy told me about the circumstances and events Aaron got into, the look on his face, gazing at Amber told me how much he truly loved her. I also noticed that Aaron often waited until she finished speaking before he spoke. Half the men I disliked always cut in when their wives and girlfriends are speaking.

Amber told Aaron, "I can imagine how happy we'll be, darling; but if you stop loving me later on, I will have a home and our children. My mother showed me the cost of being a powerless woman. And then I look at your mum and I know so much more; I love her for that!"

"Mum and Daniel will gladly add to the mix. But I don't know if she's going to live with him or whether he'll move into our old home."

"They should start afresh, in a new place," Roy said.

"Why?" I asked.

"A future requires a clean slate. I don't want the past."

Amber moved around us and went over to him and asked. "What troubles you?"

"So many things are going to change now. Where will our lives be three years from now?" Amber sympathetically tried to comfort him. I needed to talk to Roy, but I certainly wouldn't do it in front of them.

Amber said, "We are going to be the very best friends London can imagine."

"I like the sound of that," Aaron told her.

"We are eclectic. Your love is a broadcaster and novelist. You're a journalist. My love is a champion for employment and I am la nouvelle femme." Proclaiming her self-identity thrilled her, I could tell.

"We are going to become what we want," she said with a joyous lust for life!

Aaron said, "Roy's melancholic, he's had so much to worry about, but now, cous, it's your time and ours." With that, Aaron spun Amber into a waltz.

I looked away from them. "Let me take care of you, Roy. Don't you know how much..."

Roy said, "Yes, I feel it, Eugene." I kissed him because I truly felt he was coming to me. When he pulled back, I could see him shed some of his bashful ways. His eyes were now talking to me intimately. Amber was watching us and she was heartfelt, I could feel it. I also knew I wanted to write her character from now on, instead of Roy continuing to write about her.

Roy said, "Read the Kama Sutra—prepare to become a goddess of love."

She told Aaron, "I don't need any books. I have imagined you naked many times. Anaïs Nin is a novice compared to the decadence I will make of my tabula rasa. I'll do anything, providing it doesn't leave me disgraced in the eyes of God."

Roy said, "But you told your dad you'd make yourself a Godless lesbian."

"This is one of the reasons why Helena dislikes men. Women have to be figurative because men tend to be literal. I'd never give up my faith and certainly not for sex. Only a cunt does that." With Parliament behind us, we all laughed because hearing her use that word with *her* accent, so French yet something else; gave it a certain—piquant as they say in France.

"Roy, I don't see you laugh so often, but I'm going to make you laugh more. I want to inspire my new friends. You guys are the first men to become my mates. My other friends are all girls in Europe: but you are my first men. Yes, it's nice!"

"*I'm* your first man," Aaron replied.

"Don't be so obvious, of course you are—idiot!" Roy laughed again. "But I will also have Daniel, my new father-in-law! He's smart. Your mother's face when she said she asked him to marry her: so incredible. All your hard work to find someone for her to consider and he was in your life all along!" She laughed beautifully.

* * *

Walking across the Millennium Bridge towards the Tate Modern, Donna suddenly came to a stop and looked away, clearly distressed. "Roy, I don't know if I can do this. The Tate looks like a concentration camp, I've always hated it."

"If you can't, I'll text Pedro..." She pulled her suit together, buttoned the jacket and then grabbed my hand and took a full breath. Smiling people walked past us from north to south, coming and going across the bridge.

"No love, I'm breaking up with him. I must do this. I can't just text him." Donna braced herself and I led her towards the Tate's austere looking façade that held millions of treasures and at the same time, held deadly associations.

Inside the Tate café, people were wandering about behind us. I watched Pedro's face as he studied Donna. It reminded me of when I broke up with Brian and so I felt for both of them. He was very nicely turned out in a seersucker jacket and a blue-white T-shirt. Knowing what was coming made me a bit depressed, but I had to get over that because Donna needed me.

"Pedro, the love I feel for this man shocks *me*. I wake up and go through my day, hoping he'll know I'm thinking of him. Love is mysterious and amazing." I could see him slowly cracking under the weight of the truth, that wasn't just in Donna's words; her truth was in her Being. Reading Eugene's chapters taught me to be more insightful and critically aware of other people.

"When I met your daughter and son-in-law, it reminded me of what I don't have. But because you're decent and lovely, I told myself it didn't matter. But something strange happened. I realised my son's fiancée, and Roy, this man here is my family. I thought I could make your family mine. But I am not destitute, even though I felt like I was for a long time." Donna reached out for his hand. "In your bed, I came alive again because you're great."

"But it wasn't enough," Pedro said.

Maybe it was because of Eugene, but I spoke out loud.

"Pedro, people in love don't live in bed; they get out in the world and change things." They both stared at me.

Donner earnestly told him, "For the first time in years, Pedro, you brought intimacy and passion into my heart and that resuscitated me. But Daniel makes sense of my life in the future because I'm no longer living in the past." Her voice and her eyes pleaded with him.

He told Donna, "I never thought dying would feel like this." Pedro's face was mask-like. He stood up and looked at both of us and then he bowed and walked off into the crowd. Donna covered her face.

"Mum, let me go and bring him back so—"

"No! I will not apologise for loving Daniel. Pedro is a great guy and everything, but Daniel is exactly who I need to live with. I'm not about to deny my husband." Her perseverance was something I tried to learn because I admire that.

"And you're that sure of him?"

She moved closer. "Daniel's got intelligence and incredible sex appeal. Pedro is sexy, yes and he's got a good heart. But I can see my life with Daniel's family. He loves Aaron. And his mum hasn't got her claws in her kids. Daniel is on good terms with life. His kindness is remarkable and I love that about him. He's got balls."

I must have made a funny face or something. "What? I'm no menopause matron. I've felt everything with Daniel. He's into tantric sex." I was startled. "Let's get out of here and I'll tell you." I got up and escorted her away from the table and we made our way out, away from students, tourists and couples.

Back on the Millennium Bridge walking towards St Paul's Cathedral, Donna was calmer. "Pedro has a lot going for him. No man that good sits alone every night rotting away. Daniel needs me: he *was* wasting away. A few bitches found their way to him because he was trying to be something he's not: a goy Playboy. Daniel's much too Hebrew to be that hollow; casting away everything that historically makes us who we are, just to be 'trendy'."

"What does Daniel love about you most?"

"The morning after we made love he said, I defied victimhood. He told me Aaron and I inspired him to explore Black psychological studies. Donna stopped and said, "One morning, he got up and stared at me. He was bollocks naked; with me in the nude in his bed. And he said: I have 'Goddess power'. He told me I give him cerebral orgasms."

"Wow, fuck yeah! Marry him!" Donna high-fived me.

"And what about the good doctor *you're* seeing? Are you doing it right?"

"Tantric he's not, but he can turn an hour into eternity. I've been hanging out with him so much I'm beginning to talk like him. I think I'm in love, but I don't know because I've really only ever loved Aaron, you, Zara and Humphrey."

"If you feel empty and meaningless alone; and you feel blessed with him, believe me; that is when you *know*." I hugged her tightly because unlike the ruffians who fucked and fertilised me into existence: Donna was my God-given mother.

* * *

Amber met Helena at the Diana statue in the Rose Garden at Hyde Park as they agreed. On a bright sunny day like that, Helena told me she was very hopeful. I spoke to her the day before. The beauty of the roses in the green landscape made everything seem tranquil and calm, but Helena was deeply anxious. She arrived early and Amber arrived on time. Helena told me, much to her surprise; Amber was wearing a lilac blue soft leather tight fitting trouser suit with her hair in a post-punk pinned-up style. Amber glided in her Jimmy Choo Emily 85 blue suede stiletto sandals and Helena wanted to have sex with her there and then.

Amber made her way directly towards Helena and greeted her by taking both her hands rather than cheek to cheek. Helena knew the difference. The people who were coming and going in the background didn't matter to either of them.

"I'm glad we've made this time, Helena. Let me come to the point because I get dizzy from everybody else's chaos. No one else could be my maid of honour. That is *your* place. Our life hasn't disintegrated because of your family's... requirements of my husband."

"Amber, you are not married yet, he's your fiancé."

"Please don't annoy me! I came for this meeting to put to rest the stupid mess from before. So—Aaron and I will be married soon and I want my best girl to help me with everything. Our friends from school and college will of course be invited. Two people from my work at the V&A, your brothers and their wives."

"I sense you are angry with me." They walked in circles around the little pool and statue of Diana the Huntress.

"Your family get everything they want because you have the money to buy everything you desire. My husband, yes, my *husband* is not for sale. I don't know if you're building your life on *Sex and the City*, but that nonsense is fiction!" Helena was going to speak, but Amber held up her red leather hand and stopped her.

"No, darling! I am speaking; I am not yielding as I have throughout my life. You are unhappy because you have not apologised to me for trying to take a child from my husband's life. What you wanted would have caused so much trouble! Your ego is out of this world on a diva-nova! When you think it all out, you will regain my love. Paying for this wedding means nothing: you have millions."

"I'm sorry." Amber looked at her and she didn't believe Helena, so she walked off while Helena watched her backside swing left and right.

At Michael and David's, the house was exceptionally cool and shaded as we got things together for Sunday dinner. Massimo watched Michael and David's sons in the kitchen and then Michael called Massimo and me into the living room.

Massimo said, "This is such a wonderful home." As I've said before, Michael and David's life is the one thing I envied.

Michael was in linen trousers and a red silk shirt, and David was in jeans and a white see-thru shirt. Massimo wore a tailored Italian suit. We could hear David and Michael's sons in the other rooms and Massimo kept saying. "They have life in them." Unlike Massimo's sons who looked like overdressed manikins, Michael and David's sons were charged with virile energy, the kind you see in a football team.

"Michael! Please help me with Helena because all she has done these last two days is cry. She's my only girl."

"Massimo, I have no special secrets to share with you about this. My husband was panic-stricken when he thought he'd lose his son. And it took ages to get one of my sons to respect my life after his mother and I divorced. Eugene has brought you to me for advice, so let me honour his trust." Massimo nodded to Michael and me. "You have paid the tribute that Amber asked for. That was her punishment for you. I don't know if you are familiar with 'an act of contrition'."

"It's an examination of conscience. Rather like Yom Kippur's Day of Atonement." Michael walked away from David and went to Massimo and pulled him close and spoke in his ear. Some strange Italian vibe covered them in kinship.

"I was born and lived with no money as a child. I played on the streets of Rome and loved it. When I was bad, my father took off his belt and skinned my arse. When my mother put camphor oil on my arse after a beating, she or Papa gave me, I loved her as much as when she took me to swim or to the movies." I watched Michael talk and gesture to Massimo and I knew Massimo could feel Michael's truth as much as David and I did. Michael continued to speak honestly.

"Once, I was very rude to my sister's husband. Papa grabbed my belt and yanked me through the streets until we got to their house. I had to apologise to him and my sister. I was seventeen. It hurt more than a beating." Massimo screwed up his face, clearly indicating he got the message. "You and Helena have to speak to Donna and Aaron because you underestimated their dignity."

"Pardon me," David said. "You both did something terrible. To impugn Aaron's manhood to his granddad and discredit him, just to indulge your daughter!"

Michael said, "I'm talking to Massimo, don't do that!"

"He made matters worse. I'm an LGBT Activist. Remember the shit I went through when my ex-wife went to Adrian and tried to dirty my name. In my house, I have the right to share in a conversation."

"Massimo knows he was wrong, don't shame him. How is a man to recover if he is constantly shamed?"

David told Massimo. "Your daughter has to go to Amber and Donna and beg their pardon. Her behaviour is wilful. I mean for God's sakes, you're the parent: talk to her!"

Michael said, "Don't get Nigerian on him. We are trying to help, not bury the man." David confronted Michael and pointed in his face.

"Nigerian, get Nigerian... What the fuck is that?" Their sons came into the room.

Michael, told him, "You and your father—"

David gestured dramatically at Michael. "Oy, OK, yeah! I've changed. We've changed."

Michael's 25-year-old angelic youngest son, Roberto said, "Not that again."

Cesare, Michael's 30-year-old eldest, broodingly handsome son, said, "Papa! I've told you, no foreplay in front of the children. You both get worked up too easily."

David's 24-year-old son, Adrian, said, "Yes, dad, at your age, you might peak too early." Adrian was one of those good-looking cool Black guys Europeans always wanted to hook up with. His Italian brothers gave him loving man-hugs.

David pulled Michael closer and kissed him and their sons were at ease with them. Massimo noted the ease among David and Michael's sons.

"Massimo, in my Jamaican and Nigerian culture, you and Helena acted 'out of order'. The two of you must honestly apologise to them for what you attempted to do. Take Donna and Aaron somewhere."

Massimo said, "Maybe your family's restaurant: I heard it's super."

David quickly said, "It's fully booked for the next two months; take them to *your* favourite place." Their sons gestured for us to go in for lunch. Massimo came and took my arm.

"Helena was right to ask me to talk to you. I don't want to upset your friends too. Bernard and I mistakenly tried to help my little girl."

David said, "Don't do that, Massimo! Manipulation might work on Eugene, but face what you did. I speak for Michael when I say there will be no peace for any of you until you restore your integrity." Their sons took note and so did Massimo. We stepped back and let David and Michael lead us into dinner. I comforted Massimo because now he couldn't hide his shame from anyone.

* * *

I stood in Helena's Knightsbridge flat and even though she was surrounded by all the luxuries she had; she was destitute. Dressed in all her finery, there was nothing Helena could wear to hide her face. She was distraught when she recounted what happened.

"I went to Amber and Donna and even as I said the words: 'I apologise for my conduct. Asking for Aaron's child was vain and wrong. I jeopardised your marriage, Amber, and I upset you and Aaron and you too, Donna, so I ask you to please forgive me'. And you know what happened?"

"Just say it, Helena."

"Amber looked so angry. But she said. 'I forgive you because if I had to live without you, I couldn't stand it. I love you, darling. But I have to stand up for myself because no woman should be robbed when she gives so much of herself to people she loves'. I agreed with her. And Donna said: 'Always remember what you're feeling now Helena and you'll never go off the rails again'."

Helena tore at her clothes, gasping to breathe and she looked like she was going to scream! "It was like Donna knew the shame I was feeling!" Helena then gasped and sobbed. Everything in my soul reached out to her. I asked her if she wanted me to stay so she could lie down and I'd cook her something in her fridge or cupboard and she thanked me and I made her dinner.

After dinner, when we sat in her living room, she told me that she'd never let another woman see her in her current state. For all our differences, we were still connected.

"I'm a new age woman. I know right from wrong. How did I do that? What's the matter with me?" I pulled her into my side and let her rest her head on my shoulder. I then sang her a lullaby my mother used to sing to me. For whatever reason, sitting there with her like that took me back to 1972 when I was a teenager. I hung out with my friends from GLF, and with the girls in the Women's Movement who taught me so much. How this woman found a place in my heart I don't know, but I love her.

CHAPTER FORTY

23rd September 2018

Regardless of living in the same house and listening to everything Aaron told me about his sessions with Dr Liebermann; it took the wedding to make me see how little I really knew Daniel. The second-hand news I heard about their battles did not prepare me for Daniel's gregarious personality or his robust masculinity. I'm only truly aware of this right now because when Eugene is editing or writing, he's stressed the reliability of facts that's fed through our minds. And his writing style inspires me to follow his lead. So, as I watched Daniel waiting for Donna to appear in her wedding dress, I felt the weight of his authority and power as Aaron had never mentioned to me.

In keeping with Jewish tradition, at the end of Rosh Hashanah, Donna and Daniel's wedding took place out in the open, under the chuppah up in the hills of Jerusalem. The wedding was populated with friends from around the world whose lives were affected by Donna and Daniel. I wasn't surprised that friends flew in from the Caribbean, Africa, Spain, America and London to see Donna now she was fully recovered because survival is life-affirming. I was, however, surprised that Daniel had so many friends. Some were his fellow medics; others were his friends and then there was his massive family network across Europe whose expansion was due to their marriages.

I felt the deepest happiness for Donna. Maybe it's because I love her more than any other woman I've ever known. After all, she was more than a mother to me. The sacred signs and symbols of the Holy Land were all around us. Being in Jerusalem felt like nowhere else I've ever been. The air was scented with something that kept playing in my memory bank: it went back to Jamaica, my old church and the smell of the land. Jerusalem smelled of frankincense, sandalwood and cloves, mixed with manure and soil. The scenes from hilltops reminded me of every film epic of Christianity and the Roman Empire I'd ever seen.

Added to all this was the faces of the families. Daniel's family were there in number and they all looked like men and women who'd give you an argument about anything and laugh out loud at the drop of a Yamaka. What I like about Jewish faces is that they are filled with suspicion and mirth. The same could be said for African Caribbean's, but there is far less anger in the faces of Jewish people I've been introduced to. Daniel's family ranged from teenagers to elders aged ninety-two. There was no doubt that they were all from Europe, but obviously, the Holy Land united us all.

It was Donna's 'family' that made the wedding look like a counterculture 'happening' because of her friends' age, their racial heritage and their lived lives. Donna walked towards Daniel, between Harold and Violet, since her parents were obviously not there. Harold and Violet never looked more important, or impressive, escorting their 'daughter'. Donna looked like she was in a state of bliss walking pass me, Aaron and Amber, Saul and other members of our family.

Donna's friends had made her a Grecian classic style drape dress with a hood that dropped back and hung from her shoulders down her back. The amazing thing about the dress is that it was the colour gold, rather than white. Suggesting Donna looked like a Greek goddess is absurd, but she did look regal. With her hair up and her gold dress down to the ground, everyone looked at her mesmerised by her loving face and physical grace. Daniel looked at her as if he could have made love to her in public.

I didn't understand the words of the ceremony, but everything was done according to Jewish tradition, under the chuppah and eventually, Daniel stamped on the glass and broke it and everyone yelled Mazel tov! I felt great and took Eugene's hand. Donna and Daniel looked wonderful and quite transformed from the period before their wedding.

Because we were out in the open, the faces of Jewish, Italian, Caribbean and Africans really made it feel like an event with worldwide delegates. I'd seen celebrities' trashy weddings; but

Donna and Daniel's wedding had an atmosphere that was ripe with life and death, spiritual bloodlines, family blood and Jewish survival, as well as African triumph.

* * *

Roy proudly introduced me to people left, right and centre, but I still couldn't keep track of everyone. I kept thinking about how I was going to write this up because Daniel's family background revealed that he was much beloved and some women clearly ached for him. I wanted to explore that, but I reminded myself it's Aaron and Donna's story; however, it had become more than that now. The mill of people around us was very diverse. One of the things I couldn't get over was the smell of the air and the defused golden light of Jerusalem.

Donna continually introduced us by saying: "This is my son, Aaron, his fiancée, Amber, my Godson Roy and his partner Dr Eugene Martins, the Broadcaster." I nodded so much I felt like an automaton. Daniel also walked us around the hired open venue and introduced us to his family. They were all prosperous family business people. Everyone was indicatively dressed for a wedding and they welcomed Donna with a range of felicitations that included comments about her gold-coloured sequin classical Greek styled wedding dress. In the Reception Room, I could feel people's joy for her and Daniel.

In spite of everything Roy recounted to me about Aaron's experiences with his family and friends, the lightness in my own body and the energy from Daniel and Donna's friends told me so much more about what kind of people they were. There must have been almost three hundred people there and no one commands that level of love and loyalty from friends without genuine benevolence in their soul. Various languages popped in and out of my ears, moving among the guests.

A man in his fifties, with a distinctly east London sarcastic voice, said: "If he gives you any trouble, call me!" The man looked like a stand-up comedian.

Daniel affectionately said, "Fuck off Harry!" and turned to Donna. "That's a bum I've known since we were kids." Donna patted the man's face.

As we circled the venue, a cacophony of various languages in conversation became increasingly peppy. We found ourselves among two groups of Donna's vivacious friends. I'd been told earlier; these Black women were dressmakers and friends of Violet's. They were talking to a group of Jewish ladies they all knew in Hackney and Camden and they were gesturing as if they were dancing on the spot.

The Bankolé and De Farenzino families were there. Daniel was introduced to them a few months earlier, but he hadn't met Michael's business partners Carlos, JJ and their son, Brian: Roy's ex-boyfriend. JJ stood head and shoulders above everyone around him because he was six foot seven, as broad as a door frame and embodied the kind of strength you only see in African Americans.

JJ asked, "Lady Donna, how'd you feel now?" He held out his hands to her, and the diamond-encrusted watch he was wearing set off the colour spectrum. The 20-carat Asscher-cut diamond ring on his dark brown hand was almost the last word, but after he kissed Donna's hand, JJ's husband, Carlos reached out for him and he had a larger yellow diamond on his middle finger and he was wearing diamond earrings. They reeked of glamor and danger.

I asked Roy, "What's their story?" because I'd never seen any guys like them. He pulled me aside to a spot on the terrace out of earshot and whispered to me. As he spoke, everyone in view blurred into the sun and eventually came back into focus because Roy's statement really impacted on me mentally.

"They're kingpins." He pulled me in tight and whispered in my ear. "They used to work for the Secret Service carrying out 'Hits'." My face froze and I slowly pulled back to take another look at them in between all the Jewish faces. "When I was going out with Brian, if any white people in America messed with him, he'd say to me: 'daddy and papa can rub them out'. I said how and he told me about their work and the fact they still had international ties that could remove any motherfucker."

"They're fucking sexy, aren't they?"

"Full of spunk on the streets and in bed from what I learnt as a trusted member of their family. They've got so much money. Apart from Humphrey and Donna, I've never seen a more intense love and devotion between anyone else I've ever met."

"Is their money legal or illegal?"

"Their wealth comes from their LGBT Arts Programme." In their silk suits and custom made what have you, they owned their space. JJ gave Donna an envelope which I found out later was big-time money. Roy held my hand tightly and pulled me over to them.

JJ said, "Donna, no matter what—you need help, pick up the phone."

Carlos moved in and pointed his index finger up to heaven. "We're taking care of that 'thing' it's almost done." Donna leaned in and whispered to both of them. I've seen gangster films, watched Blaxploitation, and read psychological thrillers, but nothing in that genre matched the power both men held.

I think Daniel felt the same threat as I did when he said, "Hello, I'm the husband; really well behaved and seriously in love with her." Carlos gave out a big laugh. He reached out for a man hug and Daniel offered his hand which Carlos cupped and his perfect 4C's giant 30-carat rock pulled eyes towards him.

Daniel asked, "Should I kiss your ring?" And JJ threw his head back and laughed. Daniel's brothers and sisters and a few of their friends crowded in.

JJ said, "This is Lady Donna's day, so I'll keep my vulgarism to a minimum." Donna told people, "These are two of my dearest friends, Jeff and Carlos. Jeff is the President of an LGBT Arts Foundation. His husband, Carlos is President of a Talent Agency representing some of the biggest African American and Hispanic names in Art and show business. Tell them what business was like last year, Jeff."

"We made over 100 million." The moment that was said, it seemed like the spotlight shone on JJ and Carlos.

Daniel's overdressed elder cousins from Frankfurt said, 'Fuck!'

Carlos replied: "Regularly!" He winked at JJ and I shivered because they were so cocky and gorgeous together. They didn't even need to kiss, we got it!

Roy staggered forward laughing as people around us watched him. I'd never seen that particular look on Roy's face before. I think his response was due to the fact he knew them as well as he did.

JJ said, "See what you missed, kid?" That's when Brian doffed his head at me.

Donna told Daniel, "Roy used to go out with their son, Brian." Brian moved forward. He was an unusually handsome Black guy who looked like a star. There was nothing Puff Daddy, or any of the other hip-hop guys had done regarding style that Brian didn't embody. I felt sure that Rosa, as well as Daniel's brothers and sisters, were talking about us in Yiddish.

Brian pointed at Roy and told me. "It takes a madman to deal with this guy."

"Yes, I'm crazy about him," I replied and Daniel reached out and gave me a terrific man hug.

"That is a fantastic return of service, Eugene!" Roy then pulled me in and kissed me on the neck.

Roy said, "Is it any wonder I love this guy, mum." I don't know if he heard himself but I heard Roy and then he and Donna walked away from us, as JJ, Carlos and Daniel shared looks of contemplation before we all began speaking again.

Later on, Donna introduced Solly Bankolé and his parents to Daniel's family with detailed background information on how they met. However, Daniel's family looked more interested in the fact Solly agreed to introduce them to some of his friends who they might do business with because Daniel's brothers, like all of us, knew who the Bankolés were.

Solomon told Donna, "This is the start of your new life. If there's anything, you have trouble with—"

"My situation with my clients and Miriam's family is costing me money."

"Call my office. We'll go through what's what and get them off your back. Based on what Cynthia told me, I know how to get your clients full attention."

Six different men came over to Donna and pledged their loyalty to her. I didn't know who they were, but I clocked Rosa watching them from a distance. Daniel introduced Donna to more of his friends and she gracefully accepted their congratulations when Michael came over to tell her what he needed to say. "Lola and Tony couldn't have done anything more. Your make-up and hair are..." He kissed his fingers. "The dress is perfect. The only thing left for you to do is take it all off and let your hair down tonight." Even though it was a touch, risqué, Daniel liked the way he said it. I think that's because of Michael's Italian accent, and his splendour. Unlike guys who think it's important to be effeminate,

Michael, as a gay dad had the kind of sassy butch masculinity that sizzles.

"I have ordered a one-year supply of great Italian wines for your home. Hopefully, it will make your first year together mellow and tipsy. If either of you has problems of any kind," he gave Daniel a card, "call me. I will arrange things, so we see you often." Roy told me that Michael was well in with JJ and Carlos.

I didn't know where Roy was, so I joined Michael and he pulled me next to his side. "Eugene! I love your last program on Black Jewish stars in show business." Michael pulled Daniel towards him. "Daniel, this is a man to know. He's helped me and my husband. I vouch for his friendship."

I said, "He's drunk. I do love this wedding. It's very—something!"

Daniel said, "Uncanny."

"Yes!" I said joyfully. "That's it. It's strangely familiar but unexperienced."

Daniel told us. "Because of Aaron and Donna, *I've* imagined many things I was unfamiliar with. Customs and things like that. I'm so glad all this is now going to fill my life," he replied, pointing at people.

Donna told him, "Tonight, I'll show you more than customs."

Michael said, "Tonight, *everyone* here will be revealing themselves."

"Well, climax is my favourite word," Donna replied

Daniel told her, "I can promise you more than that."

I knew it! Donna had to be polymorphic. Roy chose to see her as a drama star, but to me she embodied the sexual fecundity of Mediterranean women. But I couldn't write about it because Roy kept cutting it out.

Daniel put his arm around her waist and walked her away from us. Ten minutes later, the photographer was taking pictures and I watched various groups hustle into formations of families. Daniel and Donna posed with his mother, his brothers and sisters, as well as his uncles. Then there were photos of Harold and Violet with Donna and Daniel's family. I watched closely as Roy and Aaron fit in with both families, but most of all, Daniel told everyone.

"If it weren't for this terrific guy, I'd have never been introduced to his mother." There were all kinds of photos of Daniel and Donna with Aaron and Amber, but the most significant moment that imprinted itself on my mind was the photograph they took where Aaron kissed his mother's face and Daniel kissed Aaron on the cheek. That was the moment I saw love between the three of them I had not examined deeply but understood so fully. I glanced at Roy and Amber and I felt their adoration because my love was also unreserved.

CHAPTER FORTY-ONE

14th March 2019

"*Roy!*" someone called out and I answered another question. As Aaron's best man, I can say the wedding was exactly what everyone expected, considering it cost £270,000. Helena took my hand as we stood in the ballroom and watched Aaron and Amber prepare for their first dance as husband and wife. I could feel Helena's tension as she gripped my fingers.

Months earlier, Amber was going to hire Hampton Court and invite her school friends, her parents' family, her friends at the V&A and friends from around Europe. Amber then extended the invitations to Aaron's staff, colleagues, Donna's friends and Daniel's family. That meant there were going to be over 250 guests and the cost was astronomical. Eventually, the plans got so big, Aaron told Amber to "stop it". He arranged a dinner at our house and asked Daniel to speak to the families.

In our packed living room, for the first time, I witness Daniel's ascension from counsellor to Head of the Family. Daniel explained to everyone involved the damage they were inflicting on each other. All parties involved felt humble. What was interesting to me was, instead of shaming people, Daniel explained the mental damage they were self-inflicting and then living with. I had no say in the wedding, but Daniel made me think about my own bullshit.

After that, Aaron and Daniel hired Kenwood House, a beautiful white Regency mansion on Hampstead Heath for the reception and so it was only a short trip from the synagogue where the wedding ceremony was enshrined by Jewish tradition. As the 'best man' and 'maid of honour', Helena and I took our responsibilities very seriously.

We took care of both of them, especially in the final week. Looking over at the orchestra of twenty men and women in black and white formal dress, Aaron looked so gallant and suave in his grey suit, purple waistcoat, white shirt and cravat. All of the men were in the same colours, but we wore totally different suits from Aaron. Amber's bridesmaids wore dresses in various styles all in the shade of yellow moon.

Amber's incredible Oscar De La Renta wedding dress, along with the pearl necklace, diamond earrings and bracelet, showed her at her best. She really looked like a princess. At the other end of the ballroom, the orchestra began a brief overture and I watched Aaron prepare himself to start the waltz. Everyone around the ballroom was enchanted by the sight of them. No matter how wealthy the guests were; Aaron and Amber were the stars under the Regency splendour of the room with all its décor, paintings, and wedding furnishings.

The orchestra played the 1949 Miklos Rozsa Waltz from *Madame Bovary*. Amber wanted it because it was one of her favourite moments in the film, when Emma Bovary reaches the heights of her ambition just before she goes on to destroy herself.

* * *

Today is my birthday and I feel seventy. But it's also Aaron and Amber's wedding day. After a bath in every oil and salts Michael and David had, I got dressed and looked fifty. David and Michael told me I always looked different in a tux. The months that passed leading up to Aaron's wedding were eventful. Now, the wedding was as beautiful as all the families had hoped. I looked at Bernard and Massimo with their wives and they were all enchanted by the sight of Amber happily married to a man they knew they could not rule. They played their power games with Aaron and he showed he was prepared to fight anyone who tried to control him.

Now he waltzed Amber around the splendour of Kenwood House, as the one hundred perfectly dressed guests gazed at them. As they danced, Aaron and Amber spoke intimately. They looked out of this world because they captured the elegance of the Regency past although we were all in modern dress. Nevertheless, at weddings, people always seemed just a bit old-fashioned. I have a particular fondness for period dramas, so

I was pulled into the loving elegance of their dance and the happy faces of Aaron and Amber's parents.

I saw envy and joy in Helena and Amber's friends who wanted husbands as handsome as Aaron to make them look as beloved as Amber was, waltzing around the ballroom.

After their dance, Amber took her father's hand and he gracefully danced her around the ballroom. Aaron took Jean's hand and danced with her, but that poor woman had no sparkle. It wasn't until Aaron changed partners and danced with his mother that the light moved off Amber and Bernard and onto Donna and Aaron.

They danced perfectly and suddenly everyone burst into applause.

I asked Helena, "Are you alright?"

"Yes, I feel strange though."

"You got past the worst day and so you're going to be fine now."

"You know, considering all the girls and women who are friends of mine, you were the only one I could talk to about that day."

"You were very upset. But I think *that* day and on *my* worst day when Roy broke up with me. It set something in stone for you and I." Helena smiled at me, and I know she agreed. Of course, I could remember our difficult days vividly.

The orchestra changed from the waltz to Cole Porter's *Begin the Beguine* and *Easy to Love*. Aaron and Donna obviously worked out the routine that was far more beguiling than anything on the TV show *Strictly*, which I detest. Everyone could see that Donna and Aaron learnt their dance from old Hollywood movies. As I watched them, it made me wish my mother was still alive, because I felt terribly single.

Aaron handed Donna off to Bernard and then Aaron took Helena's hand and danced with her. I wish I knew what they were saying. Before long, everyone in different families were dancing together, but of course, I noticed Roy had no one to dance with. He stood among the families, not so much single as I am, but alone. The orchestra stopped and Aaron made his way to Amber and took her hand. In the white, orange and lavender decorated ballroom, he spoke to everyone.

"Amber and I are blessed with two beautiful mates. Helena, come forward; Roy—get out here, mate!" Both of them came forward, but they were reticent in different ways. They moved out of the crowd and went to the centre of the ballroom. Roy looked good and Helena never looked better. Amber and Aaron kissed them on the cheek and the camera crew moved in. Helena said thank you and good luck to Amber and managed to be casual even though during the wedding ceremony, she cried tenderly as she watched Amber say her vows.

Roy looked at everyone and people fell silent, waiting for him to speak. He eyed Donna and Daniel then he looked at all the families present. Violet and Harold knew there was something wrong. I felt it. He gave a shy smile to the Bankolés and De Farenzinos, and then focused on JJ and Carlos in among the 100 guests.

"I can only say that acts of kindness and honour will sustain your marriage. A great friend taught me that we live in a world of impermanence. With that in mind, Aaron, take inspiration from your mother, unlike men, she is an eternal inspiration of love I believe in. God bless you both." He walked away and handed the microphone to Bernard. Roy seemed changed to me. It wasn't just the intensity in his eyes, as he spoke to people; he had somehow regressed. The stature that developed in him when he was going out with me had diminished.

It was then, I remembered the best days of my life with Roy. We were with Amber and Aaron for a weekend. On that Friday night, we spent the evening watching the series, *Old Jews Telling Jokes*. All four of us rolled around laughing.

The next day we played bubble football. I was shocked that Amber didn't object to roughing it, as a girl from a wealthy family background might have. She got into scruffy gym clothes and trainers and played for two hours. Watching everyone covered in the inflated bubble, like creatures from another planet in see-thru plastic, bumping and zigzagging around the gym was hilarious. We had lunch at *Breakfast Club* Spitalfields and then went to a gallery for a private showing of erotic art. I told them nothing on display was more erotic than making love to Roy.

Amber asked us to rate ourselves as lovers. Aaron said 9, Roy said 7 and I said 10. Aaron said there are no tens and Roy said,

'Eugene *is* a 10'. That conversation led us to dinner and Aaron confessed how difficult it was to want Amber and have to keep himself cool. Amber said she 'squeezed her lips' to cope and that made all three of us blush. That evening we went out dancing at the gay bar in Dalston. When we got back to Roy's place, I made love to him and afterwards, I left his bedroom to go to the bathroom and out in the hallway, I bumped into Aaron. I pushed my chest out and led with my cock. I thought he was going to make some snide comment about my age or the fact he was gym fit with a six pack. But he said: 'Sexy motherfucker shaking that ass!' and I was reminded of the first time I went to his place for the Prince memorial.

On Sunday, we hired a couple of XK Jaguars and took them for a run down to Brighton. Making time, speeding and 'sort of' racing Aaron and Amber was nice. Over lunch, we had a lot to talk about concerning what class we belonged to. Roy said we're the Revisionist Class. 'We've overturned traditions an evolved into Revisionist'. He spent an hour on the subject and we listened to his wisdom.

On the drive back, we got to London in time for six o'clock. It was one of the loveliest pink sky evenings I could remember in ages. While I was doing supper, Amber took off her clothes and went out onto my shielded balcony in her Manolo Blahnik shoes in the nude and caught the breeze. She reminded me of women in Helmut Newton photographs I'd seen in the 1980s. She was without shame, false modesty, or arrogance.

When Aaron returned from the bathroom and saw Amber standing in the pink evening light, he took off his clothes and went out onto the balcony to join her. Roy came from the bedroom to help me prepare the food, but when he saw Aaron and Amber out in the evening haze; he got undressed and joined them too.

The ascending shades of their skin, from cream to honey and brown; along with the fitness of their youth stopped me cooking. I turned off the stove, went out onto the balcony and put my outstretched hands around all of them. The boys were on my left and right and Amber held pride of place beside Aaron. Right then, each of them felt like they were mine.

* * *

Amber moved between all her wedding guests and family, speaking French, German, Italian and English. She wasn't just the bride; she was the centre of attention. Her finishing school could claim some of the credit for her elegance, but her thoughts spoke of her intelligence as she posed and answered questions.

I hovered around behind Amber's chic father and dowdy mother, and I heard Jean say: "Stop looking at her like that. You gaze at Amber as though she's one of your conquests."

"My daughter is everything you are not. Therefore, she fascinates me; I'm proud of her." She called him an adulterous bastard.

"Thank you for reminding me. Ms Dalio must be aching for me now," he told Jean and eyed her with utter contempt and then he walked off and left her.

The next time I saw Bernard, he was dancing with his mistress, as the DJ worked with the orchestra within the lights show. He played House Techno classics and the orchestra played in conjunction with the techno grooves from his mixing desk. To my surprise, Bernard was a very nifty mover. I was also stunned at how well Daniel danced. All at once, I wanted to dance if only to remind myself that although I was in my mid-sixties, I had plenty of moves and grooves in me.

The highlight of the dance was when Amber and Aaron dance with Roy and Helena. A medley of House-Techno grooves bolstered by the orchestra played and they switched partners and danced with each other for ten minutes that showed me Helena and Amber no longer held acrimony towards each other. Dancing in their haute couture exclusive fashions, they moved as freely as street dancers who knew how to perform at dance shows brought into Sadler's Wells Theatre.

After all the trouble their parents had caused, along with Helena's brothers and sisters-in-law who first struck me as stiff narcissists, they clapped and cheered Helena, Amber, Roy and Aaron on, while swaying and grooving to the music.

I had some more bubbly and joined in with everyone because no matter how I felt, we were at Kenwood House for a wedding that was beautifully planned. The food, drinks, service, joy and celebration were Aaron and Amber's joyous day. A curious moment occurred when Michael came to dance with me.

He said, "Their love conquered their family's stupidity. Believe in your love and you will win in the end." How my best friend dispelled my angst, I don't know. I looked across the room and felt genuine relief and happiness for the bride and groom.

CHAPTER FORTY-TWO

May 2019

Daniel and Aaron put in 70 minutes' work at the gym and then they jogged along The Bishops Avenue in Hampstead; one of the most salubrious areas in London. The tree-lined street was scattered with blossom as they ran, followed by their personal trainer four feet behind them.

"I'm still on a high from our honeymoon; I've never seen Paris the way Amber knows it: Rive Gauche and all that. Amber said Helena is more 'Right Bank'. Bernard's friends were really hospitable to us: took us to loads of posh places. Then the Riviera was amazing! Amber was..." He laughed. "She's gorgeous." They laughed with an unspoken understanding. Their personal trainer told them to focus and both of them turned to him at the same time and said, "Shut the fuck up!" They pulled faces, high fived each other and ran a bit faster.

Back at the gym, Daniel told him what he discerned from the two sessions he had with Roy. They came out of the showers and dried off. Since they were alone, Daniel spoke freely and hid nothing, so Daniel ended by saying. "Roy is clinically depressed." Aaron couldn't say anything, so they put their clothes on, combed their hair and then a couple of Lebanese guys entered the locker room.

Daniel and Aaron were almost ready to go. "Tomorrow my Rabbi's coming to the house."

Aaron thought he heard one of the men say, 'Jews' and a sneer twisted the other man's face. Both of them were in their mid-twenties. Aaron turned from the mirror and walked right up to them as they started to undress.

"What did you just say?" he asked in a threatening and contemptuous tone. Both of them looked all over the place but not at Aaron. "I better be mistaken about you because if that was some anti-Semitic shit, I'll make you sorry, you dig?" They quickly looked at him and then averted their eyes. Aaron told me they were typical inflammatory gutless internet trolls.

Daniel shouted, "My son is talking to you, numb-nuts!" Then he closed in on them.

"I didn't say anything," one of them replied and the other guy acted like a recalcitrant rich college boy, who had disrespect stamped on his face.

Aaron slapped the non-verbal guy hard in the face. "Britain doesn't need more bigots."

Daniel told them, "Fuck off and don't come back!" They put their gym clothes back in their bags and they left quickly.

Aaron told Daniel. "My father also said, 'slap them down when they take a shot'." They high-fived!

Daniel pulled up in his Range Rover and parked in front of his house across the road from his other house where Rosa lived with her grandchildren, Ursula and son-in-law. When he got out of the car, Rosa was in her front garden and she called over. Daniel and Aaron spoke to her briefly before they went in. His neighbours offered their felicitations and he happily waved because he'd known them for over twenty years and as a group of well-to-do Jewish families; everyone within a one-mile radius clubbed together. Daniel also knew he became even more popular because of his new family.

Inside the house, the stripped walls and half-empty dining room was stark. After dinner, Donna said to Daniel, "My whole day is ruined now." He took her hand. "I've got your family across the street, and *your* parents in Wimbledon who want us to be family. But Roy saved my life. When the agony of losing Zara and Humphry tore my mind apart, I took all those pills, but Roy got to me in time. After that he took out my vomit and washed my underwear. He *is* my family, so I'm not abandoning him." Amber clearly didn't know and she was distressed. Donna read her face perfectly. "Not just me, Aaron was suicidal too. Roy saved him as well."

Amber told her, "Mama, I didn't know he love you like that."

"Well, he does. He loves both of us. What are we gonna do for him? Why did he break up with Eugene?"

"Without getting into medical privacy, Roy has had a psychotic break." Donna began crying and Amber comforted her. "Don't say that Danny, don't. When he first came to England—"

"Mum please," Aaron interrupted. "The past is the past."

"Not if it's destroying him now! Daniel, tell me what's wrong with Roy?" "Donna, doctor-patient confidentiality is governed by ethics and UK Law."

"Then how can I help him?" Donna asked.

Daniel watched them and struggled to speak. "Roy told me he worships this family, even you, Amber; although he's only known you for a while."

Aaron said, "Then, is there anything I can do, Papa?"

"Yes. Now I'm going to break the law. Donna, Amber, let me talk to Aaron." Donna touched Amber on the shoulder and they headed out, but Donna told them, "You're my husband and you're my son. A boy came into my life and years later, he saved my life. That man is a part of our family, fix it." Daniel hadn't seen her like that, but as a psychiatrist, he understood a great deal. Donna marched Amber out and she turned back to tell Daniel, "Love you."

Daniel went to the cabinet wrapped in plastic, poured two glasses of bourbon and gave one to Aaron. The patchy spotlights on the wall showed that the lights in the ceiling were not completed.

"Roy told me a lot of things. In my medical opinion, Displacement lies at the heart of Roy's breakdown. This is brought on by, adverse childhood events that disrupted healthy development and emotional regulation. This could include physical or emotional abuse, sexual abuse, bullying—What is that look? You know something." Aaron tried to keep his mouth shut. "You have to tell me. Does it involve you?"

"No, it happened in Jamaica."

"Based on my knowledge of Franz Fanon's psychiatric studies of Black men's psychosis, I can help him. So now you are compelled to tell me." They gave each other a nod.

* * *

The insistent knock at my front door would not stop, so finally I dragged myself out of the chair and stumbled through the hallway to open the front door. I suddenly heard the sounds of the Barbican estate flood back into my ears when I looked at Aaron standing in front of me. He looked tanned and self-possessed.

"Glad you realised I wasn't going away. Yes, I will come in, thank you," Aaron said as he pushed passed me and headed through the hall and into the living room. There were half-eaten meals on dirty plates all over the living room floor and tables, as well as the kitchenette area.

"You're in a worst state than Roy. I hear he called you and you told him to 'get fucked'."

"Yeah, so what? That leaves him available for you any time you want." Aaron stared at me and pointed at a chair without saying a word and demanded I sit down.

Aaron said, "Let me tell you what yesterday was like and why I'm here." He told me how a good day with Daniel at the gym got worse as they had family dinner.

"Daniel advised me to tell you about Roy. Do you know that Roy's haunted by his past?" I said no. "Years ago, my dad diagnosed Roy as having mental health problems. He underwent...care. Well, our whole family were doing everything to get him well." Whatever the look on my face was he reacted to it.

"His mother and father were poisoning him, but he didn't die quick enough, so his father viciously beat him up because he's gay."

"He's told me."

"Yeah, did he say that his father dropped dead from a heart attack while he was kicking his twelve-year-old guts in?" I saw tears in his eyes. I nodded.

"And did he tell you his mother called some guys she knew to kill him?" The tears fell from his eyes. It must have taken Aaron a minute to continue.

"Those thugs sexually assaulted him, with belt and bottle." Aaron lost his breath and struggled to breathe. "Roy found where the leader lived. So, he got a jug of acid and threw it in his face." The horror of that played on Aaron's face.

"The rest of those thugs went back to Roy's mother and killed her. Did he tell you that?" I shook my head. "Roy escaped to London. His grandfather lived here. But he's lived with that trauma. His mum *hired* motherfuckers to kill him, but *he* blames himself they killed her. He twists that into all kinds of religious shit. My dad and another doctor helped him to recover."

I jumped to my feet and shouted right in his face. "I need something out of a relationship that's more than taking care of an emotional cripple."

"Don't say that," he replied, shaking his head repeatedly. "You're the only man he's had a happy romantic relationship with."

"Bullshit!" I replied and shoved him in the chest.

"No. Truth, my friend." Roy hadn't confided in me to that extent. He was always replete with mystery, it's one of the things I like, but that kind of life in Jamaica I had never imagined.

"I'm not here to tell you lies. I know you! You're Dr Eugene Martins. You wrote the one great romantic novel about Caribbeans in Britain. My parents love your book, I've read it. You didn't get the Man-Booker Prize, but 90% of Black Brits respect you for the love story you gave us in that novel. Roy adores you. I know everything about his love for you."

"Bollocks!"

In a knowing and cocky manner, he said, "You love European Art cinema and you detest the Conservative government. When you were sixteen, you had your only sexual experience with a girl, which you hated. As the only Black student at Cambridge, a white guy, who will remain nameless, became your first love. Loganberries and ice-cream on flapjacks are your favourite food. Your agent is the only white guy who considers you more a scholar than a 'black'. You can cum three times if everything is right."

I was stunned Roy told him about that.

"Your parents loved you even more after you 'came out'. Mate, Roy idolises you because you're intellectual and a romantic! I was so jealous of you because you've made Roy happier than I could."

I turned my back on him.

Aaron walked up behind me. "His ex, Brian, has all that money but he's an American that called Roy a nigger—out of 'affection'. Roy hung him out to dry for that insult and to this day Brian doesn't know he got played!"

Roy lied to me about that.

"Narj is an Art whore, he'll fuck for fame. You, mister, you are gallant and Roy responds to your camaraderie and sex appeal."

"I don't believe you," I flatly replied.

Aaron grabbed my arm and turned me around. "If it wasn't for Amber, I'd have rather cut my wrist again than say you're better for him than me!" I grabbed his arm, twisted it, and looked at his wrists and there were scars there.

"Mum overdosed and I thought I lost her, so I cut my wrist. If Roy hadn't forgotten his train tickets, mum and I would be with dad and my sister." He told me to get him a drink. I went and poured him a large rum. He came for it and took a gulp. "The thought of dad, mum and Zara gone drove me insane. I begged Roy to make love to me and bring me back. Roy's blood is in me. His spunk is in me. And his breath is in me." Whatever I looked like he reacted. "I adore Amber with the deepest love that's in my heart. I love Roy from the depth of my soul. My mother is at the core of my conscious psyche. Do you really think weak lying men's philosophies or orthodoxy is what I live by? Especially this bunch of crypto-fascist Brexiteers."

"No, I think you're your own man."

"That's only been possible because people's bigotry has shown me what type of scum they are. I'll never bow to that. I know you're fucking loaded but are you big enough to be a really big man?"

"What do you mean?" He emptied the glass.

"I've sat up many a time listening to Roy tell me about people you introduce him to and conversations you have that educate and thrill him." I shrugged him off and he went and helped himself to another drink.

He snuck around me as I faced away and he said, "Remember the night you made love to Roy out on that balcony; in front of London."

It was one of our great nights.

"Are you honestly telling me you didn't feel that you defied every bigot to become the man of your own making: a hero to the man you love."

"Shut up!"

"Roy told me afterwards you were high!" Even a DJ couldn't have said it better so I looked away. "At three o'clock in the morning, you intimately strolled around the Barbican kissing and talking to Roy about the future. Do you deny that passion and that hope?"

"What else has he told you?"

"I know what you fear and what you hope for. I know how *good* you are." Nothing I wrote about Aaron prepared me for how confrontational he really is.

"You think app sluts want a relationship with a man your age?" That felt like a kidney punch. "Roy is everything you need." I showed him the door.

"Fuck that, you're going to listen to me. Amber and Roy share the same quality I look for in people I love—integrity. Women have offered me pussy instead of sharing their dignity and I've never fallen for it." He came back at me like we were in a boxing ring.

"But when I was seeing Roy, he still ended up in your bed."

Aaron grabbed me by the shirt. "He grew up hating sex. When he had *me*, he learnt to enjoy it because I was suicidal and wanted him to save me so we started making love. Brian and his other boyfriends didn't give him that. With us, we found passionate life. I was the light that obliterated the homophobic darkness inflicted on him. And Roy is the Black purity that replaced what I lost and what I needed. After my father was killed, I dreaded being white." He backed away. "I still hate people thinking I'm white." He opened the door and went out onto the balcony to cool off. I felt like he was a heavyweight knocking me around.

"Oh yeah, despite what you think, I'm not gay. Now I know Roy loves you, I'd never violate your dignity or betray my wife." He seized oxygen into his fists when he told me, "True, I've been scared at times, so I reached out to Roy. But don't be a schmuck! Reach out and bring your man home!"

Talk about 'Use the Force'. I stared at Aaron and then I watched him eyeball me. Perhaps I have allowed myself to be weakened by Roy's insecurities. I went and got my mobile and then called Roy. I started sweating through my vest even as I dialled and waited. Aaron walked to the other side of the room and soon, Roy answered and I told him, "Baby, it's me; I'm going out of my mind. I'm aching with misery."

"What's brought this on?"

"Are you kidding me? You took all the joy out of my life when you left. I'm wasting away. Come over, now—get in a cab." I could feel my insides shaking.

"I can make everything right if you're also feeling empty and dead. Roy, we need love. Come to me." I listened to him and then ended the call.

Aaron came towards me, "What did he say?"

"He said if I really forgive him, he's on his way." Aaron took off his jacket.

"Go take a shower and I'll clean up and get out."

"I don't know if I'm still angry with you."

"Fix this mess and we'll talk. Maybe you'd like to see the house." He went and picked up the plates and I went to the bathroom.

* * *

When Roy stood in my doorway in white jeans and a black sweater, his face was tense and yearning. He was so young at thirty-two. But he'd aged since I saw him last. I yanked him inside, slammed the door and smacked his face. He didn't react, so I hit him again and grabbed his shoulders.

"I've been starving, drinking, wanking, and crying!"

With aching tenderness, he said, "Forgive me, please. There's something rotten in me that makes me ridiculous. I hate it. Can you help me?"

"Tell me every rotten thing about your life as a child. All of it."

"I can't, it's sordid and revolting."

"Nothing you say will stop me from loving you." He looked like a kid who'd been told he was going to be granted happiness and freedom. I mean the joy that is tangible to Black people. A life where hatred won't destroy our faith in the world we live in."

"My parents hated me because I don't want to have sex with women."

He backed away from me. "So, they tried to kill me." He looked distraught uttering those words. "It killed them instead." He looked me right in the eye.

"I'm glad they're dead. Normal people don't feel like that. But I got my chance to prove to God I'm not irredeemable. I took care of Donna and Aaron. When they married, I felt I had nothing."

"Don't you understand the meaning of love? We've spent all these months examining how Donna and Aaron's love changed Amber and Daniel's lives."

"Writing about them showed me things I didn't understand but you've made me see things I've never felt. I'm not a misfit, I love being with you. Here, all those days writing. Discussing life. You taking me to your friends. And your face when you introduce me to everyone." I touched his face. "You never have sex with me. You always make love to me. It's wonderful."

He lifted his hand as if he was an invalid, but he touched my cheek and his cool hand soothed me. I've never seen anyone more lovesick, perhaps except for Helena when she confessed her shame to me.

"Roy, I don't want to die alone in misery. I'm too old for that. Will you look after me, and let me take care of you?" His expression shifted from melancholy to gay, as he nodded. He pulled me in closer and closer still and I felt he was changing as life came back into him.

CHAPTER FORTY-THREE

June 2019

As *always*, I noted how people dressed because it reveals how they've decided they want to be seen. In the reception room of their Albion Square home, Amber entered the room. Through the V&A, Amber discovered Emma Peel's costumes in *The Avengers*, so she wore a blue jersey zip-up catsuit and low heel lace-up boots. She no longer had an Ingénue persona; she had become the woman of her own invention. Her inquisitive face and her athletic body were the epitome of sexual desire. As she greeted everyone, the freedom of her body and the swing in her hair made her all the more vital and alluring.

During their engagement, Amber and Donna decorated and furnished their home with beautiful bric-a-brac from previous eras and I could see Amber's elegance and Aaron's taste in modern techno style. The entire house looked like a curated exhibition, but it was very family and friends cosy.

Daniel and Donna watched Amber and so did her parents. It was clear to me that Donna and Daniel had a love life that made them tactile and telepathic, whereas Jean was distant and lifeless. Bernard's behaviour on the other hand, was rakish. It struck me how like her father Amber was. I was standing at the far end of the large reception room and I watched the way Massimo and Helena kept an eye on Amber and it reminded me of when I first saw them. Massimo's camaraderie and pride in Bernard were matched by Helena's obsession with Amber.

When Roy and Aaron entered the room, my insides jumped. Roy had on a pair of black leather trousers, mountain boots and a T-shirt. Since that incredible day back at the Barbican, he had reclaimed his courage. Aaron strutted around in jeans, trainers and a white shirt which epitomised his manly London swagger. Both of them had their hair cropped, which made them look tough. Roy made his way towards me and I watched him; engulfed by a haphazard and amorous spirit. I remembered him uninhibited and naked in my bed, begging me for everything. Now he glanced lovingly at me and took my hand.

I raised my voice. "People, a quick announcement. Since you're *like* family to me and are family to Roy, I wanted you to know Roy and I have agreed on a Civil Partnership."

Donna happily yelled 'Oh my god!' Clearly, Daniel was doing her good, so she looked great as she got up and came to us from the other side of the room.

Roy said, "Eugene, I changed my mind." My balls tightened. Aaron and Daniel yelled, 'What!' Then Bernard and Jean, Massimo and Helena fidgeted and wobbled as if they were quivering in limbo.

Roy said, "Get this, you-old-hippy, I want to marry you. I'm not going to be your lover; I must be your husband. Can you stand it?"

Helena screamed and dashed towards me and Massimo looked so proud of her because she had changed.

I told him, "You fucking son of a bitch! Don't do that to me. I'm sixty-four!"

"Yeah, and prodigious."

"Get that right! I'm happy to marry you and proud to be your husband." The greatest and I do mean the most elusive genuine smile filled his lips. I clutched him and kissed him about the face and he laughed and couldn't stop laughing.

Bernard said, "Aaron, when I first heard about you, your friends and family, I knew you hadn't just saved my daughter's life. What I never imagined is that you and your friends would change *my* life. All of you have shown me the futility of living unhappily and so I tell you all. I'm ending my marriage because our life together means nothing." Bernard glared at Jean and I felt he detested her.

Donna and Daniel clearly didn't care but Massimo went to Jean to comfort her. She picked up her handbag to leave and Amber crossed the room to talk to her. Jean said, "You think your marriage is the answer to life, but it isn't. Your husband will use you and then neglect you until he finds a mistress, or you take refuge in Helena's bed." Donna was clearly angry.

Amber confronted Jean and spoke with great authority. I watched Helena and I saw the intensity in her eyes as she watched Amber and her mother. I also felt the rage in Amber and I think Massimo did as well.

With rigid formality, Amber declared, "Aaron will always be my loving husband." Her Germanic tone was sharp. "On our honeymoon, he proclaimed that my vagina is regal." Jean's face stiffened, her father's mouth opened and Helena concealed a laugh that left a salacious smile on her face, but Donna cast a glance at Daniel which made him raise an eyebrow.

Amber's confrontational stance towards her mother was ferocious. "Your declarations and lies almost ruined me as a child. You said men are sexually brutal and every woman learns to live with that." Jean nodded her head to confirm.

Bernard said, "I've never had brutal sexual relations with your mother."

Amber pointed at Jean. "My husband doesn't make me do *anything* I don't want! When it comes to intercourse Aaron's passion is outstanding. And he knows the majestic pleasures of cunnilingus." Jean was horrified. "Yesterday, he almost made me pass out!" Helena looked at Aaron, who was as cool as a rock star. Daniel looked proud of him. Bernard turned from Amber to Aaron and then back to Jean. Apart from Roy, who obviously knew him inside out, we were flabbergasted.

Accusingly, Amber pointed in Jean's face. "I had to go to my other mother for advice about my wedding night. Donna helped me, but it turned out Aaron was afraid of hurting me, so he was delicate." Amber placed her hands in prayer. "In the name of everything holy, you cannot curse me with misery." Amber turned Jean around by her shoulders and marched her to the door. Jean and Bernard were taken aback for different reasons I'd say. "Get out!" Amber stated. "I want no misery in my house! My home is for fabulous people. When you have recovered your heart, come back."

Bernard followed Amber to the hall and everyone in the room eyeballed each other. Amber slammed the door and when she came back into the living room, she kissed and caressed Aaron and stood in front of him.

Amber stated, "I will not suffer at anyone's hands anymore!" Helena and Massimo exchanged looks and Amber faced Aaron.

"I don't have to. I am your devoted ally, as I said in our wedding vows, darling." She turned to us. "When we were in Paris, I took him to *Le Pré Catelan* restaurant in Bois de Boulogne. I felt so beautiful. The night we went to Montmartre and Pigalle, everyone wanted to talk to us. Not because I am Audrey reincarnated. But I am loved. *My* husband wants me to be psychologically and financially secure. That is love." Bernard took her hand and kissed it. Silence filled the room as we all eyed each other cautiously.

"Mate, Donna, come with me," Roy said. "Eugene, bring the thing." Donna was a bit confused, but she went with the flow and followed Roy. "Mate, where's your bedroom?" Aaron led us out of the reception room, upstairs.

"Mummy, doesn't the house look wonderful!" Donna obviously agreed.

"Amber has a great eye for beauty," Aaron said.

Albion Square was a conservation area of renovated Victorian houses and a lovely private garden in the middle of the square. You'd never think such beautiful houses could be in a poor Borough like Hackney. Aaron's grandparents gave them 'marriage money'; therefore, he used it to make the house the home for his family to be. Upstairs, the spacious master bedroom was decorated in their wedding colours. There was a 19th century tête-à-tête S-shaped loveseat in the bay window: and a leather boxed bed was covered with lace and satin sheets and pillows, as well as two exquisite chiffonnière, and an art nouveau dresser screen.

I closed the door and Roy said, "I wrote this for you." I took two manuscripts out of my satchel. "It's a romantic novel." Confused, Aaron and Donna searched his face. "I based the story on what you both went through to get married. In my first version, it was biographical. So, I read some of Eugene's other novels and rewrote the romance as a fiction inspired by all of you." Donna was astounded.

Aaron asked, "How long have you been working on this?"

"Not long." Something private and sacrosanct passed between them.

His rewrite was totally different from my version of events and characters, but it was always his dream and not mine. I was fine with his version because it didn't violate my friendship and confidentiality with Helena. That's why I let him rewrite it and I promised to give it to my publisher for consideration.

"Wait!" Aaron said. He dashed out into the hallway, leaned over the banister, and called, "Darling, come up, you've gotta see this."

A minute later, Amber was in the bedroom. Aron put his arm around her and gave her the manuscript. "Roy wrote this. It's a novel inspired by what me and mum went through to get married." She looked at it and took Roy's hand and held it.

Roy told her, "Even though it's not biographical, you'll recognise yourselves. Think of it like a 'mash-up' romance."

"Mama, you told me you love him. Now I understand why." Amber looked heartened and surprised. "Roy, come, I'll show you the house and we'll talk." She led Roy away and I watched Aaron. He took his mobile to make a call and left me with Donna. She slipped her arm threw mine and we went back downstairs.

Bernard was sitting on the stairs intensely speaking in French on his mobile. From his bon vivant voice, right down to the way he gestured, I was certain he was talking to his mistress.

As we walked through the reception room, Donna asked me what I knew about the book and I told her it was Roy's thank you to them for rescuing him from his former brutal life. Helena came into the room and asked for a minute with me.

"I'm thinking about your wedding chéri. Donna, if I may?" Helena led me towards the hall and we went downstairs into the kitchen diner, rather like the setup Aaron and Roy had in their house, only this one was in silver and orange. Massimo was fixing himself a cold plate when Helena called him over to join us.

"If Eugene will let me, I would like to plan his wedding reception at the house in Ascot. He has been so wonderful for me over the last year, I'd like to host it. You can give me instructions, Eugene."

"No need, Helena. I love you for offering and for what we have. I love it."

Massimo said, "Money doesn't matter; please allow my daughter this gesture."

"Helena, why are you doing this?" She turned away from people and pulled her farther and I in close.

"I did something terrible. The shame is still in me. I asked Papa to steal life from them." She flushed and gasped. Massimo consoled her so it didn't look like she was falling apart and I intensely felt the kinetic energy between them.

"Without our sacred friendship, the only one I've had with a man, I'd—" We watched her pull herself together and Massimo and I gave her strength. A smile came to her face that proved she was no woman in peril; she had guts and dignity.

Helena said, "Will you speak to Roy about my wedding gift?" I was about to reply when Aaron came and tugged my arm. Amber gave Helena a kiss on the cheek and took her into the garden. Aaron led me upstairs to a guest room. It was also nicely furnished in a Scandinavian style. He closed the door and stepped up to me.

"I've got in the way with Roy before. It won't happen again. I've spoken to Roy and my lawyer. I've signed over my share of the house at Greenwood Road to you. The documents will be with you tomorrow."

Considering everything Roy told me about Aaron and what I imagined, there was a distinct difference between my perception and the truth.

"Why are you being kind to me?"

He took time to consider before he replied, "Roy's agreed to continue mental health treatment with Daniel. Roy said, he'd go mad without you. Those are not words. That's the truth." We couldn't talk for quite a few seconds.

"Dealing with Roy's life isn't easy. Coping with my own was even more difficult. So, considering my past with Roy and Amber's past with Helena, other people had *their* doubts, but Amber and I didn't." He became lost in his own thoughts. "Amber's a joy to me." I can say it now. When he smiles, Aaron's irresistibly handsome. "Mate, you don't have a home of your own."

"My friend is staying in Paris because of this Brexit bullshit so he offered me the Barbican flat for a great price. It will be a fresh start for us."

"Save your money. I want to get out of your way and giving you the house will show my respect to Roy. Besides, at this stage of your life, a mortgage—"

Infuriated, I said. "Yes! I know! I'm sixty-four and what? I only have fifteen good years left?"

"You've got your own TV show, black magic in your pants, and a PhD—man! That's the fucking trifecta."

"I'm not helpless!"

He always makes me so defensive. I know it's because I am a bit jealous of him.

"OK. We'll make the house our home." Aaron gave me that look I'd seen when he eyed Donna, Amber, and Daniel. In spite of my resentment towards him, only a fool couldn't see he was kind.

By late afternoon, everyone was in Aaron and Amber's splendid spring garden eating and drinking. I watched and heard Aaron with everyone. The sun shone warmly and I felt acutely alive. Aaron led Harold and Violet over to Rosa, Daniel and his brother and sister Nathan and Ursula. They exchanged thoughts on Caribbean and Jewish culture.

At the same time Amber brought Michael and David to talk to her father. I overheard them chatting about the latest exhibition at the V&A. As a former art dealer and agent, Michael had a lot to say and David wanted to know what new role Bernard had recently been appointed to by his government. Michael and David had a long chat with us to explain they would be 'best men' to each of us.

Another Star from Stevie Wonder's *Songs in the Key of Life* jumped out of the speakers and filled the air with the sound of drums! Amber screamed and we all turned to her. Her face was filled with joy! "Boulevard de la Croisette, Cannes! Our honeymoon, mon amour chéri!" Amber danced towards Aaron and he approached her with some funky Latin dance moves. She told everyone, "We danced on the Boulevard de la Croisette coming back from the beach."

"My angel, I'll love you more next year and the year after that," he proclaimed. They were perfect together as they danced. Michael, David, Massimo and Bernard, began a conversation about happy marriages.

However, it was Roy who told us, "Eugene, I respect the work you do but the kindness you show people is why I love everything about you. You drive carefully, you fuck beautifully, you listen thoughtfully." For the first time, I sensed Bernard and Massimo weren't shocked. Daniel pulled Donna towards Amber and Aaron and both newlyweds shared a conversation between them.

Solly and Alice happily spoke to Helena and Daniel's family. Rosa and Ursula were fascinated by Helena and something in the music kept us all moving. Roy came up to me and I put my arm around him and he said, "This must be the first time in ages, I haven't felt alone at one of these gatherings." Suddenly, I felt deeply fragile. Aaron watched us and winked at me.

I told Roy, "I know. I've been alone at these things for over ten years." I felt a strong weight in my chest.

"Although I'm not your first love, I'm glad to be the last one."

"Shut up, or I'll start crying." I buried my head in his neck and told him what Helena offered to do for us.

"Say yes." I nodded.

For whatever reason, Donna and Daniel came to us. "Are you alright, Bubala? You need anything?" Marriage made her even more lovely and truly beautiful.

Roy and I looked up at both of them and said: 'you'. Daniel touched my face and Donna kissed Roy.

Aaron came from out of nowhere and said, "Papa, I know my dad is watching and my sister is smiling for us." That clearly impacted on Daniel. Helena came over with Amber and joined us, so we spoke about our wedding. In time, Roy and I eased Helena from the group and we told her, we'd happily accept her wedding gift, which genuinely pleased her. She asked when and we both said the first week of September. Aaron dashed away but then soon rushed back with four bottles of wine.

The sun on the flowers transformed the garden into Technicolor. Aaron told us, "Each season, we'll throw a party." Amber swayed as he handed out the bottles and he took a swig and handed it off to Donna and she took a mouthful and past the bottle to Daniel, who took a gulp and passed it on. Soon, everyone just drank from the bottles.

Massimo turned to Michael and rushed into Italian at 100-words a minute until he threw his arms around him and then continued to talk. Daniel weaved and moved between people as he brought Donna to Amber and Aaron. Whatever he told her made Donna pat his bottom. Rosa watched him, enchanted, as she spoke to Nathan and Ursula. Aaron tapped a bottle with a fork and we all quietened down as the music played.

"The Mrs wants to throw *soirees* to meet brilliant people in London. I'm up for that, but there's no one better than my family.

So, every season, expect to come over for a feast." They shook the bottles and cheered.

The following day Helena emailed me a picture that captured Aaron and Donna with Amber and Daniel. Beside them, Roy and I looked incredibly happy.

"Oy!" Aaron told everyone. "I'm not made of money so bring Caribbean, Jewish and Italian stuff with you!" Absolutely everyone laughed and that's when Aaron and Donna blew us all a kiss.

THE END